Jack Vance

Wild Thyme and Violets
and Other Unpublished Works

Jack Vance

Wild Thyme and Violets

AND OTHER UNPUBLISHED WORKS

Published by Spatterlight Press

Cover art by Howard Kistler

ISBN 978-1-61947-153-5

Spatterlight Press LLC

Spatterlight
P R E S S

340 S. Lemon Ave #1916
Walnut, CA 91789
www.jackvance.com

CONTENTS

Reaching for the Essence*

by Paul Rhoads†

It is with a mixture of gratitude, and a certain sense of entitle-ment, that I accepted the proposition to write this Foreword. To say nothing of how the V.I.E. launched a complete and correct set of Vance texts into the digital age, nor of how the 'unpublished' texts here in question have, to the contrary, already been published by the V.I.E., nor again how — thanks to Spatterlight Press which, judging by its roster, is largely an extension of the V.I.E. project — Vance's stories are now integrally available as 'e' or POD books, and further, as wide availability was a major goal of the V.I.E.: I beg to proclaim myself not merely happy, but proud.

The present volume uses the title, and republishes the contents, of V.I.E. Volume 44.‡ That volume, which also used the phrase "unpub-lished works", included three texts which *had* been published: "The Kragen", a shorter and earlier version of *The Blue World*, and revisions by Vance of "Guyal of Sfere" and "I'll Build Your Dream Castle". The V.I.E. deemed these texts sufficiently different from their alternates to merit separate publication. A place had to be found for them, and that place was V.I.E. Volume 44, as now this Spatterlight book. Regarding "Guyal of Sfere"; Vance imposed a later style on his revision of this very early work for republication as a stand-alone story. The difference

---

* Spoiler Alert!

† Editor-in-chief of the Vance Integral Edition, and author of *Winged Being: Thoughts on Jack Vance and Patient Explanations of the Obvious.*

‡ Less some 200 pages of V.I.E. addenda.

of mood is such, however, that we felt it inappropriate to publish the revised version in the original context of *Mazirian the Magician**, but that the revision was too significant to leave unpublished.

Before I begin a discussion of the major unpublished works, I would like to mention certain V.I.E. editorial matters which, besides their inherent interest, shed some light on the points I wish to make further on.

The editorial job of the V.I.E. was often not trivial, as anyone will tell you who troubles themselves to investigate the conflicting evidence in published versions of certain texts, to say nothing of manuscripts and other sources such as correspondence with publishers. For many reasons the V.I.E. canon should be confidently understood as the source of authentic Vance, or "his stories as he wanted them published". There are, however, two problems I wish to mention. One concerns *The Star King*. There is no other evidence for this text than the original magazine publication and the later book version. The differences between the two are not insignificant. They are stylistic, and the book version includes additional descriptive text and an expanded and somewhat changed ending. There was controversy among V.I.E. editors about the status of stylistic aspects of each version which suggested editorial changes. But finally, we chose to follow the magazine version because of the character of the ending, which presented a problem similar to *Gold and Iron*.†

The ending of *Gold and Iron* had been altered from what had originally been written, or at least what was originally conceived. In casual discussion, Jack forcefully contradicted me when I noted that Roy Barch and Komeitk Lelianr get married; when I read him the text to prove my point, he insisted he had never written it that way. The evidence of the manuscripts, however, tells the opposite story. V.I.E. editorial policy was to publish Vance as he wished, so to correct that ending was unproblematic for the V.I.E.;‡ still, one may wonder how Vance could have actually penned an ending he not only did not

---

* Vance's title for *The Dying Earth*.

† Published previously as *Slaves of the Klau* and *Planet of the Damned*.

‡ This policy also led to the change of the Tschai title from *The Wankh* to *The Wannek*.

remember, but vigorously argued was so illogical he could not possibly have written it! My theory is that prior to finalizing the manuscript, perhaps prior to writing more than a lost outline — or even simply after having imagined the story but as yet written nothing — Vance discussed it with his publisher, and the latter gave him an instruction, perhaps in the form of a "suggestion", with which the author, understandably interested in good professional relations, complied. Decades later he recalled the story as originally conceived. *Gold and Iron* was abridged for publication in an Ace double (as *Slaves of the Klau*, with *Big Planet*), and here was an opportunity to correct the ending; but it is not corrected. The abridgement however was not necessarily by Vance himself, or if it was, he did not necessarily review the ending. We can suspect this because Vance never cared to revisit his work, and was capable of carelessness when he did. In a preface to an Underwood-Miller collection of early stories entitled *Lost Moons* (1982) Vance referred to certain of his revisions as "a lick-and-promise operation, rather like putting rouge on a corpse". His abridgement of "Crusade to Maxus" (we know he did the abridgement in this case) was particularly careless, consisting of a few brutal cuts which render part of the story incoherent. "Crusade to Maxus" was additionally altered by an editor to give it an anti-capitalist spin; I mention this as an example of the non-trivial character of some of these problems.

The problem of *The Star King* is related to that of *Gold and Iron* because the romantic aspect of the ending was likewise altered in a "non-vancian" direction. There was no direct evidence of how this had happened, but we had accumulated information about Vance's stylistic evolution and the ways editors sometimes altered his prose. The problem for the V.I.E. editors was resolved, though not by unanimous decision, in rejection of the book version. I have come to feel, however, that the book version had more merit than had been allowed. The authenticity of the magazine/V.I.E. version is unproblematic and, at the very least, the book ending remains suspect, but the ideal text of *Star King* may not yet have seen the light. Such a text, though to a lesser degree, would resemble the indispensable and superior V.I.E. version of *Languages of Pao*, which combines two quite different versions by a process of careful addition (an interesting story itself).

A more serious problem involved the Ellery Queen novels.* We did not initially intend to publish these, and only received permission to do so very late. For this reason, the otherwise tediously rigorous V.I.E. methods were slackened, and at least one important mistake was made. This was the removal of the phrase *his own darkness* from "Strange She Hasn't Written".† I recall being consulted on the issue, and the phrase in question is discussed in Chuck King's preface to Volume 14 bis. But now, for reasons of "textual integrity" rather than "textual evidence" (to express myself in V.I.E. jargon) I am sure this phrase is original and authentic. Taken in the context of the whole it even reveals itself as the keystone phrase of the whole story!

These matters, as I suggest above, relate to what follows. They involve Vance's method of writing by, one might say, addition, which arises out of an artistic necessity peculiar to himself, as well as Vance's approach to the problem of evil.

Let us turn, then, to the rare and marvellous (with two ells, in the vancian manner, if you please) gems presented here, for the first time in a universally available publication! These include two movie treatments, two mystery novels, and three other texts harder to classify. Vance preferred that the V.I.E. not publish another treatment, the very prescient "The Port of New York", which involved terrorists menacing that city with an atom bomb in the hold of a ship. The text, which is half a page long, ends with a memorable joke: *Alternate happy ending: New York is destroyed.* Vance had spent time in New York writing science fiction scenarios for *Captain Video,* but clearly did not care for the place; above all he was irked by the snobbish disdain of many New York artists and intellectuals for what has recently become known as "flyover America". This is understandable when one appreciates how Vance's work so largely emerges from the fading frontier spirit of rugged self-reliance and discovery, characteristic of the American hinterlands. Having been born in California in 1916, Vance was in touch with this spirit through the living memory of people around him. His attitudes and tastes crystallized in disdain for the vices of urbanity, a sentiment

---

* V.I.E. Volume 14 bis.

† published originally as *The Four Johns*

to which he gives full rein in such stories as "The Insufferable Red-headed Daughter of Commander Tynnott, O.T.E." (published also as "Assault on a City"), or "Ullward's Retreat".

Of the treatments, "Clang" dates from about 1984. The treatment was never optioned, but was prescient: in 2011 a movie was made about gladiatorial robots. "Real Steel" is close enough to "Clang" that one is tempted to suspect, not plagiarism exactly, but that "Clang" may well have been the source of the concept; when one is familiar with how Hollywood movie ideas are processed, juggled, bought, sold and reworked before an actual film is produced, the suspicion becomes easy to entertain. The differences between the two stories however, are revealing. By the 1980s Vance had long given up interest in the themes — if not the decor — of science fiction, in favor of what he called "my kind of stories". The pugilistic robots in "Real Steel" become humanized and elicit empathy, in the spirit of Asimov and the still-growing excitement about artificial intelligence; in "Clang", however, the hairless bi-pedal monocephaloid (to use Vance's formulation) boxing machines never rise above the status of interesting objects, and can elicit no more human sympathy than a refrigerator.

The whys and wherefores of the "The Magnificent Red-hot Jazzing Seven" (1974) are explained too well by its author to require comment. Let it be known however, that Jack Vance, casting aside his pen, devoted the last decade of his life to jazz; singing, playing ukulele, harmonica, kazoo, washboard and jug-bass with daily enthusiasm, even going so far as to cut a CD of classic tunes and his own compositions (available from Spatterlight!). In younger days, Vance achieved sufficient proficiency on the cornet that pros of his acquaintance allowed him in their jam sessions. As a journalism student at Cal, he reviewed jazz clubs. A consuming passion, which frequently erupts into his stories, Vance resolutely and defiantly restricted jazz to an area within a triangle defined by three points: Bix Beiderbecke, Jack Teagarden, and the 1920s — which is to say: the musical heroes and halcyon days of his youth. This genre he unapologetically extolled to the detriment of all others — though, in one of many vancian paradoxes, he occasionally admitted admiration for Debussy and other classical composers. Despite his bonhomie, Vance was a discreet and private man, but in the preamble to "The Red-hot Jazzing Seven" are to be found some of the most heart-felt and personal lines he ever committed to paper.

The main event in this volume, however, are Vance's major unpublished works. They are qualified as unfinished, but the painter Whistler famously remarked that a painting should be finished at every stroke, and replacing "painting" and "stroke" with "story" and "word", Vance lived this maxim, for these beautifully written texts leave one with little or no sense of being un-finished. "The Genesee Slough Murders" stands as a somewhat short Joe Bain novel. But is any Vance novel ever long enough?

Vance's practice was to begin with an outline. These outlines however were often more than half the length of the published version. But Vance really began his work with a long labor of imagination, elaborating his story out of characters, which he developed, in turn, out of what he called an "atmosphere". I have heard Vance discussing this, and these genitive atmospheres, or waking dreams and fantasies which seem to have imposed themselves upon him, were the real foundation of his writing. He then built his texts in a certain manner which is akin to a process of addition. There were never, for example, any foundational or intermediate stages; the 'outlines' do not include anything like notes to himself about what he means to do later, unelaborated and rough, mapping out of sequences, and so on. The last section of "Cat Island" does include such a phrase:

Further episodes trace the history of Cat Island...

This, recounts nothing. It is a place-holder, a structural indication void of content. It is also practically the only such phrase I have found in these texts, the exception that proves the rule. What follows, however, is in the characteristically engaging vancian manner:

"...the hinterlands are opened up to development. Vast mouse-ranches come into being..."

Hinterlands developed; mouse-ranches: here is vancian substance; the story already exists! This phrase, as its stands, is the sort of thing we often find in Vance, in his thumbnail culture sketches for example. Vance readers eventually feel, not that Vance's work is never finished, but there could always be more. Other writers create texts like a house of bricks, all parts conspiring to weld up a solid and finished object to which nothing can be, or need be, added; but just as Vance's worlds seem to extend ineluctably in the ten directions of space and time, so his prose is like an aqueous substance coursing the watersheds and valleys of imagination, flowing and flooding where and as far as it may, constrained or dammed only by the exigencies of publication. One thinks of Morreion's numberless circumambulatory tours of his planet, the vastness of the Big Planet horizons, the always-expanding prospects of the Gaean Reach and unplumbed depths of the Beyond; or again, the infinite preciousness he claims for each fragile, evanescent spark of sentience swimming the infinity of existence — myriads of unforgettable characters emerging, however briefly, then disappearing into unfathomable distance, an unknowable infinity of faces and adventures. Each story is like an incident in the vancian meta-story, infinite in time and space, total in import, of which one can never have more than a fleeting and dream-like glimpse. Provoking such a glimpse can even seem like Vance's most profound motivation, the ultimate purpose of each novel. His phrases are pervaded with the patience and sympathy which such a motivation must cultivate. We are left with the sense that any section, however long and elaborated, is not yet too long, the pace never too slow. The efforts he lavished on the evocation of countless taverns, bars and hostels, houses, towns and cities, trees and landscapes, ships and conveyances of all kinds, betray a curiosity of vast scope for which no fact, however apparently banal, can be irrelevant, and for which no act, however seemingly inconsequential, lacks unsuspected importance. As the poet Navarth remarked: "Do you realize that a crook of my finger disturbs the farthest star?" With Vance, finally, each word grasps at a disappearingly expansive notion. Sometimes those words murmur to us how their author left them behind in an almost self-derogatory frustration, traces of a yearning unmeasurable in scope, and indeed, the late work is a tranquil flood; *Ports of Call* would have been even longer than *Lyonesse* or *Cadwal*, had Vance's eyes not failed him so miserably.

"The STARK"* exemplifies the vancian gaze into infinity in an amusingly concrete manner, dating from an early period (1954) when, hoping to provoke publishing opportunities in the genres, he attempted to write real science fiction. Perhaps originally conceived as a novel, it develops as something like a plan for an open-ended series of novellas. Readers will recognize an aspect of a proto-backstory of the vancian universe, such as we encounter in *Tschai*.

The Alastor novels also were intended as an open-ended series, and there is a trace — a most intriguing hint — of a fourth Alastor book, indited in blue ink in Jack's spidery hand:

> Alastor 458: Pharism: The Connatic reads a letter: There is a most evil man in this region. He destroyed something beautiful. The cursar's report: there was always an extra dimension: perhaps a fabric of guesses or an extravagant figure of speech, or an emotional reaction by which Bertold revealed his effervescent personality.

The phrase: "the Connatic reads a letter" is analogous to: "the telephone was ringing in the dark"; a mysterious communication casts a light into darkness, revealing more puzzles than it resolves. Both phrases, redolent of the vancian atmosphere, are gambits in his alchemical quest to transubstantiate mental vapors into verbal gold. Such phrases do not belong to a plan; they are already story. The *Pharism* outline, evoking some vast and secret tragedy, is alive with tension between destruction of the beautiful, and effervescence of personality. This might puzzle us unduly were there not a panoply of effervescent vancian villains, destroyers of innocence and beauty. Typically vancian, characteristically nietzschean, the phrase quivers with embryonic potential; it projects a shadowy prolongation of the Alastor series which disappears into a fog of might-have-been, which yet, somehow, "is". If so much can be said for this scrap, how much more may we not hope from the substantial texts of this book!

---

* The text includes illustrations following Vance's own sketches, prepared by Joel Anderson for the V.I.E. and adapted for Spatterlight Press by Christopher Wood.

"Cat Island" is a very early text (1946) which none-the-less exemplifies that species of story Vance later, in efforts to push away the science fiction label, was driven to call "my kind of story". It is a raging adventure, about domestic cats; it deals with the foundations of society and war, framed as zany comedy; it is filled with psychological insight, covered in the whipped cream of ironic inconsequentiality; it is philosophical, yet patriotic. Unlikely conjunctures, vivid in these scant early pages, map Vance's literary essence. Here is his relation to the genres: the vancian mode of transformative originality. "Cat Island" is no more "adventure", "romance", "western", "comedy", "mystery" or "science fiction" than *Bird Isle*, or *Ports of Call*. It is all of them, and none of them. It is Vance's kind of story. Read all his work in its light, and taste the full flavor of his art.

But if science fiction is what you want, nothing in Vance can satisfy more than "The STARK". Its premise is the only cosmic cataclysm Vance ever contemplated, the greatest worth bothering to imagine: imminent destruction of the earth. The problem is solved, as it must be in science fiction, by technology: replacement of the planet by a machine free to wander space, and no greater technological gadget was ever imagined! Technology is power, and power is liberty. But such a feat, gaining this power and liberty, is only possible if all of humanity directs itself to the single goal of human salvation. The real problem then is political, and the real goal is philosophical. Only a unified world, coordinated and directed by unified understanding and will, can effectuate the secular miracle of human salvation. Politics, not technology, is the source of liberty.

This puzzle is a basic 20th century theme, and Vance resolves it in surprising ways, particularly for a man who, with most of his generation, and against too many of his fellow artists, was a cold warrior. First president Anker voluntarily relinquishes power to Russian Communist dictatorship; then a conflict born of bigotry and folly compromises completion of the star ark, and easy-going, practical and clear-minded Sam Eavens saves the day through resolution and decisive action. The virtues embodied by Anker and Eavens are typically American.

Two years previously (1952) Vance had already treated this theme in *Gold and Iron*, where earth is colonized by a culturally superior race.

This superiority is recognized by the American protagonist in a spirit of good-natured realism. Reminiscent of H. G. Wells' Eloi, however, Lekthwan superiority lacks something which leaves it defenseless against the savagery of the enslaving Klau. Only the typically American combination of resilience and resolve, characterized by Sam Eavens in "The STARK", can meet the challenge.

Life requires many things, both the theoretical power of the Lekthwan and the moral power of the American attitude as Vance understood it. Perhaps Vance is suggesting that moral power is more important than technological power. "The STARK", however, suggests something larger — for, after Earth's population is saved, nothing changes. The STARK, like the Gaean Reach itself, is just the world in another form. The ebb and flow of political, technological, moral and cultural conflict continues unabated, expressed in a tesseract of social evolutions over decades and centuries as the STARK plies its way from to star to star.

At an even more basic level we find something in these stories which underlies many aspects of Vance's work, such as the Historical Society and the Institute, those Olympian observers and adjusters of culture. This "something" is Vance's life-long fascination with Oswald Spengler. Spengler's thesis, greatly popular in the pre-war time of Vance's youth, may be simply stated: cultures rise, flower, then decay and fall. Spengler's thought is a popularized version of hegelian ideas, which are alive today in other forms, such as the cultural and historical relativism which, depending on your perspective, are wreaking havoc or provoking welcome changes in the arts, education, social fabric and so on. But Vance's work is nourished by reaction to many intellectual currents, for example scientism, another specter from the 19th century. I have called scientism the religion of materialism, and Vance was a great observer of religion, himself a half-hearted mystic. Social Darwinism arose out of scientism, in which some see a root of 1930s fascism and others a source of the thinking in such books as *The Bell Curve*. These old ideas, debated in other terms prior to the second world war, constantly take new forms and menace us, or succor us if you prefer, with new hypotheses and attitudes. Vance has given us most useful accounts of them, in *The Cadwal Chronicles* for example. This is the cultural air we breath; bracing winds or noxious gases, they are the atmosphere from which Vance works his gold.

Vance struggled with the riddle of spenglerian fate: can it be evaded? Can society — that society out of which Vance's art springs, and for which it is created—renew itself in the face of inevitable decay? Despair is not obligatory, but there are good reasons to think Spengler was right. If many Vance stories end well, in the traditional comic mode, less hopeful messages can be slipped between the lines. The agents of Cadwal saved themselves; might they have failed? might they fail next time? might their success be a sort of failure? For all his playful explorations, Vance's attitude may be more profoundly hegelian than Spengler's: he resists historical determinism and adopts a stance of sheer observation. The "historical development" of which Hegel spoke was a flowering of culture through human history to its perfection in his own time. But this hegelian progress is neither temporal nor spatial; certain cultural phenomena are prior to others, but only theoretically. No state of culture necessarily tends to develop into another in the same place, nor are any subject to theoretically necessary decay. For example, in the hegelian perspective Chinese culture is more and less evolved than certain others, but has remained constant for millennia. Vance is an observer and taster of cultures, not a prophet of historical doom or paradise like Hegel's followers Spengler and Marx. Vance leaves his readers room to hope.

Events on the STARK are alarming. At one point, all human knowledge is destroyed and scientists work to create a superior race. The result is a brood of monsters which enslaves humanity. If such themes return in later work, Vance never again takes them to such extremes. The events of "The STARK", however, are useful to keep in mind when encountering their more subtle and ironic versions, such as the situation on Fader in *Night Lamp*.

The larger vancian theme has another major aspect, personal and psychological, and "The Telephone was Ringing in the Dark" offers an essential elucidation. This theme, the evil which lurks in the hearts of men, is neither softly christian nor coldly manichean, but darkly and vigorously nietzschean. It is well-exposed in such stories as *The House on Lily Street* and *Bad Ronald*, where Ronald Wilby and Paul Gunther are essentially the same sort of characters as Kokor Hekkus and Howard Alan Treesong. But vancian good-guys also have dark sides. It can be argued that Kirth Gersen is an assassin, that Glinnes Hulden is a reactionary, and that Glawen Clattuc is a racial supremacist. As for Myron Tany, though this seems to be too subtle for some readers, his heartlessness, if understandable by reason of his youth and nothing out of the ordinary, causes him the sort of pain and remorse which most of us must bear. In Vance evil is everywhere. "The Telephone was Ringing in the Dark" however presents us with a unique case, a radical exposition of a ubiquitous vancian flavor: in this story everyone is bad. We have something like this in *Strange She Hasn't Written,** and *The View from Chickweed's Window*; in the latter, however, Lulu's extra-legal revenge — or adjustment of cosmic disequilibria — cannot be qualified as unjust, though the calculated dose of schadenfreude she indulges is diluted with very little christian forgiveness, while Robert cannot forgive himself his past misdeeds. If Mervyn Grey, of *Strange She Hasn't Written*, is less bad than he might have been, his weakness is enough to cut him off from his heart's desire, a fate Lulu's Robert seeks to inflict upon himself; seeing no hope of redemption, and by corollary no divine retribution, he seeks to insure his own punishment. Since we do not learn of Mervyn's evil until the end, it colors the story in a way reminiscent of "Telephone", since we only understand bit by bit that our protagonist, Garnet Marsh, is neither hero, nor particularly good, nor even properly protagonistic. Still this story is unique; there is (if we except the vague and foolish Amy, submerged and drowned in the ambient criminality) no innocence.

Garnet Marsh is not precisely evil, but the annoyance to which he is subjected (which he himself feels it would be better to ignore) startles him from a degenerative state. Thus revivified, he involves himself in petty, irrational and sometimes criminal activities, inspired by revenge. These mix him up with unsavory and murderous people, who manipulate him. He goes, one might say, from one zombie state to another, a distressing and sobering but altogether vancian situation. What at the outset gives him back the vitality he lacks, is a fortuitous

---

* Published as *The Four Johns*.

event; but this new lease on life only returns him to morbid sterility. His fate is like that of Jorjol, in *Domains of Koryphon*,* where a gift, a privilege in appearance advantageous — in Jorjol's case being raised by Uther Madduc rather than out among the tribes — contains the seeds of his chaotic disaster. "Telephone" holds an extreme position in the vancian context and is thus a vantage from which the full import of other stories reveal themselves.

Furthermore, as always with Vance, there are surprising phrases which can open alarming perspectives:

> Automobiles passed below, sentient metallic oblongs, neither bird, beast, fish nor insect, the human polyp within functioning as nerve-pulp.

It is also, like the other "mysteries", a vivid picture of California life in all its crazy diversity.

Finally, there is "Wild Thyme and Violets". Though rife with vancian echoes, this story resembles nothing else in Vance's œuvre. It relates perhaps most closely to *Bird Isle* as a sort of feckless romp, but this time in a darkling world. Lucian, the central character, if he can be called that, is a hapless painter who — like the hero of *Wyst* — lodges a beautiful mute in his miserable hut. Beyond that, parallels are few. The incidents are comic and poetic, yet more and more dire. The marquis Paul-Aubry is the eeriest of vancian villains. His doings, motivated by wan curiosity, derive from a solipsism so suffocating he is intrigued only by his own incapacity to feel. Merely to provoke himself he indulges in pointless destructions, petty or horrific, all to no avail. This portrait I suspect to be a revelation of an aspect of Vance's own personality, more generally revealed by his dispassionate and ironic literary stance. Vance's personal solution, rather than the weird destructions of his marquis, was artistic creation through which a vast array of experience could be indulged (shades of Kokor Hekkus!). Self-conscience so acute that it culminates in moral detachment — for why one thing rather than another? — is profoundly vancian.

---

* Published as *The Grey Prince*.

Lucian, like Cugel, is a ne'er-do-well of imagination, doomed to bad luck. Unlike Cugel he is endowed with a tender heart. Events at Gargano, which need not have turned so dire, end up discouraging poor Lucian, who happily retains the resilience to move on. But he is not really the central character, any more than the marquis, or the naive mayor, Parnasse, or Mersile, the mountebank. The story is expressive of pure atmosphere where, like "Telephone", and if there is no real evil — for the marquis is "evil" without malice — no one is actually good. Crafty deceptions and ribald tricks are the norm. Alicia is too entrapped in her vagaries to embody benevolence, and Lucian's love seems to meet her elusive personality at no definite point, though she accepts it with docility.

What to make of such a tale? It is most vancian! Until *Ports of Call*, nothing strikes so clearly the subtle note of vancian morality: skeptic, amused and bemused, broad but distant, slyly nietzschean: life is to be lived to the full by each, according to his, mostly dim, lights and subject to his, generally feeble, powers. The ensuing currents and counter-currents provoke roil in the cosmic fabric, which imparts a particular import. What is it? Perhaps because "Wild Thyme" remains an outline, with certain chapters distilled to a single phrase, we here touch most closely Vance's starting point, one of his atmospheres out of which his kind of stories are born. Its color is sienna, tinged with blue-grey and burgundy. You will see it and you will not forget it.

Wild Thyme and Violets
and Other Unpublished Works

CAT ISLAND

1

ONE TERRIBLE NIGHT at sea a large ship foundered among the toppling waves. The sole survivors were a number of cats, thirty-two in all, who managed to clamber aboard a life-raft. Through lightning and thunder, wind and spume, they clung for dear life, while the typhoon drove the raft across the dark waters like a trifle of chaff whisked on the breeze. Drenched, cold, miserable, the cats secured themselves to the ropes and gratings arranged for that purpose.

When morning dawned the wind died and the sea calmed, but the horizon delineated only an inscrutable wet wilderness.

For three days the raft drifted, and many were the dangers and alarms, and many the expressions of discomfort and despair. The timid cats crouched miserably in the center of the raft, avoiding as best they might any glimpse of the sea and the salt spray which stiffened their fur. The most daring cats, despising the idea of risk, alert for thrills, paced about the edge of the raft, the better to spy land, or perhaps to catch a careless fish.

At dawn of the fourth day the raft drifted upon the beach of an island. With one accord the cats leapt ashore, where they quenched their thirst at a nearby spring and appeased their worst pangs of hunger on crabs and other crustaceans whom they found crossing the beach. Hereupon, a period of several hours was devoted to rest, the cleansing and ordering of fur.

With their most urgent needs satisfied, the cats held a council. Among the group were three elderly cats to whom the others gave deference and looked for leadership. Two of these, in the interests of harmony, effaced themselves and sat with tails modestly folded at the outskirts of the gathering. The third, a large Maltese named Peter, was elected temporary chairman. After a moment of deliberation he addressed the group.

"Comrades in adversity! Through the caprice of the elements we have been delivered upon this pleasant island. Indeed it is wild, undeveloped, and a far cry from the ease of our former homes. Still, compared to the rigors of the life-raft, or the dark wet depths, it is a veritable garden of Arcadia. Seemingly no connection with civilization exists, however, and who knows how long Destiny may impound us upon this forgotten cranny of the world?"

Faces were glum at this aspect to the situation. Only upon the life-raft had the comforts of the familiar hearth, the private saucer of milk, and the soft cushions of the basket seemed more dear. There were murmurs of discouragement, but also proposals were advanced as to how best to convey a message of distress to the appropriate authorities.

Sadly none of the concepts appeared effective in the ultimate view. Peter dismissed them in turn with a few caustic remarks.

"The suggested use of smoke-signals is not only nuncupatory, but also inept in that —" he made a sweeping gesture about the blank horizon "— what eye is there to see? Also, the plan to capture and train carrier pigeons is scarcely more feasible, even recognizing that the native genius of these estimable birds brings them unalterably back to the hands which trained them. The venture would terminate in an episode of birds being taken from the cote, hurled into the air, the same birds quickly wheeling and returning to the same cote, their messages unread."

"Perhaps we could construct a radio transmitter and send SOS messages," suggested a young black cat. "I see a perfectly splendid place for an antenna — from the tip of that cocoanut palm to the crag of rock there on the hillside. I could climb that tree in a jiffy, even carrying a coil of wire!"

"I know the Morse codes for SOS!" called out another cat in excitement. "Three dots, three dashes and three more dots. Or," somewhat doubtfully, "is it the other way around?"

"In that case our message would read 'OSO'," said a white cat named

Snowball. "It might well be construed to mean: 'Stay away!' or 'Do not save us'."

Peter's long gray tail twitched. "In any case, inasmuch as none of us has thought to bring with him a small broadcasting unit, nor the supplies necessary for the construction even were one of us trained in electronic principles, we must abandon this illusory but otherwise exalted proposition. I become increasingly convinced that, discounting miracles, we must plan to remain where we now find ourselves for an indefinite period."

In general the response to Peter's conclusion was doleful twitching of the whiskers and even a few ears laid back in depression. "We must make the best of the situation," declared Peter, "and indeed we will! We are American cats, heirs to glorious tradition! We have our health, our courage has been proved by the tempestuous days and nights on the deep! We find ourselves new pioneers and we will establish a settlement — nay, a community, a principality even! So shall we prosper!"

This rousing exhortation was greeted with acclamation and cat-calls, together with spirited lashing of tails. With renewed confidence the thirty-two cats faced the future.

2

At the prospect of indefinite residence upon the island the castaway cats gave the landscape a more thorough examination. "Our first thoughts must be toward a permanent place of habitation," declared Peter.

"I see some hills," called a pretty young Persian named Kitty, who had climbed halfway up a cocoanut palm. "Perhaps we could find caves."

"The suggestion, in certain of its aspects is sound," said Peter, perhaps a trifle ponderously. "Still, under careful analysis it cannot stand the test of practicality."

"Why not?" demanded Banjo, a yellow tortoise-shell, who, secretly enamored of Kitty, felt compelled to second her proposals.

"It must be remembered," explained Peter, fixing upon the brash Banjo a lambent yellow stare, "that caves are wont to occur in a rocky terrain — basalt, trap, flint, limestone, and like formations. We must ever bear in mind the necessity of convenient sanitary facilities. The lee of that bluff —" and he indicated a knoll fronting a wide beach of soft white sand "— would, to my mind, prove a more satisfactory location."

Much was said pro and con, with the lee of the bluff finally selected, and the cats set off to inspect the site of their new home, running and bounding across the sand, leaping over driftwood and seaweed in a brisk and carefree manner.

Beside the bluff they halted once more. A cat called Timothy spoke. "What will we name our new home?"

For a space the group was silent; then came a torrent of suggestions. Each had a proposal to put forward. Some were fanciful, even elaborate; others were terse. Some were sentimental; still others tended in an ideological direction, upon which controversy might be expected.

It was the sage Peter who once more resolved the situation. "What we require," he said, "is a name at once sonorous, dignified, inspiring and expressive. Grace and vigor must go hand in hand. What could be more appropriate than —" he paused.

"Than what?" came the excited chorus.

" 'Cat Island'?" murmured Peter.

Approval was immediate, unanimous, and as the cats paced off the bounds of their new village, they insensibly began to think of themselves, not as castaways, but as settlers, homesteaders — in short, Cat Islanders.

Further episodes trace the history of Cat Island: the hinterlands are opened up to development. Vast mouse-ranches come into being; the mouse herds are guarded by a new breed of rough and ready young cats known as 'muskits' (in analogy with 'cowboys').

An airplane crashes on the beach; the cats learn that the USA is at war with a cruel enemy.

Shortly thereafter Cat Island is invaded by a contingent of the enemy. The cats acquit themselves notably.

The cats coordinate their efforts with the US Marines. The night before a landing by the marines the cats sneak into the enemy's barracks and steal all the trousers.

In the morning the US Marines land, and the enemy is too embarrassed to leave their barracks and are easily captured. It is a gallant action for which the cats receive commendation.

The Genesee Slough Murders

Chapter I

ON THE AFTERNOON OF Saturday, June 15, Sheriff Joe Bain encountered several persons in the full vigor of life, who, to their horrified amazement, would shortly be killed by a mysterious enemy.

The day began in an ordinary fashion. Joe's seventeen-year-old daughter, Miranda, scrambled eggs for his breakfast, while he drank a cup of coffee and read an editorial on the front page of the morning *Clarion*:

> ### AN UNCOMFORTABLE DILEMMA, AN ACCEPTABLE COMPROMISE
>
> Often in life one set of praiseworthy endeavors collides head-on with another set. This predicament is currently our own. The tree-shaded waterways of San Rodrigo, Contra Costa, San Joaquin, Sacramento, and several other counties, are esthetic assets to our beautiful state. The fields and farms surrounded by these waterways are a source of wealth to those who till them, and by economic convection to the whole population. The line of division between land and water, namely the levees, have become a cause of bitter conflict. The levees must be strong and sound to prevail against the spring floods. On the levees grow lordly cottonwoods, poplars, oaks, willows, weeping willows; mulberry, fig and elderberry trees; wild rose and blackberry tangles, to create many miles of delightful vistas. Alas! the roots weaken the levee on which the trees grow.
>
> The Army Engineers, to protect the waterways, are

engaged in removing the trees and lining the banks with rip-rap. Conservationists, nature-lovers, yachtsmen, ecologists, a number of plain ordinary crack-pots, as many plain ordinary trouble-makers, intend to halt the work, and they mean Now. The Sierra Club, a responsible and far-sighted organization, has instituted legal action to halt the levee stripping.

Where does the *Clarion* stand on this difficult question?

We would hope for a compromise.

On islands and berms where the levees are not endangered, let the trees stand! But where the roots weaken the levee and imperil the economic well-being of our county — regretfully they must go.

Beauty is meaningless to farmers whose fields are flooded. They earn no more money; they pay no more taxes.

Which leads us to the basic thrust of this editorial.

San Rodrigo County has the fourth lowest tax rate of any county in California, and one of the lowest gross incomes. As a result our public buildings are ghastly Victorian jokes; our school system is barely adequate; our Sheriff's Department is a languid and amateurish operation working by fits, starts, spasms and frantic improvisation.

We must accept a bitter reality. We need to pay higher taxes. Only then will we be able to attract able career officials who will bring San Rodrigo County into the Twentieth Century.

We need the tax money.

The trees endanger the fields which provide tax money.

Hence, with regret, the trees must go.

Today a number of people will gather along Genesee Slough to prevent any further stripping of the levees.

How shall we regard this demonstration? We hope that appropriate laws will be enforced.

Joe flings aside the paper in annoyance. "Howard Griselda has lost none of his zeal. He's on my back again."

Miranda tries to soothe him. The telephone rings; she goes off to answer. "Who's that?" Joe asks.

"Oh, just someone."

Joe goes down to his office. The night has been relatively calm; two cars stolen and a burglary.

The department is chronically short-handed; Joe has put a trusty, Dave Merrick, to work as relief despatcher, handling the radio during slack hours. Dave is twenty-one, a ham radio operator, whose crime was stealing his father-in-law's airplane and cracking it up. Joe considers him impulsive and naive rather than criminal, and allows him considerable latitude. Besides he can use the help.

Joe goes out to look over the scene of the burglary. The victims are Victor and Jessie deGiorgio. While they attended a wedding their house was entered, and goods to the value of $1200 were stolen.

They live in a frame house under five big oak trees, at the center of a vineyard. Joe looks around the premises. He asks, "Who knew the house would be empty?"

"Just the family; that's all. We don't tell our business to nobody."

"Looks to me like somebody knew you'd be out of the way for awhile. Who lives in that house yonder?" Joe points across the field.

"Just some poor-class people. Hicks is their name. I never talk to them; they never talk to me."

"They might have noticed something; I'll go have a word with them."

Joe drives up the sand road to the Hicks house. A dog barks. Chickens move aside. Under a tree is an old pick-up. A young man is working on a fancy hot-rod. Joe thinks he looks sullen and shifty. "You're Mr. Hicks?"

"That's right. What can I do for you?"

"You live here with your family?"

"They're back in Arkansas for a bit. Me and my brother stayed home."

"I see. Where's your brother?"

"Inside the house. What's the trouble?"

"Somebody robbed the deGiorgios last night. I wonder if you noticed anything unusual."

"No sir. Not a thing."

"How about your brother?"

"Not a thing, so far as I know. In fact we weren't home."

"Where did you go?"

"Into Aurora. We looked at some stuff in Monkey Wards; we got some hamburgers. Then we came home."

"You drove your pick-up?"

"That's right."

"What time do you think you got in?"

"About ten I guess."

"You didn't go out this morning to buy groceries, for instance?"

"No sir. How come you're so interested?"

"Just suppose," says Joe, "that you noticed the deGiorgios leave, all dressed up, and decided to rob their house. Where would you hide the loot?"

Tom Hicks laughs. "I sure don't know. I never thought about it."

"The attic? Or maybe the barn?"

"I can't understand why you're talking like this, Sheriff."

"Because of the way your pick-up is pointing. It's facing down the driveway. I think when you came home at night you'd drive up to the front door."

"Sometimes I turn it around."

"Show me how."

Tom Hicks says, "Why all the interest in how I turn the pick-up?"

"Because it looks to me like you drove up to the barn, turned around, unloaded, and pulled up to where you are now. I can't see any other reason for the pick-up to be where it is."

"You're getting mighty fancy, Sheriff. Wasn't anything like that."

"Let's go take a look in the barn."

"Now just a minute. I don't think that's the right thing to do. It's against my civil liberties."

"I can get a warrant in two shakes. Also don't say anything you wouldn't want to hear in court. Do I look at your barn the easy way or the hard way?"

≈

Joe makes them load the stuff back on their pick-up; all drive to the deGiorgios.

Joe tells the deGiorgios: "I figure the young one will get off with a warning; the oldest one will draw about six months if it's his first offense…Could you use six months worth of work out of these two miserable wretches?"

"I could use some help, sure. If they'd work."

"What do you say, boys? Do you want to go to jail or work six months for Mr. deGiorgio? And I mean work. Because if there's any soldiering you'll be back in the soup."

The choice is grudgingly made.

Joe goes home for lunch. Miranda is again on the telephone. "Who are you talking to? Seems all you do is languish on that damn blower."

"Oh, just somebody."

"I see."

Chapter II

Joe and four deputies drive out to the Genesee Slough, where the demonstration against the levee stripping is already underway. Hippies are perched in trees, men and women sit on the levees blocking the path of a bulldozer. A tall handsome woman of about 30, distinguished by a striking pile of red hair, marches back and forth. Joe watches her in awe; a Celtic war-goddess wearing a white trench-coat and shades. In the water a barge supports an enormous power-shovel. Dusty Rhodes, the operator, watches the demonstration with sardonic detachment.

Howard Griselda, smoking a pipe, ambles up to Joe. "Well, Sheriff, what do you think?"

"I'm beyond thought. I'm just watching and hoping it's all a dream. That red-headed lady looks to be a fearless adversary."

Griselda grunts. "What do you propose to do?"

"As of this moment, nothing."

"They're interfering with the work; they're trespassing on the levee."

"If I told them to disperse, and they just laughed at me, I'd feel an awful fool."

"The Sheriff isn't supposed to play the fool; he's supposed to take effective action."

"I didn't say 'play', Howard; I said 'feel'."

Griselda puffs a cloud of smoke from his pipe. His nephew and employee, Lloyd Griselda, an intense young man of twenty-four, is taking pictures of the demonstration. Lloyd Griselda has a round bull-dog face, blond curly hair, conservative mutton-chop sideburns.

In the high branches of a cottonwood stands a tall hippie. He jeers at Dusty Rhodes, and to make his feelings absolutely clear he urinates toward the barge: a perfect half-parabola sparkling in the sunlight. Somebody calls out in rapture: "Oh please! Do it again!"

Griselda looks at Joe. "Well, Sheriff?"

"Well what?"

"I saw an indecent act."

"So did I."

"Well?" asks Griselda.

"Were you offended?"

"To some extent."

"Want to sign a complaint?"

"No."

"I don't either."

The hippy in the tree climbs down. He decides to lead an attack against the barge and runs up the plank. After a brief tussle Dusty Rhodes hurls him over the side.

Griselda looks at Joe. "What are you going to do?"

"About which?"

"I thought I noticed an act of assault."

"The operator doesn't look too outraged."

Griselda nods with profound understanding.

"Out of curiosity," Joe asks, "what kind of editorial do you plan to write about my feeble behavior?"

"You've said it all right there."

"Now Howard, be honest. Do you really want those trees pulled out?"

"Did you read my editorial this morning?"

"I did. You said you wanted the trees cut down so you can get money enough to fire me. I almost feel like joining the demonstrators. In fact, unless my eyes deceive me that's my daughter out there, protecting her household."

Griselda has already stalked away to confer with his nephew Lloyd.

Joe walks down the levee to where Miranda stands under a weeping-willow: a long-legged dark-haired saucy-faced girl, now wearing a semi-hippy costume, also a headband stuck with two jaunty feathers.

Joe looks her over. "What are you doing out here?"

"I'm protecting the beauty of California."

"Those are awful tight shorts you're wearing, speaking of beauty. I wouldn't take a deep breath if I were you."

"Oh, funny Daddy, you're so square."

"Strange how one man can cultivate so many different reputations. Howard Griselda, now, thinks I'm a lazy hound for not leading all these people off to justice…That rangy red-headed lady is giving me the eye. She thinks I'm God's gift to the fair sex. What's her name?"

"I don't know her name. She came with the Aurora delegation; I think she's in charge of something."

"She looks like a real goer. Good Lord, here she comes."

The red-headed lady strides down the levee to confront Joe. She has sparkling icicle-blue eyes; she stands as tall as Joe, not even counting the amazing pyramid of red curls on her head. "I understand that you are Sheriff Joe Bain." Her voice is cold and clear. Her dispassionate gaze makes Joe feel like a Russian peasant.

"I have that honor."

The woman is Suzanne Staffe. She orders Joe to arrest Dusty Rhodes for assault.

"Assault on who?"

"On this person here, Dakota Slim."

The hippy comes forward, and adds his own expostulations to those of Miss Staffe. Lloyd Griselda comes up and takes pictures of the three, to Joe's annoyance.

Dusty Rhodes, a tall saturnine man in tan whipcord, saunters past; his relief has arrived. Dakota utters an unmentionable phrase. Dusty Rhodes pauses, shrugs, goes his way. Dakota runs screaming after him; Rhodes seizes him by the nape of the neck and seat of the pants, runs him down the bank and pitches him into the tules.

Suzanne Staffe demands that Joe take action. Joe says: "The main thing I saw was Dakota charging Dusty."

Suzanne Staffe makes a brittle comment, and Joe complains: "Everybody wants me to destroy their enemies!"

"I'll destroy my own enemies!" screams Dakota Slim.

Joe looks up into the tree from which Dakota had urinated and assesses the distance to the barge. "You'll never reach the deck."

~

Joe drives to Cap'n Henry's Riverview Haven for a beer. When Joe returns to the demonstration the sun is low and the mob has dwindled. Howard Griselda has gone; Lloyd Griselda is sitting in his red VW, hoping for some dramatic event. Joe looks around and finds Miranda. They drive back down the levee to Cap'n Henry's and have dinner. Joe doesn't want to be bothered or even recognized; he takes a table to the back, in the shadows.

Miranda has been much impressed by Suzanne Staffe. "Don't you think she's striking? So poised!"

"She reminds me of those Aubrey Beardsley pictures you got hanging in your room," says Joe.

"You're so unperceptive, Daddy. She's an exciting person to be around. I'd like to do something important too — not just get married and start keeping house."

"I sure as hell don't want you to start keeping house without being married."

"Don't be silly! I'm only half in love, anyway."

Joe is startled by the sudden change in subject. "Indeed? Who is the lucky fellow?"

"Well — I don't really know his name."

"You mean you don't know his real name?"

"I don't know any of his names. I don't even know what he looks like. He telephoned our house on a wrong number; we got to talking and he's called back every day since."

"The attachment can't be too serious."

"It is in a way. I've never met anyone like him."

Joe shakes his head in wonder. "If he can do this over the phone, what a high-powered cuss he must be in person. How old is he?"

"I've never asked him."

The demonstration is the sole topic of conversation. The dining room is a pleasant place overlooking Genesee Slough, with docks in front and a marina to the side. Cap'n Henry has been incapacitated; his wife, Leona

Eklund, runs the place. She is a dynamic assertive, very blonde lady of forty-five, thin as a mink, wearing over-young clothes and too much make-up. Cap'n Henry sits at the bar, wearing a nautical cap and drinking an occasional glass of beer. He has a bland red face; he speaks very little and walks slowly with a cane. Leona likes to think of herself as an alluring seductress; she dances to the juke-box with Ralph Henigson, who owns a big cabin-cruiser. Cap'n Henry watches without apparent interest.

Suzanne Staffe comes into the dining room with Dakota Slim. Leona Eklund confronts them. "I've had trouble with this person, and I don't allow him in the dining room!"

Suzanne Staffe draws herself up. "He's here as my guest."

Joe tries to make himself even more inconspicuous. "There's a fight I definitely don't want to have to break up," he tells Miranda.

But Leona Eklund sniffs and turns away. Lloyd Griselda appears. He speaks a moment or two to Suzanne Staffe; she gives her head a regal nod; Lloyd takes flash-pictures.

Another altercation: Leona Eklund refuses to serve Dakota Slim because he has no driver's license. "How do I know how old he is? I can't see his face!"

Suzanne Staffe and her friends leave in disgust, to Joe's relief. Twilight falls across the water; bats flicker through the trees. The dining room is now almost empty; custom has shifted to the bar. Joe and Miranda finish dinner and leave. Joe checks into headquarters; everything quiet.

They drive home. Miranda takes a shower and goes to bed with a book; Joe sits down with a can of beer to watch a baseball game.

A half-hour passes. Joe gets ready to take a shower. The doorbell rings. Joe hesitates out of caution and distrust. He switches on the outside lights. Howard Griselda stands outside. Joe lets him in. "What the devil are you doing here, Howard?"

Griselda looks around. "Home alone?"

Joe thinks his manner strange. "More or less. My mother's up at Halfway House for the summer. What's on your mind?"

"Oh, nothing much. Just thought I'd drop in for a chat."

"I'm game if you are. Have a beer?"

"No, thanks."

"Well, what did you want to talk about?"

Griselda slowly stuffs his pipe. "You asked about that red-headed woman. I think she's planning to enter politics."

"So long as she doesn't run for Sheriff, it's great by me. What does she do for a living?"

"She's an attorney; she's just gone into partnership with James Malony in Aurora."

"Well, that's interesting news. Do you have anything else to tell me?"

Griselda stuffs his pipe. "Well, I've got a little problem."

The doorbell rings; this time it's a city policeman. "Good evening, Sheriff. We had a report of a prowler."

"A prowler? That would probably be Howard Griselda."

"No, this was somebody trying to get in your windows."

"Hmm. Let's check around a bit."

Joe looks in the kitchen and the back porch: all okay. He knocks on Miranda's door. "Yes Daddy?"

"Can we come in? We want to look under your bed."

"Come in."

The house is checked: no sign of a trespasser. The policeman leaves, Griselda is smoking his pipe with great energy. Joe asks, "So what's your problem?"

Griselda shrugs. "It can wait." He unceremoniously takes his leave.

Joe rubs his chin in perplexity. "Isn't that the strangest thing. Is Griselda going mad? What in the world was he doing around here?"

No solution to the problem is forthcoming; Joe goes to bed.

━

The next morning is Sunday. Joe calls into headquarters. Another quiet night. A hit-and-run attracts Joe's attention. The victim was LaVon Kellums, an outboard motor mechanic at Riverview Haven. Deputy Wardell, returning from the demonstration, found him staggering along the road at 9 o'clock. Wardell called for an ambulance, then tried to extract information, but Kellums, in a state of shock, could report nothing. Wardell took Kellums' wristwatch, which had been smashed and had stopped at 8:07.

After the ambulance had taken Kellums to the hospital, Wardell had driven to Slough House. At the service station Wardell asked Bill Quarles the proprietor if he had paid any heed to passing traffic.

Quarles said, no, nothing particular, except that at about eight o'clock a red VW coming from the direction of Pleasant Grove had almost missed the bridge, owing to speed and erratic driving. Several other cars had passed later, all coming from the east, toward Pleasant Grove. The red VW Quarles saw might well have been the car which had struck Kellums, since the cracked crystal of Kellums' watch shows microscopic flakes of red enamel.

≈

Joe goes to see the victim. LaVon Kellums is a man of twenty-five, of medium height, with a flat undeveloped face. His eyes are small and pale blue, his kinky blond hair is worn in a nondescript ruff. He is vague, almost incoherent in his remarks. Joe derives no information from the interview.

Chapter III

Joe goes home. Miranda is talking into the telephone.

"Your phantom lover, I presume," says Joe.

Miranda breaks off the conversation with dignity. "He's a very nice person."

"Why doesn't he come over and call on you? Not that we need any more Romeos hanging around this place."

"I don't know. I've asked him to come over, but he says no."

"He's probably baby-sitting the kids while his wife works."

Miranda shakes her head. "I don't think so. He sounds — well — almost noble, with very high principles."

"Maybe he's a priest."

Miranda changes the subject.

During the afternoon Joe telephones Lloyd Griselda and asks him to come down to headquarters. Lloyd arrives with a truculent Howard Griselda, who wants to be present while Joe questions Lloyd. Joe refuses. Lloyd Griselda then wants to have a lawyer. Joe says, "Sure, if you insist. It makes you seem awful guilty."

"No such thing," says Howard Griselda. "He doesn't want to be tricked!"

"How can he be tricked if he tells the truth?"

Howard and Lloyd confer a moment, then Lloyd says, "I'll be glad to make a statement to you."

"Very good. Come this way then."

Joe takes Lloyd into his office. "I'll be recording the statement. The tape will pass into the next room where a stenographer will type up the statement for your signature."

"I guess that's all right."

"These questions are in regard to the hit-and-run accident involving LaVon Kellums at about 8 o'clock on the evening of Saturday, June 15. What were your movements from, say, seven o'clock on?"

"After leaving the demonstration I drove to the Riverview Inn, arriving there about seven-thirty or maybe a little later. I took some pictures. Then I met my uncle, Howard Griselda, and he accompanied me home."

"He was in your company at eight o'clock?"

"That's right."

"You mean from the time you left the Riverview Inn?"

"That's right."

"I'm a little puzzled here. You drove from the demonstration to the Riverview Inn in your own car?"

"Yes."

"And you met Howard Griselda at the Riverview Inn?"

"I met Howard Griselda there, yes."

"How did he get from the demonstration to the Riverview Inn?"

"You'll have to ask him that."

"You don't know?"

"What has it got to do with the accident?"

"What I'm trying to get at, which car did you drive back to Pleasant Grove in?"

"In my car."

"That's a red VW?"

"Yes."

"Where was his car?"

"I couldn't say out of my own personal knowledge."

"When you met him at Riverview Haven, was he in his car?"

"No."

"Where was he?"

"In my car."

"Where did he enter your car?"

"Does it make any difference?"

"I want to establish how much road you covered in the company of Howard Griselda."

"I picked him up at his home."

"So we finally get it worked out. You drove from the demonstration to Pleasant Grove, picked up Howard Griselda at his home, and both of you drove to Riverview Inn?"

"Yes."

"Why in the world didn't you say so? Is it a crime to be seen riding with Howard Griselda?"

"Naturally not."

"At Riverview Haven, you went in to take pictures?"

"Yes."

"And Howard Griselda waited in the car?"

"Yes."

"Why was that?"

"He chose not to go in."

"I'm profoundly puzzled by all this. He sat in the car while you went in to take pictures?"

"Yes."

"Why didn't he go in?"

"You'll have to ask him that."

"Let's go on. What time did you leave Riverview Haven?"

"I'm not sure. About nine o'clock."

"Nine o'clock? I didn't leave till about that time."

"I'm only making an estimate."

"You drove the car?"

"I drove the car."

"Let's see. You live in an apartment out the south end of town?"

"That's right."

"You drove Howard Griselda home, then went home yourself?"

"Yes."

"Stranger and stranger. Howard Griselda came out to my house at about ten o'clock. Were you with him?"

"What's that got to do with the hit-and-run case? That happened at eight o'clock?"

"Kellums' watch stopped at eight. Maybe his watch was wrong. For all I know you dropped Howard Griselda off at home and drove back out to Genesee Slough."

"Well, I didn't."

"You can't prove it. You haven't proved anything yet. You could have dropped Howard Griselda off and still got back to Genesee Slough in time to run over LaVon Kellums."

"No, I couldn't have done so."

"You can't prove it. You haven't covered the time. I think I'd better arrange a line-up and see if Kellums can pick you out."

"I was with Mr. Griselda when he went out to your house."

"Why did you go out to my house?"

"That has no bearing on the case."

"Maybe not, but you're sure trying to keep something quiet. So you were in the car when Howard Griselda was visiting me."

"That's right."

"And afterwards you drove Mr. Griselda home."

"Yes, I did."

"And went home yourself immediately after?"

"I did."

"Why did you take pictures of Miss Staffe at Riverview Inn?"

"She asked me to do so. For the paper's picture file."

"You drove all the way to Pleasant Grove, picked up Howard Griselda, drove all the way back to Riverview Haven, just to take some pictures of Miss Suzanne Staffe?"

"What difference does it make what my motives were? I didn't run over LaVon Kellums and Mr. Griselda is a witness to this."

"OK, that's all."

The statement is brought out. Lloyd reads it and signs it. Joe takes it to Howard Griselda. "This is all most peculiar. Do you verify all these crazy activities?"

Griselda, looking somewhat downcast, reads the statement. "It seems generally accurate. I'll sign it."

"But why, Howard, why? All this nocturnal activity when a man your age ought to be home in bed."

"My activities are none of your affair, Joe."

"I sure hope they're not, speaking as Sheriff. You state that you were in Lloyd's company from seven-thirty to ten o'clock."

"Approximately those times. He ran into no one during this period."

"Well, temporarily I'll have to accept that. You can write a news story to the effect that my main suspects are Lloyd Griselda and his uncle Howard Griselda, but that I had to let them go for lack of evidence, especially after Lloyd carefully washed his car and ironed out some dents in his fender."

"I don't like your implications, Joe."

"Sorry, but run the story as I gave it to you."

"I'll do nothing of the sort."

Two days pass. Joe gets a complaint from Ralph Henigson, owner of the Dodge agency in Aurora. He keeps a big cruiser at Riverview Haven, and he asserts that a local character named Bill Jiggs has threatened to blow up his boat. "This old coot scares me, because he's vicious. The water skiers don't dare go near him; he shoots them with a BB gun."

"What's he mad at you for?"

"He doesn't like the wake my cruiser kicks up. It's a big boat; it's bound to make a wave; nothing I can do about it, except crawl past his houseboat."

Joe doesn't want to offend Ralph Henigson, a man of influence. "I'll have a word with him; maybe we can work out a compromise. You go slow past his mooring and he won't blow up your cruiser."

Joe catches Bill Jiggs at Riverview Haven, buying gasoline from Leona Eklund, who is impatient with Jiggs and suggests that he buy his gasoline elsewhere. Jiggs says he's going to report her to Standard Oil and have her franchise taken away. Leona Eklund gives back as good as she gets, and Bill Jiggs is steaming when Joe talks to him. Jiggs claims that Henigson makes a practice of cruising full-speed along the slough, setting up five-foot waves which bounce his houseboat up and down. Joe explains that this is one of the hazards of living in a houseboat; Jiggs walks off shaking his head.

A grisly discovery is made which seems to exculpate Lloyd Griselda. At low tide a fisherman discovers a red VW sunk in the slough where it ran off the road. Inside are the bodies of a young woman and a baby. Her driver's license says she is Ileda Wilkin of Pomona. Joe calls her address, to find that it is three years old, that no one knows anything about her.

Two days pass. On the night of June 20 three people are killed. Leona Eklund is shot through the window of her home. Ralph Henigson is shot aboard his cabin cruiser. Dusty Rhodes is shot in the doorway of his trailer.

The bullets are 30 caliber and all have been fired from the same gun.

Chapter IV

Joe investigates: Leona Eklund, Dusty Rhodes, Ralph Henigson; someone hated all three.

He suspects Dakota Slim, who lives in a commune on a tule island, subsisting on natural produce: tule flour, roots and foliage; acorns, mud-clams, cat-fish, blackberries. He also checks out Bill Jiggs.

Chapter V

Miranda talks on telephone to her phantom lover. Joe finally lays down the law. "This is preposterous. Tell this unseen Lothario to show his face or else!"

"Daddy, please don't be coarse. He's frightfully intelligent; he knows everything about everything."

"If he's so damn intelligent, ask him who killed those three people."

"All right, I will ask him."

Miranda asks. "He says he knows, but he doesn't want to say."

"Oh?" Joe, in spite of himself, is impressed. "And why not?"

"He says that under the circumstances he might do the same thing."

"Tell him that the father of the girl he loves is jumping around like a scalded cat trying to locate the killer."

"He knows that too, but he doesn't care."

"That's a fine how-de-do. Ask him how he knows."

Miranda's unknown admirer will reveal nothing of his claimed knowledge, and Joe is troubled and uneasy.

≈

The calls abruptly cease. Miranda is first on edge, then worried. Joe becomes infected with her mood. The telephone silence seems almost sinister.

Joe tried to find who the caller was. Miranda can supply no clues, except that he loved the sea and wanted to sail to the most remote part of the Indian Ocean.

Chapter VI

Joe goes out to Bill Jiggs' houseboat. Jiggs is an irascible old man, suspected of much petty illegality, such as lamp-fishing by night from a hole in the floor of his houseboat, and shooting at water-skiers.

Jiggs looks Joe over with suspicion, then says, "Yeah, come aboard; I thought at first you was the game warden."

Joe inspects the houseboat. He sees a shotgun, a rifle, a BB gun. "Which of these do you use to tweak the water-skiers with?"

Jiggs scowls. "What's it to you?"

"There's been complaints."

"I see. Well, I don't know nothing about it. There's bees and wasps flying around here. If some jackass of a water-skier gets stung while he's racketing around and breaking up my crockery I ain't gonna worry one bit."

"Maybe you better move your boat."

"I was here first."

"That may be, but suppose you put somebody's eye out?"

"I'm a better shot than that. With them big rear-ends sticking out, how could anyone miss? If I was to do such a thing."

"What caliber is that rifle?"

".30-'06. Why?"

"Some people got killed by a .30-'06 a week or so ago."

"Not by that .30-'06."

"Do you mind if I check it out?"

"Sure I mind."

"Well, I might have to check on it anyway. You threatened Henigson."

"If you was sent bouncing around by his monster of a boat you'd threaten too. What are we supposed to do? Sit here and take all that big-time guff? I thought this was supposed to be America."

"You called Mrs. Eklund names, and vowed to get even."

"Why not? Henry's been cashing my checks for years. She made him put a stop to it because she didn't like to see me in the bar. She's trying to be real spiffy, and I guess I'm not what she calls high-class!"

"You told Dusty Rhodes you'd see him in hell before he moved you out with his rig."

"I might just have done that."

"Everything considered, I think I better check out your rifle."

"Keep away from my belongings, Sheriff, unless you got some legal right to do so."

"You got any idea who shot these people?"

"I haven't given the subject any thought."

Joe goes to look at a parcel wrapped in newspaper. "What have you got here?"

"Nothing much of anything."

"A young striper maybe?"

A headline catches his eye:

DESCENDENT OF CLIPPER-SHIP DESIGNER DIES AFTER LONG ILLNESS.

Donald Stang, age 20, whose great-great-grandfather was Donald Stang, designer and builder of the famous clipper-ship *China Pearl*...

The remainder is torn away.

Joe looks at the date. Pleasant Grove *Clarion*, June.

Chapter VII

Joe fires the .30-'06 into a bucket of water, takes the bullet and returns to Pleasant Grove.

He goes to the office of the Pleasant Grove *Clarion* where he reads the rest of the paper. Howard Griselda asks him how his investigation progresses.

"I have three investigations going on. Who was the hit-run artist? Who killed Mrs. Eklund, Ralph Henigson and Dusty Rhodes? Who's been phoning my daughter? I just solved two of the problems."

"You found who was calling your daughter?"

"Yes. Donald Stang, or so it would seem."

"Hmm. The hit-run driver?"

"Your boy Lloyd is off the hook. It was a lady named Ileda Wilkin, who ran her car into the slough. We can close the books on that one."

Chapter VIII

Joe goes to the hospital. Young Donald Stang had half a double room, with a telephone. An old man in the bed opposite had little information. "He knew he was dying and made no complaint. All the nurses cried when he died."

If Donald Stang had in fact been calling Miranda, if he knew the identity of the murderer, Joe wonders where he got the knowledge. The old man says, "Donald never mentioned any murder. He spent a lot of time talking on the telephone."

Joe visits Donald Stang's family. "Did he leave any papers?"

There are papers: sketches of sail-boats, islands with palm trees, sunsets over the ocean.

"A diary? A journal?"

"No."

"Did he have any friends? Anybody he might have confided in?"

They didn't know.

≈

Joe wonders what to tell Miranda. He decides that she has a right to know the truth. Miranda is extremely upset. Presently she says, "I wonder how he knew anything about the murders? What about the old man who shared the room. Could he be the murderer?"

Joe hasn't thought of this. He checks on the old man and learns that he was hospitalized three days before the murders and so could not possibly be guilty.

Chapter IX

Joe has been trying to find Ileda Wilkin's next-of-kin. The Pomona police are no help. Her address is two years outmoded; no one remembers her.

In her purse is the picture of a bearded man.

Joe goes out to the commune to talk to Dakota Slim. On the way he stops where Ileda Wilkin ran through the brush. In the weeds he finds a flashlight. He proceeds to the commune, and finds Dakota Slim. He hears a subdued 'Oink' from a big hippy wearing a straw hat.

"Oink, is it," says Joe. "I'll give you oink."

"Don't fool with him," says Dakota Slim. "He's trained in yoga."

"Be that as it may," says Joe. On a hunch he pulls out the picture from Ileda Wilkin's purse, also her driver's license. "Any of you people know this girl or this man?"

Ileda Wilkin's sister lives at the commune. The man is her husband. "He's gone straight, and Ileda says he's the squarest of the square!"

"What is his name? I want to tell him his wife is dead."

"LaVon Kellums."

Chapter X

Joe drops into the outboard-motor shop. "How come you didn't tell me Ileda Wilkin was your wife?"

"You didn't ask."

"Well, what happened out there? You weren't hit like you said you were."

LaVon Kellums smiles sourly. "I was hit. I tried to stop a car, and it ran me down."

"So why didn't you come forward and identify your wife?"

Kellums shrugs stonily. "She was dead. The kid was dead. I didn't care about anything else."

"I see. In the meantime the county pays the funeral expenses. Did you think of that?"

Kellums shrugs again.

"You had a big flashlight. What kind of car hit you?"

"A Volkswagen. I think it might have been red."

"So you were in the car. Who was driving?"

Kellums freezes. "Ileda."

Joe says, "Let me see your driver's license."

"What for? I'm not driving anything."

Joe holds out his hand. "Give. Don't forget, your position is pretty shaky."

"I don't have any. I got busted."

"Why?"

"Driving under the influence."

"Little by little it comes out," says Joe. "I suspect you were driving that night. You ran the car into the ditch, and you had lots of reasons for keeping quiet about it."

"That's your story."

"It's my guess…Well, in your shoes I might have done the same thing."

"You going to take me in?"

"I don't know what I'd charge you with, unless you care to confess something."

LaVon Kellums gives a hoarse chuckle and bends over his work. "Not bloody likely."

"You couldn't identify the driver of the car that hit you?"

"No."

≈

Joe thinks, finally, at last, I got that mess cleared up. Not that it does anybody any good.

Chapter XI

The investigation has petered out. Joe is at a loss as to what to do next. Nobody seems to have any real reason to kill either Mrs. Eklund, or Dusty Rhodes, or Ralph Henigson, let alone all three.

Suzanne Staffe calls on Joe, in her capacity as attorney for Dakota Slim. Cap'n Henry won't serve Dakota Slim or his ilk; Suzanne Staffe insists that such discrimination is unconstitutional, and she wants Joe to enforce this point of view upon Cap'n Henry.

Joe is doubtful. "I don't believe the Supreme Court has gone all the way on this as yet —"

"I'll make it a test case, with great pleasure."

"Don't do that," says Joe. "I'll have a word with Cap'n Henry one of these days."

"Why not now?"

With her red hair, classic features and flashing blue eyes Suzanne Staffe is regally beautiful. Joe gallantly agrees. "You ever been married, Suzanne?"

"No."

Joe and Suzanne Staffe drive out to Genesee Slough. At Riverview Haven business is proceeding as usual; Cap'n Henry seems capable of managing the business without the assistance of his wife.

When Joe and Suzanne Staffe arrive he is out fishing with old Bill Jiggs. Joe and Suzanne have lunch. Out of idle curiosity Joe asks why Lloyd Griselda was taking pictures of her.

Suzanne Staffe laughs scornfully. "Mr. Griselda was taking pictures of someone else whom he did not want to put on his guard."

Joe rubs his chin. "Now who might that have been??" He thinks back. "Not me, certainly. Why take a picture of me? What was I doing that was so interesting?"

Suzanne Staffe watches him with curiosity. "Whatever is the trouble, Sheriff?"

"Nothing much. Hardly anything at all. I just thought of something."

Suzanne Staffe insists on telephoning Howard Griselda, in order that Cap'n Henry's policy of discrimination be brought to public attention. Griselda says he'll meet them at Riverview Haven.

~

Howard Griselda ambles into the restaurant with Lloyd. They join Joe and Suzanne Staffe. Howard Griselda takes out his pipe, stuffs it with tobacco with easy condescension.

Joe says, "You know, Howard, I believe you'd give half your fortune to get the goods on me."

"What are you complaining about now, Sheriff?"

"I'm not complaining; it's too funny. I just figured it out a minute ago. Your boy Lloyd doesn't know my daughter Miranda. He sees me with a pretty young thing; he thinks he's going to catch me in the act. He takes pictures, he gets you so excited that you hot-foot out to my house in order to hear me explain away my crimes. You sure look silly in this one, Howard."

Griselda says, "I'm only a journalist, Joe. My job is to keep the public informed."

"I'm surprised you didn't run the story anyway. The headline is a natural:"

LAST NIGHT SHERIFF JOE BAIN
DID NOT SEDUCE AN UNDERAGE FEMALE.

Griselda blows out a cloud of smoke. "That aspect didn't occur to me."

Some hippies chug up in an old rowboat. Dakota Slim enters the dining room with his friends. The waitress won't serve them. Suzanne Staffe orders Joe to arrest the management. Joe says he can't arrest anybody unless they commit a crime or unless he has a court order.

Cap'n Henry returns with Bill Jiggs and LaVon Kellums. He tells the waitress, "Forget it. Serve them just as if they was human."

"Leona wouldn't have liked it," sniffs the waitress.

"There goes the trip to Washington," Joe tells Suzanne Staffe. "Cap'n Henry is now on your side. Even old Jiggs is allowed in. Now if I could only catch that murderer we could all go home happy."

Howard Griselda valiantly returns to the attack. "I suppose you haven't made any progress on the case?"

"I wouldn't say that," says Joe. "In fact I got a pretty good notion — but I better not disclose anything more. The murderer might hear me. Just say as usual:"

SHERIFF JOE BAIN BAFFLED;
TRIPLE MURDERER STILL AT LARGE

Joe rises to his feet. "I'll bid you all good evening."

Howard Griselda says sardonically, "After the next election, Joe, come to the office; maybe I can put you to work writing my headlines."

"I sure hope it doesn't turn out like that," says Joe somberly. He departs into the twilight.

"What a strange man!" says Suzanne Staffe. "He seems to have the instinctive intelligence of a wild animal!"

Howard Griselda gives a sour grunt. "He's as unprincipled as a tom-cat, if that's what you mean. One of these times he won't land on his feet."

≈

Lloyd Griselda goes out to his car where it's parked under the cotton-woods. A figure stirs in the shadows. "Is this your car?"

Lloyd Griselda peers into the murk. "Yes, why do you ask?"

"You might like to know that I'm going to kill you."

Lloyd Griselda's knees become loose. "Just a minute! You've got the wrong man. I've never done anything to you!"

"Yes you have. When I needed help, when I begged for your help, you drove past and knocked me down with your car. My wife bled to death and my baby smothered. Three other people passed me by. I swore I'd kill them and I did."

"That's no reason to kill me!" blurts Lloyd. "I didn't know you were in such trouble!"

The voice is implacable. "You refused me help. You killed my wife and baby."

A flashlight snaps into LaVon Kellums face. Joe Bain says, "That'll do for now. I'll take that gun. Give it here!"

LaVon Kellums fires at the flashlight, which Joe had been holding far to the side. As he fires, Joe tackles him and takes the gun.

≈

Lloyd Griselda is indignant. "You used me for bait. You knew he was out to kill me!"

"It was the only way to get him to rights," said Joe. "I hadn't an ounce of evidence against him."

Howard Griselda says in a voice quivering with emotion, "Suppose the man had fired his gun instead of taking time to explain himself? You'd be morally responsible for the murder!"

"I was pretty sure LaVon would want to talk a bit," says Joe reasonably. "After all, he had something to say: his wife lays dying, he tries to flag down a car and Lloyd here knocks him into the ditch. It's enough to make anybody upset. Just consider yourself lucky, Lloyd."

Lloyd draws a deep breath. "I'm lucky all right. I might have been killed just then!"

"Sometimes we have to take risks to get results," Joe tells him. "It all worked out pretty well."

LaVon Kellums is in jail. Suzanne Staffe has agreed to defend him. She and Joe leave the courthouse. The time is close on midnight.

Joe says, "I'm so weary, but in a nice easy way. Let's not talk crime any more. Look at that full moon up there; it makes me want to relax. How's the Scotch situation up at your place?" He puts his arm around her waist. She is unexpectedly flexible. Joe stops to look around the parking lot.

Suzanne asks, "What's the trouble?"

"It's just like Lloyd Griselda to be skulking around with his camera…I don't see him anywhere…"

"Let him skulk," says Suzanne Staffe. "I'm old enough."

The STARK

The Voyage and the People

Contents:

DIMENSIONS AND DATA

Length of STARK:	
Including caps	24.6 miles
Excluding caps	23.0 miles
Diameter:	2.34 miles
Number of transverse sections:	124
Outside shell:	2.6" chrome-nickel steel
Mass of shell:	5.5×10^{10} lbs.
Number of decks:	456
Total area of decks:	7.3×10^{11} ft^2
Total mass of decks:	8×10^{12} lbs.
Total mass of STARK:	9.6×10^{12} lbs.

KEY TO FIGURE 1:

Skin	Code Color	Thickness	Radius	Number of Decks	Function
A	Black	1300'	1300'	90	Drive, raw material, storage, energy, production
B	Gray	2000'	3300'	200	Food synthesis and processing
V$_1$	White	300'	3600'		Vacant (spare storage)
C	Green	800'	4400'	34	Agriculture, vivaria, repository and museum
D	Blue	600'	5000'	32	Park, recreation, services, distribution, administration, schools
V$_2$	Orange	300'	5300'		Vacant (stadia, public assembly)
R	Red	900'	6200'	90	Residential

Note: Colors and letter references not supplied on author's diagrams.

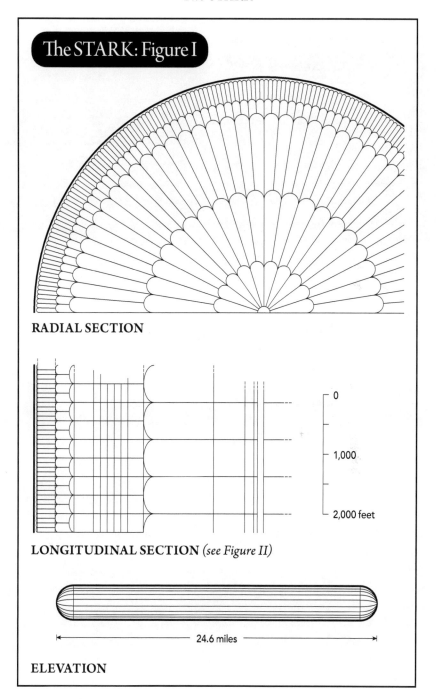

The STARK: Figure I

RADIAL SECTION

LONGITUDINAL SECTION *(see Figure II)*

0

1,000

2,000 feet

|← 24.6 miles →|

ELEVATION

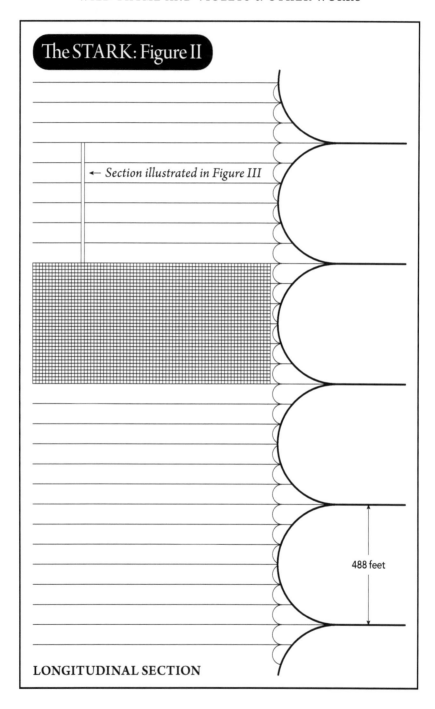

The STARK: Figure II

← *Section illustrated in Figure III*

488 feet

LONGITUDINAL SECTION

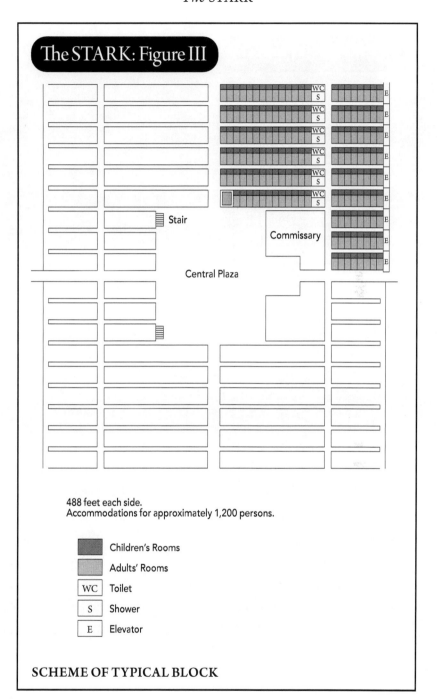

The STARK: Figure III

Stair

Commissary

Central Plaza

488 feet each side.
Accommodations for approximately 1,200 persons.

Children's Rooms

Adults' Rooms

WC   Toilet

S   Shower

E   Elevator

SCHEME OF TYPICAL BLOCK

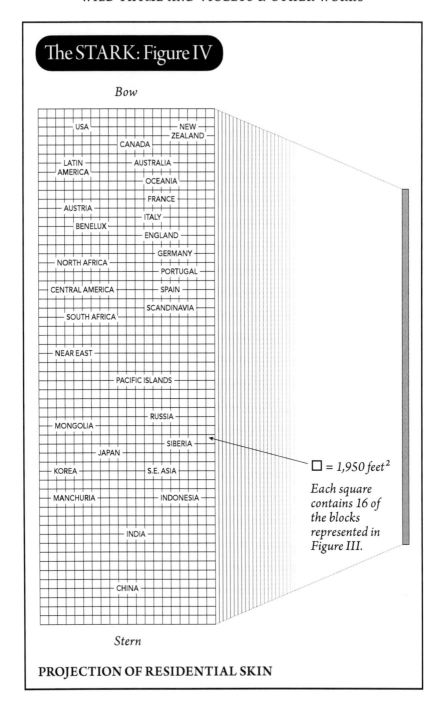

The STARK: Figure IV

PROJECTION OF RESIDENTIAL SKIN

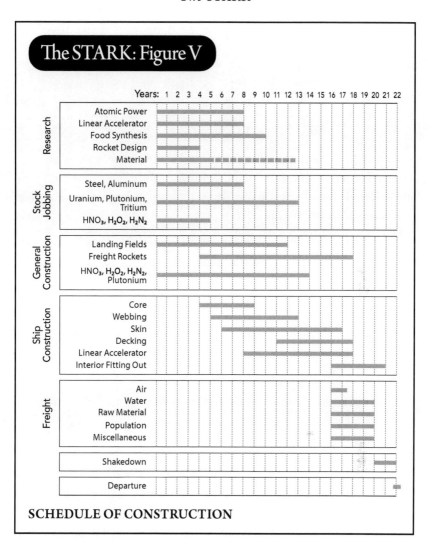

The STARK: Figure V

SCHEDULE OF CONSTRUCTION

I

RA 18h, 40m; Dec + 31°

Part 1: *What Strange Impulse?*

Carl Mitchell, research assistant at Mt. Wilson Observatory, is summoned before Dr. Herbert Spiers, director of observatory, for disciplinary action. Mitchell was caught altering research data apparently to fit a private hypothesis of his own — a minor, but rather disreputable, act which has forfeited him the respect of his associates.

Spiers curtly asks for an explanation. "What impulse, what strange impulse, caused you to do a thing like that?"

Mitchell obstinately has nothing to say.

Spiers becomes angry. "I can sign a criminal complaint against you — mutilating observatory property!"

"Go ahead," says Mitchell. "That's your privilege."

Spiers is puzzled. "Why, Mitchell? If I could understand, perhaps I wouldn't be so harsh with you."

"Dr. Spiers — whether or whether not you're 'harsh' is my smallest concern."

Spiers is even more puzzled. "I'm going to look into this." He calls for the plate Mitchell was discovered mutilating.

Mitchell grabs it, breaks it.

Spiers aghast, furious, bewildered. "What do you hope to gain?"

Mitchell finally breaks down, tells his story. He had been idly checking photographs of a region in Hercules, near Cerberus, taken a day apart during June, when he noticed an object with the remarkable parallax of 1.187" per day.

Such an object, he reasoned, must be either an asteroid or undiscovered planet in a plane out of the ecliptic.

He drove up to the observatory. It was a night of poor seeing; Mitchell had no trouble getting the 100" reflector. He turned the telescope to RA 18h, 40m; Dec + 31° — close to point toward which the sun is moving.

He saw object, a dim red spark. He checked it through spectroscope: a star, Type N, with positive radial velocity of 200 m/s.

Mitchell returned to library, checked other plates, found no proper motion. Star's absolute magnitude was 24.7 — almost dark. Its distance is .00724 parsec, .0244 light-year.

In confusion Carl Mitchell went to sit at table in the library. He checked his figures, hoping to find mistake.

A colleague came up, asked what's going on — why he looked so absorbed. Mitchell said, "Nothing too much." Friend went about business; Mitchell continued to think: "In about 22 years this star will pass very close to the sun. If I report this, what will happen?" He pictured panic, riot, revolution. If he kept quiet nothing would be noticed for ten or fifteen years more, given reasonable luck.

He made his decision, scraped at emulsion — and was caught in the act.

Dr. Spiers finds it hard to comprehend the magnitude of the situation.

"Well, well," says Dr. Spiers. "You took rather a weight on your shoulders, didn't you, young fellow?"

"I suppose so," says Mitchell proudly.

Dr. Spiers stands up. "You destroyed observatory property, but even worse is the intolerable presumption of using your callow 24 year old brain to decide the fate of the world. The cost of the plates will be deducted from your salary. Get back to your work, and in the future, when important decisions are to be made, consult your superiors."

"You mean, if I find another star that's going to wipe the Earth out of existence, to tell you about it?"

"Exactly."

Part 2: *The Eye Of Lucifer*

President James Anker makes secret flight to Geneva, meets British Prime Minister, Lionel Catridge, and USSR Premier Tchapenko.

Both are suspicious, ill at ease, in the dark as to purpose of the meeting.

Anker explains situation, exhibits photographs and statements. The Russians and British are first incredulous, then awed.

Anker takes them to a window, points up toward Vega. They look through a small telescope at the blood-red star. "The eye of Lucifer," mutters Catridge.

When Anker tells them his plan for survival, they are astonished. Anker is a simple straightforward man with utter faith in human intelligence and capacity for achievement. He believes that it is possible to succor not a chosen few, but every man, woman and child on the planet. Anker's preliminary sketches show a cylinder 23 miles long, 2.34 miles in diameter, to be assembled in orbit around the Earth, and propelled by the thrust of a linear accelerator.

"Such a vessel is admittedly a tremendous undertaking," says Anker, "but human survival is a tremendous goal. Would it involve greater effort than that expended in World War II?"

Tchapenko, stubborn, proud, is still hostile. He refuses to cooperate. "You take care of your people; we'll take care of ours!"

Anker and Catridge both argue with him. "It's essential that the scientific talent of the entire world be focussed on the single problem, without regard to race or politics. Two escape projects quadruple the difficulty of each — half as much mental power for twice as much work."

Tchapenko shrugs. It is a competitive world, wherein the most suitable will survive. The most suitable, he intimates, will be a few thousand Russian Communists.

He starts to leave. "Wait," says Anker.

Tchapenko turns. "Well?"

"Tomorrow we broadcast the imminence of danger to the entire world. Regardless of your plans — ours will be to carry every man, woman and child to a new world."

Tchapenko shrugs. "As you will." He starts out, pauses, turns back. His face is red. He realizes that in the face of such a program no scientist, technician, craftsman or laborer would delay an hour before leaving Russia for the West.

He snaps his fingers. "I could march on the West tomorrow."

"Come, Tchapenko," Catridge pleads. "Our hour has come. Are we to meet it at each other's throats — or are we to put aside old grudges, help each other to life?"

Tchapenko comes forward. The three shake hands. "There is no more cold war."

Part 3: *The Speech*

President Anker is to make a special address in an hour.

— • —

- In Davenport, Iowa, Archie McKay is celebrating his divorce in a bar.
- In the office of the Morgantown, Virginia *Democrat*, a young reporter is assigned to cover the TV broadcast of the speech, and write the story for the late edition, the *Democrat* not being a subscriber to wire-service.
- In San Bernardino, California, a sharpshooting real estate speculator has just suckered a rancher out of a large tract of desert land, where a building boom is expected.

— • —

President Anker comes on the air. In simple words he explains the cataclysm which in 22 years will burn Earth to a cinder; he describes the vessel which will rescue mankind. Each individual will be assigned a living space approximately a thousand cubic feet, exclusive of recreation area — more room than he is assigned on a trans-Atlantic liner. The vessel will take the human race safely and comfortably across space to a new planet among the stars.

How long will they be in space?

He doesn't know. It certainly will be a long time — twenty years at absolute minimum, most probably longer. It will be the most remarkable adventure the human race can imagine.

— • —

Archie McKay, celebrating his divorce, examines the model of the space-ark the President displays in the saloon's TV set. He thinks he is watching space-opera.

The real estate promoter runs out to find the rancher in order to sell back the property.

The cub reporter, gasping and sucking air, can't take notes for excitement. What a story! What a break he's been assigned to handle it!

—•—

The President makes a plea for cooperation, calmness and faith. He asks the citizens to display good judgment, to quiet rumor, avoid sensationalism, and above all, have confidence in themselves and the innate genius of the human race.

—•—

The reporter jumps up, runs out screaming, "Stop the press!" He babbles for foot high headlines: The World Is Coming To An End.

He is astounded when the cynical lantern-jawed night editor slugs him.

The foolish young reporter looks up from the floor. "Why did you do that?"

Archie McKay has his eighteenth highball. A commentator says something about the world coming to an end.

Archie sings, jokes, has a great time.

The bartender says, "What a hangover you'll wake up to."

The promoter finds the rancher, but nothing doing. The rancher heard the speech too.

Everywhere around the world people go outside and look up into the sky toward Vega, where baleful Lucifer hangs still invisible.

Part 4: *Challenge and Response*

The World Survival Authority meets, an interim chairman is selected, a schedule established, various commissions and authorities appointed.

The question of government of the Star-Ark, or STARK, the headline abbreviation, arises. Up to now it's been a question everyone has carefully been avoiding. Palyushkin, Russian representative on the WSA, is a stern austere dedicated Communist. He makes mistake of commenting that he hopes that capitalistic exploitation of the worker will be ended along with end of the Earth — and the fat is in the fire.

Vigorous polemics from all sides. Congressmen fulminate. "We've kept the world free of Communism this long; we're not going to cave in at this last hour of Earth's history."

President confers earnestly with congressional opponents. "We've got to forget pride, all our old scale of values!"

Congressmen obdurate. "Let the Russians make the concessions — we've made enough. We won't be ruled by the Communists — on this world or any other!"

"Nobody's going to rule anyone," says the President.

"Oh no?" jeer his opponents. They cite examples of Commie infiltration into most important posts.

"Let 'em infiltrate — so long as they work. The main thing is the STARK."

"We'll have to think it over."

A delay. Schedules not being met on account of suspicion and dilatoriness. Secret despatches from American Embassy in Moscow report disturbing news of Russian impatience, further talk of going it alone. The world is splitting up. The President spends a sleepless night. In the morning he dissolves Congress.

Congress refuses to be dissolved, begins impeachment proceedings.

Anker declares martial law, sends a battalion of troops to Capitol Hill.

Congressmen indignant, outraged. What kind of democracy is this? Anker is as bad as the Communists!

Anker appears. He is smiling, but he looks as if he is about ready to cave in. He makes a speech, trying to pacify the dissolved Congress. He justifies his actions on the ground that the grimmer the emergency, the more democratic processes must be curtailed. "This is the grimmest emergency imaginable, hence liberties are curtailed to an extreme. It has become necessary to establish what is in effect an authoritarian government.

"This is what they will expect aboard the STARK until the ship gets shook down; why strain at the idea now?"

A Congressman shouts, "If we got to have a dictator, we don't want you!"

Anker smiles. "You're not getting me. I also must obey the new source of authority. His name is Palyushkin, new chairman of WSA."

Anker bows, walks out of the chamber. At the door he turns and says quietly, "I hope and pray I have made the right decision."

II

Soup

Erich Kohlmeier, an atomic physicist, originally a German refugee, addresses the graduating class of '63 at Cal-Tech.

"The world is literally blowing up in your faces — but why despair? You have before you the greatest adventure of man! In a sense this graduating class is lucky; man needs your ability as man has never needed ability before!"

He cites difficulties and problems of constructing STARK. Inefficiency of chemical rockets is the current headache. Kohlmeier reveals that it's touch-and-go whether or not chemical rockets can convey enough material into orbit. Total mass of STARK is enormous; rockets are undependable, and consume monstrous quantities of fuel.

Martin Waber, graduating *magna cum laude*, has opportunity to speak to Kohlmeier. They discuss atomic space-drive. Kohlmeier describes the linear accelerator, some of the attendant problems, i.e. synchronization of motor fields, thermodynamic gradients, minimization of hysteresis in electrodes. Also important is necessity of vast quantity of uranium; energy required to accelerate STARK is of astronomical order, and uranium fission yields only 3.6×10^{20} ergs/lb. If some means of directly converting atomic energy to thrust, or even to electricity, were known, problems would be tremendously simplified. Kohlmeier remarks that atomic physicists everywhere in the world are devoting eighteen hours a day to these problems. If they don't succeed, the STARK may or may not be completed; the human race may or may not survive. And even in the event it does manage to win free, it will be by the skin of the teeth.

Waber asks Kohlmeier if he ever knew Serge Iazkov, a Polish physicist. Kohlmeier becomes agitated by his recollections. He and Iazkov were in the same compound after World War II, working on Russian atomic bomb. He remembers Iazkov as a schizophrenic, alternating between mysticism and furious excesses of emotion. Iazkov possessed a marvellous intuitive sense which Kohlmeier describes as almost clairvoyant.

Iazkov, recklessly defying camp regulations which insisted on concentration of effort, performed a set of private experiments which blew up the camp. He spoke facetiously of his work as 'boiling a cauldron of soup'.

Kohlmeier escaped in the confusion of the explosion; he knows nothing of what happened to Iazkov.

Martin Waber tells him that Iazkov's son Don is a freshman at Cal Tech. Don believes that Iazkov had converted matter directly to thrust.

Kohlmeier thinks not. Explosion was due to simple exceeding of critical mass. Peculiar, of course, that Iazkov had not taken simple precautions... Kohlmeier leaves.

Waber becomes convinced that Iazkov is alive. He sets out to find him.

He becomes conscious of a mysterious force, or personality in the background, which he can't identify. It seems intent on misleading him, frustrating his efforts to find Iazkov. The longer he seeks, the more strongly he becomes convinced that Iazkov has made some fundamental discovery.

His search takes him through various levels of society, different continents — affords a picture of the world preparing for the great exodus.

He attends a convention of biologists, botanists, entomologists, zoologists, ichthyologists, etc. — trying to decide exactly what plants, animals to preserve.

He visits a performance of *Lucifer Comes* — a weird extravaganza: ballet symbolizing human futility in the face of cosmic force.

He mingles with the criminals that thrive in a world from which (so they consider) all basis for normal morality has been removed.

He narrowly escapes death in the civil war raging in India.

He finds that Iazkov is a member of mystical sect, and lives in Tibet.

Waber arrives to find Iazkov dying from radiation sickness; just as Iazkov is about to talk, he is killed by mysterious agent. (Identity and motivation of this agent not completely worked out.)

Waber returns to U.S., and by organization of information he has accumulated, reconstructs Iazkov's cauldron of 'soup'.

The resultant cell generates thermo-electric power, and upon the injection of tritium, emits a narrow beam of gamma radiation, alpha and beta particles, the latter at a velocity of .9999 c — generating tremendous thrust.

Wave length of emitted radiation suggests that temperatures at certain microscopic nodes rise to a degree sufficient to annihilate matter. Energy is drained from cell by thermo-electricity and by emissive beams. Massive shielding necessary — but efficiency of cell extremely high.

Waber's enemy reveals himself; Waber kills him with beam from cauldron.

III

The Big Job

Sam Eavens, expediter on hull construction, works on N4B-14-G3 (North quadrant, Segment 4, Quarter segment B, Longitudinal section 14, Green skin, Deck 3), with a construction crew, whose foreman is a big raw-boned rough-neck named Utah Brassold.

Eavens is former salesman, easy-going, gregarious, with not too much construction experience, but good organizational sense.

Utah works with a furious energy, but undergoes irrational spasms of humor, fury, enthusiasm. He has no regrets about leaving Earth; he enjoys the excitement, the atmosphere of emergency, participation in the Big Job. Utah's crew is assembling the web, butt-welding hundred foot lengths of steel rod to form cables. A Polish crew is working behind them installing collars where the catenaries branch off.

Utah has no use for the Poles, considers them fair game for ridicule.

The Polish foreman, also the Polish expediter have protested several times. Sam has so far managed to prevent real trouble. Atomic thrust units are beginning to replace the old chemical rockets; the flow of material has quadrupled. The pressure is on; Utah daily becomes more obstreperous.

Sam comes back on the job after a day off to find work at a standstill, with Poles and Utah's crew bristling at each other like strange dogs. Material is tangled together, men floating idly around, breathing up oxygen.

The Polish expediter is missing. Evidence indicates that Utah has given him an orbit (punching hole in oxygen tank; thrust sends him out into space).

The Polish Commissar appears. Polish foreman blames Utah.

Commissar talks to Sam Eavens. "What's the truth of this?"

Eavens doesn't know. He's just come on job. There's no proof of anything. Eavens promises better cooperation in future.

He talks to Utah — who is amused by turmoil. He tells Eavens to keep the Commies out of his hair if he wants to avoid friction. Eavens tries to explain that politics has no present application, insists on the need for cooperation, but it's like talking to a stone wall.

A new Polish expediter, a young pink-cheeked lad just out of technical academy, comes on the job. He takes work very seriously, starts immediately to give instructions to Utah.

Utah tells his crew, "One false move from this jerk, he gets an orbit!"

The young expediter makes the move, Utah starts to give him the orbit.

The Polish crew interferes.

A big fight between the two crews among the cables. Material destroyed, welding gas burnt up, men killed. Looks like a full-scale battle forming between all Commies and all Westerners. Disaster!

Eavens tells Utah, "Give yourself up! You're the cause of this. Do you want to wreck the whole project!"

"I don't much care."

Eavens says, "I'll have to take you in myself..."

Utah laughs at him. "If you think you're man enough."

Eavens and Utah fight among the webbing. Eavens wins, Utah gets an orbit.

Work slowly, cautiously resumes. At 3:30 Eavens' relief comes on the job. "What kind of a day did you have?"

"Oh just so-so. Had a little trouble... See you tomorrow..."

IV

Moving Day

Fred Smith, Captain of Civil Order Squad, goes out on his last patrol. Tonight he will catch the last ferry up to the STARK, now laden, stocked, populated, and gradually increasing its orbit.

San Francisco is deserted. A few cars are parked in the street, some locked as if owners already aboard the STARK feared theft. The sun is shining, the air is crisp, the bay is blue. Never has San Francisco looked more beautiful, more forlorn.

Smith looks through houses, making sure no-one is left behind — invalids, babies, etc. Block-Wardens theoretically have checked off the residents of each block; Smith is making a last check. On the porch of a house Smith meets an old man placidly smoking.

Smith passes time of day. The old man's attitude conveys that he plans to stay behind.

"I'm just as happy to sit here. You've got a hard pull up there…Some folks I hear are already living the good life."

"Yeah…"

The old man is referring to the outrider globes. At the height of construction over two thousand freight-elevators shuttled back and forth, conveying thousand ton loads sometimes three or four times daily. During the last two years a number of top Russians constructed globular shells around a thousand of these units, furnished them in sumptuous style, and proposed to live in them instead of aboard the STARK.

Smith and the old man talk a few minutes longer. "I hear some folks went down into the Carlsbad Caves, figuring to come out after the excitement," says the old man.

"They won't come out to much."

"Oh, they're confident. Got 'em food and water; they figure to live for years underground if necessary."

"In a hundred thousand years, maybe the world will be cool…They won't live to see it." Smith starts to move on. "Well, old man, this is last call. Better get on down to the depot."

Old man placidly smokes pipe. "There's a woman and her daughter up on third floor. Woman's a Christian-Ender; she's old and don't make no difference — but you ought to make her give up the girl."

"I'll go up and check," says Smith.

"There's also a man living somewhere around," says the old man. "Watch out for him."

Smith goes up steps, meets man coming down. Smith is wary. Usually these men are criminals fearful of registering. Man makes move for gun. Smith beats him to it, gets gun.

Man says, "Don't point that thing at me — I'm on my way down to depot."

"There's no rush," says Smith. "Let's take a look for the women who are upstairs."

"They're not in," says the man.

"We'll look anyway. Upstairs!" He herds man up at gun-point.

In the top apartment they find body of old woman, several days dead. Man disclaims knowledge. In next room find body of girl, also dead, freshly killed.

Smith looks at man. "Well?"

Man protests. "So what? I took nothing away from them…They were going to die in a few days anyway."

"Logic is a great thing," says Smith.

The old man sees Smith come out alone.

"Seems like I heard a shot," says the old man.

"That might well be," says Smith. "There's some horrible things running loose around these buildings. It'll be worse after the STARK goes…Earth will be a pretty hard place. Better change your mind, old man."

"No, don't think I will…I'll see it end."

"Well — so long," says Smith.

"So long."

V
The Judas Goat

The time is Departure minus four months — shakedown year. The STARK has been gradually widening its orbit. Freight-carriers convey up last minute cargoes — soil, sea-water, trees, minerals, hematite, limonite, carnotite, pitchblende, clay, sand, rutile (which may be used to yield metal and oxygen), artifacts for the museum.

The populations are adjusting to life aboard ship; turmoil, disorder, griping goes on.

The inner echelon of high-ranking Communists confer. They speak of destiny — long-range planning — the necessity of leaving nothing to chance. The Secretary for Political Action listens with a wry smile. Quietly he announces that nothing has been left to chance.

The last carrier arrives from Earth. Lucifer hangs behind the Sun like an orange behind a grapefruit.

The STARK accelerates, widens its orbit, moves off at a tangent.

Alan McNarty is member of a group of hard-shell conservatives — who call themselves the Young Turks, and, like the Communists, believe in the need for long-range planning, dynamic action, control of the future.

McNarty proposes a plan to take over the government of the ship. Once the Young Turks are in power, McNarty prophesies a golden era of democracy, free enterprise, etc. The Young Turks are interested but cautious. "How can so few of us successfully take over the ship?"

"Easy! We gain control of a few strategic points: bridge, central energy panel, air-temperature panel. The time is now! Before the Communists make a move of their own!"

One of the plotters is George Kadares. His father is Paul Kadares, former editor of *Liberal Arts Monthly*. George tells Paul Kadares of plot; Kadares is horrified. He goes to a meeting of the Turks, argues against the projected *coup*. "You might gain temporary control of the ship — but you can't possibly control the feelings, emotions, desires of the ship's population. That's the future political complexion of the

STARK, and you can't control that through an ill-conceived, half-baked uprising! To gain power you've got to earn confidence — not make yourself suspected of authoritarianism!"

McNarty claims the Russians are up to the same kind of scheme; the only hope of the West is to seize the initiative!

Kadares demurs. "Let the Russians take the ship over — what do they gain? Nothing but resentment. The West benefits."

McNarty slugs him; the Young Turks carry out their plan. Various parties deploy through the ship.

On the bridge the Control Authority watches Lucifer pass the sun. The skins of each are torn apart; radiation from the interior blasts out, sears Earth.

The Young Turks come, take over the control room. Western representatives of the Authority protest; the Russians try to fight. McNarty kills a man. The Turks take over the strategic spots. The *coup* is a success!

The new group starts to broadcast to ship — but the news is already going out over loudspeaker system. The Young Turks are identified as Fascists, Oligarchs. The Young Turks hastily cut off the voice, broadcast their own version of the seizure, but the harm has been done.

A group of armed Communists appear from secret hiding places, subdue the Young Turks. Clearly they have known all along what has been going on. Now they have a reason for extending military control over all the ship. The Young Turks have been a set of dupes.

The Turks stand trial; all are convicted, quickly executed. McNarty is last to go. He remains confident to last. He seems puzzled as Russians prepare to shoot him.

"Wait," he says, "there's a mistake! You're not supposed to shoot me! Call in Kryzenkov!"

Kryzenkov appears. He is successor to Tchapenko, now dead. "Why have you bothered me?"

"Obviously," said McNarty, "because these men were about to shoot me."

"Naturally," says Kryzenkov.

"But I've set the whole thing up for you!" cries McNarty. "I've obeyed your specific orders! You can't abandon me now!"

Kryzenkov smiles. "Can we do anything else? Be sensible, McNarty!"

McNarty, frothing in frustration and fury, is executed along with the other Young Turks.

VI

Avant-Garde

Cory Chevis, a flamboyant *avant-garde* artist, has been assigned to a bachelor cabin in Pennsylvania 40K (deck 40, block K, in Pennsylvania section of the U.S.A.). Next door lives Arne Schiffko, a rather mysterious figure. Chevis is not working. Every day the bulletin board in the plaza lists jobs to be filled, but Chevis is busy painting abstract compositions.

On Earth he worked with Public Information Office, animating morale cartoons; now he wants to devote all his time to painting. Arne Schiffko encourages him.

A number of jobs go unfilled; Clyde Ballard the Block-Warden, an ex-Army officer, berates Chevis for his slackness.

Chevis defends himself. "I'm perfectly willing to work."

"On your own terms, eh? Well, we can't have that here. We're a highly organized society; there's no place for undisciplined effort."

A new notice is posted: To secure the new issue food card, a certificate of employment must be produced. (There is no actual need of labor; there are many more hands than jobs, but the Interim Commission wants to maintain in the population's minds the idea that food results from work — that the STARK is not a paternalistic institution.)

Cory Chevis is annoyed by the new regulation, but since he wants to eat, he goes to Block-Warden Ballard and asks for job.

He is assigned job of painting corridor in the Food-Synthesis Skin, where metal corrodes unless protected. Chevis is exasperated. He wants some kind of creative painting.

"Create on your own time," says Block-Warden Ballard. "But if you want to eat — paint those corridors."

Chevis returns to his cabin, rages to Schiffko at what he considers an unenlightened attitude. He goes to work, and paints designs in corridor. Pleasant designs, but the unimaginative foreman objects. Chevis argues, and gets fired.

He returns to Penn 40K, visits the Block-Warden. "How about letting me paint landscapes on the walls around the plaza? That's a good job for me."

"Can't be done. We want to keep the place neat. Here's a job for you — sorting trash, right out against the outer skin. It's a little messy of course." Ballard grins.

Chevis is infuriated. "Go chase yourself, you lard-faced slob!"

"No work, no eat."

Schiffko and Chevis go for a long walk. Schiffko encourages him to use his initiative. Chevis posts a sign on the bulletin board offering to paint portraits for food coupons.

Commies have pretty well infiltrated ship. In every square there is at least one member. The Commie in Penn 40K, Alois Pontverde, sees notice, tears it down.

Chevis attacks him, they fight. Chevis wins, hammers his sign back up in place.

Case is reported to highest levels; top Commies are interested. Here is what seems to be a clear-cut case of resurgent private enterprise — individualism in a dangerous guise. Commies resolve to nip the matter in the bud. They have no direct leverage in the United States, although they more or less dominate the Interim Commission which sets broad policy matters.

Chevis gets a few nibbles on his offer — but Commies scare off the customers.

Chevis gets hungry. He steals food card from Block-Warden Ballard. No-one knows of theft except Schiffko, but Chevis gets picked up. Chevis accuses Schiffko of betraying him. Ballard, a decent sort at heart, feels sorry for Chevis, but has no choice except to do his duty.

Chevis is notorious. Commies label him a degenerate drone, or a parasitical knave. All the stops are pulled out. They coin a word: "Chevis" becomes a synonym for unprincipled scrounger.

Chevis goes before Segment Court. TV cameras trained on him — a *cause célèbre*! Public opinion is by and large against him. Chevis can offer no articulate defense. Schiffko propounds that in taking the food card Chevis was availing himself only of what rightfully belonged to him, that when Block-Warden Ballard prevented Chevis from making his own livelihood, he became obligated to feed him.

Court is adjourned. The judge is approached by member of the Interim Commission who stresses the necessity of convicting Chevis. "Order and discipline must be maintained!"

The judge is visited in his chambers by Schiffko. The judge hints that Chevis may face a long term at hard labor for his anti-social conduct.

Schiffko argues against. Judge protests that he can only interpret the law.

Schiffko points out the old common-law has no application, that the judge has it in his power to make important juridical advances, to pioneer a new common-law geared to the new realities — to the effect that any governing system must provide scope for human creativity, and the mechanisms whereby an individual may market his production.

Schiffko departs. The judge thoughtfully reads anonymous letters of intimidation.

The judge convenes court. He is intensely nervous. He reads his decision: Chevis is not guilty. The Interim Commission is in fact the offender; Chevis is the damaged party. The judge rules that government is bound by an unwritten contract to provide an environment where the individual may market the products of his personal effort.

Chevis was ready to fulfill his part of the contract; the government was not. Chevis is therefore not guilty.

The decision creates a furor. The United States Interim Sub-Commission quietly accepts its validity.

The judge responds to a knock on his door. Schiffko is standing outside. Judge surprised. Schiffko comes; they talk. Schiffko mentions that a new medium of exchange is being issued, based on the erg.

Judge says, "That's all very well — but just what are you doing here?"

Schiffko looks at his watch. Door opens. It is Pontverde with gun, to assassinate judge. He is taken aback at the sight of Schiffko.

Schiffko says, "Before you kill anyone — you had better check with Kryzenkov."

Pontverde hesitates.

"If you don't, I will," says Schiffko. He dials telephone, asks for Kryzenkov.

Kryzenkov comes on the phone. Schiffko asks him, "Do you think it good policy to assassinate the judge? Consider public opinion."

Kryzenkov surprised, says uneasily, "No, no, definitely not!"

"Tell your man Pontverde."

Kryzenkov speaks to Pontverde. Pontverde leaves.

Judge heaves deep sigh, asks Schiffko, "Just who are you?"

Schiffko says, "I am one who lives for the future; I am the *avant garde*. But I also derive my direction from the past. Perhaps you can call me a Socratic Liberal. There are others like myself."

"Perhaps you should join together," says the judge. "One man alone is hardly a match for the intricate organization of the totalitarians."

"Very true," Schiffko agrees. "And as a matter of fact — there is a loose organization. You'll probably be hearing more of us."

The judge grins. "Not, I hope, in my professional capacity."

VII

The Most Effective Weapon

Life is not too hard; most of the population never had it so good. Each national group adjusts in different and characteristic manner, but there's a wide-spread feeling of let-down. The pressure of planning, administrating, construction of the STARK is over; actual voyage is anti-climactical.

A large number of older men, accustomed to giving orders, or at least taking responsibility for their own livelihood — farmers, executives, owners of businesses — fall victim to boredom. There isn't enough to occupy their minds, absorb their energies. Many undergo nervous disorders.

A rash of societies, political alignments, associations for the promulgation of various ideas breaks out.

WESTERN ALLIANCE: A loose group with no fixed program, dedicated to the liberal traditions of Western Europe and America.

ASIATIC LEAGUE: A group preoccupied with racialist theory. They feel that the colored races lack a proportionate share of voice in governing the ship.

HUMANISTS: Their goal is the blending of all races into one, with one language, one tradition, one ethos. By this means they hope to avoid future war on the future home of man.

NON-CONFORMISTS: In opposition to the Humanists, they insist on individualism, which by their creed is more important than justice, life or death.

GOLDEN RULE SOCIETY: These people are indignant that the Commies have taken privileges to themselves. They feel that rewards should go to those who have achieved.

THE OPTIMUM HUMANS: A group which advocates eugenic breeding and selective birth control to improve the race.

THE CATHOLIC LEAGUE: —

SOCRATIC SOCIETY: A group small in number, with incommensurate influence. Associate membership is open to anyone; full voting membership is by invitation. The Commies are intensely suspicious of the Socratics.

THE ECUMENISTS: —

THE SOCIAL ECOLOGISTS: —

The Communists have more or less infiltrated the strategic and prestige-laden posts. In general, they make no effort to proselyte new members. The ill-advised revolt of the Young Turks gave them leverage; they labored, organized, strove — nothing was too much effort — and succeeded in controlling strategic positions around the ship. Now they are relaxing, relegating authority. The rank and file is discontented, because the rewards have been nowhere commensurate with the efforts.

Bob Cole runs into old friend, Jolly Hinsdale, who avoids him.

Cole is puzzled and angry. "How come?"

Hinsdale blurts out that he wants nothing to do with a turn-coat.

Cole says, "You mean because I joined the Communist party?"

"That's right."

Cole laughs. "You've got the wrong idea, Hinsdale."

"Maybe so," says Hinsdale bitterly. "At least I've got my honor."

"I've got mine too," cries Cole angrily. "I've done nothing to be ashamed of."

"You joined the Commies — that's enough to turn any man's stomach."

Cole holds his temper. "You're living in the past, Jolly. Times have changed. Everything's changed, including the means by which a man gets ahead in the world."

"Some things no decent man stoops to."

"Look, you used to belong to the Chamber of Commerce and Lion's Club."

"So what?"

"You joined for one reason: to sell more insurance. I joined the Commies for the same reason. Let me tell you how it happened..."

Cole describes his job — inspector on algae tray, working under Alex Cargus, a Commie.

Cargus was sour and cynical. All his life he'd been a militant Commie — got his head broke in demonstrations, etc. His reward was this miserable position. He passed more and more work and responsibility to Cole, while he amused himself with women working on his processing belt.

At last Cargus gets promotion; Bob Cole expects to be promoted also — because he is only man who knows how to run the tray.

Instead a stranger is sent in — a kid hardly dry behind the ears, son of top Commie. Bob Cole is expected to teach him.

"I saw the only way to get ahead was to join the party. I did so."

"And that's why I called you a turn-coat."

"Look, Hinsdale — face reality. What am I betraying? Nothing.

The word no longer has a political meaning. I just want an even break aboard ship."

Hinsdale stalks off unconvinced.

A few minutes later Cole is summoned to the office of the Quadrant Commissar. Commissar has no official standing; his responsibility is only to Communist Party. He is an Italian who speaks no English. The office is a pleasant pavilion among orange trees in the Blue Skin.

Commissar talks to Cole and offers him promotion.

Cole says, "What do I have to do?"

"Join the Socratics. Keep us informed."

"In other words — spy!" says Cole bitterly.

"Exactly."

"No," says Cole. "I'll spy for no-one."

"You're not a good Communist," says the Commissar.

"Not that good."

Commissar conducts him around pavilion. "Space — privacy — foliage. Almost like living in the country. You could have a villa like this if you contributed decisively to Party welfare."

"No," says Cole.

The Commissar appeals to his better nature. "The Socratics are planning aggressive tactics."

"How do you know?"

"We can put two and two together as well as the next one. Do you want to see the ship in chaos?"

"No." Cole is finally persuaded to join Socratics and use his own judgment about reporting news.

He attends Socratic meeting, meets Hinsdale. "What are you doing here?"

Cole tells him candidly.

Hinsdale takes him to Arne Schiffko; with grim amusement he introduces Cole as Commie spy.

"Observer," says Cole frigidly.

"Observe away," says Schiffko. "In fact we're having a secret meeting. You can attend."

Cole goes to secret meeting. Beautiful women, talented men, philosophers, scientists, the intellectual cream of the ship. They plan various functions and activities which seem to Cole completely innocent.

Arne Schiffko introduces him as a Communist observer; all laugh at him.

Cole is furious. "Who do you think you're fooling. I know you're up to something — you're plotting — naturally you wouldn't do it in front of me!"

"You've heard all the plotting we ever do," says Schiffko.

"You mean to say you have no political interests?"

"Not at all — of course we do. But our weapon is a subtle one."

"What is the weapon then? Or is it a secret?"

"We have no secrets. The weapon is called mimesis."

In deep thought Cole reports to Commissar. He gives Socratics a clean bill of health. Commissar annoyed. He is carrying book: English Grammar.

"Yes," he says, "I am learning English. So much around the ship happens in English that I can't understand."

Cole laughs. "Now — do I get a villa?"

"No. You have proved nothing against the Socratics."

Cole looks at English Grammar, laughs. "You're a living proof, Commissar."

VIII

The Passing of the Old

USSR Premier Kryzenkov (the 'Fat Man') in effect is most powerful man aboard ship. He is a Communist, and also an Optimum Human. He exercises power not so much through the use of naked force, but by the fact that he controls distribution of privileges: the outrider ships (propulsion units enclosed in aluminum and plastic globes), farm produce, fresh meat, luxury goods such as cameras, scientific equipment.

Kryzenkov maintains two bubbles. He lives in one, attended by servants and concubines; in the second is his private hot-house, winery, distillery, cattle and poultry ranch, abattoir and dairy. He plans to preempt another, which he will landscape into a private wilderness.

Each nation polices its own region. There has been formed, in addition, an elite Security Guard, to protect the STARK's drive, generators, air and food production. Its loyalty is theoretically given to the STARK itself, without reference to persons, races, or nations, but in effect the Security Guard is Kryzenkov's private army. He uses power so subtly that by and large the population of the STARK considers him a harmless sybarite.

His son Arkady is a different kettle of fish, a lewd, reckless young scoundrel.

A Buddhist Festival is underway in Asia. The religious aspects are not to the forefront: one of the events is a western-style beauty contest. The crowning of Miss Asia.

A nineteen year old Burmese girl is winner. Arkady Kryzenkov becomes enamored, drags her off. There is disturbance. The Asians riot. Arkady is in trouble.

The Security Guard appears, rescues him. Some Asians, also some of the Elite Guard are killed. A tough young Esthonian, Irban Katskaya, takes charge of Miss Asia. He decides that she's too good for Arkady, takes her to Esthonia, sets up housekeeping. Miss Asia has little to say about any phase of her destiny.

Arkady traces Miss Asia, and is furious about what has happened. He catches Kryzenkov in a drunken pliable mood. The next day an edict appears making inter-racial marriages, formal or informal, contrary to approved policy, totally forbidden to Security Guard. They are an elite group; the stock must remain pure.

Asia is infuriated by announcement. Corridors are blocked off; Caucasians roughed up, killed. The Chinese Communists suffer complete loss of face. They change name, but lose all influence.

The dominant factions in Asia are Classicists, Pan-Asiatics.

The Esthonian SSR is still subject to Russian law. A detachment of Russian police comes to arrest Irban Katskaya.

The Esthonians riot, lynch Russians.

Martial law. Esthonia declares itself free of Russia, proclaims independence. Latvia, Lithuania do the same.

Russians turn nausea gas through air-ducts. Irban Katskaya, former

Security Guard, knows code to Segment air-generator. He slips down, turns valves. Gas comes out in Moscow. Arkady Kryzenkov, meanwhile, has turned nerve gas into ducts; gas kills two million Russians.

Communists confer, decide they can't suffer loss of prestige. They don't dare use gas again. They start deploying troops through Baltic decks.

Troops are ambushed, garroted, stabbed, etc. A hard lesson is learned: a section determined to resist can hold its own against trained troops greatly outnumbering its population.

All Europe revolts, declares independence. In Western Europe, former colonial powers slyly rub salt in wounds by relinquishing all claims to former colonies.

In Esthonia, Miss Asia is caught on plaza and lynched by Esthonian women, who irrationally blame her for trouble.

Irban Katskaya kills a dozen of them with tommy-gun, himself becomes a refugee. He tries to flee to West, but is captured by ex-comrades in Security Guard, taken out to Kryzenkov's bubble.

Kryzenkov orders him locked up. Irban Katskaya has become a symbol to a vast number of people; he therefore is a tool, a lever against the public imagination. Kryzenkov wants him kept until he can contrive some use for him.

They listen to a broadcast from England. A member of the Socratic Society discusses current events in the light of the past, and traces the development of contemporary political thought.

The Socratics, he says, represent the genius of Occidental civilization, stemming to the liberal Athenians, developing toward the West.

Communism and the elite Optimum Humanism, on the other hand, is the genius of the Oriental mind, having developed from the Sumerian priest-kings, through Xerxes, Darius, the Byzantines, etc.

Kryzenkov ruefully admits the cool cleverness of the Socratic speaker, who has deftly tied Oriental Absolutism, Communism, and Optimum Humanism in the same package.

Arkady blames their difficulties on Irban Katskaya, and is annoyed at the thought of Irban getting off so easily. He gives orders for Irban to be flogged.

Captain of Security Guard, former comrade of Irban's, is disgusted. He says, "I am a soldier, not a torturer."

Arkady says, "I am giving you commands."

The captain replies, "I have had previous commands in regard to this person."

"I am superseding these."

The captain bows, conducts Arkady into sound-proof chamber. Arkady follows; the captain hands him a whip, points to Irban, who is standing free. He says, "I am placing Irban in your custody. If you want any flogging done, do it yourself."

Arkady takes whip, stands irresolute; he does not dare to make a move. He doesn't know whether captain will protect him or not, but suspects not. He flings down whip, departs.

Irban says, "I better follow him, since I'm in his custody."

The captain shrugs, turns away. It's no longer his responsibility.

Irban leaves room.

Kryzenkov has come to a hard decision. The Socratic ideas have a great deal of effect throughout the ship. Kryzenkov weighs his two philosophies — Communism and Optimum Humanism. The word 'Communism' no longer has practical advantage, associated as it is with the Russian attempts to preserve the paper structure of its empire. Communism is an idea which has outgrown its use.

Kryzenkov jettisons it. He makes a speech in the name of Optimum Humanity, liberating *de jure* all the former satellites — although they already are free *de facto*.

Irban Katskaya has made his way to ferry-barge, escapes.

Arkady wants to shoot him, or order his recapture. Kryzenkov chides Arkady for his childishness, and wearily refuses to take the trouble.

IX

The Secret

The Optimum Humans have changed their name to the Order of Service, to justify their monopoly of privileges and power. They give lip-service to the doctrine of 'Rewards to Those Who Serve'.

They make use of advertising agency methods in their attempt to saddle Socratics with epithets: 'Cephalo', 'Eggheads', 'Elite'.

The contest between Order of Service and Socratics is quiet but none-the-less deadly.

Wanda Lavanchine, daughter of member of Order of Service, is good-looking girl of eighteen, with an alert and inquiring mind.

She hears her father make guarded reference to "the secret" — but he refuses to explain. She'll learn when the time comes.

Wanda visits the STARK, where she meets Donald Carmone, a student of astro-physics at Columbia University, a young man of strong enthusiasms, strong prejudices.

Wanda visits Columbia and finds it much more stimulating and interesting than the exclusive 'finishing-school' atmosphere of the Order of Service Academy for Young Women.

Her parents protest but she has her own way and registers at Columbia, concealing her Order of Service origin. She signs up for astro-physics, and meets Donald Carmone again.

They go out together; Donald still unaware of her origin. He strongly disapproves of the Order of Service; Wanda is amazed at the extent of his feeling and that of most of her new friends. Donald complains that the cycle has made its full turn now: that the early Marxists were idealists; the Stalinists were syndicalists, the Optimums, a self-appointed aristocracy, now degenerated into the ultra-conservative *status quo* Order of Service.

Donald is particularly exercised by the fact that the observatory is situated in one of the outrider ships, and open only to specially licensed students. "Here we are, in the middle of space — ideal conditions for study of the universe! But observatory is locked off. What's the point of studying astro-physics!"

"Well — they say there's no time at the telescope for anyone but the staff."

"There must be *some* time!"

"I'll find out."

Donald suspiciously asks how.

Wanda confesses her background. Donald is taken aback, but says he'll forgive her if she can find out why astronomy students aren't given access to telescope.

Wanda goes out to her home-globe, makes guarded inquiries. Her father evades. She discovers that astronomers plan to attend a special convention.

She reports to Donald. They arrange to visit observatory at this time. Wanda thinks that perhaps here is the 'secret' to which she's heard references.

They stealthily cross intervening space to the observatory, investigate. Nothing of any great moment.

Donald looks through telescope, marvels at clarity of vision. Objective is 100 foot parabolic mirror of mercury; star images are magnified into perceptible disks.

They look back at Earth; surface is incandescent. They look ahead to Alpha Centauri. Donald looks, frowns, swings the spectroscope into place.

Velocity of STARK is not at all what it should be — only a third.

Donald and Wanda look at each other in astonishment. Donald says bitterly, "It's the Order of Service. They've cut acceleration down purposely, they don't want to reach Alpha Centauri…"

Astronomers come back. Donald and Wanda are trapped. They signal to STARK, report what they've discovered.

Socratics send out boat for them. Order of Service is nervous. They realize that they're about to be discredited — and will be in luck if aroused populations don't tear them to pieces.

X

Fall of the Order

The Order of Service has been discredited, but for some peculiar reason the population of the STARK tolerates them and their tyranny.

There are a number of other strange symptoms among the peoples — lassitude, neurosis, transvestism.

Guido Zarcone, a psychologist, is worried enough to abandon his other research, and track down source of the disturbance.

His investigations take him throughout ship. In Manchuria he finds population relatively undisturbed, and stealthily staging gladiatorial combats.

He studies their diets, finds they eat none of a certain carbohydrate which has become a staple to the rest of the ship. Zarcone investigates this carbohydrate, catches an Order of Service man in the act of adulterating it with estrogen and anti-testosterone.

The Order of Service man, to conceal the evidence, swallows it, dies in convulsions.

Zarcone makes report, diet is adjusted; Order of Service is now in very bad repute.

XI

Project N^n

The Order of Service has disappeared, been absorbed. The Socratics have been shouldered with responsibility of governing STARK, which they reluctantly undertake. They govern as little as possible, setting broad policy. National groups govern themselves through local organization, with little interference from Socratics.

The outrider bubbles are awarded to Heroes of Achievement — persons who have contributed to welfare of humanity.

The Socratics embark on a monumental task, under direction of Martin Waber, who has grown into a man of tremendous erudition and perspective. They plan to collate and systematize the entirety of human knowledge.

This is a vast job, involving first a new theory of categories and information evaluation, a new logic of arrangement, a new symbology to systematize the recording of disparate fields of knowledge. The project is expected to yield a tremendous harvest of new knowledge, to lead research into a hundred unsuspected directions. The program is named Project N^n to symbolize the vastness of the scope and the magnitude of the rewards.

Project N^n gets underway. Years pass. There is slow progress — slower than was calculated.

The Centauri group grows brighter ahead. If there are habitable planets here, the attendant problems of colonization will force an indefinite postponement to Project N^n.

Martin Waber, after much soul-searching, gives secret orders to decelerate, thereby lengthening by several years the time necessary to reach Proxima Centauri.

This is social dynamite; it was for just such an offense that the Order of Service was discredited.

Ferdinand Sabroth is Waber's nephew, an associate member of Socratics. He is an amoral young opportunist, with much of Waber's intelligence and a tremendous drive to power. The retiring quality of the Socratics, in his mind, has created a power vacuum; he plans to fill it.

He learns of Waber's decision to slow STARK and tries naked blackmail. He wants full Socratic membership and an outrider globe.

Waber pleads with him, emphasizes the benefits of the New Synthesis.

Sabroth jeers. "You're just as bad as the old Order of Service — playing God!"

Waber pulls a gun with intent of killing Sabroth. Sabroth outwits him, gets gun.

Waber appears to be broken. He sags into a chair. He admits the fault of paternalism in the Socratics, concedes that no matter what the consequences every man must determine his own destiny.

Sabroth threatens him. "Get a move on — do what I ask or I'll bust the Socratics wide open."

Waber thinks, then reaches for a microphone.

"What are you going to do?" says Sabroth.

"I am about to make an announcement to the ship, admit my error. And turn you in for blackmail."

"You fool! You'll wreck everything!"

Waber says, "Ferdinand, perhaps I am clairvoyant — but I have a feeling that a concession to you, giving you the head-start you demand would be worse for the human race than the end of the Socratics."

He reaches for the mike.

"Wait," says Ferdinand Sabroth. "You win. We'll call it quits. Forget I spoke to you."

"No," says Waber. "I have a duty to perform."

Sabroth sees his entire future go glimmering. In desperation he argues with Waber, not to be selfish, not to sacrifice the Socratics for the sake of his own vanity.

"The least I will do," says Waber stonily, "is see you behind bars, for blackmail."

Sabroth glumly calculates the pros and cons of the situation. If he spilled the beans about the Socratics, he'd still go to jail; but when he gets out, the power vacuum may be filled. It's to his interest to preserve situation as is until he can get another chance to make a play for power. He swallows the bitter pill, surrenders himself.

Waber smiles grimly to himself as Sabroth is taken away. He gives orders for deceleration of STARK to be abandoned until Project N^n is back on schedule.

XII

The Hero

Ferdinand Sabroth is visited in jail by a remarkable and complex woman named Ariel Angiello — who inspires fascination both through her beauty and the infrangibility of her emotions. In certain aspects, she is similar to Sabroth. They recognize this similarity, and each distrusts the other the more.

Ariel wants something of Sabroth's — perhaps the leverage that Sabroth held over Waber. She tries to pry this knowledge from Sabroth, who won't talk.

Sabroth asks her what she wants it for. She explains that she is motivated by a desire to live a life on a high key — it may be harsh, intense, it may even be short, but it won't be monotonous. The Socratic Society is waning, she believes; its strength and sternness has become an ivory-tower complex. She plans to exploit what she diagnoses as weakness.

Sabroth sees she would be more dangerous as an ally than as an enemy, and tries to get her in trouble.

She outwits him, makes several attempts to assassinate him.

Sabroth is turned loose. He goes to Waber, who greets him without animosity. Sabroth proposes that he take an outrider globe, go ahead to scout Proxima and Alpha Centauri. These are ten years ahead of the

STARK, but a small ship, operating on high acceleration, could go and return in a year.

Waber says, such an expedition is already being formed: a dozen scientists and their wives. Sabroth notices that one of the names is Ariel Yare. He inquires, "Who is Yare?"

Waber laughs. "Old man who has married beautiful young woman."

Sabroth visits Ariel, asks what she's up to.

She tells him frankly that when the globe returns from Alpha Centauri, there will be no-one alive but Ariel Angiello.

"Ariel Yare, isn't it?"

She laughs. "That's a good joke."

The globe is on the point of departure. Sabroth tries to join expedition without success.

Expedition about to leave.

Sabroth, in space-suit, climbs out on skin of STARK, lets tangential force throw him across gap to scout ship.

He sneaks inside, hides, where he can watch what's going on.

Expedition starts.

He thwarts an attempt of Ariel's to poison everyone on the ship, but is discovered, denounced. He accuses Ariel, but no-one believes him. He is locked up. Ariel visits him. Sabroth sees she is planning best use to make of him, debating whether or not to kill him.

Ship reaches Proxima Centauri. Nothing, no planet. Goes on to Alpha, double star. They spot several planets, land on one.

Sabroth escapes from cell while others are out on surface of planet.

Ariel comes running back, Sabroth hides. Ariel goes to his cell with apparent intent of killing him; Sabroth surprises her, disarms her, locks her in cell.

"Where are the others?"

"Forget about them. You and I — we'll be partners. We'll return to the STARK…"

Sabroth studies her in fascinated horror, then goes out to see what's happened to others.

They're all dead — victims to some peculiar condition of the planet. Sabroth believes Ariel responsible.

He returns to ship, sets out food, oxygen on surface of planet. Ariel watches in apprehension.

"What do you plan to do?"

"I certainly don't dare take you back to STARK. I'm the criminal, the uninvited. I'd be executed, just on your word. It's your life or mine."

She begs him not to put her out, weeps, pleads... Sabroth tells her that if he could see her as a woman, as a human being he might have some pity... But he can't.

Ariel says she didn't kill the others; instead she tried to save them.

Sabroth laughs.

"I can prove it!"

"How?"

"Come out, I'll show you."

They go out together to scene of disaster; Ariel tries to kill Sabroth by same means others died. She thinks she's succeeded, calls him all kinds of a fool, sneers, taunts him.

Sabroth has expected this, and saves himself, overtakes her on way back to ship. Ariel dies in some kind of accident peculiar to planet.

Sabroth is alone. He thoughtfully starts back toward STARK, realizing he's in a hell of a fix. At last he's master of a globe, a legitimate hero who ought to get globe on return. Except circumstances are too accusing.

On the STARK — the ship appears out of nowhere, slides quietly in among other outrider globes.

No-one notices for an hour or two. When Martin Waber goes aboard he finds ship empty. Log reports data regarding Centauri — an unfavorable environment.

The mystery of the explorer ship is tremendous sensation aboard STARK.

Sabroth visits Martin Waber, and taking suitable precautions, tells story. Waber believes him, applauds his courage. He gives orders to change course to Sirius, put ship back on acceleration.

Sabroth has saved STARK 10 or 20 years of decelerating, re-accelerating. Waber offers some kind of reward; Sabroth turns it down.

"What I've learned about myself is reward enough..."

XIII
A Matter of Justice

The Socratics, not interested in governing, have been operating on the principle that the least government is the best. They have no taste for the job, but are more interested in the intellectual advances of the time. As a result, clever criminals are taking advantage of gaps in legal mechanism, and have been doing very well.

Gordon Guerard is one of these criminals, and has his heart set on an outrider globe.

Paul Hunter, a Canadian physicist, has contrived an experimental test for the Force-Time hypothesis of Leon Rakozny, which makes gravitational field, or continuum curvature, a function of spin of atomic particles. Each vortex acts like a tiny egg-beater; in the aggregate they stir up a gravitation field proportional to their number.

Paul Hunter multiplies spin of a proton to the 10th power. A flicker of light appears on the oscillograph indicating a fraction of a dyne.

Hunter is drunk with exultation — the first man to create artificial gravity!

He addresses the Socratic Society on the implications of his work. At the moment he sees no way of manipulating the new phenomenon to any practical advantage. He uses, for analogy, a cork floating in the center of a pond. A man standing on the bank can thrash in the water with a stick, disturb the cork, but he has little control over the motion.

The experiments however open up an entire new field of research.

The Socratic Society acclaims him as a hero, and votes him tenancy of an outrider bubble, which pleases Hunter. He plans to equip bubble as Institute for Advanced Research.

On his way back to the laboratory, Hunter is beat up by thugs.

Gordon Guerard is behind the attack. The first globe available in years — going to a scientist!

To make an impression he orders Hunter beat up. Then he calmly approaches Hunter, demands that Hunter assign him rights in the bubble. If Hunter refuses — he'll be beat up two or three times more — then given an orbit.

Hunter accedes without any protest — to surprise of Guerard.

Hunter tells friends, "The situation is deeper than my personal pride. There's a problem here which I've got to think out. Some research as meaningful as synthetic gravity. These lumps," he rubs his head, "correspond to Rakozny's Force-Time hypothesis, which gave me the lead in the other problem."

"What are you going to do?" his friends ask.

"I've got a brain which I've dedicated to research. What is research but the service of mankind? If anything else, it becomes self-indulgence. The service of man needs another problem solved — and that most pressingly."

Hunter studies history. He makes a pilgrimage throughout the ship. He talks to all kinds of people, visits Asia in disguise.

He finally prepares a report for Socratic Society which he announces as more important than his previous discussion.

He poses the problem: how to govern humanity? How to insure freedom, the full scope of individuality, rewards to the virtuous, punishment to the evil, without the apparently inevitable lapsing into decadence and license?

He submits that the Socratics have been pursuing an incorrect policy, based on anachronistic ideals. "To over-simplify, let's divide humanity into the Good, the Average, the Bad. The Socratics are Good, no question of that. They are honest men, living austere lives, rewarding persons whom they feel so deserve with the richest prize they can give — an outrider bubble. The theory is that the Hero should be rewarded."

"This, I submit, is unrealistic. The honest governor living a Spartan life is merely protecting parasites."

The Socratics protest. "You want us to become depraved, tyrannical?"

"No, by no means. I suggest that those who enjoy the fruits of law and order be required to maintain law and order. The Socratics are poorly adapted to be rulers; their function is to guard, to serve as tribunes. Those who are richest, who have the most to protect, they must be responsible. An average person — who suffers loss from a criminal must be able to recover damages from the upholder of order."

The Socratics dubious. "How about Heroes? How do we reward achievement?"

"Achievement is its own reward. I suggest —" and Hunter grins "— that we appoint Gordon Guerard the first Chief Marshal."

"But — he's a crook! Criminals should not be legitimized! Crime does not pay!"

"Let's let Guerard worry about that. If you suppress him, there are thousands to step into his shoes. They already know that crime *does* pay. The shock comes when they see the criminal forced to pay back, forced to serve instead of victimize."

"Well, we'll try it. You tell Guerard."

"Gladly."

Guerard receives the news wryly. "Hunter," he says, "I made a mistake when I tangled with you. You've got too many brains. But I'm going to go you one better. Here. Take back your globe. The tables are now turned. You are now the Chief Marshal. I know when I'm licked."

Hunter, to his intense dissatisfaction, finds himself Chief Marshal.

XIV

Socratic theory encourages regionalism, believing that human development is best served by a multi-angled approach.

The policy carries with it attendant evils: a degree of jingoism, parochialism. Brazilian children, for instance, are taught from textbooks similar to those used in Brazil on old Earth, with a map of old Brazil hanging on the wall. Similarly with most of the other national groupings.

The observatory reports increasing density of matter in space ahead, with attendant erosion of ship's skin. An accessory meteor guard is designed — a globe of plastic foil anchored only at bow and stern and distended by centrifugal force.

It is suggested that this globe be painted to represent the features of old Earth, at a scale of 1 inch to 29 feet.

Work on the project starts. Meridians and latitudes are laid out, continents delineated, oceans tinted blue-green with spray of metallic ions.

Border dispute between Honduras and Nicaragua over province which both claim results first in fights, then killings, then riots, then war, which spreads through Latin America, and over greater part of STARK.

A coalition of India, Indonesia, China win nominal victory; Socratic Order declared subversive; in reaction against Socratic ideas, a policy of uniformity, synthesis goes into effect.

XV

The new leaders call themselves the Transcendentalists. The basis of their beliefs stem from mysticism and oriental metaphysics.

A new interest in para-psychology arises, which had been shadowed by the materialistic bias of Socratics.

XVI

No habitable planets by Sirius. STARK heads for Procyon. Philologists convene to formulate a new universal language, based on environment and realities of the STARK.

XVII

The Transcendentalists ruthlessly press standardization of everything aboard ship. Socratics have gone underground. A new atmosphere of violence and fear aboard STARK.

Scientists ordered to abandon research; current level of technology frozen, for the reason that any new break-throughs might disturb standardization procedures.

Fundamental research becomes a crime; research tools and equipment are destroyed. The Transcendentalists consider what to do with the Knowledge Bank — the great systematization of knowledge begun under Martin Waber.

Underground group devises method for saving Bank — re-recording in miniature? Diversion of attention?

The record is concealed somewhere — perhaps in a human brain, or a series of human brains, maintained in artificial medium.

XVIII

Transcendentalists in efforts to achieve uniformity order a synthesis and amalgamation of all racial, cultural, linguistic and psychological differences. They break up the national groupings, mingle the races, encourage inter-racial mating.

Craft guilds and trade associations assume more importance. After a few generations these associations occupy the same positions as the former national divisions; Transcendentalists have merely changed one type of organization for another.

XIX

In the effort to secure smooth amalgamation of the races, inter-racial procreation is encouraged, rewarded. As a result the STARK becomes crowded. Birth control ordered — without success. A contraceptive agent is administered to the entire population of the STARK. It has unforeseen effect: everyone aboard the ship is rendered permanently sterile. The race apparently has committed suicide.

One exception — babies in gestation at time of universal sterilization are unaffected. These few babies now represent the hope of the race.

They are carefully collected into a series of antiseptic creches, nurtured and raised with loving care — but sheltered and protected from contact with reality. There are not too many of these children and they have been scientifically matched with future mates.

One of these, a girl, detests her future mate. She says so, but her ideas meet with no sympathy.

She breaks loose, runs away, hides. A reward out for her; anyone sheltering her will be punished.

She takes up with a scruffy young mechanic; they live quietly together, violating laws right and left, dodging the cops. Then one day — as cops are patrolling — a baby screams!

A startling sound — there have been no babies for seventeen years.

Girl is found. Evidently males are not sterile when mating with normal women.

XX

After two or three generations — the STARK is almost deserted. There are very few young people and children, but great bulk of population is sixty, seventy, eighty and over.

The laws, rules, regulations reflect the tastes, interests, concerns and safety of the old people. Youth is discriminated against.

Youth bands together, rebel. There are a few brisk battles — Young versus Old. The Old surrender voluntarily.

XXI

Another generation passes. The STARK is for the greater part deserted. The new race lives up forward; the Stern is a kind of wilderness inhabited by wild men, criminals, desperadoes, fugitives.

A new frontier. Adventure!

XXII

The criminals band together, raid the Bow for women, begin to breed. The STARK is divided into two groups, antagonistic, irreconcilable, and mutually incomprehensible. The Bow is more numerous, with higher degree of civilization than the barbarians of the Stern.

The Bow has established defenses against the Stern barbarians — but a band of barbarians makes their way forward, kills the rulers of the Bow, becomes the new Imperium.

The Stern rulers send greetings to their erstwhile comrades, who now rule the Bow. "Now all of us may enjoy the wealth of the Bow." The new Bow rulers are not sympathetic. They don't want to share their spoils.

A war between Bow and Stern.

XXIII

A star ahead with planets that appear habitable. Great excitement aboard the STARK. Scout ships sent ahead. Worlds look good. Now is time of decision. Everybody is uneasy.

Planet appears below.

Well — who wants to leave?

There is considerable hemming and hawing — but it develops that no-one wants to leave the STARK, which is now home. A scout ship discovers that in spite of appearances the planet is unsuited to human life.

No colony is possible. And the STARK population suddenly revises its emotional position. Now that they can't land, the planet seems infinitely desirable.

The STARK is restocked with raw materials, and continues into space, now vaster and darker and bleaker than ever before.

XXIV

A mad emperor rules STARK. He indulges in practices of the most unpleasant sort. Certain groups protest, using tradition and ancient law as their foundation. The emperor kills them all, and decides to change the records to prevent any further annoyance.

He orders all records destroyed, a new set prepared, in which it shall be written that he, the Emperor, was Deus Progenetrix — that he built the ship, fathered the race, etc.

Museum refuses, barricades the corridors. In vain — the Myrmidons swarm in, kill the curators, ransack the treasures and artifacts, burn books, papers, film.

Every reference to the past is expunged. The image of Earth on the globular meteor-guard painted over.

XXV
Time of the Freaks

Mad Emperor orders biological experiments to suit man for his chosen habitat: deep space.

A new man is designed with body temperature lowered to 60°

(vapor pressure of blood thereby falling to about 13 mm. Hg, which vein walls are able to contain). A tank of H_2O_2 takes the place of lungs.

First man to walk in space without protection, survives — but can't stand pressure inside brain-pan, dies in pain.

Other men designed with thicker skulls, lower portal of pain, higher Vitality Factor. Some weird creatures ensue: the Freaks. They cling to life so strongly as to make killing them almost impossible. They break loose, massacre scientists, strangle Emperor, take over STARK. Normal men are slaves. Freaks are as fantastic mentally as they are physically; STARK becomes an unrecognizable caricature of original vessel.

Red and blue binary appears ahead, with planets. They are uninhabitable to ordinary men, fine for Freaks. They tumble out of STARK in a mad tumult, brawling and shouting.

STARK is quiet. Men creep out of holes, thankfully accelerate STARK away from the planet by the red and blue binary.

XXVI

Of the Freaks left aboard ship, most are killed in revenge against years of torment.

A few Freaks survive — those lucky enough to resemble normal humans. They dare not admit being Freaks, but their children sometimes show Freak stigmata, and are persecuted.

Freak human hybrids are good stock, with high vitality and intelligence; the persecution now serves no good purpose.

One of these Hybrids performs some signal service, saving lives of many humans. As a result, Freaks are legitimized — but no Freaks are left. Stock has been absorbed back into race.

XXVII

Orthodoxy aboard STARK — in reaction against madness and license of Freaks. Priests of the cult of Deus Progenetrix (the Mad Emperor) rule the ship. The Emperor's version of events is taken for truth — no tradition of old Earth remains.

In the schools, cells of young students begin to question Orthodoxy. They are persecuted as atheists. Historians attempt research. A number of hypotheses to account for the STARK are made — some close to the truth.

A group of scientists, hypothecating origin on a planet, calculates its mass and density from air pressure and the artificial G, its constituents from analysis of STARK components, time of leaving Earth by measure of radioactivity.

Someone finds map of Earth underneath paint; paint secretly removed. There's a picture of Earth!

Priests up in arms over heresy; sway mass of populace with fake portents. Scientists in bad way. They discover records concealed long ago when Transcendentalists first gained power over Socratics. All the vastness of human knowledge and lore restored to the human race.

XXVIII

Ahead is dim red star with planets. One is habitable. Scouts from the STARK find a number of cities, relicts of high civilization — but no intelligent race. Very odd. Inhabitants could not have been gone very long, a few months or years. Where did they go? Why? *Marie Celeste* type mystery.

The world is dim, cold, unpleasant. No-one wants to land, except unreconstructed Orthodoxists. They want to leave STARK and the hateful new liberalism.

Orthodoxists put down, STARK leaves, and presently overtakes a vast space-vessel quite similar to STARK.

A cautious approach is made, a degree of communication established. Those aboard the vessel are inhabitants of the deserted planet — creatures adapted to darkness and chill of the planet. They are fleeing the catastrophe which is about to devastate their planet.

Aboard STARK rages great controversy — whether or not to return and rescue Orthodoxists. Finally it is decided to do so; STARK starts back. A group of obstinate men sabotages rescue, causes delay. They are apprehended, and for a punishment promised whatever may be the fate of the Orthodoxists. If the catastrophe is by heat — they shall be burnt to death; if cold, they shall be frozen, etc.

STARK is too late. Dim red star enters dust cloud. Apparently Orthodoxists are doomed to extinction by cold.

But the star disturbs the equilibrium, cloud is sucked into star, bringing new hydrogen, new energy. Star flares up into bright warm orange sun. When STARK arrives they find Orthodoxists in the pink. World is now a fine place, although it would be too hot and bright for original inhabitants.

Saboteurs are given same fate as befell Orthodoxists — put down on planet. Once more STARK takes off.

XXIX

STARK approaches a magnificent Earth-type world — sunny, green mountains, blue seas, plains, meadows. No intelligent inhabitants. Characteristic proteins of planet not incompatible with human. In short — an ideal world.

A number of men and women — about a third of population — want to land. The planet is named Earth.

The rest of the people aboard STARK are hesitant. They all have different reasons for not liking planet. Some think it's too hot, others too cold. Too wet — too dry. Too small — too large. All these want to stay aboard the STARK, and move on across space.

They stay in orbit a year, restocking with raw materials, helping colonists get settled. Then STARK continues out across space — and apparently this will be its function: seeding the universe with men.

WILD THYME AND VIOLETS

Outline

I

THE FOUR HUNDRED HOUSES of Gargano, blocks of white- or color-washed stone, occupy numberless tiers and levels up the slopes of a gray limestone mountain. Wisps of smoke float above mouldering tile roofs; a few dispirited trees can be seen: fig, orange, mulberry. At the center of town is the plaza, with the cathedral looming above. Opposite stands the inn, with benches and tables under a trellis. The mayor's mansion looks down a short avenue to the right.

The surrounding country is somewhat bleak. On the hillside grow a few olive trees, wild thyme, asphodel, thistle, groups of slender cypress. Outcroppings of gray limestone scar the slopes; a few poverty-stricken families live in caves, which they have fitted with stout timber doors. Stretching away to the southeast are the marshes, where the folk of Gargano graze their goats and geese. The air is dry and pungent with the odor of herbs. Near the town stands the castle of the Marquis del Torre-Gargano: an extravagant edifice in the rococo style, with mullioned windows, turrets and bartizans, high balconies and sky-walks. In the moat grow water-lilies and bulrushes. The gardens are somewhat neglected; the roses bloom profusely but underneath are dry weeds.

In the castle live the saturnine Marquis Paul-Aubry Alcmeone del Torre-Gargano and his seventeen-year-old daughter Alicia, who is dumb. Their life is very quiet; the Marquis chooses to entertain no one. Alicia is something of an enigma: a pensive girl who paints exquisite little pictures of flowers in water-color. No one knows why she cannot speak.

Saturday in Gargano is market day. The plaza is cluttered with color: fabrics and copperware, fruits, melons, spices, glassware, sandals. A blind gypsy plays the guitar. A pair of officers in blue, black and tan uniforms drink wine under the bower outside the inn and ogle the town girls. Mersile, a traveling mountebank, sits on the steps of his horse-drawn caravan, appraising the crowd. Etheny, his idiot helper, erects a booth decorated with thaumaturgical symbols. A priest, Father Berbolla, darts a frowning side-glance at the booth. He shakes his head at the mountebank and goes his way to the inn.

A blue and gold barouche, the paint faded and the gold-leaf somewhat tarnished, clatters across the square, on its way to the castle. Within, straight and still, sits the Lady Alicia, returning from a visit with her cousin. The folk of Gargano cannot understand her inability to speak. Has she never learned? Or perhaps she is bewitched. Certain devout old ladies cross themselves as the carriage passes.

Behind, running and bounding, comes Lucian, the town ne'er-do-well. He is tall, gaunt, with russet hair, flaming green eyes. Lucian lives in a chronic state of near-starvation. He owns a few frayed brushes, a pot or two of paint; he paints signs, portraits, fences — anything by which to glean a few florins. He runs after the carriage hoping to catch a glimpse of Alicia, whom he adores. He clutches a nosegay of wild thyme and violets which he tosses into the carriage. Alicia pays no heed.

The innkeeper bawls at Lucian, who has been engaged to work a few days at the inn. Lucian regretfully turns aside, and is unlucky enough to jostle Parnasse, the mayor, and is angrily reprimanded for his carelessness.

II

Parnasse is a large full-blooded man, given to vehement gestures and large curses. Contradictions appear in the character of Parnasse: he is pompous but earthy, generous but mean, shrewd but foolish. His wife Clotilde is barren, and Parnasse has suffered many crude jests on this account. Parnasse longs for a son, but Clotilde obdurately fails to produce even a daughter.

Parnasse goes to his mansion and flings himself on his couch to rest, to concentrate, to muster his energies.

A gong sounds. He marches upstairs to Clotilde in her bed-chamber. "You have taken the extract?"

Clotilde, an amiable woman of good proportions, assents. "To the edge of a surfeit."

"And the exercises?"

"All, everything; the entire regimen."

Parnasse checks a chart on the wall, mumbling and muttering. He pulls out an elaborate watch. "At this instant the moon enters Sagittarius; the hour is at hand!"

III

At the inn Lucian rushes back and forth in his capacity as roustabout, scullion and waiter. Father Berbolla enters, takes a seat and orders a frugal meal, smiling a small patient smile. Lucian serves this precise meal, at which Father Berbolla stares in astonishment. He calls the innkeeper. "See what this dunderpate has brought me!"

Lucian too late realizes his ungenerous error; the innkeeper's patience is at an end; Lucian is discharged on the instant.

He ambles back to his hut on the marshes. On the road he spies a bit of yellow stone. He takes it home, grinds it to a powder, mixes it with gum, and tests it on a board. Very pale, but nonetheless useful. Lucian's palette by necessity is improvised. For red he uses triturated pomegranate rind; for green, the juice expressed from crushed dock leaves. Saffron stolen from the inn gives him yellow. Soot is black; chalk is white. Muds and slimes provide a range of browns, grays, and even orange. Blue? He uses powdered lichen to doubtful effect.

IV

Marquis Paul-Aubry and Alicia sit at their luncheon. The room is octagonal, very high, and paneled in white wood, with a border of graceful green festoons, from which depend peaches and apricots. A large window overlooks the rose garden and a hazy vista to the south over the marshes. The table is covered with damask; at the center is a low silver vase of yellow roses. Alicia wears a white gown; her skin is pale. She sips verbena tea. Marquis Paul-Aubry is elegantly thin. His skin is as pale as that of Alicia, with a bluish undertone. His hair is black and dressed severely close to his head; his features are stern, austere. His deportment is controlled by a rigid schedule from which he never departs.

He eats half a brandied peach, a biscuit, and takes a glass of white wine.

Footsteps sound in the hall. Into the room rushes the stable-man, in a state of fury. He buffets the Marquis, who topples to the floor. The groom glares and makes a fist, then departs; the Marquis, stern but urbane, picks himself up, dusts his knees with a napkin and resumes his seat. He displays no emotion, because he feels none. How could any person of breeding react to a circumstance so coarse and insipid?

Alicia goes to her bedroom and sits by the window watching the sky. On a nearby branch a bird sings. Alicia listens intently. Suddenly she smiles, and whistles the notes through her teeth.

The bird flies away; Alicia sadly watches it depart over the marshes.

She descends to the rose garden, and sitting on a marble bench pulls petals from blown blossoms. A little heap forms at her feet.

The Marquis saunters to the stables. He instructs the stableman regarding the horses and receives a surly acquiescence.

The Marquis turns and for a moment contemplates the stableman's son. The pink-cheeked boy wears a blue smock; his hair is brown and overlong. With a woebegone face he forks manure into a cart, and will look neither at the Marquis nor his father.

Marquis Paul-Aubry turns away with a sigh. It must be a disease from which he suffers! Other folk feel emotion; why is he so denied?

V

Mersile stands in his booth. He sells balms, elixirs, papers imprinted with magic signs. For those who so require he casts horoscopes, lances boils, pulls teeth. When business is slack he plays a concertina while Etheny, his half-wit helper, performs a jig.

Parnasse approaches the booth. After a glance right and left, he asks in a husky voice: "How may a barren woman be rendered fertile?"

"There is a single certain method," Mersile tells him: "The expert use of hypnosis!"

"Ah!" breathes Parnasse. "This then is the answer! But how do I proceed?"

"Not you! Only an adept can perform the feat!"

Parnasse hires Mersile to do the work, wincing at the price.

"Conditions must be absolutely correct!" Mersile declares.

"So much goes without saying," Parnasse declares. "What do you suggest?"

"A condition where every attribute conduces to the happy consequence we have in mind. Etheny!"

Mersile sends Etheny to the mansion to hang appropriate symbols in Madame Clotilde's bedroom. "Tomorrow the ceremony will take place."

Clotilde has gone to the cathedral. She vows a hundred candles to each of several saints if they will assist her to conceive a child. She implores the advice of Father Berbolla in regard to poor Parnasse, who suffers so many frustrations. "Only today he has gone to take counsel from the thaumaturgist!"

Father Berbolla is shocked. "Here are evil advices. Can you not dissuade him?"

"Only by conceiving, which so far has been beyond my capability."

Father Berbolla will pray for her, and he feels obliged to sprinkle her chamber with holy water, against the possibly baneful influence of Mersile.

VI

Parnasse and Clotilde eat their supper: boiled meat and broth, a brace of roast fowl, pig's feet.

Parnasse tells her of his preparations and admonishes her: "Attend at all times to our goal, which is fecundity! Be fruitful! Bring forth! Conceive! I can only do what is possible; you must do the rest."

"What is left after the possible?" Clotilde inquires somewhat stupidly. "The impossible?"

"You are purposely obtuse," cries Parnasse. "It is not all that difficult!" He sends for Lucian, who presently appears, puzzled and hungry.

"Here is Madame Clotilde," states Parnasse. "Take note: she is without child, flat as a halibut. I wish you to paint her in a state of full gestation, and at once. Is all this clear?"

"What of my fee?"

"A detail! We can arrange the matter at any time. The important thing is that you start work instantly."

"I must buy paint and canvas, but, in all candor, I have no money."

"Obtain what you need; I will pay any reasonable charges. When will you start?"

"I will do my sketches now, if your excellency can provide paper and a bit of charcoal."

"Clotilde will see to your needs."

"A bit of bread and meat, and a bite of cheese — these to steady my hand as I sketch."

VII

One morning before dawn Alicia leaves the castle. The first frost of autumn lies on the land. She walks up the hillside, watches the sky take on color. She seems to be seeking something, but what? Who knows? Least of all Alicia. Overhead a flight of geese fares south croaking and moaning. In the west the full moon grows pale; in the east the sun rises. Alicia suddenly becomes alarmed and hurries back to the castle.

VIII

Clotilde is pregnant! Parnasse has confided in no one. Clotilde has provided no information. But the news has suddenly become general property.

Parnasse is irritated to find his intimate business in so many mouths. With rather poor grace he accepts congratulations, then grows proud and, taking a glass of wine here, a taste of plum brandy there, presently he is in good spirits. He knows the remedy for barrenness, he informs his admiring cronies. Indeed! And will he share his secret? Parnasse winks and makes a cryptic sign. Everyone speculates as to which of the expedients proved the most effectual: Prayer? Hypnosis? Cabalistic symbols? The pregnant portrait? Parnasse waggishly shakes his head. "None of these! As your mayor, as your comrade and fellow citizen of Gargano, I will demonstrate the sleight upon any of your wives, nieces or daughters."

IX

The priests engage Lucian to paint an altar-piece. They supply an advance of money sufficient to buy paint and varnish. Lucian instead buys food: bread, cheese, bacon. On his way home a dog steals the bacon. Lucian pursues the dog across the marsh.

X

Lucian paints the altar-piece with paints mixed of pitch, soot, chalk, sulfur, red clay. In the central cartouche sits a madonna and child. Lucian uses Clotilde as a model and absentmindedly includes her pregnancy. The priests are critical; they refuse to pay his fee. Lucian throws up his arms and storms away. The priests inspect the unfinished painting which, for the sake of economy, they decide to use despite the somewhat questionable subject matter.

XI

All-Hallows Eve is at hand: an important festival at Gargano. The priests lock themselves in their cells, and recite troubled Aves and Te Deums.

In Gargano the custom is most rigid: a maid wearing white is deemed innocent and may not be subjected to amorous proposals.

Marquis Paul-Aubry and Alicia appear at the fête. The Marquis wears a black and steel-gray uniform, black shako. His nose is hooked and pinched, his mouth has a sour dyspeptic droop. Alicia is frail as a fairy in a ballerina costume: a tunic of spangled white satin and white tights, a tutu of fluffy white gauze. A cloche of white satin confines her hair; she seems excited and unusually vital. Lucian, costumed as Caliban, sees her and becomes almost faint with longing, but she is swept away by three revelers: a pierrot and two punchinellos. They hoist her upon a table and toast her with goblets of wine, urging her to drink, to dance, to sing; they are young bravos of Montfalcone and unaware of both her identity and her inability to speak. Alicia looks this way and that, wearing a bewildered half-smile. The Marquis, at a little distance, watches with saturnine detachment, envying the revelers their spontaneity. How beautiful is Alicia, this pale dumb creature whom he has sired! How beautiful and how mysterious! But does she feel? Is she sensate? What color are her perceptions? Can she imagine pain? horror? futility?

A cup of wine is upset; a flow of red stains Alicia's stockings; she looks down ruefully.

The two punchinellos lift her down from the table; the pierrot whirls her around in a series of drunken capers. Alicia becomes puzzled and alarmed; her eyebrows raise; her eyes shine in the torchlight.

The Marquis watches from the side. What has she sensed? Does she exult? apprehend?

The three revelers whirl her away, off behind the inn. Alicia makes no sound of protest; the pierrot and the punchinellos believe her acquiescent and take her into a hay-room. Alicia gasps and holds back, to no avail. She no longer wears pure white; the prohibition is dissolved. The Marquis still watches critically from a little distance. Does she realize what is about to happen? He returns to the square and sips a glass of wine.

Lucian in wild anguish comes to tug at his arm; the Marquis thrusts him off with a frown of distaste. Lucian babbles of Alicia's plight; the Marquis turns his back. Lucian rushes to Alicia's aid; he is buffeted back into the darkness.

The Marquis yawns fastidiously. Perhaps after all he will interest himself in the matter. He finishes his wine, and languidly saunters to the hay-room. He stands in the opening waiting for a sensation to come over him. A single cresset illuminates the room. Alicia, her garments in disorder, lays passive in the hay. The two punchinellos have finished with her; the pierrot prepares himself, but now he is annoyed by the Marquis' sneer of disapproval. "Hence troll; we have no need of you here."

The Marquis considers the situation, whips forth a rapier and with the casual ease of a man stepping on an insect, impales the pierrot. The punchinellos croak in dismay and flee. The pierrot lies on his back, kicking and groping like an upturned beetle.

The Marquis watches dispassionately, interested only in the fluctuations of his own awareness. Surely his pulse is beating somewhat faster? Alicia props herself up on her arms, and watches glassy-eyed. Feebly she tries to cover her naked legs. The Marquis orders Lucian to bring up his carriage; Alicia is taken back to the castle.

The Marquis wipes his rapier on the dead pierrot and returns to his table.

XII

Alicia, wearing a night-dress, stands by her window. At Gargano the fête continues, but less exuberantly. The colored lights swing more slowly; the music is fitful. Alicia looks up into the dark sky. The stars are white, remote, pure. Alicia stares up in mournful fascination; how peaceful is the dark sky; how loving are the stars! She steps forward. Dark air rushes past her; she falls into the moat. Lucian, who had followed the carriage and since has been skulking about under the cypress trees, flounders into the water and drags her forth, limp and listless.

Almost beside himself with joy he carries her to his hut on the edge of the marsh, and lays her upon his pallet. He builds up his fire, boils tea, removes her soiled garments and throws them into the fire. He dries her with adoring hands, and talks to her in a soft voice: "You threw your life away; I found it and took it for myself and now you are my very own."

Alicia lies in a half-daze. Lucian speaks on in a husky voice: "Never again will you suffer or know desolation!"

Alicia turns her head and looks at him. Lucian strokes her hand. "Speak to me: tell me that you love me, as I love you."

Alicia's lips twitch: an attempt to speak? A grimace?

XIII

The Marquis sits alone at his breakfast. He drinks coffee from a tall silver cup. Cadwal, his steward, appears with news regarding Alicia.

The Marquis considers the situation, but finds no stimulation. He is indifferent.

Cadwal says delicately: "The artist Lucian is notorious both for excessive conduct and indigence."

"The qualities would seem — after a period of disequilibrium — to nullify each other," remarks the Marquis.

The steward bows curtly and withdraws. Marquis Paul-Aubry sips his coffee, eats a slice of fruit-cake. Then he goes to stand by the window. He thinks of the kicking pierrot. Is there such a thing as emotion-by-association? His hands close; his pale knuckles show white.

Father Berbolla presents himself at the castle. Lucian's conduct is an impertinent scandal; what does the Marquis propose to do?

He had not considered the matter from this perspective. The fact that anyone should impute to him a concern, or even an opinion, comes as a notable surprise. He can only affirm and corroborate a condition so self-evident as to seem a banality: the matter is nothing to him. When Alicia sees fit, she will return to the castle. If she chooses to stay, why should she be thwarted? Each person must cut his own trail through the Hyrcanian jungle of the future. Try as he may, he cannot fathom Father Berbolla's evident preoccupation with this matter.

"We are children of the church together," Father Berbolla asserts. "If you refuse to succor a pair of errant souls, then, in all good conscience, I must."

The Marquis offers the priest coffee and fruit-cake, and the conversation shifts to other matters.

Father Berbolla and the Mother Superior go to Lucian's hut. Despite Lucian's pleas they take Alicia away to the convent.

XIV

Father Berbolla talks to Alicia who sits passively. The candles flicker; she is fascinated. Father Berbolla suggests that she take vows, and devote her life to good works. Alicia's eyelids droop.

Lucian meanwhile has contrived a mad plan for the rescue of Alicia. He becomes confused and wanders into the Mother Superior's chamber, where she is washing her feet. Lucian runs wild-eyed from the building. He is seized and taken before the mayor, and consigned to jail. Alicia slips away and returns to the castle.

XV

Marquis Paul-Aubry, in the throes of ennui, wanders about the castle. He shatters a porcelain figurine and studies the shards. Did the act provide a sensation? He secures a volume of illuminated psalms and tears out page after page and feeds each in turn into the fire, watching the colors alter, go dark, shrivel into flakes of soot.

The stable-boy peers through the doorway. The Marquis appraises him from the side of his face, then moves slowly forward. The boy smiles a trembling half-smile. The Marquis kicks him: once, twice, three times. The boy, holding his adorable buttocks, rushes from the castle.

Standing at the window the Marquis sees him wandering off down the hill. He frowns, purses his lips, and selects a dagger from the wall display. Leaving the castle, he strides on long thin legs down the hill.

He waits behind a hedge. The boy comes past. The Marquis chirrups. The boy halts, and peers over the hedge. In a sudden flurry of arms and legs the boy is hacked and slashed.

The Marquis considers the corpse. His nostrils are flared; the pupils of his eyes are dilated. He examines himself. How to distinguish between simple sensation and veritable emotion? If a roaring lion suddenly leapt from behind the hedge, the Marquis no doubt would make a recoil action, to some greater or lesser degree, but could this gross reflex by any device of casuistry be termed an emotion? The Marquis suspects not. Curious, curious. Well, at least the affair had been stimulating. He so seldom went abroad into the fresh air; he must do it more often.

XVI

Gargano is shocked by the murder. Who could commit so monstrous a deed? Parnasse confers with the Marquis, who frowns and taps his chin with his stick. Yes, yes, he will certainly look into the affair.

XVII

The winter passes. Clotilde swells enormously and at the seventh month gives birth to quadruplets. One resembles Mersile the mountebank; the second resembles the priest; the third is gaunt, long-nosed and red-haired like Lucian; the fourth is most like Etheny the idiot.

Parnasse comes to survey the litter. His eyes gleam and he jerks at his beard. Clotilde watches from the corner of her eye.

XVIII

The Marquis breakfasts with Alicia, then goes to walk in the countryside, wearing a black and red coat, gray trousers, black boots with moleskin gaiters. The landscape is dark and dreary; the trees have not yet put forth leaves. He passes Lucian's hut and looks within. A stool supports a half-finished portrait of Alicia. The Marquis considers the painting, and prods it with his stick.

He saunters into Gargano and takes a glass of warm tokay with cloves at the inn. Parnasse enters.

The Marquis in his mind's-eye sees himself assaulting Parnasse, cutting the heavy throat, hacking the red cheeks, plunging a great cutlass into the heavy midriff, then standing back as the huge red and pink hoses of Parnasse's guts come tumbling forth. The corpse would smell abominably. The Marquis gives a grimace of fastidious distaste. Parnasse is too strong-blooded, too ruddy and thick; the best murders are delicate and mild. Someday it might be amusing to lower a beautiful young girl by the hair into a vat of perfume.

He returns to the castle. Alicia sits staring into the fire. The Marquis stops to reflect...She would put forth no blood whatever, only a pale ichor, faintly scented of violet. The effort would hardly be worth the nuisance. He goes one step, then pauses again. If they could converse and discuss the matter, what would she say?

Someone has come to the door. Cadwal announces Lucian.

Lucian makes a fervent presentation. "Sir, I have been released from prison only this last hour. My crime, as I construe the argument, is the zeal of my service to the Lady Alicia."

"I wouldn't be too certain of this," replies the Marquis. "As I recall, you were accused of voyeurism at the convent…No matter. What are your present purposes?"

"At one time I begged that she put her life into my keeping. She did not then reject my proposal, and I have come to learn how matters stand now."

The Marquis nods approvingly. "Well spoken. You wish then to resume the custody of the Lady Alicia?"

"If she is of a mind to it."

"Aha, indeed. Well then, I neither render permission nor withhold it. You must persuade the Lady Alicia, as the matter lies between yourselves."

Lucian bows, nearly weeping with gratitude. He turns to where Alicia sits brooding.

The Marquis saunters politely across the room and watches over his shoulder. Lucian smiles down into Alicia's face; she stares into his eyes. He speaks, holds out his hand. Slowly she rises. The Marquis turns and leaves the room. When he comes back they are gone.

The Marquis gazes out the window. Dusk is gathering across the marshes. He goes to a long disused chamber where he dons a harlequin costume and a black domino as well. By a private way he slips out from the castle.

His feet are agile and light; occasionally he cuts a caper. In the lane he hears a sound of singing: three little girls, returning home from taking sheep into paddock.

The harlequin leaps forth; one must escape, which is a pity. With a squirming crying bundle under each arm he jumps the ditch on feet of air, and flits into the dark woods.

XIX

Mersile the mountebank declares his competence to find the murderer. He will use hypnosis.

XX

Lucian and Alicia sit in their hut before a small fire. As Alicia looks into the fire tears form in her eyes and stand glistening. Lucian knows why she weeps; he wants to weep himself.

XXI

The Marquis wanders around the castle. He halts before an ancient portrait. With a knife he chips away the paint, flake by flake. After ten minutes he becomes bored with the work and goes to the window. The time is late afternoon. The sun sets in the marshes, a cold vermilion rind.

XXII

Lucian sets forth to earn, beg or steal a few bites of food for himself and Alicia. At the inn he makes caricatures of a group of officers, and receives a silver coin, with which he buys a sausage, a crusty loaf, a cheese and a bottle of wine.

Approaching the hut he stops short, astounded by a flickering of shadows: a frantic motion like the flurry of an enormous moth... Lucian peers through the window. The harlequin stands panting above a crumpled body.

Lucian craftily throws a jug of turpentine upon the harlequin and applies a torch.

The harlequin bounds flaring down the dark road, and off across the marsh.

Lucian is composed and elegant. He arranges Alicia on the couch, and paints a portrait: a face wide-eyed, luminous, glowing with dreams too splendid to be spoken.

XXIII

The funeral takes place in morning mist. Alicia is carried to the crypt of her ancestors, in a little valley above the castle. A few people walk behind the hearse: the Marquis, some aged aunts, the castle servants, Lucian.

When all are departed Lucian comes back to sit by the crypt. His expression is rapt; he seems to be listening.

Rain starts to fall. Lucian shivers and returns to his hut to find a number of angry people waiting for him. The town marshal, acting upon information, has discovered a harlequin suit under his bed.

The townspeople start to cudgel Lucian. He leaps to the roof, roaring in anguish. "I killed no one; I was in jail while the murders occurred!"

Parnasse reluctantly steps forward. "True. He is not the harlequin."

Someone inquires, "Then how to explain these garments under the artist's bed?"

An urchin whispers to Parnasse; he saw Etheny the idiot bringing a parcel to the hut.

XXIV

Etheny is dragged howling to the gibbet. Father Berbolla urges him to confess, that he may be shriven. The Marquis stands to the side, saturnine, dispassionate. Etheny makes a frantic gesticulation: "He gave my orders! There he stands!"

The Marquis laughs. The onlookers are appalled by the scope of Etheny's madness.

Parnasse gives a stern signal; Etheny is hauled aloft, to hang kicking and jerking.

The folk of Gargano take a wan satisfaction in the working of justice. Once more they assure each other that all may sleep soundly in their beds. The Marquis smiles sadly to himself…Why not? The killings were as tiresome as any other activity. Perhaps for a period he will indulge in charities and good works, and gain the love of the townspeople.

XXV

The evening is calm and still. A new moon hangs over the mountain. Lucian comes across the hillside and approaches the crypt. He stands beside a cypress tree. He hears a soft strange sound, and looks in all directions.

The sound — if it existed — is gone. Lucian slowly returns to his hut. He makes a pack, rolls up the portrait of Alicia. Flinging a cloak around his shoulders, he leaves the hut and walks off down the pale road.

CLANG

Concept and synopsis for screen-play

TIME:
Fifty years hence.

PLACE:
Los Angeles.

GENERAL THEME:
The spectacular sport of 'Pugilistics': prize-fights between robots of quasi-human appearance eight feet tall.

ENVIRONMENT:
Different in some aspects from now. People look about the same, wear clothes differing from ours in decorative details, ride in small electric cars which guide themselves safely and quickly from place to place. Public transit straddles freeways; there are occasional glimpses of a novel architecture.

Laws safeguard every aspect of the environment; the 'Consumer-Report' mentality is in power. Food is sterile, if nutritious; life is secure and sanitary.

Perhaps too secure, too sanitary!

The average citizen lives a sensible and placid life; he is obliged to divert his emotions and competitive urges into professional sports, and he heightens the intensity of this participation by gambling: an activity controlled by organized crime.

Gambling is the characteristic disease of society, even though institutional gambling — i.e., the casinos at Las Vegas — have been outlawed.

The ordinary sporting event is ultra-polite and very safe. Tennis-players must wear plastic bubbles to protect their faces; football has become a well-padded version of touch-tackle. Boxing has been totally outlawed; no sport now gratifies the average man's taste for vicarious violence.

EXCEPT !!! for the dramatically violent and spectacular sport of 'Pugilistics', which cannot be outlawed since the participants are robots, usually constructed to simulate half-human creatures of fearful appearance.

NOTE:

The flavor and conditions of society can readily be suggested by a few casual and even entertaining incidents, and need not be the topic of exposition.

BACKGROUND TO 'PUGILISTICS'

The robots fight in three classes: lightweight, middleweight and heavyweight; these latter up to eight feet tall, weighing maybe two tons.

Each fighter displays a distinctive personality: some are brutal and massive, others are quick, given to sudden slashing attacks, then a dancing retreat. They show many varieties of visage, sometimes awful, sometimes noble, and sometimes it seems as if the fighters generate a personality of their own, and 'come alive', as it were, and this is especially noticeable if the fighter is a veteran of many bouts, since it learns by experience, and in fact must be programmed by a skilled human technician who laboriously loads the brain with every practical tactic, feint, maneuver and reaction.

The fighters are constructed in special shops, by pugilistic engineers, each notable for the distinctive qualities of his products. There are many such shops, but to build a heavyweight fighter of championship quality and program it with all its moves, is an expensive production. The 'Syndicate' (a euphemism for organized crime) never lacks for money, and covertly provides the backing for several shops, most notably 'Sweigart's Robotics', which regularly turn out superbly destructive fighters.

Bouts consist of four-minute rounds with two-minute intervals between. Fights continue until one robot is disabled and then mercilessly destroyed, to the outcries of the crowd and a special kind of passionate music which has evolved over the years to fit the emotional extremes of the occasion.

This particular spectacle, though with a distant relationship to gladiatorial combat and the bull-ring, is unique in human history.

The story-line indicated below takes advantage, as fully as possible, of the wonderful visual effects latent in the theme.

MAIN CHARACTERS

Joe Perkins, protagonist, is about 30, thin, sinewy, with a sensitive bony face and a wry disposition. He is the partner of

Henry Tamm, about 45, stocky, energetic, restless, sometimes reckless. Tamm and Joe operate a waterfront machine-shop which produces specialty parts for submarine drilling and mining of the ocean floor. Joe spends much of his time at sea or under the sea, and is not a man of the city. Tamm manages the shop. Unlike Joe, he is a dedicated gambler, losing much and winning little. Time and time again Joe explains that he can't outsmart the Syndicate, to which Tamm grits his teeth and vows to get his own back.

Dill Archer: pugilistic engineer with talent and optimism, but no business acumen. He operates the Bell Robotic Shops. His wife Fariana has run off with a Syndicate operator, leaving Dill with a daughter *Ellen*, now about 20, pretty, straightforward, practical, with a hatred first of the pugilistic business, which she is now stuck with. Even more she hates the Syndicate, which, so she is quite aware, has robbed and cheated them outrageously.

Vince Hackett, an engineer employed by Dill Archer, has his eye on Ellen, but she evades him.

STORY

Joe Perkins delivers components to an off-shore mining rig in an ocean skimmer. Upon his return he finds Tamm intently watching a prize-fight between a pair of heavyweights: 'Blue Belial' and 'Awful Claude' — the latter a Bell robot.

Blue Belial dismembers Awful Claude and reduces him to a heap of twitching metal, to the music of glory and destruction, which accentuates the emotions of both exaltation and tragedy.

Tamm seems glum, but says nothing. Joe recognizes the symptoms. "How much are you in to this one?"

"Plenty. In fact, too much."

The video screen glows to show the distraught face of Dill Archer. "Did you see the fight?"

"Naturally. What else would I be watching?"

"They got at Claude!"

"What do you mean?"

"I mean they stirred up his brains! Didn't you notice? He should have won that fight!"

"So where do we stand now?"

"I'm wiped out. I put everything and more than everything on Claude."

Archer turns his head and looks away; a female voice from an unseen source can be heard: "Mr. Archer is busy at the moment! He can't talk to you!"

A second voice, light, easy, menacing, speaks: "He doesn't need to talk. Just have him give me my money."

Archer walks away from the screen. Joe and Tamm hear his voice: "I don't have any money. Not right now."

"Sure you do! You win, we pay. We win, you pay. That's how the game goes."

The screen is turned off. Tamm runs from the office. Joe calls: "Where are you going?"

"They're about to kill old Dill!"

Joe, growling and cursing, runs after Tamm.

They arrive at Bell Robotics. Archer has been beat up. Ellen is tending him and raging with fury against the two men who dealt so rudely with her father, and, according to them, this was just for starters.

It turns out that Tamm has advanced Archer money for expenses; Archer now can pay back nothing except plans, models, expertise. Tamm asks Archer: "How much to pay off your bets?"

"Thirty grand. I'll have to give up title to the shop."

Tamm turns to Joe. "We can swing that, right, Joe? We'll advance Dill the money and take Bell Robotics for security."

"I don't want Bell Robotics! This isn't my field!"

"We can't lose! Dill is a genius!"

"Then why isn't he rich instead of lying there half-dead?"

Joe meets Ellen's eyes. He hesitates, then throws his hands into the air. "Whatever you say."

"Wonderful!" yells Archer. "Hackett, go back to work; the shop is staying open!"

::::

Through some mysterious source the Syndicate learns of the arrangement, and is dissatisfied, because they want no outsiders in the game. Next day the bagman collects the thirty thousand, and immediately thereafter, an explosion destroys Bell Robotics and maims Dill Archer.

Ellen however has put certain invaluable records in a vault; these are secure and salvaged.

::::

Joe and Tamm willy-nilly find themselves in the robot business, to Joe's disgust. They start building robots. Most of the components are off-the-shelf; the rest can easily be fabricated.

The group discovers or deduces that Vince Hackett is a pipeline to the Syndicate. Tamm wants to take him far out to sea, and let him walk home. Joe says no; Hackett may somehow be useful.

For practice the shop builds a lightweight fighter, named 'Steel Mosquito'. It goes up against a fighter built by Sweigart Robotics in a big money fight, whereupon it loses, and unaccountably. Analyzing the film, Joe sees that the Syndicate fighter had illegally clamped the Mosquito's feet magnetically so that it could not jump back to evade demolition.

A new Mosquito is built. False information is fed to the Syndicate through Hackett. This time the Mosquito destroys the Sweigart robot, to win over a hundred thousand dollars.

In the morning Vince Hackett does not show up for work. Joe finds his body aboard the skimmer and quickly transports it to the garage of

Saul Cermolo, the Syndicate boss, where it is discovered by the police on a tip from Joe.

::::

The group builds a heavyweight known as the Black Angel. To program the memory circuits, a man must enclose himself in the shell, and the robot is subjected to various stimulations. The human responses become its program. This is a tedious job, though not a great deal of skill is necessary, since the moves may be enacted at half-speed, and then programmed for use as fast as the mechanism can tolerate. This job was formerly performed by Hackett and Archer; now it falls to Joe.

The big fight approaches. The Black Angel will face the new Sweigart Scorpion.

Angel is tested against other heavyweights and reacts with encouraging savagery.

Syndicate types come out to the shop, including the head honcho Saul Cermolo. Various menaces. Tamm hotly refutes.

Tamm keeps guard over Angel by night. Joe, out romancing with Ellen, is summoned to the shop. Activity! Interlopers run off through the dark. Joe enters shop to find Tamm killed and Angel sabotaged in a clever fashion, at the neck joint.

Angel is repaired. Knowledge in regard to the Scorpion is lacking. Joe is lowered on a line from a high helicopter, and climbs down through sky-light. He sees the Scorpion being tested: an awesome machine with mauls the size and weight of anvils, by which it batters the heads of its adversaries.

Joe is detected and chased back and forth and finally escapes the way he came.

The fight: 'Black Angel' and 'Copper Scorpion' lumber into the ring: a pair of terrible contrivances, the more awful for their half-human semblances.

The preliminary music sounds: sad, sweet, the music of destiny.

The fight begins.

Angel holds its own until Scorpion batters its head and springs its neck, thereby disrupting the circuits. In desperation, and despite pleadings from Ellen, Joe surreptitiously slips into Angel and guides it himself. This is dangerous.

The fight proceeds. Scorpion is puzzled by Angel's unorthodox maneuvers, but throws massive blows which daze and bewilder Joe, so that he cannot prevent Angel from staggering and falling to one knee. Cries from the crowd, as they sense destruction and the orgiastic catharsis.

Angel lurches erect, manages to grip Scorpion's arm and pinion it, then with the other bend Scorpion's head over backward, so that Scorpion tumbles and falls. With a great straining effort, Angel lifts Scorpion high and dashes it to the ground.

Angel stamps on Scorpion's head and the metal features contort and crumple in a grotesque mask.

Instead of tearing Scorpion to bits, Angel leaves the ring and marches from the arena.

In a glass-enclosed balcony suite, Saul Cermolo and other top Syndicate brass have been watching the fight. As they dolefully take account of their losses, the outer door bursts open.

Angel stands dramatically framed in the opening.

Angel lurches into the room. It pushes over a big table to block the opening and systematically seizes, crushes and destroys the entire company, despite their weapons: all the top brass of the Syndicate! Then Angel punches a hole through the wall into the next suite. Joe staggers out of Angel, looks around the room, then slips through the hole into the next chamber, just as the door bursts open and the police surge into the room.

::::

The peculiar behaviour of 'Black Angel' is blamed upon defective circuits. Immediately there is a call for legislation to ban this potentially dangerous spectacle, or at the very least remove all destructive impulses from the circuitry so that robots could be made of harmless foam, and conduct athletic dances instead of fighting.

::::

With profits from fight, Joe and Ellen go off on some new venture.

The Magnificent Red-hot Jazzing Seven

Concept and synopsis for screen-play

TIME: 1927.

PLACE: The Midwest, including sections of Des Moines, Chicago and Cooneysburg, a town in southern Indiana.

This is intended as a new member in the sequence which began with THE SEVEN SAMURAI and continued with THE MAGNIFICENT SEVEN. In this version, the protagonists are not Japanese warriors or cowboys, but jazz musicians.

※

JOE BUSH, AN OVER-THE-HILL cornet-player, now works as night-clerk in a cheap hotel in Des Moines. He can no longer play his horn because an ex-fiancée hit him over the head with a bottle of Old Smiley, wasting the gin and knocking out Joe's front teeth, thus destroying his embouchure.

Into the hotel comes a pair of old friends: Rusty Hinch and Floyd Bean, with Ginger, Bean's brat of a daughter, about ten years old. Hinch and Bean operate the Blue Goose, a roadhouse near Cooneysburg, in the southern part of Indiana, on the Cooney River.

Hinch and Bean desperately need Joe's help. The Riverview Hotel at Cooneysburg has lately been taken over by big money and renovated. Only the best bootleg is served and most discreetly. A fancy orchestra, Roger Wickersham and his Society Aces, complete with harp, violin and vocal trio, play for all the local functions, to the detriment of the

Blue Goose, which no longer can compete, and so must take draconian measures to survive.

Therefore Hinch and Floyd Bean implore Joe to assemble his old band and come down to Cooneysburg and help them fight back, before the Blue Goose goes under.

Joe says: "Why not hire a local group?"

"The problem is finance. They all want money up front. With you it's different."

"Not that much different."

"Right now we're short! As soon as the Blue Goose gets on its feet, we all make out! You can count on it!"

Joe shows the gap in his teeth. "I can't even blow up a balloon, let alone play my horn. Also the band is scattered far and wide."

"But they are alive?"

"Oh sure, they're alive. Some just barely, and Cal Abbott is in jail."

"When does he get out?"

"What difference does it make? There is no such thing as a toothless cornet-player."

"Get some teeth at the store."

"That costs money."

"How much?"

"A couple hundred bucks."

Ginger has been looking at a newspaper. "Here it says: 'Teeth fixed cheap! We'll pull every tooth in your head for fifty dollars!'"

"I don't want any more teeth pulled. I want them back in."

Hinch and Floyd Bean confer aside. Reluctantly they bring out a hundred and twenty dollars. "This is all we can raise. Get your teeth and bring the band down to Cooneysburg."

Ginger protests. "You should make him sign a paper!"

"Paper? What kind of paper?"

"If he can't remember how to play, then he's got to give the teeth back."

"Shut up, kid," says Joe. "Go sit on that fire hydrant out there."

"Joe, you have got to help us! You are our last resort!"

Joe dubiously takes the money. "I'll give it some thought."

A rainy afternoon on the South Side of Chicago. The Salvation Army Band is marching along the street, playing 'Onward Christian Soldiers'. Joe Bush shuffles along behind, among the other bums, his coat collar turned up. He takes a few steps forward, mutters to Mike Swanson, the tuba player, and the tuba gives a jerk of surprise. At a corner the Band swings smartly to the right. Joe and Mike Swanson continue ahead and break into a trot, and so disappear into the darkness.

Charley Lamar is discovered playing piano in a honky-tonk bootleg joint.

As Joe and Mike Swanson arrive, a big Packard Phaeton drives up. The driver gets out: a flashy type in a black Fedora with a pearl stickpin in his dove-gray tie. He flicks the ash off his cigar and enters the joint.

Joe and Mike follow, and renew acquaintance with Charley Lamar, who agrees to join the group. Joe asks: "Who is that dude with the pearl stickpin?"

"That's Sure-shot Baxter; he's a gambler and he'll bet on anything, if the odds are right."

"Really." Joe casually starts a conversation with Sure-shot. "Nice car you got."

"Yep. First-class. I dress first-class, I eat first-class and I drive first-class."

"I'll tell you something you won't believe. Do you see Charley Lamar over yonder?"

"Sure I see him."

"If you tried to give that car of yours to Charley, he'd turn you down cold."

"You're dam right I don't believe it."

"You got a difference of opinion. I'll give you odds of ten to one." Joe puts down a hundred dollars. "I got my money where my mouth is. I say that I'm right and you're wrong."

"A hundred bucks, eh? At ten to one?"

"That's my picture of the odds. Maybe you don't care to risk ten bucks?"

"Oh I don't mind a risk or two if the odds are right. Here's my ten. You got a bet."

"Good enough: an easy ten-spot. Hey, Charley, come over here a minute."

Charley comes over to the table. "What's the problem?"

"I've got a bet with this gentleman. I claim that you wouldn't take his car if he gave it to you."

Charley frowns. "You might be right. I'm afraid of them things. If God wanted us to ride in cars, he'd have given us wheels instead of toe-nails."

"There's your answer," says Sure-shot and reaches for the money. "I don't lose the easy ones."

"Wait a minute!" Joe cries. "He didn't definitely say 'yes'. Let's do this right. Where are the keys?"

"Right here."

"See if Charley will take them."

Sure-shot tosses the keys to Charley, who looks at them disdainfully. "What good are these things to me?"

Sure-shot laughs indulgently. "I think you just lost your bet."

"That still wasn't a 'yes' or a 'no'," says Joe. "Give me a fighting chance! Where is the owner's certificate?"

"Right here."

"Sign it off."

"That's a lot of trouble just to win a measly hundred bucks," grumbles Sure-shot. He signs off the certificate. "There it is. Now: are you going to take the car or not?"

Charley says: "On this occasion I think I will."

Joe cries out in outrage: "You just lost me a cool hundred bucks!"

Sure-shot collects the bet and can't help gloating: "I'll give you a hint that is worth a lot more than a hundred bucks. Never tussle with the pros! They call me Sure-shot! Do you know why? Because I never lose! That was an easy hundred bucks, because I knew the odds."

"Live and learn," says Joe. "Well, no hard feelings on my part. You taught me a good lesson. Let me buy you a drink. Waiter! Set 'em up!"

"Next round is on me," says Sure-shot. "Waiter, go find what Charley is drinking and fix him up. He just made me a hundred bucks."

After a few minutes the waiter returns. "Charley is no longer with us. He took off a few minutes ago, driving a big car."

"That's funny," says Sure-shot. "I thought he couldn't drive!" He looks around for Joe and Mike, but they have also departed.

Somebody asks Sure-shot: "You won a hundred bucks but you gave away your car. How do you figure it?"

Sure-shot rubs his chin. "It's the principle of the thing that counts."

※

The big Packard drives through the suburbs of Davenport, Iowa, and pulls in front of a neat white bungalow. On the porch, confined to a wheel-chair, sits Bill Bangs, former trombonist with the Red-hot Jazzing Seven. He is basking in the sun, but nevertheless well bundled up against a draught. His wife stands nearby, a stout red-faced woman with a fussy, somewhat domineering manner. She disapproves of Bill's old associates and is convinced that it was the musical life which brought Bill to his present condition, halfway between life and death. When she states as much to Joe, Mike and Charley, Bill nods in weary confirmation. "Yes dear…Quite right, dear."

Joe manages to mutter a few words into Bill's ear, then takes Mrs. Bangs somewhat aside to comment upon the lovely wisteria bush. In the background Mike Swanson listens to Bill, then slips away.

Mrs. Bangs is firm. "It's time you gentlemen were leaving. The slightest excitement is bad for Bill."

"What a pity!" exclaims Joe. "He was once a fine musician! Do you play yourself, Mrs. Bangs?"

In the background Mike Swanson sneaks through the foliage carrying a trombone case.

"I sing at church and that is the extent of it. Now you must go since it is time for Bill's tonic."

"Of course! We wish nothing but good health for Bill!"

"It's pretty late in the day for that, when you musicians, with your drinking and all, put him in the shape he's in!"

"Good-bye, Mrs. Bangs."

"Good-bye." The camera follows as Mrs. Bangs turns away and pours a dose of a dark rancid-looking liquid into a glass and carefully adds a spill of powder. She turns to give the potion to Bill, but the wheelchair is empty.

Camera swings to the street where Bill, wearing pajamas and bath-robe, is loping toward the Packard, which is already in motion, owing to the general fear of Mrs. Bangs. Bill doesn't bother to open the door but vaults into the back seat, and the Packard roars off down the street. Camera follows Packard as Mrs. Bangs advances into the foreground and halts, arms akimbo, looking after her fleeing husband.

⁂

The Packard stops in front of the jail. Joe says: "He should be getting out just about now."

The group goes into the waiting room, and Joe asks the clerk when Slim Everts is to be discharged.

The clerk raises his head and listens. "Maybe never, unless he cools his act."

Joe looks into the next room to find Slim Everts trying to recover his clarinet from the property clerk, who denies its existence.

Joe quiets Slim and calls in the Warden. "My friend wants his clarinet. He is now a free man and can play anywhere he likes."

"Technically, that is correct."

"Well then: where is the clarinet?"

The warden apologetically takes them to his cottage, where his fat eight year old son is alternately practicing on Slim Everts' fine Selmer clarinet and trying to get the dog to blow a tone.

⁂

Joe, Mike, and Charley file into a room in a hospital, where three doc-tors are gravely inspecting a man reclining rigid in a hi-tech chair, where he is wired up to all manner of electrical devices, etc.

Davy Dixon the banjo player has been in a train wreck and while he has suffered no organic damage he remains in a state of catatonic coma. He sits rigid with eyes closed and the doctors are baffled by his case.

Joe asks the nurse: "Where is his banjo?"

"In the closet, with his other effects."

Joe gets the banjo. "I don't like to do this to an old friend, but I suppose in a case like this compassion must be put aside."

Joe sets the banjo excruciatingly out of tune. He then puts it into

Davy's grasp, and arranges Davy's hands as if he were playing. Then he draws the limp fingers across the strings, eliciting a horrid discord.

On the third stroke Davy's eyebrows twitch. On the next, he gives a faint grimace. On the next, the eyes pop open. Davy looks down at the banjo. "This son of a bitch has been tuned by a cow."

Joe turns to the awed doctors. "I believe that you will now find him cured."

❊

The musicians attend a circus. (Or a carnival or a tent-show.) One of the acts is 'Professor Solinsky and his Trained Kodiak Bears'.

The Professor and his shambling beasts perform. One rolls a hoop; two play catch with a medicine ball; another bangs on a toy drum, while Professor Solinsky jumps around barking orders and snapping a whip.

Joe speaks a few words to the bear beating the drum. It hesitates only an instant, then tears off the bearskin and runs away from the carnival with the musicians, while the crowd shouts and jeers and presently cries of 'Hey rube!' are to be heard.

❊

The Red-hot Jazzing Seven, once more at full strength, rolls south through rural Indiana and presently arrives at the Cooney River. Five minutes later they are in Cooneysburg.

The time is evening. At the Riverview Inn Roger Wickersham and his Society Aces are playing for dancing at an outdoor pavilion under Japanese lanterns. The tune is 'My Little Gypsy Sweetheart' and Roger Wickersham sings an earnest baritone vocal refrain.

The group drives on. A mile out of town they arrive at the Blue Goose. They park the Packard, then stand and listen a moment. From inside is coming the sound of a strange raucous music. The group look at each other in wonder and go into the Blue Goose.

The music comes from the Catfish Spasm Band, which is now playing a raffish version of 'Shake That Thing'. The instrumentation consists of guitar, washboard, tub bass, and harmonica, with doubling on kazoo, comb, jug, and tin whistle.

— 109 —

Four or five customers sit hunched here and there over bottles of near beer and water-glasses of bootleg booze.

Rusty Hinch and Floyd Bean are overjoyed to see Joe and the band. Ginger is more cautious. "Make him show you his teeth before you get too friendly."

As they talk, the Catfish Spasm Band plays in the background.

Joe brings up the subject of money. As before, Rusty says: "Right now things are a bit lean, but when the crowds start coming back, then we'll all make money."

Ginger says: "Daddy, you make sure that I'm to be the featured attraction."

"Get lost, kid," says Joe. "We got serious business to talk about."

The band meanwhile has been unlimbering their instruments. One by one they go to sit in with the Catfish Spasm Band. First, Charley sits down at the piano. The tune is 'Royal Garden Blues'. Then Mike Swanson sits down with his tuba, and immediately knocks out a terrific tuba solo. Then one at a time, each adding a dimension to the music: banjo, clarinet, trombone, drums which by some cinematic miracle are on the bandstand, and finally Joe Bush takes over the cornet lead.

Out in road people driving past hear the music. They pull over, park and come into Blue Goose, where a sudden new life has come into being.

⁂

Episodes, encounters, raids and retaliations follow hard on each other. The Riverview begins to lose business as people flock to hear the great new band at the Blue Goose.

The management at the Riverview Inn strikes back with a waltz contest.

The Blue Goose retaliates with a Charleston contest, and here should be some great visual effects.

The Riverview Inn scores big when the Rotary Club stages its annual charity extravaganza at the Riverview Inn. The Blue Goose has only a single recourse: to sponsor an entry, which will be a contingent from the Catfish Spasm Band disguised in black derbies and long black beards: The House of David Stompers, playing *fralich* music on kazoo, washboard and jug.

At the last minute, the management of the Riverview Inn gets the entry disqualified, on grounds of moral decrepitude or something similar, to the anguish of Rusty Hinch and Floyd Bean.

The Volunteer Fire Brigade sponsors a portly gentleman singing 'On the Road to Mandalay'.

The Riverview Inn sponsors a lady in a beaded dress playing 'My Rosary' on the zither while her sister sings contralto.

The Cooneysburg Gazette sponsors a comic team which does a version of 'Mr. Gallagher and Mr. Shean'.

The Farmer's Grange sponsors a trio who play 'The World is Waiting for the Sunrise' on banjo, clarinet and duck-call.

At the last minute the Blue Goose manages to introduce a surprise entry: Floyd Bean's obnoxious daughter Ginger, who sings 'That's My Weakness Now (boop-boop-a-doop)', and wins the contest.

Thereafter, whenever the Red-hot Jazzing Seven start to play, Ginger leaps up on the bandstand to sing, mug and cavort. The band will have nothing of this: "We don't need no canaries!" "This is a jazz-band, not a zoo." "Get away from here, you ugly little pest!"

One night Floyd, worried because Ginger is missing, finally finds her locked in her room, tied to a chair, gagged, with bread and water on the table beside her, and a big padlock on the door.

❋

Episodes and counter-episodes:

At the Riverview Inn the management is becoming nervous. At the Blue Goose, business is booming.

Joe asks Rusty to start paying a salary to the band, but Rusty has a dozen reasons why the band will still have to wait.

❋

The Riverview Inn tips off the feds as to bootleg booze at the Blue Goose.

On the day of the raid, the Blue Goose is comfortably placid. Ginger spots the big black sedans of the Feds: "Raid!"

The Feds alight from their cars, advance upon the Blue Goose. They thrust open the doors. The bar is now a soda fountain; the customers are all engaged with marshmallow delights, banana splits and chocolate sundaes. On the band-stand Charley plays the piano while Slim sings 'Danny Boy'.

Non-plussed, the feds depart. As soon as they are gone, the soda fountain swings around on a turn-table; the bar returns to the room. Ginger goes around with a basket, collecting plaster-of-paris sundaes and banana splits.

"A near thing!" says Rusty Hinch. "Those thugs at the hotel have pushed me too far!"

Rusty and Floyd Bean plan revenge.

The Ladies Aid Society has planned a *soirée dansante* for Saturday evening, at which they will serve punch and chicken salad sandwiches.

A window in the hotel kitchen is open. Directly below is the big earthenware crock, holding about twenty gallons, in which the ladies are busy mixing punch, laughing and chatting as they work.

When the ladies are not looking—maybe Ginger distracts them in some way, like coming in with two big mastiffs, Rusty Hinch's face appears at the window. He looks around and pours a bucketful of clear liquid into the crock.

Ginger and the mastiffs are expelled; the ladies return to the punch, and find it very nice, in fact, quite nice indeed.

At the soirée all is going splendidly. Roger Wickersham and the Society Aces play 'Softly, as on a Morning Sunrise' while the quality of Cooneysburg, dressed in their best, dances, sips punch and discusses art.

Scene shifts to the kitchen. The ladies come in and sing out: "More punch needed! It's ever so good, and we're running low!"

Again Rusty pours a bucket of white lightning into the crock.

The camera returns to the dance-hall. The Society Aces are now playing 'Yes Sir That's My Baby' with a kind of lumbering Gothic pep, and there is great activity on the dance-floor. Coats have been discarded; the men are dancing with heads low and elbows high; the ladies, as they are whirled through the evolutions of this jigging fox-trot, stylishly kick their legs up behind. Several couples start doing the cake-walk, and the hall becomes a scene of neo-Roman debauchery.

Whistles sound; the Feds are back. Dozens of the town's gentry, including the Reverend Woskerly, are hustled out into the wagon.

*

The management of the Riverview Inn is disgraced. They are forced to sell out to a pair of local entrepreneurs and depart for greener pastures in Cape Girardeau, Missouri.

The local entrepreneurs are Rusty Hinch and Floyd Bean. The Red-hot Jazzing Seven learn the news with mixed emotions. They have won the good fight; the forces of vulgarity have been dispersed! Now it is time to reap the benefits of victory!

The Seven approach Rusty Hinch, now wearing a nice suit, in his office at the Riverview Inn. Rusty is somewhat uncomfortable, but puts on a breezy attitude. "Boys, you did a great job! I'll never forget it, nor will Floyd either!"

"Right!" says Floyd.

Joe says: "Now that we'll be playing here at the hotel, I think it's time to talk contract."

Rusty Hinch clears his throat. "As a matter of fact, we've renewed with Roger Wickersham."

"What!"

Floyd says: "Sorry, Joe, but we simply had no choice. Roger wants Ginger to sing with the orchestra, and we've got her career to consider."

*

The Seven depart Cooneysburg in the old Packard. The time is evening. At the outdoor pavilion Roger Wickersham is playing for a college prom. Ginger's squeaky voice can be heard singing: "— whatcha gonna do, whatcha gonna do, on a dew-dew-dewy day."

The band rolls up its eyes and drives on. They stop by the Blue Goose to pick up the drums. The Catfish Spasm Band is again on the stand, whaling away at some mournful sad-sweet blues.

The Seven return to the Packard and pile in. From the Blue Goose the music sounds dim and sad. The Seven drive away down the road and the tail-light recedes into the distance and is gone.

*

NOTES:

This piece is supposed to be a mellow perspective over the idyllic aspects of the Twenties, as they never were but as we would like to think of them.

There are no real villains here, nor any real evil-doing: only great music, wonderful visual effects and humor, which is here better understated than otherwise. Also, nostalgia by the ton. There is little if any sex and less violence. Love-interest? I don't see an obvious place for it. Something might be contrived, if necessary, so long as it does not, and here not means NOT, involve some purported female singer with the Red-hot Seven. This is taboo. Good jazz bands don't use canaries; just bad ones.

The incidents and episodes are, of course, not graven in stone, but define the flow and scope of the story, and perhaps may be refined or otherwise improved upon.

I have recently noticed on the radio a surprising amount of time being given to old tunes of the '20s and '30s: not just jazz, but popular music of the day played by such orchestras as Isham Jones, Ben Pollack, Coon-Sanders, Harry Reser, Rudy Vallee, and the like.

I won't go so far as to predict a big popular upsurge or a fad for the music of the '20s, but I seem to feel it in the air. This piece might well catch the breaking edge of the wave.

THE KRAGEN

Chapter I

AMONG THE PEOPLE of the Floats caste distinctions were fast losing their old-time importance. The Anarchists and Procurers had disappeared altogether; inter-caste marriages were by no means uncommon, especially when they involved castes of approximately the same social status. Society of course was not falling into chaos; the Bezzlers and the Incendiaries still maintained their traditional aloofness; the Advertisermen still could not evade a subtle but nonetheless general disesteem, and where the castes were associated with a craft or trade, they functioned with undiminished effectiveness. The Swindlers comprised the vast majority of those who fished from coracles; Blackguards constructed all the sponge-arbors in every lagoon; the Hoodwinks completely monopolized the field of hood-winking. This last relationship always excited the curiosity of the young, who would inquire, "Which first: the Hoodwinks or hood-winking?" To which the elders customarily replied, "When the Ship of Space discharged our ancestors upon these blessed floats, there were four Hoodwinks among the Eighty-Three. Later, when the towers were built and the lamps established, there were hoods to wink, and it seemed nothing less than apposite that the Hoodwinks should occupy themselves at the trade. It may well be that matters stood so in the Outer Wildness, before the Escape. It seems likely. There were undoubtedly lamps to be flashed and hoods to be winked. Of course there is much we do not know, much concerning which the Dicta are silent."

Whether or not the Hoodwinks had been drawn to the trade by virtue of ancient use, it was now the rare Hoodwink who did not in some measure find his vocation upon the towers, either as a rigger, a lamp-tender, or as full-fledged hoodwink.

Another caste, the Larceners, constructed the towers, which customarily stood sixty to ninety feet high at the center of the float, directly above the primary stalk of the sea-plant; there were usually four legs of woven withe, which passed through holes in the pad to join a stout stalk twenty or thirty feet below the surface. At the top of the tower was a cupola, with walls of split withe, a roof of gummed and laminated pad-skin. Yard-arms extending to either side supported lattices, each carrying nine lamps arranged in a square, three to the side, together with the hoods and trip-mechanisms. Within the cupola, windows afforded a view across the water to the neighboring floats — as much as two miles or as little as a quarter-mile distant. The Master Hoodwink sat at a panel. At his left hand were nine tap-rods, cross-coupled to lamp-hoods on the lattice to his right. Similarly the tap-rods at his right hand controlled the hoods to his left. By this means the configurations he formed and those he received, from his point of view, were of identical aspect and caused him no confusion. During the daytime, the lamps were not lit and white targets served the same function. The hoodwink set his configuration with quick strokes of right and left hands, kicked the release, which thereupon flicked the hoods or shutters at the respective lamps or targets. Each configuration signified a word; the mastery of a lexicon and a sometimes remarkable dexterity were the Master Hoodwink's stock in trade. All could send at speeds approximating that of speech; all knew at least four thousand, and some six, seven or even nine thousand configurations. The folk of the floats could in varying degrees read the configurations, which were also employed in the keeping of the archives, and other communications, memoranda and messages.*

On Tranque Float, at the extreme east of the group, the Master Hoodwink was one Chaezy Zander, a rigorous and exacting old man with a mastery of over eight thousand configurations. His first assistant, Sklar Hast, had well over five thousand configurations at his disposal. There were two further assistants, as well as three apprentices, two riggers, a lamp-tender and a maintenance withe-weaver, this latter a Larcener. Chaezy Zander tended the tower from dusk until middle evening: the busy hours during which gossip, announcements, news and notifications regarding King Kragen flickered up and down the fifty-mile line of the floats.

Sklar Hast winked hoods during the afternoon; then, when Chaezy Zander appeared in the cupola, he looked to maintenance and supervised the apprentices. A relatively young man, Sklar Hast had achieved his status by working in accordance with a simple and uncomplicated policy: without compromise and with great tenacity he strove for excellence, and sought to instill the same standards into the apprentices. He was an almost brutally direct man, without affability, knowing nothing of either malice, guile, tact or patience. The apprentices disliked but respected him; Chaezy Zander considered him over-pragmatic and deficient in reverence for his betters, notably himself. Sklar Hast cared nothing one way or the other. Chaezy Zander must soon retire; in due course Sklar Hast would become Master Hoodwink. He was in no hurry; on this placid, limpid, changeless world, time drifted rather than throbbed. In the meantime, life was easy and for the most part pleasant. Sklar Hast owned a small pad of which he was the sole occupant. The pad, a leaf of spongy tissue a hundred feet in diameter braced by tough woody radial ribs, floated in the lagoon, separated from the main float by twenty feet of water. Sklar Hast's hut was of standard construction: sea-plant withe bent and lashed, then sheathed with sheets of pad-skin, the tough near-transparent membrane peeled from the bottom of the sea-plant pad. All was then coated with well-aged varnish, prepared by boiling sea-plant sap until the water was driven off and the resins amalgamated.

---

* The orthography had been adopted in the earliest days and was highly systematic. The cluster at the left indicated the genus of the idea, the cluster at the right denoted the specific. In such a fashion ⠿ at the left, signified *color*, and hence:

White	⠿	•
Black	⠿	•,
Red	⠿	••
Pink	⠿	•.•
Dark Red	⠿	• .•

and so forth.

On the pad grew other vegetation: shrubs rooted in the spongy tissue, a thicket of bamboo-like rods yielding a good-quality withe, epiphytes hanging from the central spike of the sea-plant — this rising twenty or thirty feet to terminate in a coarse white spore-producing organ. Most of the plants of the pad yielded produce of benefit to man: fruit, fiber, dye, drug or decorative foliage. On other pads the plants might be ordered according to aesthetic theory; Sklar Hast had small taste in these matters, and the center of his pad was little more than an untidy copse of various stalks, fronds, tendrils and leaves, in various shades of black, green and rusty orange.

Sklar Hast reckoned himself a lucky man. As a Hoodwink by caste and Assistant Master Hoodwink by trade he enjoyed a not inconsiderable prestige. Standing before his hut, Sklar Hast watched the gold and lavender dusk and its dark pastel reflection in the ocean. The afternoon rain had freshened and cooled the air; now the evening breeze arose to rustle the foliage and brush susurrations across the water...Chaezy Zander was growing old. Sklar Hast wondered how long the old man would persist in fulfilling the rigorous exactitude of his duties. True, he showed no lapse whatever in precision or flexibility of usage, but almost insensibly his speed was falling off. Sklar Hast could out-wink him without difficulty should he choose to do so; a capability which Sklar Hast, for all his bluntness, had so far not demonstrated. Useless folly to irritate the old man! Sklar Hast suspected that even now he delayed his retirement mainly out of jealousy and antipathy toward Sklar Hast.

There was no hurry. Life seemed to extend ahead of him as wide and lucid as the dreaming expanse of water and sky which filled his vision. On this water-world, which had no name, there were no seasons, no tides, no storms, no change, very little anxiety regarding time. Sklar Hast was currently testing five or six girls of orthodox Hoodwink background for marital suitability. In due course, he would make a choice, and enlarge his hut. And forever abandon privacy, Sklar Hast reflected wistfully. There was definitely no need for haste. He would continue to test such girls as were eligible, and perhaps a few others as well. Meanwhile, life was good. In the lagoon hung arbors on which grew the succulent sponge-like organisms which when cleaned, plucked and boiled, formed the staple food of the Float-folk. The lagoon teemed likewise with other edible fish, separated from the predators of the ocean by the enormous net which hung in a great hemisphere from various buoys, pads and the main float — this a complex of ancient pads, compressed, wadded and interlocked to create an unbroken surface five acres in area and varying from two feet to six feet in thickness. There was much other food available: spores from the sea-plant fruiting organ, from which a crusty bread could be baked. There were in addition other flowers, tendrils and bulbs, as well as the prized flesh of the gray-fish to take which the Swindlers must fare forth in their coracles and cunningly swindle from the ocean, which horizon to horizon, pole to pole, enveloped the entire surface of the world.

Sklar Hast turned his eyes up to the skies, where the constellations already blazed with magnificent ardor. To the south, half-up the sky, hung a cluster of twenty-five middle-bright stars, from which, so tradition asserted, his ancestors had fled in the Ship of Space, finally to reach the world of water. Eighty-three persons, of various castes, managed to disembark before the ship foundered and sank; the eighty-three had become twenty thousand, scattered east and west along fifty miles of floating sea-plant. The castes, so jealously differentiated during the first few generations, with the Bezzlers at the top and the Advertisermen at the bottom, had now accommodated themselves to one another and were even intermingling. There was little to disturb the easy flow of life; nothing harsh nor unpleasant — except, perhaps, King Kragen.

Sklar Hast made a sour face and examined those three of his arbors which only two days before had been plucked clean by King Kragen, whose appetite as well as his bulk grew by the year. Sklar Hast scowled westward across the ocean, in the direction from which King Kragen customarily appeared, moving with long strokes of his four propulsive vanes, in a manner to suggest some vast, distorted, grotesquely ugly anthropoid form swimming by means of the breaststroke. There, of course, the resemblance to man ended. King Kragen's body was tough black cartilage, a cylinder on a rectangle, from the corners of which extended the vanes. The cylinder comprising King Kragen's main bulk opened forward in a maw fringed with four mandibles and eight palps, and aft in an anus. Atop this cylinder, somewhat to the front, rose a turret from which the four eyes protruded: two peering forward, two aft. During Sklar Hast's lifetime King Kragen had grown perceptibly, and now measured perhaps sixty feet in length. King Kragen was a terrible force for destruction, but luckily could be placated. King Kragen enjoyed copious quantities of sponges and when his appetite was appeased he injured no one and did no damage; indeed he kept the area clear of other marauding kragen, which either he killed or sent flapping and skipping in a panic across the ocean.

Sklar Hast's attention was attracted by a dark swirl in the water at the edge of the net: a black bulk surrounded by glistening cusps and festoons of starlit water. Sklar Hast ran forward to the edge of the pad, peered. No question about it! A lesser kragen was attempting to break the net that it might plunder the lagoon!

Sklar Hast shouted a curse, shook his fist, turned, ran at full speed across the pad. He jumped into his coracle, crossed the twenty feet of water to the central float. He delayed only long enough to tie the coracle to a stake formed of a human femur, then ran at top speed to the hoodwink tower.

A mile to the west the tower on Thrasneck Float flickered its lamps, the configurations coming with the characteristic style of Durdan Farr, the Thrasneck Master Hoodwink: *"...thirteen...bushels...of...salt... lost...when...a...barge...took...water...between...Sumber...and... Adelvine..."*

Sklar Hast climbed the ladder, burst into the cupola. He pointed to the lagoon. "A rogue, breaking the nets. I just saw him. Call King Kragen!"

Chaezy Zander instantly flashed the cut-in signal. His fingers jammed down rods, he kicked the release. *"Call...King...Kragen!"* he signaled. *"Rogue...in...Tranque...Lagoon!"*

On Thrasneck Float Durdan Farr relayed the message to the tower on Bickle Float, and so along the line of floats to Sciona at the far west, who thereupon returned the signal: *"King...Kragen...is...nowhere... at...hand."*

Back down the line of towers flickered the message, returning to Tranque Float in something short of sixty seconds. Sklar Hast read the message as it left the Bickle Tower, before reaching Thrasneck, and rushed over to the side of the cupola, to peer down into the lagoon.

Others had now discovered the rogue kragen and set up a shout to the tower, "Call King Kragen!" Sklar Hast shouted in return, "He can't be found!" Chaezy Zander, tight-lipped, was already dispatching another message: *"To ... the ... various ... intercessors ... along ... the ... line. Kindly ... summon ... King ... Kragen ... and ... direct ... him ... to ... Tranque ... Float."*

Sklar Hast pointed and bellowed, "Look! The beast has broken the net! Where is Voidenvo?"

He swung down the ladder, ran to the edge of the lagoon. The kragen, a beast perhaps fifteen feet in length, was surging easily through the water, a caricature of a man performing the breast-stroke. Starlight danced and darted along the disturbed water, and so outlined the gliding black bulk. Sklar Hast cried out in fury: the brute was headed for his arbors, so recently devastated by the appetite of King Kragen! It could not be borne! He ran to his coracle, returned to his pad. Already the kragen had extended its palps and was feeling for sponges. Sklar Hast sought for an implement which might serve as a weapon; there was nothing to hand: a few articles fashioned from human bones and fish cartilage. Leaning against the hut was a boat-hook, a stalk ten feet long, carefully straightened, scraped, and seasoned, to which a hook-shaped human rib had been lashed. He took it up and now from the central pad came a cry of remonstrance. "Sklar Hast! What do you do?" This was the voice of Semon Voidenvo the Intercessor. Sklar Hast paid him no heed. He ran to the edge of the pad, jabbed the boat-hook at the kragen's turret. It scraped uselessly along resilient cartilage. The kragen swung up one of its vanes, knocked the pole aside. Sklar Hast jabbed the pole with all his strength at what he considered the kragen's most vulnerable area: a soft pad of receptor-endings directly above the maw. Behind him he heard Semon Voidenvo's outraged protest: "This is not to be done! This is not to be done! Desist!"

The kragen quivered at the blow, twisted its massive turret to gaze at Sklar Hast. Again it swung up its fore-vane, smashing the pole, slashing at Sklar Hast, who leapt back with inches to spare. From the central pad Semon Voidenvo bawled, "By no means molest the kragen; it is a matter for the King! We must respect the King's perquisites!"

Sklar Hast stood back in fury as the kragen resumed its feeding. As if to punish Sklar Hast for his assault, it passed close beside the arbors, worked its vanes, and the arbors, sea-plant stalk lashed with fiber, collapsed. Sklar Hast groaned. "No more than you deserve," called out Semon Voidenvo with odious complacence. "You interfered with the duties of King Kragen, now your arbors are destroyed. This is justice."

" 'Justice'? Bah!" bellowed Sklar Hast. "Where is King Kragen? You, Voidenvo the Intercessor! Why don't you summon the great gluttonous beast?"

"Come, come," admonished Semon Voidenvo. "This is not the tone in which to speak of King Kragen."

Sklar Hast thrust himself and his coracle back to the central float, where now stood several hundred folk of Tranque Float. He pointed. "Look. See that vile beast of the sea. He is plundering us of our goods. I say, kill him. I say that we need not suffer such molestation."

Semon Voidenvo emitted a high-pitched croak. "Are you insane? Someone, pour water on this maniac hoodwink, who has too long focused his eyes on flashing lights."

In the lagoon the kragen moved to the arbors of the Belrod family, deep-divers for stalk and withe, of the Advertiserman caste and prone to a rude and surly vulgarity. The Belrod elder, Poe, a squat large-featured man, still resilient and vehement despite his years, emitted a series of hoots, intended to distract the kragen, which instead tore voraciously at the choicest Belrod sponges.

"I say, kill the beast!" cried Sklar Hast. "The King despoils us, must we likewise feed all the kragen of the ocean?"

"Kill the beast!" echoed the younger Belrods.

Semon Voidenvo gesticulated in vast excitement, but Poe Belrod shoved him roughly aside. "Quiet, let us listen to the hoodwink. How would we kill the kragen?"

"Come! I will show you how!"

Thirty or forty men followed him, mostly Swindlers, Advertisermen, Blackguards and Extorters. The remainder hung dubiously back. Sklar Hast led the way to a pile of poles intended for the construction of a storehouse. Each pole, fabricated from withes laid lengthwise and bound in glue, was twenty feet long by eight inches in diameter, and combined great strength with lightness.

Sklar Hast found rope, worked with vicious energy. "Now — lift! Across to my pad!"

Excited by his urgency, the men shouldered the pole, carried it to the lagoon, floated it across to Sklar Hast's pad. Then, crossing in coracles, they dragged the pole up on the pad and carried it across to the edge of the lagoon. At Sklar Hast's direction, they set it down with one end resting on the hard fiber of a rib. "Now," said Sklar Hast. "Now we kill the kragen." He made a noose in the end of a light hawser, advanced toward the kragen, which watched him through the rear-pointing eyes of its turret. Sklar Hast moved slowly, so as not to alarm the creature, which continued to pluck sponges with a contemptuous disregard.

Sklar Hast, crouching, approached the edge of the pad. "Beast!" he called. "Ocean brute! Come closer. Come." He bent, splashed water at the kragen. Provoked, it surged toward him. Sklar Hast waited, and just before it swung its vane, he tossed the noose over its turret. He signaled his men. "Now!" They heaved on the line, dragged the thrashing kragen through the water. Sklar Hast guided the line to the end of the pole. The kragen surged suddenly forward; in the confusion and the dark the men heaving on the rope fell backward. Sklar Hast seized the slack, and dodging a murderous slash of the kragen's fore-vane he flung a hitch around the end of the pole. He danced back. "Now!" he called. "Pull, pull! Both lines! The beast is as good as dead!"

On each of a pair of lines tied to the head of the pole fifteen men heaved. The pole raised up on its base; the line tautened around the kragen's turret, the men dug in their heels, the base of the pole bit into the hard rib. The pole raised, braced by the angle of the ropes. With majestic deliberation the thrashing kragen was lifted from the water and swung up into the air. From those watching on the central pad came a murmurous moan of fascination and dread.

The kragen made gulping noises, reached its vanes this way and that, to no avail. Sklar Hast surveyed the creature, somewhat at a loss as how to proceed. The project thus far had gone with facility: what next? The men were looking at the kragen in awe, uncomfortable at their own daring, and already were stealing furtive glances out over the ocean. Perfectly calm, it glistened with the reflections of the blazing constellations. Sklar Hast thought to divert their attention. "The nets!" he called out to those on the float. "Where are the Extorters? Repair the nets before we lose all our fish! Are you helpless?"

Certain net-makers, a trade dominated by the Extorter caste, detached themselves from the group, went out in coracles to repair the broken net.

Sklar Hast returned to a consideration of the dangling kragen. At his orders the ropes supporting the tilted pole were made fast to ribs on the surface of the pad; the men now gathered gingerly about the dangling kragen, and speculated as to the best means to kill the creature. Perhaps it was already dead? Someone posed the question; a lad of the Belrods prodded the kragen with a length of stalk and suffered a broken collar-bone from a quick blow of the fore-vane.

Sklar Hast stood somewhat apart, studying the creature. Its hide was tough; its cartilaginous tissue even tougher. He sent one man for a boat-hook, another for a sharp femur-stake, and from the two fashioned a spear.

The kragen hung limp, the vanes swaying, occasionally twitching. Sklar Hast moved forward cautiously, touched the point of the spear to the side of the turret, thrust with all his weight. The point entered the tough hide perhaps half an inch, then broke. The kragen jerked, snorted, a vane slashed out. Sklar Hast sensed the dark flicker of motion, dodged and felt the air move beside his face. The spear-shaft hurtled out over the pond; the vane struck the pole on which the kragen hung, bruising the fibers.

"What a quarrelsome beast!" declared Sklar Hast. "Bring more rope; we must prevent any further such demonstrations."

From the main float came a harsh command: "You are mad-men; why do you risk the displeasure of King Kragen? I decree that you desist from your rash acts!"

This was the voice of Ixon Myrex, the Tranque Arbiter, a Bezzler of great physical power and moral conviction, a man with recognized powers and large prestige. Sklar Hast could not ignore Ixon Myrex as he had Semon Voidenvo. He considered the dangling kragen, looked about at the dubious faces of his comrades. They were hesitating; Ixon Myrex was not a man to be trifled with. Sklar Hast walked truculently to the edge of the pad, peered across the intervening water to the shape of Ixon Myrex.

"The kragen is destroying our arbors, Arbiter Myrex. The King is slothful about his duties, hence —"

Ixon Myrex's voice shook with wrath. "That is no way to speak! You violate the spirit of our relationship with King Kragen!"

Sklar Hast said in a reasonable voice, "King Kragen is nowhere to be seen. The Intercessors who claim such large power run back and forth in futility. We must act for ourselves. Cross the water to my pad. Join us in killing this ravenous beast."

Ixon Myrex held up his hands, which trembled in indignation. "Return the kragen to the lagoon, that thereby —"

"That thereby it may destroy more arbors?" demanded Sklar Hast. "This is not the result I hope for." He took a deep breath and made his decision. "Where is the rope?"

Arbiter Myrex called out in his sternest tones, "You men on the pad! This is how I interpret the customs of Tranque Float: the kragen must be restored to the water, with all haste. No other course is consistent with custom."

Sklar Hast waited. There was an uneasy stirring among the men. He said nothing, but taking up the rope, formed a noose. He crawled forward, flipped up the noose to catch a dangling vane, then crawling back and rising to his feet he circled the creature, binding the dangling vanes. The kragen's motions became increasingly constricted and finally were reduced to spasmodic shudders. Sklar Hast approached the creature from the rear, careful to remain out of reach of mandibles and palps, and made the bonds secure. "Now — the vile beast can only squirm. Lower it to the pad and we will find a means to make its end." The guy ropes were shifted, the pole tilted and swung; the kragen fell to the surface of the pad, where it lay passive, palps and mandibles moving slightly in and out. It showed no agitation, nor discomfort; perhaps it felt none: the exact degree of the kragen's sensitivity and ratiocinative powers had never been determined.

In the east the sky was lightening where the cluster of flaring blue and white suns known as Phocan's Cauldron began to rise. The ocean glimmered with a leaden sheen, and the folk who stood on the central pad began to glance furtively along the obscure horizon, muttering and complaining. Some few called out encouragement to Sklar Hast, recommending the most violent measures against the kragen. Between these and certain others furious arguments raged. Chaezy Zander had descended from the tower, to join Semon Voidenvo and Ixon Myrex, obviously in disapproval of Sklar Hast's activity. Of the Caste Elders only Elmar Pronave, Jackleg and Master Witheweaver, defended Sklar Hast and his unconventional acts.

Sklar Hast ignored all. He sat watching the black hulk with vast distaste, furious with himself for having become involved in so perilous a project. What had been gained? The kragen had broken his arbors; he had revenged himself and prevented more destruction. On the other hand he had incurred the ill-will of the most influential folk of the Float, including Ixon Myrex and Chaezy Zander: no small matter. He likewise had involved those others who had trusted him and looked to him for leadership, and toward whom he now felt responsibility.

He rose to his feet. There was no help for it; the sooner the beast was disposed of, the more quickly life would return to normal. He approached the kragen, examined it gingerly. The mandibles quivered in their anxiety to sever his torso; Sklar Hast stayed warily to the side. How to kill the beast?

Elmar Pronave crossed over from the main float the better to examine the kragen. He was a tall man with a high-bridged broken nose and black hair worn in the two ear-plumes of the old Procurer Caste, now no longer in existence save for a few aggressively unique individuals scattered through the floats, who used the caste-marks to emphasize their emotional detachment.

Pronave circled the hulk, kicked at the rear vane, bent to peer into one of the staring eyes. "If we could cut it up, its parts might be of some use."

"The hide is too tough for our knives," growled Sklar Hast. "There's no neck to be strangled."

"There are other ways to kill."

Sklar Hast nodded. "We could sink the beast into the depths of the ocean — but what to use for weight? Bones? Far too valuable. We could load bags with ash, but there is not that much ash to hand. We could burn every hut on the float as well as the hoodwink tower, and still not secure sufficient. To burn the kragen would require a like mountain of fuel."

A young Larcener who had worked with great enthusiasm during the trapping of the kragen spoke forth: "Poison exists! Find me poison, I will fix a capsule to a stick and push it into the creature's maw!"

Elmar Pronave gave a sardonic bark of laughter. "Agreed; poisons exist, hundreds of them, derived from various sea-plants and animals — but which are sufficiently acrid to destroy this beast? And where is it to be had? I doubt if there is that much poison nearer than Sankeston Float."

Sklar Hast went again to survey the black hulk, and now Phocan's Cauldron, rising into the sky, revealed the kragen in fuller detail. Sklar Hast examined the four blind-seeming eyes in the turret, the intricate construction of the mandibles and tentacles at the maw. He touched the turret, peered at the dome-shaped cap of chitin which covered it. The turret itself seemed laminated, as if constructed of stacked rings of cartilage, the eyes protruding fore and aft in inflexible tubes of a rugose harsh substance. Others in the group began to crowd close; Sklar Hast jumped forward, thrust at a young Felon boat-builder, but too late. The kragen flung out a palp, seized the youth around the neck. Sklar Hast cursed, heaved, tore; the clenched palp was unyielding. Another curled out for his leg; Sklar Hast kicked, danced back, still heaving upon the Felon's writhing form. The kragen drew the Felon slowly forward, hoping, so Sklar Hast realized, to pull him within easier reach. He loosened his grip, but the kragen allowed its palp to sway back to encourage Sklar Hast, who once more tore at the constricting palp. Again the kragen craftily drew its captive and Sklar Hast forward; the second palp snapped out once more and this time coiled around Sklar Hast's leg. Sklar Hast dropped to the ground, twisted himself around and broke the hold, though losing skin. The kragen petulantly jerked the Felon to within reach of its mandible, neatly snipped off the young man's head, tossed body and head aside. A horrified gasp came from the watching crowd. Ixon Myrex bellowed, "Sklar Hast, a man's life is gone, due to your savage obstinacy! You have much to answer for! Woe to you!"

Sklar Hast ignored the imprecation. He ran to his hut, found chisels and a mallet with a head of dense sea-plant stem, brought up from a depth of two hundred feet.* The chisels had blades of pelvic bone ground sharp against a board gritted with the silica husks of foraminifera. Sklar Hast returned to the kragen, put the chisel against the pale lamellum between the chitin dome and the foliations of the turret. He tapped; the chisel penetrated; this, the substance of a new layer being added to the turret, was relatively soft, the consistency of cooked gristle. Sklar Hast struck again; the chisel cut deep. The kragen squirmed.

Sklar Hast worked the chisel back out, made a new incision beside the first, then another and another, working around the periphery of the chitin dome, which was approximately two feet in diameter. The kragen squirmed and shuddered, whether in pain or apprehension it alone knew. As Sklar Hast worked around to the front, the palps groped back for him, but he shielded himself behind the turret, and finally gouged out the lamellum completely around the circumference of the turret.

His followers watched in awe and silence; from the main float came somber mutters, and occasional whimpers of superstitious dread from the children.

The channel was cut; Sklar Hast handed chisel and mallet back to Elmar Pronave. He mounted the body of the kragen, bent his knees, hooked fingers under the edge of the chitin dome, heaved. The dome ripped up and off, almost unbalancing Sklar Hast. The dome rolled down to the pad, the turret stood like an open-topped cylinder; within were coils and loops of something like dirty gray string. There were knots here, nodes there, on each side a pair of kinks, to the front a great tangle of kinks and loops.

Sklar Hast looked down in interest. He was joined by Elmar Pronave. "The creature's brain, evidently," said Sklar Hast. "Here the ganglions terminate. Or perhaps they are merely the termini of muscles."

---

* The Advertiserman takes below a pulley which he attaches to a sea-plant stalk. By means of ropes, buckets of air are pulled down, allowing him to remain under water as long as he chooses. Using two such systems, alternately lowered, the diver can descend to a depth of two hundred feet, where the sea-plant stalks grow dense and rigid.

Elmar Pronave took the mallet and with the handle prodded at a node. The kragen gave a furious jerk. "Well, well," said Pronave. "Interesting indeed." He prodded further: here, there. Every time he touched the exposed ganglions the kragen jerked. Sklar Hast suddenly put out his hand to halt him. "Notice. On the right, those two long loops; likewise on the left. When you touched this one here, the fore-vane jerked." He took the mallet, prodded each of the loops in turn; and in turn each of the vanes jerked.

"Aha!" declared Elmar Pronave. "Should we persist, we could teach the kragen to jig."

"Best we should kill the beast," said Sklar Hast. "Day is approaching and who knows but what…" From the float sounded a sudden low wail, quickly cut off as by the constriction of breath. The group around the kragen stirred; someone vented a deep sound of dismay. Sklar Hast jumped up on the kragen, looked around. The population on the float were staring to sea; he looked likewise, to see King Kragen. He floated under the surface, only his turret above water. The eyes stared forward, each a foot across: lenses of tough crystal behind which flickered milky films and pale blue sheen. King Kragen had either drifted close down the trail of Phocan's Cauldron on the water, or approached sub-surface.

Fifty feet from the lagoon nets he let his bulk come to the surface: first the whole of his turret, then the black cylinder housing the maw and the digestive process, finally the great flat sub-body: this, five feet thick, thirty feet wide, sixty feet long. To the sides protruded the propulsive vanes, thick as the girth of three men. Viewed from dead ahead King Kragen appeared a deformed ogre swimming the breast-stroke. His forward eyes, in their horn tubes, were turned toward the float of Sklar Hast, and seemed fixed upon the hulk of the mutilated kragen. The men stared back, muscles stiff as sea-plant stalk. The kragen which they had captured, once so huge and formidable, now seemed a miniature, a doll, a toy. Through its after-eyes it saw King Kragen, and gave a fluting whistle, a sound completely lost and desolate.

Sklar Hast suddenly found his tongue. He spoke in a husky urgent tone. "Back. To the back of the pad. Swim to the float."

From the main float rose the voice of Semon Voidenvo the Intercessor. In quavering tones he called out across the water: "Behold,

King Kragen, the men of Tranque Float! Now we denounce the presumptuous bravado of these few heretics! Behold, this pleasant lagoon, with its succulent sponges, devoted to the well-being of the magnanimous King Kragen —" the reedy voice faltered as King Kragen twitched his great vanes and eased forward. The great eyes stared without discernible expression, but behind there seemed to be a leaping and shifting of pale pink and pale blue lights. The folk on the float drew back as King Kragen breasted close to the net. With a twitch of his vanes, he ripped the net; two more twitches shredded it. From the folk on the float came a moan of dread; King Kragen had not been mollified.

King Kragen eased into the lagoon, approached Sklar Hast's pad which now was deserted except for the helpless kragen. The bound beast thrashed feebly, sounded its fluting whistle. King Kragen reached forth a palp, seized it, lifted it into the air, where it dangled helplessly. King Kragen drew it contemptuously close to his great mandibles, chopped it quickly into slices of gray and black gristle. These he tossed away, out into the ocean. He paused to drift a moment, to consider. Then he surged on Sklar Hast's pad. One blow of his fore-vane demolished the hut, another cut a great gouge in the pad. The after-vanes thrashed among the arbors; water, debris, broken sponges boiled up from below. King Kragen thrust again, wallowed completely up on the pad, which slowly crumpled and sank beneath his weight.

King Kragen pulled himself back into the lagoon, cruised back and forth destroying arbors, shredding the net, smashing huts of all the pads of the lagoon. Then he turned his attention to the main float, breasting up to the edge. For a moment he eyed the population, which started to set up a terrified keening sound, then thrust himself forward, wallowed up on the float, and the keening became a series of hoarse cries and screams. The folk ran back and forth with jerky scurrying steps.

King Kragen bulked on the float like a toad on a lily-pad. He struck with his vanes; the float split. The hoodwink tower, the great structure so cunningly woven, so carefully contrived, tottered. King Kragen lunged again, the tower toppled, falling into the huts along the north edge of the float.

King Kragen floundered across the float. He destroyed the granary, and bushels of yellow meal laboriously scraped from sea-plant pistils streamed into the water. He crushed the racks where stalk, withe and fiber were stretched and flexed; he dealt likewise with the rope-walk. Then, as if suddenly in a hurry, he swung about, heaved himself to the southern edge of the float. A number of huts and thirty-two of the folk, mostly aged and very young, were crushed or thrust into the water and drowned.

King Kragen regained the open sea. He floated quietly a moment or two, palps twitching in the expression of some unknowable emotion. Then he moved his vanes and slid off across the calm ocean.

Tranque Float was a devastation, a tangle, a scene of wrath and grief. The lagoon had returned to the ocean, with the arbors reduced to rubbish and the shoals of food-fish scattered. Many huts had been crushed. The hoodwink tower lay toppled. Of a population of four hundred and eighty, forty-three were dead, with as many more injured. The survivors stood blank-eyed and limp, unable to comprehend the full extent of the disaster which had come upon them.

Presently they roused themselves, and gathered at the far western edge where the damage had been the least. Ixon Myrex sought through the faces, eventually spied Sklar Hast sitting on a fragment of the fallen hoodwink tower. He raised his hand slowly, pointed. "Sklar Hast! I denounce you. The evil you have done to Tranque Float cannot be uttered in words. Your arrogance, your callous indifference to our pleas, your cruel and audacious villainy — how can you hope to expiate them?"

Sklar Hast looked off across the sea.

"In my capacity as Arbiter of Tranque Float, I now declare you to be a criminal of the basest sort, together with all those who served you as accomplices, and most noteworthy Elmar Pronave! Elmar Pronave, show your shameful face! Where do you hide?"

But Elmar Pronave had been drowned and did not answer.

Chaezy Zander limped across the area to stand beside Ixon Myrex. "I likewise denounce Sklar Hast and declare him Assistant Master Hoodwink no longer. He has disgraced his caste and his calling: I hereby eject him from the fellowship of both!"

Semon Voidenvo the Intercessor rose to speak. "Denunciations are not enough. King Kragen, in wreaking his terrible but just vengeance, intended that the primes of the deed should die. I now declare the will of King Kragen to be death, by either strangulation or bludgeoning, of Sklar Hast and all his accomplices."

"Not so fast," said Sklar Hast at last. "It appears to me that a certain confusion is upon us. Two kragen, a large one and small one, have injured us. I, Sklar Hast, and my friends, are those who hoped to protect the float from depredation. We failed. We are not criminals; we are simply not as strong nor as wicked as King Kragen."

"You are aware," Semon Voidenvo persisted, "that King Kragen reserves to himself the duty of guarding us from the lesser kragen? You are aware that in assaulting the kragen, you in effect assaulted King Kragen?"

Sklar Hast considered. "We will need more powerful tools than ropes and chisels to kill King Kragen."

Semon Voidenvo turned away speechless. The people looked apathetically toward Sklar Hast. Few seemed to share the indignation of the elders.

Ixon Myrex sensed the general feeling of misery and fatigue. "This is no time for recrimination. There is work to be done, vast work; all our structures to be rebuilt, our tower rendered operative, our net rewoven. But Sklar Hast's crime must not go without appropriate punishment. I therefore propose a Grand Convocation to take place one week from today, on Apprise Float. The fate of Sklar Hast and his gang will be inexorably decided by a Council of Elders."

Chapter II

The ocean had never been plumbed. At two hundred feet, the maximum depth attempted by stalk-cutters and pod-gatherers, the sea-plant stems were still a tangle. One Waller Murven, a man half-daredevil, half-maniac, had descended to three hundred feet, and in the indigo gloom noted the stalks merging to disappear into the murk as a single great trunk. But attempts to sound the bottom, by means of a line weighted with a bag of bone chippings, were unsuccessful. How then had the sea-plants managed to anchor themselves? Some supposed that the plants were of great antiquity, and had developed during a time when the water was much lower. Others conjectured a sinking of the ocean bottom; still others were content to ascribe the feat to an innate tendency of the sea-plants.

Of all the floats Apprise was the largest and one of the first to be settled. The central agglomeration was perhaps seven acres in extent; the lagoon was bounded by thirty or forty smaller pads. Apprise Float was the traditional site of the convocations, which occurred at approximately yearly intervals and which were attended by the active and responsible adults of the system. Drama and excitement attended the holding of the convocations. The folk of the floats seldom ventured far from home, since it was widely believed that King Kragen disapproved of travel. He ignored the coracles of swindlers, and also the rafts of withe or stalk which occasionally passed back and forth between the floats; but on various occasions he had demolished boats or coracles which seemed to have no ostensible business or purpose. Coracles conveying folk to a convocation had never been molested, however, even though King Kragen always seemed aware that a convocation was in progress, and often watched proceedings from a distance of a half-mile or so. How King Kragen gained his knowledge was a matter of great mystery: some asserted that on every float lived a man who was a man in semblance only: who inwardly was a manifestation of King Kragen. It was through this man, according to the superstition, that King Kragen knew what transpired on the floats.

For three days preceding the convocation there was incessant flickering along the line of the hoodwink towers; the destruction of Tranque Float was reported in full detail, together with Ixon Myrex's denunciation of Sklar Hast and Sklar Hast's rebuttal. On each of the floats there was intense discussion and a certain degree of debate. But since, in most cases, the Arbiter and the Intercessor of each float inveighed against Sklar Hast, there was little organized sentiment in his favor.

On the morning of the convocation, early, before the morning sky showed blue, coracles full of folk moved between the floats. The survivors of the Tranque Float disaster, who for the most part had sought refuge on Thrasneck and Bickle, were among the first underway, as were the folk from Almack and Sciona, to the far west.

All morning the coracles shuttled back and forth between the floats; shortly before noon the first groups began to arrive on Apprise. Each group wore the distinctive emblems of its float; and those who felt caste distinction important likewise wore the traditional hair-stylings, forehead plaques and dorsal ribbons; otherwise all dressed in much the same fashion: shirts and pantlets of coarse linen woven from sea-plant fiber; sandals of rug-fish leather, ceremonial gauntlets and epaulettes of sequins cut from the kernels of a certain half-animal, half-vegetable mollusc.

As the folk arrived they trooped to the famous old Apprise Inn where they refreshed themselves at a table on which was set forth a collation of beer, pod-cakes and pickled fingerlings; after which the newcomers separated to various quarters of the float, in accordance with traditional caste distinctions.

In the center of the float was a rostrum and on benches surrounding the notables took their places: craft-masters, caste-chiefs, Arbiters and Intercessors. The rostrum was at all times open to any who wished to speak, so long as they gained the sponsorship of one of the notables. The first speakers at the convocations customarily were elders intent on exhorting the younger folk to excellence and virtue; so it was today. An hour after the sun had reached the zenith the first speaker made his way to the rostrum; a portly old Incendiary from Maudelinda Float who had in just such a fashion opened the speaking at the last five convocations. He sought and was perfunctorily granted sponsorship — by now his speeches were regarded as a necessary evil; he mounted the rostrum and began to speak. His voice was rich, throbbing, voluminous; his periods were long, his sentiments well-used, his illuminations unremarkable:

"We meet again; I am pleased to see so many of the faces which over the years have become familiar and well-beloved; and alas there are certain faces no more to be seen, those who have slipped away to the Bourne, many untimely, as those who suffered punishment only these few days past before the wrath of King Kragen, of which we all stand in awe. A dreadful circumstance thus to provoke the majesty of this Elemental Reality; it should never have occurred; it would never have occurred if all abided by the ancient disciplines. Why must we scorn the wisdom of our ancestors? Those noble and most heroic of men who dared to revolt against the tyranny of the mindless helots, seize the Ship of Space which was taking them to brutal confinement, and seek a haven here on this blessed world! Our ancestors knew the benefits of order and rigor: they designated the castes and set them to tasks for which they presumably had received training on the Home-world. In such a fashion the Swindlers were assigned the task of swindling fish; the Hoodwinks were set to winking hoods; the Incendiaries, among whom I am proud to number myself, wove ropes; while the Bezzlers gave us the Intercessors who have procured the favor and benevolent guardianship of King Kragen.

"Like begets like; characteristics persist and distill: why then are the castes crumbling and giving way to helter-skelter disorder? I appeal to the youth of today: read the old books: the Dicta. Study the artifacts in the Museum, renew your dedication to the system formulated by our forefathers: you have no heritage more precious than your caste identity!"

The old Incendiary spoke on in such a vein for several minutes further, and was succeeded by another old man, a former Hoodwink of good reputation, who worked until films upon his eyes gave one configuration much the look of another. Like the old Incendiary he too urged a more fervent dedication to the old-time values. "I deplore the sloth and pudicity of today's youth! We are becoming a race of sluggards! It is sheer good fortune that King Kragen protects us from the gluttony of the lesser kragen. And what if the tyrants of out-space discovered our haven and sought once more to enslave us? How would we defend ourselves? By hurling fish-heads? By diving under the floats in the hope that our adversaries would follow and drown themselves? I propose that each float form a militia, well-trained and equipped with darts and spears, fashioned from the most durable stalk obtainable!"

The old Hoodwink was followed by the Sumber Float Intercessor, who courteously suggested that should the out-space tyrants appear, King Kragen would be sure to visit upon them the most poignant punishments, the most absolute of rebuffs, so that the tyrants would flee in terror never to return. "King Kragen is mighty, King Kragen is wise and benevolent, unless his dignity is impugned, as in the detestable incident at Tranque Float, where the wilfulness of a bigoted free-thinker caused agony to many." Now he modestly turned down his head. "It is neither my place nor my privilege to propose a punishment suitable to so heinous an offense as the one under discussion. But I would go beyond this particular crime to dwell upon the underlying causes; namely the bravado of certain folk, who ordain themselves equal or superior to the accepted ways of life which have served us so well so long..."

Presently he descended to the float. His place was taken by a somber man of stalwart physique, wearing the plainest of garments. "My name is Sklar Hast," he said. "I am that so-called 'bigoted free-thinker' just referred to. I have much to say, but I hardly know how to say it. I will be blunt. King Kragen is not the wise beneficent guardian the Intercessors like to pretend. King Kragen is a gluttonous beast who every year becomes more enormous and more gluttonous. I sought to kill a lesser kragen which I found destroying my arbors; by some means King Kragen learned of this attempt and reacted with insane malice."

"Hist! Hist!" cried the Intercessors from below. "Shame! Outrage!"

"Why does King Kragen resent my effort? After all, he kills any lesser kragen he discovers in the vicinity. It is simple and self-evident. King Kragen does not want men to think about killing kragen for fear they will attempt to kill him. I propose that this is what we do. Let us put aside this ignoble servility, this groveling to a sea-beast, let us turn our best efforts to the destruction of King Kragen."

"Irresponsible maniac!" "Fool!" "Vile-minded ingrate!" called the Intercessors in wrath.

Sklar Hast waited, but the invective increased in volume. Finally Phyral Berwick the Apprise Arbiter mounted the rostrum and held up his hands. "Quiet! Let Sklar Hast speak! He stands on the rostrum; it is his privilege to say what he wishes."

"Must we listen to garbage and filth?" called Semon Voidenvo. "This man has destroyed Tranque Float; now he urges his frantic lunacy upon the rest of us."

"Let him urge," declared Phyral Berwick. "You are under no obligation to comply."

Sklar Hast said, "The Intercessors naturally resist these ideas; they are bound closely to King Kragen, and claim to have some means of communicating with him. Possibly this is so. Why else should King Kragen arrive so opportunely at Tranque Float? Now here is a very cogent point: if we can agree to liberate ourselves from King Kragen, we must prevent the Intercessors from making known our plans to him, otherwise we shall suffer more than necessary. Most of you know in your hearts that I speak truth. King Kragen is a crafty beast with an insatiable appetite and we are his slaves. You know this truth but you fear to acknowledge it. Those who spoke before me have mentioned our forefathers: the men who captured a ship from the tyrants who sought to immure them on a penal planet. What would our forefathers have done? Would they have submitted to this gluttonous ogre? Of course not.

"How can we kill King Kragen? The plans must wait upon agreement, upon the concerted will to act, and in any event must not be told before the Intercessors. If there are any here who believe as I do, now is the time for them to make themselves heard."

He stepped down from the rostrum. Across the float was silence. Men's faces were frozen. Sklar Hast looked to right and to left. No one met his eye.

Semon Voidenvo mounted the rostrum. "You have listened to the shameless murderer. On Tranque Float we condemned him to death for his malevolent acts. According to custom he demanded the right to speak before a convocation; now he has done so. Has he confessed his great crime; has he wept for the evil he has visited upon Tranque Float? No; he gibbers his plans for further enormities; he outrages decency by mentioning our ancestors in the same breath with his foul proposals. Let the convocation endorse the verdict of Tranque Float; let all those who respect King Kragen and benefit from his ceaseless vigilance, raise now their hands in the clenched fist of death!"

"Death!" roared the Intercessors and raised their fists. But elsewhere through the crowd there was hesitation and uneasiness. Eyes shifted backwards and forwards; there were furtive glances out to sea. Semon Voidenvo once more called for a signal, and now a few fists were raised.

Phyral Berwick, the Apprise Monitor, rose to his feet. "I remind Semon Voidenvo that he has now called twice for the death of Sklar

Hast. If he calls once more and fails to achieve an affirmative vote Sklar Hast is vindicated."

Semon Voidenvo's face sagged. He looked uncertainly over the crowd, and without further statement descended.

The rostrum was empty. No one sought to speak. Finally Phyral Berwick himself mounted the steps. He was a stocky square-faced man with gray hair, ice-blue eyes, a short gray beard. He spoke slowly. "You have heard Sklar Hast, who calls for the death of King Kragen. You have heard Semon Voidenvo, who calls for the death of Sklar Hast. I will tell you my feelings. I have great fear in the first case and great disinclination in the second. I have no clear sense of what I should do."

From the audience a man called "Question!" Phyral Berwick nodded. "State your name, caste and craft, and propound your question."

"I am Meth Cagno; I am by blood a Larcener, although I no longer follow caste custom; my craft is that of Scrivener. My question has this background: Sklar Hast has voiced a conjecture which I think deserves an answer: namely, that Semon Voidenvo, the Tranque Intercessor, called King Kragen to Tranque Float. This is a subtle question, because much depends upon not only *if* Semon Voidenvo issued the call, but precisely *when*. If he did so when the rogue kragen was first discovered, well and good. But — if he called after Sklar Hast made his attempt to kill the rogue, Semon Voidenvo is more guilty of the Tranque disaster than Sklar Hast. My question then: what is the true state of affairs? Do the Intercessors secretly communicate with King Kragen? Specifically, did Semon Voidenvo call King Kragen to Tranque Float in order that Sklar Hast should be punished?"

Phyral Berwick deliberated. "I cannot answer your question. But I think it deserves an answer. Semon Voidenvo, what do you say?"

"I say nothing."

"Come," said Phyral Berwick reasonably. "Your craft is Intercessor; your responsibility is to the men whom you represent, not to King Kragen, no matter how fervent your respect. Any evasion or secrecy can only arouse our misgivings."

"It is to be understood," said Semon Voidenvo tartly, "that if I did indeed summon King Kragen, my motives were of the highest order."

"Well, then, did you do so?"

Semon Voidenvo cast about for a means to escape from his dilemma, and found none. Finally he said, "There is a means by which the Intercessors are able to summon King Kragen in the event that a rogue kragen appears. This occurred; I so summoned King Kragen."

"Indeed." Phyral Berwick drummed his fingers on the rail of the rostrum. "Are these the only occasions that you summon King Kragen?"

"Why do you question me?" demanded Semon Voidenvo. "I am Intercessor; the criminal is Sklar Hast."

"Easy, then; the questions illuminate the extent of the alleged crime. For instance, let me ask this: do you ever summon King Kragen to feed from your lagoon in order to visit a punishment upon the folk of your float?"

Semon Voidenvo blinked. "The wisdom of King Kragen is inordinate. He can detect delinquencies, he makes his presence known —"

"Specifically then, you summoned King Kragen to Tranque Float when Sklar Hast sought to kill the lesser kragen?"

"My acts are not in the balance. I see no reason to answer the question."

Phyral Berwick spoke to the crowd in a troubled voice. "There seems no way to determine exactly when Semon Voidenvo called King Kragen. If he did so after Sklar Hast had begun his attack upon the rogue, then in my opinion, Semon Voidenvo the Intercessor is more immediately responsible for the Tranque disaster than Sklar Hast. Thereupon it becomes a travesty to visit any sort of penalty upon Sklar Hast. Unfortunately there seems no way of settling this question."

The Apprise Intercessor, Barquan Blasdel, rose slowly to his feet. "Arbiter Berwick, I fear that you are seriously confused. Sklar Hast and his gang committed an act knowingly proscribed both by the Tranque Monitor Ixon Myrex and by the Tranque Intercessor Semon Voidenvo. The consequences stemmed from this act; hence Sklar Hast is guilty."

"Barquan Blasdel," said Phyral Berwick, "you are Apprise Intercessor. Have you ever summoned King Kragen to Apprise Float?"

"As Semon Voidenvo pointed out, Sklar Hast is the criminal at the bar, not the conscientious intercessors of the various floats. By no means may Sklar Hast be allowed to evade his punishment. King

Kragen is not lightly to be defied. Even though the convocation will not raise their collective fist to smite Sklar Hast, I say that he must die."

Phyral Berwick fixed his pale blue eyes upon Barquan Blasdel. "If the convocation gives Sklar Hast his life, he will not die unless I die before him."

Meth Cagno came forward. "And I likewise."

The men of Tranque Float who had joined Sklar Hast in the killing of the rogue kragen came toward the rostrum, shouting their intention of joining Sklar Hast either in life or death, and with them came others, from various floats.

Barquan Blasdel climbed onto the rostrum, held his hands wide. "Before others declare themselves — look out to sea. King Kragen watches, attentive to learn who is loyal and who is faithless."

The crowd swung about as if one individual. A hundred yards off the float the water swirled lazily around King Kragen's great turret. The crystal eyes pointed like telescopes toward Apprise Float. Presently the turret sank beneath the surface. The blue water roiled, then flowed smooth and featureless.

Sklar Hast went to the ladder, started to mount to the rostrum. Barquan Blasdel the Intercessor halted him. "The rostrum must not become a shouting-place. Stay till you are summoned!" But Sklar Hast pushed him aside, went to face the crowd. He pointed toward the smooth ocean. "There you have seen the vile beast, our enemy! Why should we deceive ourselves? Intercessors, Arbiters, all of us — let us forget our differences, let us join our crafts and our resources! If we do so, we can evolve a method to kill King Kragen! So now — decide!"

Barquan Blasdel threw back his head aghast. He took a step toward Sklar Hast, as if to seize him, then turned to the audience. "You have heard this madman — twice you have heard him. You have also observed the vigilance of King Kragen whose force is known to all. You can choose therefore either to obey the exhortations of a twitching lunatic, or be guided by your ancient trust in the benevolence of mighty King Kragen. In one manner only does Sklar Hast speak truth: there must be a definite resolution to this matter. We can have no half-measures! Sklar Hast must die! So now hold high your fists — each and all! Silence the

frantic screamings of Sklar Hast! King Kragen is near at hand! Death
to Sklar Hast!" He thrust his fist high into the air.

The Intercessors followed suit. "Death to Sklar Hast!"

Hesitantly, indecisively, other fists raised, then others and
others. Some changed their minds and drew down their fists; others
submitted to arguments and either drew down their fists or thrust
them high; some raised their fists only to have others pull them down.
Altercations sprang up across the float; the hoarse sound of contention
began to make itself heard. Barquan Blasdel leaned forward in sudden
concern, calling for calm. Sklar Hast likewise started to speak, but he
desisted — because suddenly words were of no avail. In a bewildering,
almost magical, shift the placid convocation had become a mêlée.
Men and women tore savagely at each other, screaming, cursing,
raging, squealing. Emotion accumulated from childhood, stored
and constrained, had suddenly exploded; and the identical fear and
hate had prompted opposite reactions. Across the float the tide of
battle surged, out into the water where staid Bezzlers and responsible
Larceners sought to drown each other. Few weapons were available:
clubs of stalk, a bone axe or two, a half-dozen stakes, as many knives.
While the struggle was at its most intense King Kragen once more
surfaced, this time a quarter-mile to the north from whence he turned
his vast incurious gaze upon the float.

The fighting slowed and dwindled, from sheer exhaustion. The
combatants drew apart into panting bleeding groups. In the lagoon
floated half-a-dozen corpses; on the float lay as many more. Now for
the first time it could be seen that those who stood by Sklar Hast
were considerably outnumbered, by almost two to one, and also
that this group included for the most part the most vigorous and
able of the craftsmen, though few of the Masters: about half of the
Hoodwinks, two-thirds of the Scriveners, relatively few from the
Jacklegs, Advertisermen, Nigglers and other low castes, fewer still of
the Arbiters and no Intercessors whatever.

Barquan Blasdel, still on the rostrum, cried out, "This is a sorry day
indeed; a sorry day! Sklar Hast, see the anguish you have brought to
the floats! There can be no mercy for you now!"

Sklar Hast came forward, pale and flaming-eyed. Blood coursed down his face from the slash of a knife. Ignoring Blasdel he mounted the rostrum, and addressed the two groups:

"As Blasdel the Intercessor has said, there is no turning back now. So be it. Let those who want to serve King Kragen remain. Let those who want free lives go forth across the sea. There are floats to north and south, to east and west, floats as kind and hospitable as these, where we will soon have homes as rich and modern — perhaps more so."

Barquan Blasdel strode forward. "Go then! All you faithless, you irreverent ones — get hence and good riddance! Go where you will, and never seek to return when the teeming kragen, unchided by the great King, devour your sponges, tear your nets, crush your coracles!"

"The many cannot be as rapacious as the one," said Sklar Hast. "You who will go then, return to your floats, load tools and cordage, all your utile goods into your coracles. In two days we depart. Our destination and other details must remain secret. I need not explain why." He cast an ironic look toward Barquan Blasdel.

"You need not fear our interference," said Blasdel. "You may depart at will; indeed we will facilitate your going."

"On the morning of the third day hence, then, when the wind blows fair, we depart."

Chapter III

Barquan Blasdel the Apprise Intercessor, his spouse and six daughters, occupied a pad to the north of the main float, somewhat isolated and apart. It was perhaps the choicest and most pleasant pad of the Apprise complex, situated where Blasdel could read the hoodwink towers of Apprise, of Quatrefoil and the Bandings to the east, of Granolt to the west. The pad was delightfully overgrown with a hundred different plants and vines: some yielding resinous pods, others capsules of fragrant sap, others crisp tendrils and shoots. Certain shrubs produced stains and pigment; a purple-leaved epiphyte yielded a rich-flavored pith. Other growths were entirely ornamental — a situation not too usual along the floats, where space was at a premium and every growing object weighed for its utility. Along the entire line of floats few pads could compare to that of Barquan Blasdel for beauty, variety of plantings, isolation and calm.

In late afternoon of the second day after the turbulent convocation, Barquan Blasdel returned to his pad. He dropped the painter of his coracle over a stake of carved bone, gazed appreciatively into the west. The sun had only just departed the sky, which now glowed with effulgent greens, blues, and, at the zenith, a purple of exquisite purity. The ocean, shuddering to the first whispers of the evening breeze, reflected the sky. Blasdel felt surrounded, immersed in color... He turned away, marched to his house, whistling a complacent tune between his teeth. On the morrow the most troublesome elements of all the floats would depart on the morning breeze, and no more would be heard from them ever. And Blasdel's whistling became slow and thoughtful. Although life flowed smoothly and without contention, over the years a certain uneasiness and dissatisfaction had begun to make itself felt. Dissident elements had begun to question the established order. The sudden outbreak of violence at the convocation perhaps had been inevitable: an explosion of suppressed or even unconscious tensions. But all was working out for the best. The affair could not have resolved itself more smoothly if he had personally arranged the entire sequence of events. At one stroke all the skeptics, grumblers, ne'er-do-wells, the covertly insolent, the obstinate hard-heads — at one stroke, all would disappear, never again to trouble the easy and orthodox way of life.

Almost jauntily Barquan Blasdel ambled up the path to his residence: a group of five semi-detached huts, screened by the garden from the main float, and so providing a maximum of privacy for Blasdel, his spouse and his six daughters. Blasdel halted. On a bench beside the door sat a man. Twilight murk concealed his face. Blasdel frowned, peered. Intruders upon his private pad were not welcome. Blasdel marched forward. The man rose from the bench and bowed: it was Phyral Berwick, the Apprise Arbiter. "Good evening," said Berwick. "I trust I did not startle you."

"By no means," said Blasdel shortly. With rank equal to his own Berwick could not be ignored, although after his unconventional actions at the convocation Blasdel could not bring himself to display more than a minimum of formal courtesy. He said, "Unfortunately I was not expecting callers and can offer you no refreshment."

"A circumstance of no moment," declared Berwick. "I desire neither food nor drink." He waved his hand around the pad. "You live on a pad of surpassing beauty, Barquan Blasdel. There are many who might envy you."

Blasdel shrugged. "Since my conduct is orthodox, I am armored against adverse opinion. But what urgency brings you here? I fear that I must be less than ceremonious; I am shortly due at the hoodwink tower to participate in a coded all-float conference."

Berwick made a gesture of polite acquiescence. "My business is of small moment. But I would not keep you standing out here in the dusk. Shall we enter?"

Blasdel grunted, opened the door, allowed Berwick to enter. From a cupboard he brought luminant fiber, which he set aglow and arranged in a holder. Turning a quick side-glance toward Berwick he said, "In all candor I am somewhat surprised to see you. Apparently you were among the most vehement of those dissidents who planned to depart."

"I may well have given that impression," Berwick agreed. "But you must realize that declarations uttered in the heat of emotion are occasionally amended in the light of sober reason."

Blasdel nodded curtly. "True enough. I suspect that many of the ingrates will think twice before joining this hare-brained expedition."

"This is partly the reason for my presence here," said Berwick. He looked around the room. "An interesting chamber. You own dozens of valuable artifacts. But where are the others of your family?"

"In the domestic area. This is my sanctum, my workroom, my place of meditation."

"Indeed." Berwick inspected the walls. "Indeed, indeed! I believe I notice certain relicts of the forefathers!"

"True," said Blasdel. "This small flat object is of the substance called 'metal', and is extremely hard. The best bone knife will not scratch it. The purpose of this particular object I cannot conjecture. It is an heirloom. These books are exact copies of the Dicta in the Hall of Archives, and present the memoirs of the Forefathers. Alas! I find them beyond my comprehension. There is nothing more of any great interest. On the shelf — my ceremonial head-dresses; you have seen them before. Here is my telescope. It is old; the case is warped, the gum of the lenses has bulged and cracked. It was poor gum, to begin with. But I have little need for a better instrument. My possessions are few. Unlike many Intercessors and certain Arbiters," here he cast a meaningful eye at Phyral Berwick, "I do not choose to surround myself with sybaritical cushions and baskets of sweetmeats."

Berwick laughed ruefully. "You have touched upon my weaknesses. Perhaps the fear of deprivation has occasioned second-thoughts in me."

"Ha hah!" Blasdel became jovial. "I begin to understand. The scalawags who set off to wild new floats can expect nothing but hardship: wild fish, horny sponges, new varnish with little more body than water; in short they will be returning to the life of savages. They must expect to suffer the depredations of lesser kragen, who will swiftly gather. Perhaps in time…" His voice dwindled, his face took on a thoughtful look.

"What was it you were about to say?" prompted Phyral Berwick.

Blasdel gave a non-committal laugh. "An amusing, if far-fetched, conceit crossed my mind. Perhaps in time one of these lesser kragen will vanquish the others, and drive them away. When this occurs, those who flee King Kragen will have a king of their own, who may eventually…" Again his voice paused.

"Who may eventually rival King Kragen in size and force?" Berwick supplied. "The concept is not unreasonable — although King Kragen is already enormous from long feasting, and shows no signs of halting his growth." An almost imperceptible tremor moved the floor of the hut. Blasdel went to look out the door. "I thought I felt the arrival of a coracle."

"Conceivably a gust of wind," said Berwick. "Well, to my errand. As you have guessed I did not come to examine your relicts or comment upon the comfort of your cottage. My business is this. I feel a certain sympathy for those who are leaving, and I feel that no one, not even the most violently fanatic Intercessor, would wish this group to meet King Kragen upon the ocean. King Kragen, as you are aware, disapproves of exploration, and becomes petulant, even wrathful, when he finds men venturing out upon the ocean. Perhaps he fears the possibility of the second King Kragen concerning which we speculated. Hence I came to inquire the whereabouts of King Kragen. In the morning the wind blows east, and the optimum location for King Kragen would be to the far east at Tranque or Thrasneck."

Blasdel nodded sagely. "The emigrants are putting their luck to the test. Should King Kragen chance to be waiting in the east tomorrow morning, and should he spy the flotilla, his wrath might well be excited, to the detriment of the expedition."

"And where," inquired Berwick, "was King Kragen at last notification?"

Barquan Blasdel knit his brows. "I believe I noted a hoodwink message to the effect that he was seen cruising in a westerly direction to the south of Bickle Float, toward Maudelinda. I might well have misread the flicker, I only noted the configuration from the corner of my eye — but such was my understanding."

"Excellent," declared Berwick. "This is good news. The emigrants should make their departure safely and without interference."

"So we hope," said Blasdel. "King Kragen of course is subject to unpredictable whims and quirks."

Berwick made a confidential sign. "Sometimes — so it is rumored — he responds to signals transmitted in some mysterious manner by the Intercessors. Tell me, Barquan Blasdel, is this the case? We are both notables and together share responsibility for the welfare of Apprise Float. Is it true then that the Intercessors communicate with King Kragen, as has been alleged?"

"Now then, Arbiter Berwick," said Blasdel, "this is hardly a pertinent question. Should I answer yes, then I would be divulging a craft secret. Should I answer no, then it would seem that we Intercessors boast of nonexistent capabilities. So you must satisfy yourself with those hypotheses which seem the most profitable."

"Fairly answered," said Phyral Berwick. "However — and in the strictest confidence — I will report to you an amusing circumstance. As you know, at the convocation I declared myself for the party of Sklar Hast. Subsequently I was accepted into their most intimate counsels. I can inform you with authority — but first, you will assure me of your silence? As under no circumstances would I betray Sklar Hast or compromise the expedition."

"Certainly, indeed; my lips are sealed as with fourteen-year old varnish."

"Well then, I accept you at your word. This is Sklar Hast's amusing tactic: he has arranged that a group of influential Intercessors shall accompany the group. If all goes well, the Intercessors live. If not, like all the rest, they are crushed in the mandibles of King Kragen." And Phyral Berwick, standing back, watched Barquan Blasdel with an attentive gaze. "What do you make of that?"

Blasdel stood rigid, fingering his fringe of black beard. He darted a quick glance toward Berwick. "Which Intercessors are to be kidnaped?"

"Aha," said Berwick. "That, like the response of the question I put to you, is in the nature of a craft secret. I doubt if lesser men will be troubled, but if I were Intercessor for Aumerge, or Sumber, or Quatrefoil, or even Apprise, I believe that I might have cause for caution."

Blasdel stared at Berwick with mingled suspicion and uneasiness. "Do you take this means to warn me? If so, I would thank you to speak less ambiguously. Personally I fear no such attack. Within a hundred feet are three stalwarts, testing my daughters for marriage. A loud call would bring instant help from the float, which is scarcely a stone's throw beyond the garden."

Berwick nodded sagely. "It seems then that you are utterly secure."

"Still, I must hurry to the float," said Blasdel. "I am expected at a conference, and the evening grows no younger."

Berwick bowed and stood aside. "You will naturally remember to reveal nothing of what I told you, to vouchsafe no oblique warning, to hint nothing of the matter — in fact to make no reference to it whatever."

Blasdel considered. "I will say nothing beyond my original intention, to the effect that the villain Sklar Hast obviously knows no moderation, and that it behooves all notables and craft masters to guard themselves against some form of final vengeance."

Berwick paused. "I hardly think you need go quite so far. Perhaps you could phrase it somewhat differently. In this wise: Sklar Hast and his sturdy band take their leave in the morning; now is the last chance for persons so inclined to cast in their lot with the group; however, you hope that all Intercessors will remain at their posts."

"Pah," cried Barquan Blasdel indignantly. "That conveys no sense of imminence. I will say, Sklar Hast is desperate; should he decide to take hostages, his diseased mind would select Intercessors as the most appropriate persons."

Berwick made a firm dissent. "This, I believe, transcends the line I have drawn. My honor is at stake and I can agree to no announcement which baldly states the certainty as a probability. If you choose to make a jocular reference, or perhaps urge that not too many Intercessors join the expedition, then all is well: a subtle germ of suspicion has been planted, you have done your duty and my honor has not been compromised."

"Yes, yes," cried Blasdel, "I agree to anything. But I must hurry to the hoodwink tower. While we quibble Sklar Hast and his bandits are kidnaping Intercessors."

"And what is the harm there?" inquired Berwick mildly. "You state that King Kragen has been observed from Bickle Float proceeding to the west; hence the Intercessors are in no danger, and presumably will be allowed to return once Sklar Hast is assured that King Kragen is no longer a danger. Conversely, if the Intercessors have betrayed Sklar Hast and given information to King Kragen so that he waits off Tranque Float, then they deserve to die with the rest. It is justice of the most precise and exquisite balance."

"That is the difficulty," muttered Blasdel, trying to push past Berwick to the door. "I cannot answer for the silence of the other Intercessors. Suppose one among them has notified King Kragen? Then a great tragedy ensues."

"Interesting! So you can indeed summon King Kragen when you so desire?"

"Yes, yes, but, mind you, this is a secret. And now —"

"It follows then that you always know the whereabouts of King Kragen. How do you achieve this?"

"There is no time to explain; suffice it to say that a means is at hand."

"Right here? In your workroom?"

"Yes indeed. Now stand aside. After I have broadcast the warning I will make all clear. Stand aside then!"

Berwick shrugged and allowed Blasdel to run from the cottage, through the garden to the edge of the pad.

Blasdel stopped short at the water's edge. The coracle had disappeared. Where previously Apprise Float had raised its foliage and its great hoodwink tower against the dusk, there was now only blank water and blank sky. The pad floated free; urged by the west wind of evening it already had left Apprise Float behind.

Blasdel gave an inarticulate cry of fury and woe. He turned to find Berwick standing behind him. "What has happened?"

"It seems that while we talked, divers cut through the stem of your pad. At least this is my presumption."

"Yes, yes," grated Blasdel. "So much is obvious. What else?"

Berwick shrugged. "It appears that willy-nilly, whether we like it or not, we are part of the great emigration. Now that such is the case I am relieved to know that you have a means to determine the whereabouts of King Kragen. Come. Let us make use of this device and reassure ourselves."

Blasdel made a guttural sound deep in his throat. He crouched and for a moment appeared on the point of hurling himself at Phyral Berwick. From the shadows of the verdure appeared another man. Berwick pointed. "I believe Sklar Hast himself is at hand."

"You tricked me," groaned Barquan Blasdel between clenched teeth. "You have performed an infamous act, which you shall regret."

"I have done no such deed, although it appears that you may well have misunderstood my position. Still, the time for recrimination is over. We share a similar problem, which is how to escape the malevolence of King Kragen. I suggest that you now proceed to locate him."

Without a word Blasdel turned, proceeded to his cottage. He entered the main room, with Berwick and Sklar Hast close behind. He crossed to the wall, lifted a panel to reveal an inner room. He brought more lights; all entered. A hole had been cut in the floor, and through the pad, the spongy tissue having been painted with a black varnish to prevent its growing together. A tube fashioned from fine yellow stalk perhaps four inches in diameter led down into the water. "At the bottom," said Blasdel curtly, "is a carefully devised horn, of exact shape and quality. The end is four feet in diameter and covered with a diaphragm of seasoned and varnished pad-skin. King Kragen emits a sound to which this horn is sensitive." He went to the tube, put down his ear, listened, slowly turned the tube around a vertical axis. He shook his head. "I hear nothing. This means that King Kragen is at least ten miles distant. If he is closer I can detect him. He passed to the east early today; presumably he swims somewhere near Sumber, or Adelvine."

Sklar Hast laughed quietly. "Urged there by the Intercessors?"

Blasdel shrugged sourly. "As to that I have nothing to say."

"How then do you summon King Kragen?"

Blasdel pointed to a rod rising from the floor, the top of which terminated in a crank. "In the water below is a drum. Inside this drum fits a wheel. When the crank is turned, the wheel, working in resin, rubs against the drum and emits a signal. King Kragen can sense this sound from a great distance — once again about ten miles. When he is needed, at say Bickle Float, the Intercessor at Aumerge calls him, until the horn reveals him to be four or five miles distant, whereupon the Intercessor at Paisley calls him a few miles, then the Maudelinda Intercessor, and so forth until he is within range of the Intercessor at Bickle Float."

Sklar Hast nodded. "I see. In this fashion Semon Voidenvo called King Kragen to Tranque. Whereupon King Kragen destroyed Tranque Float and killed forty-three persons."

"That is the case."

Sklar Hast turned away. Phyral Berwick told Blasdel, "I believe that Semon Voidenvo is one of the Intercessors who are accompanying the emigration. His lot may not be a happy one."

"This is unreasonable," Barquan Blasdel declared heatedly. "He was as faithful to his convictions as Sklar Hast is to his own. After all, Voidenvo did not enjoy the devastation of Tranque Float. It is his home. Many of those killed were his friends. But he gives his faith and trust to King Kragen."

Sklar Hast swung around. "And you?"

Blasdel shook his head. "Not with such wholeheartedness."

Sklar Hast looked toward Berwick. "What should we do with this apparatus? Destroy it? Or preserve it?"

Berwick considered. "We might on some occasion wish to listen for King Kragen. I doubt if we ever will desire to summon him."

Sklar Hast gave a sardonic jerk of the head. "Who knows? To his death perhaps." He turned to Blasdel. "What persons are aboard the pad in addition to us?"

"My spouse — in the cottage two roofs along. Three young daughters who weave ornaments for the Star-cursing Festival. Three older daughters are attempting to prove themselves to three stalwarts who test them for wives. All are unaware that their home floats out on the deep ocean. None wish to become emigrants to a strange line of floats."

Sklar Hast said, "No more were any of the rest of us — until we were forced to choose. I feel no pity for them, or for you. Undoubtedly there will be ample work for all hands. Indeed, we may formulate a new guild: the Kragen-killers. If rumor is accurate, they infest the ocean."

He left the room, went out into the night. Blasdel cast a wry look at Phyral Berwick, went to listen once more at the detecting horn. Then he likewise left the room. Berwick followed, and lowered the panel. Both joined Sklar Hast at the edge of the pad, where now several coracles were tied. A dozen men stood in the garden. Sklar Hast turned to Blasdel. "Summon your spouse, your daughters and those who test them. Explain the circumstances, and gather your belongings. The evening breeze will soon die and we cannot tow the pad."

Blasdel departed, accompanied by Berwick. Sklar Hast and the others entered the work-room, carried everything of value or utility to the coracles, including the small metal relict, the Books of Dicta, the listening horn and the summoning drum. Then all embarked in the coracles, and Barquan Blasdel's beautiful pad was left to drift solitary upon the ocean.

Chapter IV

Morning came to the ocean and with it the breeze from the west. The floats could no longer be seen; the ocean was a blue mirror in all directions. Sklar Hast lowered Blasdel's horn into the water, listened. Nothing could be heard. Barquan Blasdel did the same and agreed that King Kragen was nowhere near.

There were perhaps six hundred coracles in the flotilla, each carrying from four to eight persons, with as much gear, household equipment and tools as possible, together with sacks of food and water.

Late in the afternoon they noted a few medium-sized floats to the north, but made no attempt to land. King Kragen was yet too near at hand.

The late afternoon breeze arose. Rude sails were rigged and the oarsmen rested. At dusk Sklar Hast ordered all the coracles connected by lines to minimize the risk of separation. When the breeze died and seas reflected the dazzling stars, the sails were brought down and all slept.

The following day was like the first, and also the day after. On the morning of the fourth day a line of splendid floats appeared ahead, easily as large and as rich of foliage as those they had left. Sklar Hast would have preferred to sail on another week, but the folk among the coracles were fervent in their rejoicing, and he clearly would have encountered near-unanimous opposition. So the flotilla landed upon three closely adjoining floats, drove stakes into the pad surface, tethered the coracles.

Sklar Hast called an informal convocation. "In a year or two," he said, "we can live lives as comfortable as those we left behind us. But this is not enough. We left our homes because of King Kragen, who is now our deadly enemy. We shall never rest secure until we find a means to make ourselves supreme over all the kragen. To this purpose we must live different lives than we did in the old days — until King Kragen is killed. How to kill King Kragen? I wish I knew. He is a monster, impregnable to any weapon we now can use against him. So this must be our primary goal: weapons against King Kragen." Sklar Hast paused, looked around the somber group. "This is my personal feeling. I have no authority over any of you, beyond that of the immediate circumstances, which are transient. You have a right to discredit me, to think differently — in which case I will muster those who feel as I do, and sail on to still another float, where we can dedicate ourselves to the killing of King Kragen. If we are all agreed, that our souls are not our own until King Kragen is dead, then we must formalize this feeling. Authority must be given to some person or group of persons. Responsibilities must be delegated; work must be organized. As you see I envision a life different to the old. It will be harder in some respects, easier in others. First of all, we need not feed King Kragen..."

A committee of seven members was chosen, to serve as a temporary governing body until the needs of the new community required a more elaborate system. As a matter of course Sklar Hast was named to the committee, as well as Phyral Berwick who became the first chairman, and also Meth Cagno the Scrivener. The captured Intercessors sat aside in a sullen group and took no part in the proceedings.

The committee met for an hour, and as its first measure, ordained a census, that each man's caste and craft might be noted.

After the meeting Meth Cagno took Sklar Hast aside. "When you captured Barquan Blasdel, you brought his books."

"True."

"I have been examining these books. They are a set of the Ancient Dicta."

"So I understand."

"This is a source of great satisfaction to me. No one except the Scrivener reads the Dicta nowadays, though everyone professes familiarity. As the generations proceed, the lives of our ancestors and the fantastic environment from which they came seem more like myth than reality."

"I suppose this is true enough. I am a hoodwink by trade and only know hoodwink configurations. The Dicta are written in ancient calligraph, which puzzles me."

"It is difficult to read, that I grant," said Cagno. "However, a patient examination of the Dicta can be profitable. Each volume represents the knowledge of one of our ancestors, to the extent that he was able to organize it. There is also a great deal of repetition and dullness; our ancestors, whatever their talents, had few literary skills. Some are vainglorious and devote pages to self-encomium. Others are anxious to explain in voluminous detail the vicissitudes which led to their presence on the Ship of Space. They seem to have been a very mixed group, from various levels of society. There are hints here and there which I, for one, do not understand. Some describe the Home World as a place of maniacs. Others seem to have held respected places in this society until, as they explain it, the persons in authority turned on them and instituted a savage persecution, ending, as we know, in our ancestors seizing control of the Ship of Space and fleeing to this planet."

"It is all very confusing," said Sklar Hast, "and none of it seems to have much contemporary application. For instance, they do not tell us how they boiled varnish on the Home World, or how they propelled their coracles. Do creatures like the kragen infest the Home World? If so, how do the Home Folk deal with them? Do they kill them or feed them sponges? Our ancestors are silent on these points."

Meth Cagno shrugged. "Evidently they were not overly concerned, or they would have dealt with these matters at length. But I agree that there is much they fail to make clear. As in our own case, the various castes seemed trained to explicit trades. Especially interesting are the memoirs of James Brunet. His caste, that of Counterfeiter, is now extinct among us. Most of his Dicta are rather conventional exhortations to virtue, but toward the middle of the book he says this." Here Cagno opened a book and read:

" 'To those who follow us, to our children and grandchildren, we can leave no tangible objects of value. We brought nothing to the world but ourselves and the wreckage of our lives. We will undoubtedly die here — a fate probably preferable to New Ossining, but by no means the destiny any of us had planned for ourselves. There is no way to escape. Of the entire group I alone have a technical education, most of which I have forgotten. And to what end could I turn it? This is a soft world. It consists of ocean and sea-weed. There is land nowhere. To escape — even if we had the craft to build a new ship, which we do not — we need metal and metal there is none. Even to broadcast a radio signal we need metal. None... No clay to make pottery, no silica for glass, no limestone for concrete, no ore from which to smelt metal. Presumably the ocean carries various salts, but how to extract the metal without electricity? There is iron in our blood: how to extract it? A strange helpless sensation to live on this world where the hardest substance is our own bone! We have, during our lives, taken so many things for granted, and now it seems that no one can evoke something from nothing... This is a problem on which I must think. An ingenious man can work wonders, and I, a successful counterfeiter — or, rather, almost successful — am certainly ingenious.'"

Meth Cagno paused in his reading. "This is the end of the chapter."

"He seems to be a man of no great force," mused Sklar Hast. "It is true that metal can be found nowhere." He took the bit of metal from his pocket which had once graced the work-room of Barquan Blasdel. "This is obdurate stuff indeed, and perhaps it is what we need to kill King Kragen."

Meth Cagno returned to the book. "He writes his next chapter after a lapse of months:

"'I have considered the matter at length. But before I proceed I must provide as best I can a picture of the way the universe works, for it is clear that none of my colleagues are in any position to do so, excellent fellows though they are. Please do not suspect me of whimsey: our personalities and social worth undoubtedly vary with the context in which we live.'"

Here Cagno looked up. "I don't completely understand his meaning here. But I suppose that the matter is unimportant." He turned the pages. "He now goes into an elaborate set of theorizations regarding the nature of the world, which, I confess, I don't understand. There is small consistency to his beliefs. Either he knows nothing, or is confused, or the world essentially is inconsistent. He claims that all matter is composed of less than a hundred 'elements', joined together in 'compounds'. The elements are constructed of smaller entities: 'electrons', 'protons', 'neutrons', which are not necessarily matter, but forces, depending on your point of view. When electrons move the result is an electric current: a substance or condition — he is not clear here — of great energy and many capabilities. Too much electricity is fatal; in smaller quantities we use it to control our bodies. According to Brunet all sorts of remarkable things can be achieved with electricity."

"Let us provide ourselves an electric current then," said Sklar Hast. "This may become our weapon against the kragen."

"The matter is not so simple. In the first place the electricity must be channeled through metal wires."

"Here is metal," said Sklar Hast, tossing to Meth Cagno the bit of metal he had taken from Blasdel, "though it is hardly likely to be enough."

"The electricity must also be generated," said Cagno, "which on the Home Planet seems to be a complicated process, requiring a great deal of metal."

"Then how do we get metal?"

"On other planets there seems to be no problem. Ore is refined and shaped into a great variety of tools. Here we have no ore. In other cases, metals are extracted from the sea, once again using electricity."

"Hmph," said Sklar Hast. "To procure metal, one needs electricity. To obtain the electricity, metal is required. It seems a closed circle, into which we are unable to break."

Cagno made a dubious face. "It may well be. Brunet mentions various means to generate electricity. There is the 'voltaic cell' — in which two metals are immersed in acid, and he describes a means to generate the acid, using water, brine, and electricity. Then there is thermo-electricity, photo-electricity, chemical electricity, electricity produced by the Rous effect, electricity generated by moving a wire near another wire in which electricity flows. He states that all living creatures produce small quantities of electricity."

"Electricity seems rather a difficult substance to obtain," mused Sklar Hast. "Are there no simple methods to secure metal?"

"Brunet mentions that blood contains a small quantity of iron. He suggests a method for extracting it, by using a high degree of heat. But he also points out that there is at hand no substance capable of serving as a receptacle under such extremes of heat. He states that on the Home World many plants concentrate metallic compounds, and suggests that certain of the sea-plants might do the same. But again either heat or electricity are needed to secure the pure metal."

Sklar Hast ruminated. "Our first and basic problem, as I see it, is self-protection. In short we need a weapon to kill King Kragen. It might be a device of metal — or it might be a larger and more savage kragen, if such exist..." He considered. "Perhaps you should make production of metal and electricity your goal, and let no other pursuits distract you. I am sure that the council will agree, and put at your disposal such helpers as you may need."

"I would gladly do my best."

"And I," said Sklar Hast, "I will reflect upon the kragen."

Three days later the first kragen was seen, a beast of not inconsiderable size, perhaps twenty feet in length. It came cruising along the edge of the float, and observing the men, stopped short and for twenty minutes floated placidly, swirling water back and forth with its vanes. Then slowly it swung about and continued along the line of floats.

By this time a large quantity of stalk and withe had been cut, scraped and racked, as well as a heap of root-wisp, to cure during the rigging of a rope-walk. A week later the new rope was being woven into net.

Two large pads were cut from the side of the float, stripped of rib-trussing, upper and lower membrane, then set adrift. The space thus opened would become a lagoon. Over the severed stalks sleeves were fitted with one end above water; the sap presently exuding would be removed, boiled and aged for varnish and glue. Meanwhile arbors were constructed, seeded with sponge-floss, and lowered into the lagoon. When the withe had cured, hut-frames were constructed, pad membrane stretched over the mesh and daubed inside and out with varnish.

In a month the community had achieved a rude measure of comfort. On four occasions kragen had passed by, and the fourth occurrence seemed to be a return visit of the first. On this fourth visit the kragen paused, inspected the lagoon with care. It tentatively nudged the net, backed away and presently floated off.

Sklar Hast watched the occurrence, went to inspect the new-cut stalk, which now was sufficiently cured. He laid out a pattern and work began. First a wide base was built near the mouth of the lagoon, with a substructure extending down to the main stem of the float. On this base was erected an A-frame derrick of glued withe, seventy feet tall, with integral braces, the entire structure whipped tightly with strong line and varnished. Another identical derrick was built to overhang the ocean. Before either of the derricks were completed a small kragen broke through the net to feast upon the yet unripe sponges. Sklar Hast laughed grimly at the incident. "At your next visit, you will not fare so well," he called to the beast. "May the sponges rot in your stomach!"

The kragen swam lazily off down the line of floats, unperturbed by the threat. It returned two days later. This time the derricks were guyed and in place, but not yet fitted with tackle. Again Sklar Hast reviled the beast, which this time ate with greater fastidiousness, plucking only those sponges which like popcorn had overgrown their husks. The men worked far into the night installing the strut which, when the derrick tilted out over the water, thrust high the topping-halyard to provide greater leverage.

On the next day the kragen returned, and entered the lagoon with insulting assurance: a beast somewhat smaller than that which Sklar Hast had captured on Tranque Float, but nonetheless a creature of respectable size. Standing on the float a stalwart old swindler flung a noose around the creature's turret, and on the pad a line of fifty men marched away with a heavy rope. The astonished kragen was towed to the outward leaning derrick, swung up and in. The dangling vanes were lashed; it was lowered to the float. As soon as the bulk collapsed the watching folk, crying out in glee, shoved forward, almost dancing into the gnashing mandibles. "Back, fools!" roared Sklar Hast. "Do you want to be cut in half? Back!" He was largely ignored. A dozen chisels hacked at the horny hide; clubs battered at the eyes. "Back!" raged Sklar Hast. "Back! What do you achieve by antics such as this? Back!" Daunted, the vengeful folk moved aside. Sklar Hast took chisel and mallet and as he had done on Tranque Float, cut at the membrane joining dome to turret. He was joined by four others; the channel was swiftly cut and a dozen hands ripped away the dome. Again, with pitiless outcry, the crowd surged forward. Sklar Hast's efforts to halt them were fruitless. The nerves and cords of the creature's ganglionic center were torn from the turret, while the kragen jerked and fluttered and made a buzzing sound with its mandibles. The turret was plucked clean of the wet-string fibers as well as other organs, and the kragen lay limp. Sklar Hast moved away in disgust. Another member of the Seven, Nicklas Rile, stepped forward: "Halt now — no more senseless hacking! If the kragen has bones harder than our own, we will want to preserve them for use. Who knows what use can be made of a kragen's cadaver? The hide is tough; the mandibles are harder than the deepest stalk. Let us proceed intelligently!"

Sklar Hast watched from a little distance as the crowd examined the dead beast. He had no further interest in the kragen. A planned experiment had been foiled almost as soon as the hate-driven mob had rushed forward. But there would be more kragen for his derricks; hopefully they could be noosed by the sea-derrick before they broke into the lagoon. In years to come, strong-boats or barges equipped with derricks might even go forth to hunt the kragen...He approached the kragen once again, peered into the empty turret, where now welled a viscous milky blue fluid. James Brunet, in his Dicta, had asserted that the metal iron was a constituent of human blood; conceivably other metals or metallic compounds might be discovered in the blood of a kragen. He found Meth Cagno, who had been watching from a dignified distance, and communicated his hypothesis. Cagno made no dissent. "It may well be the case. Our basic problem, however, remains as before: separating the metal from the dross."

"You have no idea how to proceed?"

Meth Cagno smiled slightly. "I have one or two ideas. In fact, tomorrow, at noon precisely, we will test one of these ideas."

The following day, an hour before noon, Sklar Hast rowed to the isolated pad on which Meth Cagno had established his workshop. Cagno himself was hard at work on an intricate contrivance whose purpose Sklar Hast could not fathom. A rectangular frame of stalk rose ten feet in the air, supporting a six-foot hoop of woven withe in a plane parallel to the surface of the float. To the hoop was glued a rather large sheet of pad-skin, which had been scraped, rubbed and oiled until it was almost transparent. Below Meth Cagno was arranging a box containing ashes. As Sklar Hast watched, he mixed in a quantity of water and some gum, enough to make a gray dough, which he worked with his fingers and knuckles, to leave a saucer-shaped depression.

The sun neared the zenith; Cagno signaled two of his helpers. One climbed up the staging; the other passed up buckets of water. The first poured these upon the transparent membrane, which sagged under the weight.

Sklar Hast watched silently, giving no voice to his perplexity. The membrane, now brimming, seemed to bulge perilously. Meth Cagno, satisfied with his arrangements, joined Sklar Hast. "You are puzzled by this device; nevertheless it is very simple. You own a telescope?"

"I do. An adequately good instrument, though the gum is clouded."

"The purest and most highly refined gum discolors, and even with the most careful craftsmanship, lenses formed of gum yield distorted images, of poor magnification. On the Home World, according to Brunet, lenses are formed of a material called 'glass'."

The sun reached the zenith; Sklar Hast's attention was caught by a peculiar occurrence in the box of damp ash. A white-hot spot had appeared; the ash began to hiss and smoke. He drew near in wonderment. "Glass would seem to be a useful material," Meth Cagno was saying. "Brunet describes it as a mixture of substances occurring in ash together with a compound called 'silica' which is found in ash but also occurs in the husks of sea-ooze: 'plankton', so Brunet calls it. Here I have mixed ash and sea-ooze; I have constructed a water-lens to condense sunlight, I am trying to make glass…" He peered into the box, then lifted it a trifle, bringing the image of the sun to its sharpest focus. The ash glowed red, orange, yellow; suddenly it seemed to slump. With a rod Cagno pushed more ash into the center, until the wooden box gave off smoke, whereupon Cagno pulled it aside, and gazed anxiously at the molten matter in the center. "Something has happened; exactly what we will determine when the stuff is cool." He turned to his bench, brought forward another box, this half-full of powdered charcoal. In a center depression rested a cake of black-brown paste.

"And what do you have there?" asked Sklar Hast, already marveling at Cagno's ingenuity.

"Dried blood. I and my men have drained ourselves pale. Brunet reveals that blood contains iron. Now I will try to burn away the various unstable fluids and oozes, to discover what remains. I hope to find unyielding iron." Cagno thrust the box under the lens. The dried blood smouldered and smoked, then burst into a reeking flame which gave off a nauseous odor. Cagno squinted up at the sun. "The lens burns well only when the sun is overhead, so our time is necessarily limited."

"Rather than water, transparent gum might be used, which then would harden, and the sun could be followed across the sky."

"Unfortunately no gum is so clear as water," said Cagno regretfully. "Candle-plant sap is yellow. Bindlebane seep holds a blue fog."

"What if the two were mixed, so that the blue defeated the yellow? And then the two might be filtered and boiled. Or perhaps water can be coagulated with tincture of bone."

Cagno assented. "Possibly feasible, both."

They turned to watch the blood, now a glowing sponge which tumbled into cinders and then, apparently consumed, vanished upon the surface of the blazing charcoal. Cagno snatched the crucible out from under the lens. "Your blood seems not over-rich," Sklar Hast noted critically. "It might be wise to tap Barquan Blasdel and the other Intercessors; they appear a hearty lot."

Cagno clapped a cover upon the box. "We will know better when the charcoal goes black." He went to his bench, brought back another box. In powdered charcoal stood another tablet, this of black paste. "And what substance is this?" inquired Sklar Hast.

"This," said Meth Cagno, "is kragen blood, which we boiled last night. If man's blood carries iron, what will kragen blood yield? Now we discover." He thrust it under the lens. Like the human blood it began to smoulder and burn, discharging a smoke even more vile than before. Gradually the tablet flaked and tumbled to the surface of the charcoal; as before Cagno removed it and covered it with a lid. Going to his first box, he prodded among the cinders with a bit of sharp bone, scooped out a congealed puddle of fused material which he laid on the bench. "Glass. Beware. It is yet hot."

Sklar Hast, using two pieces of bone, lifted the object. "So this is glass. Hmm. It hardly seems suitable for use as a telescope lens. But it may well prove useful otherwise. It seems dense and hard — indeed, almost metallic."

Cagno shook his head in deprecation. "I had hoped for greater transparency. There are probably numerous impurities in the ash and sea-ooze. Perhaps they can be removed by washing the ash or treating it with acid, or something of the sort."

"But to produce acid, electricity is necessary, or so you tell me."

"I merely quote Brunet."

"And electricity is impossible?"

Cagno pursed his lips. "That we will see. I have hopes. One might well think it impossible to generate electricity using only ash, wood, water and sea-stuff — but we shall see. Brunet offers a hint or two. But first, as to our iron…"

The yield was small: a nodule of pitted gray metal half the size of a pea. "That bit represents three flasks of blood." Cagno remarked glumly. "If we bled every vein on the float we might win sufficient iron for a small pot."

"This is not intrinsically an unreasonable proposal," said Sklar Hast. "We can all afford a flask of blood, or two, or even more during the course of months. To think — we have produced metal entirely on our own resources!"

Cagno wryly inspected the iron nodule. "There is no problem to burning the blood under the lens. If every day ten of the folk come to be bled, eventually we will sink the pad under the accumulated weight of iron." He removed the lid from the third box. "But observe here! We have misused our curses! The kragen is by no means a creature to be despised!"

On the charcoal rested a small puddle of reddish-golden metal: three times as large as the iron nodule. "I presume this metal to be copper, or one of its alloys." said Cagno. "Brunet describes copper as a dark red metal, very useful for the purpose of conducting electricity."

Sklar Hast lifted the copper from the coals, tossed it back and forth till it was cool. "Metal everywhere! Nicklas Rile has been hacking apart the kragen for its bones. He is discarding the internal organs, which are black as snuff-flower. Perhaps they should also be burned under the lens."

"Convey them here, I will burn them. And then, after we burn the kragen's liver, or whatever the organ, we might attempt to burn snuff-flowers as well."

The kragen's internal organs yielded further copper. The snuff-flowers produced only a powder of whitish-yellow ash which Meth Cagno conscientiously stored in a tube labeled: ASH OF SNUFF-FLOWER.

Four days later the largest of the kragen seen so far reappeared. It came swimming in from the west, paralleling the line of floats. A pair of swindlers, returning to the float with a catch of gray-fish, were the first to spy the great black cylinder surmounted by its four-eyed turret. They bent to their oars, shouting the news ahead. A well-rehearsed plan now went into effect. A team of four young swindlers ran to a lightweight coracle, shoved off, paddled out to intercept the kragen. Behind the coracle trailed two ropes, each controlled by a gang of men. The kragen, lunging easily through the water, approached, swimming fifty yards off the float. The coracle eased forward, with one named Bade Beach going forward to stand on the gunwales. The kragen halted the motion of its vanes, to drift and eye the coracle and the derricks with flint-eyed suspicion.

The two swindlers yet at the oars eased the coracle closer. Bade Beach stood tensely, twitching a noose, while the fourth man controlled the lines to the float. The kragen, contemptuous of attack, issued a few nonplussed clicks of the mandibles, twitched the tips of its vanes, creating four whirlpools. The coracle eased closer, to within a hundred feet, eighty — sixty feet. Bade Beach bent forward. The kragen decided to punish the men for their provocative actions and thrust sharply forward. When it was but thirty feet distant, Bade Beach tossed a noose toward the turret — and missed. From the float came groans of disappointment. One of the gangs hastily jerked the coracle back. The kragen swerved, turned, made a second furious charge which brought it momentarily to within five feet of the coracle, whereupon Bade Beach dropped the noose over its turret. From the float came a cheer; both gangs hauled on their lines, one snatching the coracle back to safety, the other tightening the noose and pulling the kragen aside, almost as it touched the coracle.

Thrashing and jerking the kragen was dragged over to the sea-leaning derrick, and hoisted from the water in the same fashion as the first. This was a large beast: the derrick creaked, the float sagged; before the kragen heaved clear from the water sixty-five men were tugging on the end of the lift. The derrick tilted back, the kragen swung in over the float. The vanes were lashed, the beast lowered. Again the onlookers surged forward, laughing, shouting, but no longer exemplifying the fury with which they had attacked the first kragen.

At a distance a group of Intercessors watched with curled lips. They had not reconciled themselves to their new circumstances, and conscious of their status as the lowest of castes worked as little as possible. Chisels and mallets were plied against the kragen turret; the dome was pried loose, the nerve-nodes destroyed. Fiber buckets were brought, the body fluids were scooped out and carried off to evaporation trays.

Sklar Hast had watched from the side. This had been a large beast — about the size of King Kragen when first he had approached the Old Floats, a hundred and fifty years previously. Since they had successfully dealt with this creature, they need have small fear of any other — except King Kragen. And Sklar Hast was forced to admit that the answer was not yet known. No derrick could hoist King Kragen from the water. No line could restrain the thrust of his vanes. No float could bear his weight. Compared to King Kragen, this dead hulk now being hacked apart was a pygmy... From behind came a rush of feet; a woman tugged at his elbow, gasping and gulping in the effort to catch her breath. Sklar Hast, scanning the float in startlement, could see nothing to occasion her distress. Finally she was able to blurt: "Barquan Blasdel has taken to the sea, Barquan Blasdel is gone!"

"What!" cried Sklar Hast.

The woman told her story. For various reasons, including squeamishness and pregnancy, she had absented herself from the killing of the kragen, and kept to her hut at the far side of the float. Seated at her loom she observed a man loading bags into a coracle, but preoccupied with her own concerns she paid him little heed, and presently arose to the preparation of the evening meal. As she kneaded the pulp from which the bread-stuff known as pangolay was baked, it came to her that the man's actions had been noticeably furtive. Why had he not participated in the killing of the kragen? The man she had seen was Barquan Blasdel! The implications of the situation stunned her for a moment. Wiping her hands, she went to the hut where Blasdel and his spouse were quartered, to find no one at home. It was still possible that she was mistaken; Blasdel might even now be watching the killing of the kragen. So she hurried across the float to investigate. But on the way the conviction hardened: the man indeed had been Barquan Blasdel, and she had sought out Sklar Hast with the information.

✳

From the first Barquan Blasdel had made no pretense of satisfaction with his altered circumstances. His former rank counted nothing, in fact aroused antagonism among his float-fellows. Barquan Blasdel grudgingly adapted himself to his new life, building sponge arbors and scraping withe. His spouse, who on Apprise Float had commanded a corps of four maidens and three garden-men, at first rebelled when Blasdel required her to bake pangolay and core sponges "like any low-caste slut", as she put it, but finally she surrendered to the protests of her empty stomach. Her daughters adopted themselves with better grace, and indeed the four youngest participated with great glee at the slaughter of the kragen. The remaining two stayed in the background, eyebrows raised disdainfully at the vulgar fervor of their sisters.

Barquan Blasdel, his spouse, his two older daughters and their lovers were missing, as was a sturdy six-man coracle together with considerable stores. Sklar Hast despatched four coracles in pursuit, but evening had brought the west wind, and there was no way of determining whether Blasdel had paddled directly west, or had taken refuge in the jungle of floats at the western edge of the chain, where he could hide indefinitely.

The coracles returned to report no sign of the fugitives. The Council of Seven gathered to consider the situation. "Our mistake was leniency," complained Robin Magram, a gnarled and weather-beaten old Swindler. "These Intercessors — Barquan Blasdel and all the rest — are our enemies. We should have made a complete job of it, and strangled them. Our qualms have cost us our security."

"Perhaps," said Sklar Hast. "But I for one cannot bring myself to commit murder — even if such murder is in our best interest."

"These other Intercessors now —" Magram jerked his thumb to a group of huts near the central pinion "— what of them? Each wishes us evil. Each is now planning the same despicable act as that undertaken by Barquan Blasdel and his spouse. I feel that they should be killed at once — quietly, without malice, but with finality."

His proposal met no great enthusiasm. Arrel Sincere, a Bezzler of complete conviction and perhaps the most caste-conscious man on the float, said glumly, "What good do we achieve? If Barquan Blasdel returns to the Old Floats, our refuge is known and we must expect inimical actions."

"Not necessarily," contended Meth Cagno. "The folk of the Old Floats gain nothing by attacking us."

Sklar Hast made a pessimistic dissent. "We have escaped King Kragen, we acknowledge no overlord. Misery brings jealousy and resentment. The Intercessors can whip them to a sullen fury." He pitched his voice in a nasal falsetto. " 'Those insolent fugitives! How dare they scamp their responsibility to noble King Kragen? How dare they perform such bestial outrages against the lesser kragen? Everyone aboard the coracles! We go to punish the iconoclasts!' "

"Possibly correct," said Meth Cagno. "But the Intercessors are by no means the most influential folk of the Floats. The Arbiters will hardly agree to any such schemes."

"In essence," said Phyral Berwick, "we have no information. We speculate in a void. In fact Barquan Blasdel may lose himself on the ocean and never return to the Old Floats. He may be greeted with apathy or with excitement. We talk without knowledge. It seems to me that we should take steps to inform ourselves as to the true state of affairs: in short, that we send spies to derive this information for us."

Phyral Berwick's proposal ultimately became the decision of the Seven. They also ordained that the remaining Intercessors be guarded more carefully, until it was definitely learned whether or not Barquan Blasdel had returned to the Old Floats. If such were the case the location of the New Floats was no longer a secret, and the consensus was that the remaining Intercessors should likewise be allowed to return, should they choose to do so. Nicklas Rile considered the decision soft-headed. "Do you think they would warrant us like treatment in a similar situation? Remember, they planned that King Kragen should waylay us!"

"True enough," said Arrel Sincere wearily, "but what of that? We can either kill them, hold them under guard, or let them go their ways, the last option being the least taxing and the most honorable."

Nicklas Rile made no further protest, and the council then concerned itself with the details of the projected spy operation. None of the coracles at hand were considered suitable, and it was decided to build a coracle of special design — long, light, low to the water, with two sails of fine weave to catch every whisper of wind. Three men were named to the operation, all originally of Almack Float, a small community far to the west, in fact next to Sciona, the end of the chain. None of the three men had acquaintance on Apprise and so stood minimal chances of being recognized.

The coracle was built at once. A light keel of laminated and glued withe was shaped around pegs; ribs were bent and lashed into place; diagonal ribs were attached to these, then the whole frame was covered with four layers of varnished pad-skin.

At mid-morning of the fourth day after Barquan Blasdel's flight, the coracle, which was almost a canoe, departed to the west, riding easily and swiftly over the sunny blue water. For three hours it slid along the line of floats, each an islet bedecked in blue, green and purple verdure, surmounted by the arching fronds of prime plant, each surrounded by its constellation of smaller pads. The coracle reached the final float of the group and struck out west across the water. Water swirled and sparkled behind the long oars, the men in their short-sleeved white smocks working easily. Afternoon waned; the rain clouds formed and came scudding with black brooms hanging below. After the rain came sunset, making a glorious display among the broken clouds. The breeze began to blow from the west; the three men crouched and rowed with only sufficient force to maintain headway. Then came the mauve dusk with the constellations appearing and then night with the stars blazing down on the glossy black water. The men took turns sleeping, and the night passed. Before dawn the favoring wind rose; the sails were set, the coracle bubbled ahead, with a chuckling of bow-wave and wake. The second day was like the first. Just before dawn of the third day the men lowered the horn into the water and listened.

Silence.

The men stood erect, looked into the west. Allowing for the increased speed of their passage, Tranque Float should be near at hand. But nothing could be seen but the blank horizons.

The dawn wind came; the sails were set, the coracle surged west. At noon the men, increasingly dubious, ceased paddling, and once more searched the horizons carefully. As before there was nothing visible save the line dividing dark blue from bright blue. The floats by now should be well within sight. Had they veered too far north or too far south?

The men deliberated, and decided that while their own course had generally been true west, the original direction of flight might have been something south of east: hence the floats in all probability lay behind the northern horizon. They agreed to paddle four hours to the north, then if nothing were seen, to return to the south.

Toward the waning of afternoon, with the rain-clouds piling up, far smudges showed themselves. Now they halted, lowered the horn, to hear *crunch crunch crunch*, with startling loudness. The men twisted the tube, to detect the direction of the sound. It issued from the north. Crouching low they listened, ready to paddle hastily away if the sound grew louder. But it seemed to lessen and the direction veered to the east. Presently it died to near inaudibility, and the men proceeded.

The floats took on substance, extending both east and west; soon the characteristic profiles could be discerned, and then the hoodwink towers. Dead ahead was Aumerge, with Apprise Float yet to the west.

So they paddled up the chain, the floats with familiar and beloved names drifting past, floats where their ancestors had lived and died: Aumerge, Quincunx, Fay, Hastings, Quatrefoil, with its curious clover-leaf configuration, and then the little outer group, the Bandings, and beyond, after a gap of a mile, Apprise Float.

The sun set, the hoodwink towers began to flicker, but the configurations could not be read. The men paddled the coracle toward Apprise. Verdure bulked up into the sky; the sounds and odors of the Old Floats wafted across the water, inflicting nostalgic pangs upon each of the men. They landed in a secluded little cove which had been described to them by Phyral Berwick, covered the coracle with leaves and rubbish. According to the plan, two remained by the coracle, while the third, one Henry Bastaff, moved across the float toward the central common and Apprise Market.

Hundreds of people were abroad on this pleasant evening, but Henry Bastaff thought their mood to be weary and even a trifle grim. He went to the ancient Apprise Inn, which claimed to be the oldest building of the floats: a long shed beamed with twisted old stalks, reputedly cut at the astounding depth of three hundred feet. Within was a long bar of laminated strips, golden-brown with wax and use; shelves behind displayed jars and tubes of arrack, beer, and spirits of life, while buffets to each end offered various delicacies and sweetmeats. To the front wide eaves thatched with garwort frond and lit by yellow and red lanterns protected several dozen tables and benches where travelers rested and lovers kept rendezvous. Henry Bastaff seated himself where he could watch both the Apprise hoodwink tower and that of Quatrefoil to the east. The serving maid approached; he ordered beer and nut-wafers. As he drank and ate he listened to conversations at nearby tables and read the messages which flickered up and down the line of floats.

The conversations were uninformative; the hoodwink messages were the usual compendium of announcements, messages, banter. Then suddenly in mid-message came a blaze, all eighteen lights together, to signal news of great importance. Henry Bastaff sat up straight on the bench.

"*Important... information! This... afternoon... Apprise... Intercessor... Barquan Blasdel... kidnaped... by... the... rebels... returned... to... the... Floats... with... his... spouse... and... several... dependents. They... have... a... harrowing... tale... to... tell. The... rebels... are... established... on... a... float... to... the... east... where... they... kill... kragen... with... merciless... glee... and... plan... a... war... of... extermination... upon... the... folk... of... the... old... floats. Barquan Blasdel... escaped... and... after... an... unnerving... voyage... across... the... uncharted... ocean... late... today... landed... on... Green Lamp Float. He... has... called... for... an... immediate... convocation... to... consider... what... measures... to... take... against... the... rebels... who... daily... wax... in... arrogance.*"

Chapter V

Four days later Henry Bastaff reported to the Seven. "Our arrival was precarious, for our initial direction took us many miles to the south of the Old Floats. Nevertheless we arrived. Apparently Blasdel experienced even worse difficulties for he reached Green Lamp Float about the same time that we landed on Apprise. I sat at the Old Tavern when the news came, and I saw great excitement. The people seemed more curious than vindictive, even somewhat wistful. A convocation was called for the following day. Since the folk of Almack Float would attend, I thought it best that Maible and Barway remain hidden. I stained my face, shaved eyebrows, mustache and hair, and at the convocation looked eye to eye with my Uncle Fodor the withe-peeler, who never gave a second glance.

"The convocation was vehement and lengthy. Barquan Blasdel resumed his rank of Apprise Intercessor. In my opinion Vrink Smathe, who had succeeded to the post, found no joy in Blasdel's return.

"With great earnestness Blasdel called for a punitive expedition. He spoke of those who had departed as 'iconoclasts', 'monsters', 'vicious scum of the world, which it was the duty of all decent folk to expunge'.

"He aroused only lukewarm attention. No one showed heart for the project. The new Intercessors in particular were less than enthusiastic. Blasdel accused them of coveting their new posts, which they would lose if the old Intercessors returned. The new Intercessors refuted the argument with great dignity. 'Our concern is solely for the lives of men,' they said. 'What avail is there in destroying these folk? They are gone; good riddance. We shall maintain our ancient ways with more dedication because the dissidents have departed.'

"One of the new Intercessors had a crafty thought: 'Of course, if by some means we can direct King Kragen's attention to these fugitives, that is a different story.'

"Barquan Blasdel was forced to be content with this much. 'How can we do this?'

"'By our usual means for summoning King Kragen: how else?'

"Blasdel agreed. 'It is necessary to hurry. These evil folk kill kragen and smelt metal from the blood. They plan mischief against us, and we must rebuff them with decisive severity.'

"There was further discussion, but no clear resolutions, which exasperated Barquan Blasdel. The convocation dissolved; we caught the evening wind to the east."

The Seven considered Henry Bastaff's report. "At least we are in no immediate peril," ruminated Robin Magram. "It appears that our surest guarantee of security is our custody of the old Intercessors, who would supersede the new officials if rescued. So here is a powerful deterrent against any large-scale attack."

"Still, we always must fear discovery by King Kragen," stated Sklar Hast. "King Kragen is our basic enemy; it is King Kragen whom we must destroy."

After a minute's silence Arrel Sincere said, "That, at the moment, is in the nature of a remote day-dream. In the meantime we must prepare for various contingencies, including demolishment by King Kragen of our new facilities. Also we must maintain a continued source of information: in short, spies must presently return to the Old Floats."

Henry Bastaff looked uncomfortably at his mates. "I will volunteer, for at least one more trip. Much effort and delay could be avoided if it were possible to sail with more assurance of reaching the destination."

Meth Cagno said, "Brunet mentions the 'compass' — an iron needle which points always to the north. The iron is 'magnetized' by wrapping it in a coil of copper strands and passing an electric current through these strands. We have copper, we have iron."

"But no electricity."

"No electricity," agreed Meth Cagno.

"And no means of obtaining electricity."

"As to that — we shall see."

Four days later Meth Cagno summoned the Seven to his workshop. "You will now see electricity produced."

"What? In that device?" Sklar Hast inspected the clumsy apparatus. To one side a tube of hollow stalk five inches in diameter and twenty feet high was supported by a scaffold. The base was contained at one end of a long box holding what appeared to be wet ashes. The far end of the box was closed by a slab of compressed carbon, into which were threaded copper wires. At the opposite end, between the tube and wet ashes was another slab of compressed carbon.

"This is admittedly a crude device, unwieldy to operate and of no great efficiency," said Meth Cagno. "It does however meet our peculiar requirements: which is to say, it produces electricity without metal, through the agency of water pressure. Brunet describes it in his Dicta. He calls it the 'Rous machine'. The tube is filled with water, which is thereby forced through the mud, which is a mixture of ashes and sea-slime. The water carries an electric charge which it communicates to the porous carbon as it seeps through. By this means a small but steady and quite dependable source of electricity is at our hand. As you may have guessed, I have already tested the device, and so can speak with confidence." He turned, snapped his fingers, and his helpers mounted the scaffold carrying buckets of water which they poured into the tube. Meth Cagno connected the wires to a coil of several dozen revolutions. He brought forward a dish. On a cork rested a small rod of iron.

"I have already magnetized this iron," said Cagno. "Note how it points to the north? Now — I bring it near the end of the coil. See it jerk! Electricity is flowing in the wire!"

The other members of the Seven were impressed. "And this iron needle will now serve to guide Henry Bastaff?"

"So I believe. But the Rous machine provides an even more dramatic possibility. With electricity we can disassociate sea-water to produce, after certain operations, the acid of salt, and a caustic of countering properties as well. The acid can then be used to produce more highly concentrated streams of electricity — if we are able to secure more metal. There is iron in our blood: I ask myself, where does the iron originate? Which of our foods contains the iron? I plan to reduce each of our foods under the lens, as well as any other distinctive substance which might yield a concentration of metal." He turned, went to the table, returned with a glistening object. "Look. A bottle of glass. Bolin Hyse has produced this bottle. He fashioned a tube of copper, fixed it to a longer tube of withe, dipped the copper into molten glass and blew. The result —" Meth Cagno inspected the object critically "— is not beautiful. The glass is gray and streaked with ash. The shape is uncertain. Nevertheless — here is a glass bottle, produced from ash and sea-ooze. Eventually, we will be building devices of great intricacy."

"Subject to the indulgence of King Kragen," muttered Sklar Hast.

Meth Cagno threw up his hands. "King Kragen bah! We shall kill him. When next a kragen is brought to the derrick, allow me to deal with it. There are tests I wish to make."

Chapter VI

On the world which had no name, there were no seasons, no variations of climate except those to be found by traversing the latitudes. Along the equatorial doldrums, where floats of sea-plant grew in chains and clots, each day was like every other, and the passage of a year could be detected only by watching the night sky. Though the folk had small need for accurate temporal distinctions, each day was numbered and each year named for some significant event. A duration of twenty-two years was a 'surge', and was also reckoned by number. Hence a given date might be known as the 349th day in the Year of Malvinon's Deep Dive during the Tenth Surge. Time-reckoning was almost exclusively the province of the Scriveners. To most of the folk life seemed as pellucid and effortless as the glassy blue sea at noon.

King Kragen's attack upon Tranque Float occurred toward the year's end, which thereupon became the Year of Tranque's Abasement, and it was generally assumed that the following year would be known as the Year of the Dissenters' Going.

As the days passed and the year approached its midpoint, Barquan Blasdel, Apprise Intercessor, instead of allowing the memory of his kidnaping to grow dim, revived it daily with never-flagging virulence. Each evening saw a memorandum from Barquan Blasdel flicker up and down the chain of floats: "Vigilance is necessary. The dissidents are led by seven men of evil energy. They flout the majesty of King Kragen; they despise the folk who maintain old traditions and most especially the Intercessors. They must be punished and taught humility. Think well on this matter. Ask yourself how may the dissidents most expeditiously be chastened?"

The other Intercessors, while politely attending Blasdel's urgencies, did little to give them effect. Blasdel daily became more hectic. At a Conclave of Notables his demands that the floats assemble an armada to invade the new floats and destroy the dissidents was vetoed by the Arbiters, Guild Masters and Caste Chiefs, on the grounds of utter infeasibility and pointlessness. "Let them be," growled Emacho Feroxibus, Chief of the Quatrefoil Bezzlers. "So long as they do not molest us, why should we molest them? I for one don't care to risk drowning for so dismal a cause."

Barquan Blasdel, containing his temper, explained carefully, "The matter is more complex than this. Here is a group who have fled in order to avoid paying their due to King Kragen. If they are allowed to prosper, to make profit of their defection, then other folk may be tempted to wonder, why do we not do likewise? If the sin of kragen-killing becomes vulgar recreation, where is reverence? Where is continuity? Where is obedience to High Authority?"

"This may be true," stated Providence Dringle, Chief Hoodwink for the Populous Equity Float. "Nonetheless in my opinion the cure is worse than the complaint. And to risk a heretical opinion, I must say the benefits we derive from High Authority no longer seem commensurate with the price we pay."

Blasdel swung about in shock, as did the other Intercessors. "May I ask your meaning?" Blasdel inquired icily.

"I mean that King Kragen consumes six to seven bushels of choice sponges daily. He maintains his rule in the waters surrounding the floats, true, but what do we need fear from the lesser kragen? By your own testimony the dissidents have developed a method to kill the kragen with facility."

Blasdel said with frigid menace, "I can not overlook the fact that your remarks are identical to the preposterous ravings of the dissidents, who so rightly shall be obliterated."

"Do not rely on my help," said Providence Dringle.

"Nor mine," said Emacho Feroxibus.

The conclave had divided into two antagonistic camps, the Intercessors and certain others supporting Barquan Blasdel, though few favored the more extreme of his propositions.

From the foliage which surrounded the scene of the conclave came a crash and a muttered exclamation. A number of men sprang into the shrubbery. There was a confused scuffle, the sound of blows and exclamations, and presently a man was dragged out into the lamplight. His skin was dark, his face was bland and bare of hair.

Barquan Blasdel marched forward. "Who are you? Why do you lurk in these forbidden precincts?"

The man staggered and blinked foolishly. "Is this the tavern? Pour out the arrack, pour for all! I am a stranger on Apprise, I would know the quality of your food and drink."

Emacho Feroxibus snorted, "The fool is drunk, turn him off the float."

"No!" roared Blasdel, jerking forward in excitement. "This is a dissident, this is a spy! I know him well! He has shaved his head and his face, but never can he defeat my acuity! He is here to learn our secrets!"

The group turned their attention upon the man, who blinked even more vehemently. "A spy? Not I. I came to find the Old Tavern."

Blasdel sniffed the air in front of the captive's face. "There is no odor: neither beer nor arrack nor spirits of life. Come! All must satisfy themselves as to this so that there will be no subsequent contradictions and vacillations."

"What is your name?" demanded Vogel Womack, the Parnassus Arbiter. "Your float and your caste?"

The captive took a deep breath, cast off his pretense of drunkenness. "I am Henry Bastaff. I am a dissident. I am here to learn if you plan evil against us. That is my sole purpose."

"A spy!" cried Barquan Blasdel in a voice of horror. "A self-confessed spy!"

"It is a serious matter," said Emacho Feroxibus, "but the truth of the matter is undoubtedly as he has averred."

The Intercessors set up a chorus of indignant hoots and jibes. Barquan Blasdel said, "He is guilty of at least a double offense: first, the various illegalities entering into his dissidence; and second, his insolent attempt to conspire against us, the staunch and the faithful. The crime has occurred on Apprise Float, and affects our relations with King Kragen. Hence, I, Barquan Blasdel, am compelled to demand an extreme penalty. Parler Denk, the new Apprise Arbiter, in such instance, can implement such a penalty by simple executive command, without consultation with the council. Arbiter Denk, what is your response?"

"Be not hasty," warned Vogel Womack. "Tomorrow the man's deed will not appear so grave."

Barquan Blasdel ignored him. "Parler Denk, what is your response?"

"I agree, in all respects. The man is a vile dissident, an agent of turmoil and a spy. He must suffer an extreme penalty. To this declaration there will be allowed no appeal."

On the following day a significant alteration was made in the method by which King Kragen was tendered his customary oblation. Previously, when King Kragen approached a lagoon with the obvious intent of feasting, arbors overgrown with sponges were floated to the edge of the net, for King Kragen to pluck with his palps. Now the sponges were plucked, heaped upon a great tray and floated forth between a pair of coracles. When the tray was in place, Barquan Blasdel went to his sanctum. King Kragen was close at hand; the scraping of his chitin armor sounded loud in Blasdel's listening device. Blasdel sounded his submarine horn; the scraping ceased, then began once more, increasing in intensity. King Kragen was approaching.

He appeared from the east, turret and massive torso riding above the surface, the great rectangular swimming platform gliding through the ocean on easy strokes of his vanes.

The forward eyes noted the offering. King Kragen approached casually, inspected the tray, began to scoop the sponges into his maw with his forward palps.

From the float folk watched in somber speculation mingled with awe. Barquan Blasdel came gingerly forth to stand on the edge of the pad, to gesticulate in approval as King Kragen ate.

The tray was empty. King Kragen made no motion to depart; Blasdel swung about, gestured to an understudy. "The sponges: how many were offered?"

"Seven bushels. King Kragen usually eats no more."

"Today he seems to hunger. Are others plucked?"

"Those for the market: another five bushels."

"They had best be tendered King Kragen; it is not well to stint." While King Kragen floated motionless, the coracles were pulled to the float, another five bushels were poured upon the tray, and the tray thrust back toward King Kragen. Again he ate, consuming all but a bushel or two. Then, replete, he submerged till only his turret remained above the water. And there he remained, moving sluggishly a few feet forward, a few feet backward.

Nine days later a haggard Denis Maible reported the capture of Henry Bastaff to the Seven. "On the following day King Kragen had not yet moved. It was clear that the new method of feeding had impressed him favorably. So at noon the tray was again filled, with at least ten bushels of sponge, and again King Kragen devoured the lot.

"During this time we learned that Henry Bastaff had been captured and condemned — indeed the news had gone out over the hoodwink towers — but we could not discover where he was imprisoned or what fate had been planned for him.

"On the third day Blasdel made an announcement, to the effect that the dissident spy had sinned against King Kragen and King Kragen had demanded the privilege of executing him.

"At noon the tray went out. At the very top was a wide board supporting a single great sponge; and below, the usual heap. King Kragen had not moved fifty yards for three days. He approached the tray, reached for the topmost sponge. It seemed fastened to the board. King Kragen jerked, and so decapitated Henry Bastaff, whose head had been stuffed into the sponge. It was a horrible sight, with the blood spouting upon the pile of sponges. King Kragen seemed to devour them with particular relish.

"With Henry Bastaff dead, we no longer had reason to delay — except for curiosity. King Kragen showed no signs of moving, of visiting the other floats. It was clear that he found the new feeding system to his liking. By then, Apprise Float was bereft of sponges.

"The Intercessors conferred by hoodwink and apparently arrived at a means of dealing with the situation. King Kragen's meal on the fourth day was furnished by Granolt Float and ferried to Apprise by coracle. On the fifth day the sponges were brought from Sankeston. It appears that King Kragen is now a permanent guest at Apprise Float...On the evening of the fifth day we launched our coracle and returned to New Float."

The Seven were silent. Phyral Berwick finally made a sound of nausea. "It is a repulsive situation. One which I would like to change."

Sklar Hast looked toward Meth Cagno. "There is the man who smelts metal."

Meth Cagno smiled wryly. "Our enterprises are multiplying. We have found a number of sources which when burnt in sufficiently large quantities produce at least four different metals. None seem to be iron. We have bled everyone on the float, twice or three times: this blood has yielded several pounds of iron, which we have hammered and refined until now it is hard and keen beyond all belief. Our electrical device has produced twenty-four flasks of acid of salt, which we maintain in bottles blown by our glass shop, which is now an establishment completely separated from the smelting."

"This is encouraging and interesting," said Robin Magram, "but what will it avail against King Kragen?"

Meth Cagno pursed his lips. "I have not yet completed my experiments, and I am unable to make an unequivocal answer. But in due course our preparations will be complete."

Chapter VII

Some two hundred days later, toward the end of the year, swindlers working the waters to the east of Tranque Float spied the armada from the east. There were two dozen canoes sheathed with a dull black membrane. Each canoe carried a crew of thirty, who wore helmets and corselets of the same black substance, and carried lances tipped with orange metal. They accompanied a strange craft, like none ever seen before along the floats. It was rectangular, and rode on four parallel pontoons. A bulwark of the black sheathing completely encircled the barge, to a height of five feet. Fore and aft rose stout platforms on which were mounted massive crossbow-like contrivances, the arms of which were laminated stalk and kragen chitin, and the string cables woven from strips of kragen leather. The hold of the barge contained two hundred glass vats, each of two quarts capacity, each two-thirds full of pale liquid. The barge was propelled by oars — a score on either side — and moved with not inconsiderable speed.

The swindlers paddled with all speed to Tranque Float and the hoodwink towers flickered an alarm: *The… dissidents… are… returning… in… force! They… come… in… strange… black… canoes… and… an… even… more… peculiar… black… barge. They… show… no… fear.*

The flotilla continued up the line of floats: Thrasneck, Bickle, Green Lamp, and at last Fay, Quatrefoil, and finally Apprise.

In the water before the lagoon lolled King Kragen — a bloated monstrous King Kragen, dwarfing the entire flotilla.

King Kragen swung about, the monstrous vanes sucking whirlpools into the ocean. The eyes with opalescent films shifting back and forth within, fixed upon the black sheathing of canoe, barge and armor, and he seemed to recognize the substance as kragen hide, for he emitted a snort of terrible displeasure, jerked his vanes, and the ocean sucked and swirled.

The barge swung sidewise to King Kragen. The two crossbows, each cocked and strung, each armed with an iron harpoon smelted from human blood, were aimed.

King Kragen sensed menace. Why otherwise should men be so bold? He twitched his vanes, inched forward — to within a hundred feet. Then he lunged. Vanes dug the water; with an ear-shattering shriek King Kragen charged, mandibles snapping.

The men at the crossbows were pale as sea-foam; their fingers twitched. Sklar Hast turned to call, "Fire!" but his voice caught in his throat and what he intended for an incisive command sounded as a startled stammer. But the command was understood. The left crossbow thudded, snapped, sang: the harpoon, trailing a black cable sprang at King Kragen's turret, buried itself. King Kragen hissed.

The right crossbow fired; the second harpoon stabbed deep into the turret. Sklar Hast motioned with his hand to the men in the hold. "Connect." The men joined copper to copper. In the hold two hundred voltaic cells, each holding ten thin-leaved cathodes and ten thin-leaved anodes, connected first in four series of fifty, and these four series in parallel, poured a gush of electricity along the copper cables wrapped in varnished pad-skin, which led to the harpoons. Into King Kragen's turret poured the energy, and King Kragen went stiff. His vanes protruded at right angles to his body. Sklar Hast said to Meth Cagno, "Your experiments seem to be as valid as with the lesser kragen — luckily."

"I never doubted," said Meth Cagno.

Sklar Hast waved to the canoes. They swung toward King Kragen, beaching on the rigid subsurface platform. The men swarmed up the torso. With mallets and copper chisels they attacked the lining between dome and turret wall. There was thirty feet of seam, but many hands at work. The lining was broken; bars were inserted into the crack; all heaved. With a splitting sound the dome was dislodged. It slid over and into the water; the men leapt down into the knotted gray cords and nodes and began hacking.

On Apprise Float a great throng had gathered. One man, running back and forth, was Barquan Blasdel. Finally he persuaded several score of men to embark in coracles and attack the flotilla. Eight black canoes were on guard. Paddles dug the water, the canoes picked up momentum, crashed into the foremost coracles, crushing the fragile shells, throwing the men into the water. The canoes backed away, turned toward the other coracles, which retreated.

Out in the lagoon King Kragen's nerve nodes had been cast into the sea. The harpoons were extracted, the flow of electricity extinguished.

King Kragen floated limp, a lifeless hulk. The men plunged into the sea to wash themselves, clambered back up on the dead swimming platform, boarded their canoes.

The barge now eased toward Apprise Float. Barquan Blasdel gesticulated to the folk like a crazy man. "To arms! Stakes, chisels, mallets, knives, bludgeons! Smite the miscreants!"

Sklar Hast called to the throng, "King Kragen is dead. What do you say to this?"

There was silence; then a faint cheer and a louder cheer, and finally uproarious celebration.

Sklar Hast pointed a finger at Barquan Blasdel. "That man must die. He murdered Henry Bastaff. He has fed your food to the vile King Kragen. He would have continued doing so until King Kragen overgrew the entire float."

Barquan Blasdel made the mistake of turning to flee — an act which triggered the counter-impulse to halt him. When he was touched, he smote, and again he erred, for the blow brought a counter-blow and Barquan Blasdel was presently torn to pieces.

"What now?" called the crowd. "What now, Sklar Hast?"

"Nothing whatever, unless you choose to kill the other Intercessors. King Kragen is dethroned; our duty is done. We now return to the New Floats."

From the shore someone called out, "Come ashore, men of the New Floats, and share our great joy. Greet your old friends, who long have been saddened at your absence! Tonight the arrack will flow and we will play the pipes and dance in the light of our yellow lamps!"

Sklar Hast shook his head, waved his hand and called back: "Now we return to the New Floats. In a week certain of us will return, and the weeks after that will see constant traffic between Old and New Floats, and out to floats still unknown. King Kragen is dead, the lesser kragen are our prey, so who is there to stop us? Now that we know metal and glass and electricity, all things are possible. Rejoice with all our good will. For now, farewell."

The barge and the canoes swung about; oars and paddles dipped into the ocean, the black flotilla receded into the east, and disappeared.

GUYAL OF SFERE

This is one of the tales from The Dying Earth. The time is the remote future. The sun gutters like a candle in the wind. Misanthropic creatures wander the forests: grues, leucomorphs, deodands. The power of the magicians has waned; those still extant spend their energies in plots against each other. In ruins along the coasts of Ascolais and Almery a few languid men and women amuse themselves until that hour when the sun finally glimmers into darkness and the earth grows cold.

GUYAL OF SFERE had been born one apart from his fellows and early proved a vexation for his sire. Normal in outward configuration, there existed within his mind a void which ached for nourishment. It was as if a spell had been cast upon his birth, a harassment visited on the child in a spirit of sardonic mockery, so that every occurrence, no matter how trifling, became a source of wonder. Even as young as four seasons he was expounding such inquiries as:

"Why do squares have more sides than triangles?"

"How will we see when the sun goes dark?"

"Do flowers grow under the ocean?"

"Do stars hiss and sizzle when rain comes by night?"

To which his impatient sire gave answers:

"So it was ordained by the Pragmatica; squares and triangles must obey the rote."

"We will be forced to grope and feel our way."

"I have not verified this matter; only the Curator would know."

"Never. The stars are above the rain, higher even than the highest clouds, and swim in a rarified air where rain can never breed."

As Guyal grew to youth, this void in his mind, instead of dwindling, becoming sedimented with wax, throbbed with a more violent ache. And so he asked:

"Why do people die when they are killed?"

"Where does beauty vanish when it goes?"

"How long have men lived on Earth?"

"What is beyond the sky?"

To which his sire, biting acerbity back from his lips, would respond:

"Death is the heritage of life; a man's vitality is like air in a bladder. Poinct this bubble and away, away, away, flees life, like the color of fading dream."

"Beauty is a luster which love bestows to guile the eye. Therefore it may be said that only when the brain is without love will the eye look and see no beauty."

"Some say men germinated in the soil like grubs in a corpse; others aver that the first men desired residence and so created Earth by sorcery. The question is shrouded in technicality; only the Curator may answer with exactness."

"An endless waste."

Guyal pondered and postulated, proposed and expounded, until he found himself the subject of surreptitious humor. The demesne was visited by a rumor that a gleft, coming upon Guyal's mother in labor, had stolen part of Guyal's brain, which deficiency he now industriously sought to restore.

Guyal therefore drew himself apart and roamed the grassy hills of Sfere in solitude. But ever was his mind acquisitive, ever did he seek to exhaust the lore of all around him, until at last his father in vexation refused to hear further inquiries, declaring that all knowledge had been known, that the trivial and useless had been discarded, leaving only that residue necessary to a sound man.

At this time Guyal was in his first manhood, a slight but erect youth with wide clear eyes, a penchant for severely elegant dress, a firm somewhat compressed mouth.

Hearing his father's angry statement, Guyal said, "One more question, then I ask no more."

"Speak," declared his father. "One more question I grant you."

"You have often referred me to the Curator; who is he, and where may I find him?"

A moment the father scrutinized the son whom he now considered past the verge of madness. Then he responded in a quiet voice, "The Curator guards the Museum of Man which antique legend places in the Land of the Falling Wall — beyond the mountains of Fer Aquila and north of Ascolais. It is not certain that either Curator or Museum still exist; still it would seem that if the Curator knows all things, as is the legend, then surely he would know the wizardly foil to death."

Guyal said, "I would seek the Curator and the Museum of Man, that I likewise may know all things."

The father said with patience, "I will bestow on you my fine white horse, my Expansible Egg for your shelter, my Scintillant Dagger to illuminate the night. In addition, I lay a blessing along the trail, and danger will slide you by so long as you never wander aside."

Guyal quelled the hundred new questions at his tongue, including an inquisition as to where his father had learned these manifestations of sorcery, and accepted the gifts: the horse, the magic shelter, the dagger with the luminous pommel, and the blessing to guard him from the disadvantageous circumstances which plagued those who travelled the dim trails of Ascolais.

He caparisoned the horse, honed the dagger, cast a last glance around the old manse at Sfere, and set forth to the north.

He ferried the River Scaum on an old barge. Aboard the barge and so off the trail, the blessing lost its cogency and in fact seemed to stimulate a counterinfluence, so that the barge-tender, who coveted Guyal's rich accoutrements, struck out suddenly with his cudgel. Guyal fended off the blow and tripped the man into the murky deep.

Mounting the north bank of the Scaum he saw ahead the Porphiron Scar, the dark poplars and white columns of Kaiin, the dull gleam of Sanreale Bay.

Wandering the crumbled streets, he put the languid inhabitants such a spate of questions that one in wry jocularity commended him to a professional augur.

This, a lank hermetic with red-rimmed eyes and a stained white beard, dwelled in a booth painted with the Signs of the Aumoklopelastianic Cabal.

"What are your fees?" inquired Guyal cautiously.

"I respond to three questions," stated the augur. "For twenty terces I phrase the answer in clear and decisive language; for ten I use a professional cant, which occasionally admits of ambiguity; for five I speak a parable which you must interpret as you will; and for one terce I babble in an unknown tongue."

"First I must inquire, how profound is your knowledge?"

"I know all," responded the augur. "The secrets of red and the secrets of black, the lost spells of Grand Motholam, the way of the fish and the voice of the bird."

"And where have you learned all these things?"

"By pure induction," explained the augur. "I retire into my booth, I closet myself with never a glint of light and, so sequestered, I resolve the mysteries of the world."

"Controlling such efficacy," ventured Guyal, "why do you live so meagerly, with not an ounce of fat to your frame and miserable rags to your back?"

The augur stood back in fury. "Go along with you! Already I have wasted fifty terces of wisdom on you who have never a copper to your pouch. If you desire free enlightenment," and he cackled in mirth, "seek out the Curator." He sheltered himself in his booth.

Guyal took lodging for the night, and in the morning went on his way. The trail made a wide detour around the haunted ruins of Old Town, then took to the fabulous forest.

For many a day Guyal rode toward the north. By night he surrounded himself and his horse in the Expansible Egg, a membrane impermeable to thew, claw, pressure, sound and chill, and rested at ease despite the avid creatures of the dark.

The dull sun fell behind; the days grew wan and the nights bitter, and at last the crags of Fer Aquila showed as a tracing on the north horizon. In this region the forest was a scattering of phalurge and daobado: these last, massive constructions of heavy bronze branches clumped with dark balls of foliage. Beside a giant of the species Guyal came upon a village of turf huts. A group of surly louts appeared and surrounded him with expressions of curiosity. Guyal, no less than the villagers, had questions to ask, but none would speak till the hetman strode up — a burly man in a shaggy fur hat, a cloak of brown fur and a bristling beard, so that it was hard to see where one ended and the other began. He exuded a rancid odor which displeased Guyal, although from motives of courtesy, he took pains to keep his distaste concealed.

"Where go you?" asked the hetman.

"I wish to cross the mountains to the Museum of Man," said Guyal. "Which way does the trail lead?"

The hetman pointed out a notch on the silhouette of the mountains. "There is Omona Gap, which is the shortest and best route, though there is no trail. None comes and none goes, since when you pass the Gap, you walk an unknown land. And with no traffic there manifestly need be no trail."

The news did not cheer Guyal.

"How then is it known that Omona Gap is on the way to the Museum?"

The hetman shrugged. "Such is our tradition."

Guyal turned his head at a hoarse snuffling and saw a pen of woven wattles. In a litter of filth and matted straw stood a number of hulking men eight or nine feet tall. They were naked, with wax-colored faces, shocks of dirty yellow hair and watery blue eyes. As Guyal watched one of them ambled to a trough and noisily began to gulp gray mash.

Guyal said, "What manner of things are these?"

The hetman guffawed at Guyal's ignorance. "They are oasts, naturally." He indicated Guyal's white horse. "Never have I seen a stranger oast than the one you bestride. Ours carry us more easily and appear to be less vicious; in addition no flesh is more delicious than oast properly braised and kettled."

Standing close he fondled the metal of Guyal's saddle and the red and yellow embroidered quilt. "Your deckings however are rich and of superb quality. I will therefore bestow you my large and weighty oast in return for this creature with its accoutrements."

Guyal politely declared himself satisfied with his present mount, and the hetman shrugged his shoulders.

A horn sounded. The hetman looked about, then turned back to Guyal. "Food is prepared; will you eat?"

Guyal glanced toward the oast-pen. "I am not presently hungry, and I must hasten forward. However, I am grateful for your kindness."

He departed; as he passed under the arch of the great daobado he turned a glance back toward the village. There seemed an unwonted activity among the huts. Remembering the hetman's covetous touch at his saddle, and aware that no longer did he ride the trail, Guyal urged his horse forward and pounded fast under the trees.

As he neared the foothills the forest dwindled to a savannah, floored with a dull, jointed grass that creaked under the horse's hooves. Guyal glanced up and down the plain. The sun wallowed in the southwest; the light across the plain was dim and watery. Another hour, then the dark night of the latter-day Earth. Guyal twisted in the saddle, looked behind him. Four oasts, carrying men on their shoulders, came trotting from the forest. Sighting Guyal they broke into a lumbering run. With a crawling skin Guyal wheeled his horse and eased the reins; the white horse loped across the plain toward Omona Gap. Behind ran the oasts, bestraddled by the fur-cloaked villagers.

The sun touched the horizon. Guyal looked back to his pursuers, bounding now a mile behind, then turned his gaze to the forest ahead. An ill place to ride by night, but where was his choice?

The foliage loomed above him; he passed under the first gnarled daobados. He changed directions, turned once, twice, a third time, then stood his horse to listen. Far away a crashing in the brake reached his ears. Guyal dismounted, led the horse into a deep hollow where a bank of foliage made a screen. Presently the four men on their hulking oasts passed across the afterglow, black double-shapes in attitudes suggestive of ill-temper and disappointment.

The thud and pad of feet dwindled and died.

The horse moved restlessly; the foliage rustled.

A damp air passed down the hollow and chilled the back of Guyal's neck. Darkness stood in the hollow like ink in a basin.

Guyal urged his horse up to the height and sat listening. Far down the wind he heard a hoarse call. Turning in the opposite direction he let the horse choose its own path.

Branches and boughs knit patterns on the fading sky; the air smelt of moss and mold. The horse stopped short. Guyal, tensing in every muscle, leaned a little forward. The air was still, uncanny; his eyes could plumb not ten feet into the black. Somewhere near was death — grinding death, to come as a sudden shock.

Sweating cold, afraid to stir a muscle, he forced himself to dismount. Stiffly he slid from the saddle, brought forth the Expansible Egg and flung it around his horse and himself. Safety. Guyal released the pressure of his breath.

Guyal of Sfere had lost his way in a land of wind and naked crags. As night came he slouched numbly in the saddle while his horse took him where it would. Somewhere the ancient way through Omona Gap led to the northern tundra, but now, under a chilly overcast, north, east, south and west were alike.

The horse halted and Guyal found himself at the brink of a quiet valley. Guyal leaned forward, staring. Below spread a dark city. Mist blew along the streets; the afterglow fell dull on slate roofs.

The horse snorted and scraped the stony ground.

"A strange town," said Guyal, "with no lights, no sound, no smell of smoke… Doubtless an abandoned ruin from ancient times…"

He debated descending to the streets. At times the old ruins were haunted by peculiar distillations. On the other hand such a ruin might be joined to the tundra by a trail. With this thought in mind he started his horse down the slope.

He entered the town and the hooves rang loud and sharp on the cobbles. The buildings were stone and dark mortar and seemed in uncommonly good preservation. A few lintels had cracked and sagged, a few walls gaped open, but for the most part the stone houses had successfully met the gnaw of time… Guyal scented smoke. Did people live here still? He would proceed with caution.

Before a building which seemed to be a hostelry flowers bloomed in an urn. Guyal reined his horse and reflected that flowers were rarely cherished by persons of hostile disposition.

"Hello!" he called — once, twice.

No heads peered from the doors, no orange flicker brightened the windows. Guyal slowly turned and rode on.

The street widened and twisted toward a large hall, where Guyal saw a light. The building had a high façade, broken by four large windows, each shielded by two blinds of corroded bronze filigree. A marble balustrade fronting the terrace shimmered bone-white behind, a portal of massive wood stood slightly ajar; from here came the beam of light and also a strain of music.

Guyal of Sfere, halting, gazed not at the house nor at the light through the door. He dismounted and bowed to the young woman who sat pensively along the course of the balustrade. Though it was very cold, she wore but a simple gown, yellow-orange, a daffodil's color. Topaz hair fell loose to her shoulders and gave her face a cast of gravity and thoughtfulness.

As Guyal straightened from his greeting the woman nodded, smiled slightly, and absently fingered the hair by her cheek.

"A bitter night for travelers."

"A bitter night for musing on the stars," responded Guyal.

She smiled again. "I am not cold. I sit and dream … I listen to the music."

"What place is this?" inquired Guyal, looking up the street, down the street, and once more to the girl. "Are there any here but yourself?"

"This is Carchasel," said the girl, "abandoned by all ten thousand years ago. Only I and my aged uncle live here, finding this place a refuge from the Saponids of the tundra." She rose to her feet. "But you are cold and weary," said the girl, "and I keep you standing in the street. Our hospitality is yours."

"Which I gladly accept," said Guyal, "First I must stable my horse."

"He will be content in the house yonder. We have no stable." She indicated a long stone building with a door opening into blackness.

Guyal took the white horse thither and removed the bridle and saddle; then, standing in the doorway, he listened to the music he had noted before, the piping of an ancient air.

"Strange," he muttered, stroking the horse's muzzle. "The uncle plays music, the girl stares alone at the stars of the night…" He considered a moment. "I may be over-suspicious. If witch she be, there is naught to be gained from me. If they be simple refugees as she says, and lovers of music, they may enjoy the airs from Ascolais; it will repay, in some measure, their hospitality." He reached into his saddle-bag, brought forth his flute, and tucked it into his boot.

He returned to where the girl awaited him.

"You have not told me your name," she reminded him, "that I may introduce you to my uncle."

"I am Guyal of Sfere, by the River Scaum in Ascolais. And you?"

She smiled, pushing the portal wider. Warm yellow light fell into the cobbled street.

"I have no name. I need none. There has never been any but my uncle; and when he speaks there is no one to answer but I."

Guyal stared in astonishment; then, deeming his wonder too apparent for courtesy he controlled his expression. Perhaps she suspected him of wizardry and feared to pronounce her name lest he make magic with it.

They entered a flagged hall and the sound of piping grew louder.

"I will call you Ameth, if I may," said Guyal. "That is a flower of the south, as golden and kind as you seem to be."

She nodded. "You may call me Ameth."

They entered a tapestry-hung chamber. A great fire glowed at one wall, and here stood a table bearing food. On a bench sat the musician — an old man, untidy, unkempt. White hair hung tangled down his back; his beard, in no better case, was dirty and yellow. He wore a ragged kirtle, by no means clean, and the leather of his sandals had broken into dry cracks. Strangely, he did not take the flute from his mouth but kept up his piping; and the girl in yellow, so Guyal noted, seemed to move in rhythm to the tones.

"Uncle Ludowik," she cried in a gay voice, "I bring you a guest, Sir Guyal of Sfere."

Guyal looked into the man's face and wondered. The eyes, though somewhat rheumy with age, were gray and intelligent and, so Guyal thought, bright with a strange joy, which further puzzled Guyal, for the lines of the face indicated nothing other than years of misery.

"Perhaps you play?" inquired Ameth. "My uncle is a great musician, and this is his time for music. He has kept the routine for many years…" She turned and smiled at Ludowik the musician, who jerked his head and contrived an acquiescent grin, never taking the flute from his mouth.

Ameth motioned to the bounteous table. "Eat, Guyal, and I will pour you wine. Afterwards perhaps you will play the flute for us."

"Gladly," said Guyal, and he noticed how the joy on Ludowik's face grew more apparent, quivering around the corners of his mouth.

He ate and Ameth poured him golden wine until his head went to reeling. And never did Ludowik cease his piping — a tender melody of running water, then a grave tune that told of the lost ocean to the west, then a simple melody such as a child might sing at his games. Guyal noted with wonder how Ameth fitted her mood to the music — grave and gay as the music led her. Strange! thought Guyal. But then — people thus isolated were apt to develop peculiar mannerisms, and they seemed kindly withal.

He finished his meal and stood erect, steadying himself against the table. Ludowik was lilting a melody of glass birds swinging round and round in the sunlight. Ameth came dancing over to him and stood close, so that he smelled the perfume of her loose golden hair. Her face was happy and wild... Peculiar how Ludowik watched so grimly, and yet without a word. Perhaps he misdoubted a stranger's intent. Still...

"Now," breathed Ameth, "perhaps you will play the flute; you are strong and young." Then she said, as she saw Guyal's eyes widen. "I mean you will play on the flute for old Uncle Ludowik, and he will be happy and go off to bed — and then we will sit and talk far into the night."

"Gladly will I play the flute," said Guyal. "I am accounted quite skillful at my home in Sfere."

Glancing at Ludowik, he surprised an expression of crazy gladness. Marvelous that a man should be so fond of music!

"Then — play!" breathed Ameth, urging him a little toward Ludowik and the flute.

"Perhaps," suggested Guyal, "I had better wait till your uncle pauses. I would seem discourteous —"

"No, as soon as you indicate that you wish to play, he will let off. Merely take the flute. You see," she confided, "he is rather deaf."

"Very well," said Guyal, "except that I have my own flute." And he brought it out from his boot. "Why — what is the matter?" For a change had come over the girl and the old man. A quick light had risen in her eyes, and Ludowik's strange gladness had gone, and there was but dull hopelessness in his eyes, stupid resignation.

Guyal slowly stood back, bewildered. "Do you not wish me to play?"

There was a pause. "Of course," said Ameth, young and charming once more. "But I'm sure that Uncle Ludowik would enjoy hearing you play his flute. He is accustomed to the pitch; another scale might be unfamiliar..."

Ludowik nodded, and hope again shone in the rheumy old eyes. It was indeed a fine flute, Guyal saw, a rich piece of white metal, chased and set with gold, and Ludowik clutched this flute as if he would never let go.

"Take the flute," suggested Ameth. "He will not mind in the least." Ludowik shook his head, to signify the absence of objection. But Guyal, noting with distaste the long stained beard, also shook his head. "I can play any scale, any tone on my flute. There is no need for me to use that of your uncle and possibly distress him. Listen," and he raised his instrument. "Here is a song of Kaiin, called 'The Opal, the Pearl and the Peacock'."

He put the pipe to his lips and began to play, very skillfully indeed, and Ludowik followed him, filling in gaps, making chords. Ameth, forgetting her vexation, listened with eyes half closed, and moved her arm to the rhythm.

"Did you enjoy that?" asked Guyal when he had finished.

"Very much. Perhaps you would try it on Uncle Ludowik's flute? It is a fine flute to play, very soft and easy to the breath."

"No," said Guyal, with sudden obstinacy. "I am able to play only my own instrument." He blew again, and it was a dance of the festival, a quirking carnival air. Ludowik, playing with supernal skill, ran merry phrases as might fit and Ameth, carried away by the rhythm, danced a dance of her own, a merry step in time to the music.

Guyal played a tarantella of the peasant folk, and Ameth danced wilder and faster, flung her arms, wheeled, jerked her head in a fine display. And Ludowik's flute played a brilliant obbligato, hurtling over, now under, chording, veering, warping little silver strings of sound around Guyal's melody, adding urgent little grace-phrases.

Ludowik's eyes now clung to the whirling figure of the dancing girl. And suddenly he struck up a theme of his own, a tune of wildest abandon, of a frenzied beating rhythm; and Guyal, carried away by the force of the music, blew as he never had blown before, invented trills and runs, gyrating arpeggios, blew high and shrill, loud and fast and clear.

It was as nothing to Ludowik's music. His eyes were starting; sweat streamed from his seamed old forehead; his flute tore the air into shreds.

Ameth danced frenzy; she was no longer beautiful, she appeared grotesque and unfamiliar. The music became something more than the senses could bear. Guyal's vision turned pink and gray; he saw Ameth fall in a faint, in a foaming fit; and Ludowik, fiery-eyed, staggered erect, hobbled to her body and began a terrible intense concord, slow measures of most solemn and frightening meaning.

Ludowik played death.

Guyal of Sfere turned and ran wide-eyed from the hall. Ludowik, never noticing, continued his terrible piping, played as if every note were a skewer through the twitching girl's shoulder-blades.

Guyal ran through the night and cold air bit at him like sleet. He burst into the shed, and the white horse nickered. On with the saddle, on with the bridle, away down the streets of old Carchasel, along the starlit cobbles, past the gaping black windows, away from the music of death!

Guyal of Sfere galloped up the mountain with the stars in his face, and not until he came to the shoulder did he turn in the saddle to look back.

The verging of dawn trembled into the stony valley. Where was Carchasel? There was no city, only a crumble of ruins...

Hark! A far sound?

No. All was silence.

And yet...

Only dank stones on the floor of the valley.

Guyal, fixed of eye, turned and went his way along the trail which stretched north before him.

The walls of the defile were gray granite, stained dull scarlet and black by lichen. The horse's hooves made a clop-clop-clop on the stone. After the sleepless night Guyal began to sag in the saddle. He resolved to round one more bend in the trail and then take rest.

The rock looming above hid the sky. The trail twisted around a shoulder of rock; ahead shone a patch of indigo. One more turning, Guyal told himself. The defile fell open, the mountains were at his back. He looked out across a hundred miles of steppe: a land shaded with subtle colors, fading and melting into the haze at the horizon. To the east he saw a lone eminence cloaked by a dark company of trees, the glisten of a lake at its foot. To the west a ranked mass of gray-white ruins was barely discernible. The Museum of Man?...Guyal dismounted and sought sleep within the Expansible Egg.

The sun rolled in sad majesty behind the mountains; murk fell across the tundra. Guyal awoke and refreshed himself. He gave meal to his horse, ate dry fruit and bread; then he mounted and rode down the trail. Gloom deepened; the plain sank from sight like a drowned land. Guyal reined his horse. Better, he thought, to ride in the morning. If he lost the trail in the dark, who could tell what he might encounter?

A mournful sound. Guyal turned his face to the sky. A sigh? A moan?...Another sound, closer: the rustle of cloth. Guyal cringed into his saddle. Floating slowly across the darkness came a shape robed in white. Under the cowl and glowing with witch-light was a drawn face with eyes like the holes in a skull.

It breathed a sad sound and drifted away.

Guyal drew a shuddering breath and slumped against the pommel. Then he slipped to the ground and established the Egg about himself and his horse; presently, as he lay staring into the dark, sleep came on him and so the night passed.

He awoke before dawn and set forth. The trail was a ribbon of white sand between banks of gray furze; the miles passed swiftly.

As he neared the tree-shrouded hillock he saw roofs through the foliage and smoke rising into the sharp air. And presently to right and left spread fields of spikenard, callow and mead-apple. Guyal continued with eyes watchful for men.

The trail passed beside a fence of stone and black timber enclosing a region of churned and scorched earth, which Guyal paused to examine. The horse started nervously; Guyal, turning, saw three men who had come quietly upon him: individuals tall and well-formed, somewhat solemn, with golden-ivory skin and jet-black hair. Their garments implied an ancient convention: tight suits of maroon leather trimmed with black lace and silver chain, maroon cloth hats crumpled in precise creases, with black leather flaps extended horizontally over each ear. Their attitudes expressed neither threat nor welcome. "Greetings, stranger," said one. "Whither bound?"

"I go as fate directs," replied Guyal cautiously. "You are Saponids?"

"That is our race, though now we are few. Before you is our final city, Issane." He inspected Guyal with frank curiosity. "And what of yourself?"

"I am Guyal of Sfere, which is in Ascolais, far to the south."

The Saponids regarded Guyal with respect. "You have come a long and perilous way."

Guyal looked back at the mountains. "Through the north forests and the wastes of Fer Aquila. At nightfall yesterday I passed through the mountains. In the dark a ghost hovered above till I thought the grave had marked me for its own."

He paused in surprise; his words seemed to have released a powerful emotion in the Saponids. Their features lengthened, their mouths grew white. The spokesman, his polite detachment a trifle diminished, searched the sky. "A ghost... In a white garment, floating on high?"

"Yes; is it a known familiar of the region?"

There was a pause.

"In a certain sense," said the Saponid. "It is a signal of woe... But I interrupt your tale."

"There is little to tell. I took shelter for the night, and this morning I fared down to the plain."

"Were you not molested further? By the Walking Serpent, who ranges the slopes like fate?"

"I saw neither walking serpent nor so much as a lizard; still, a blessing protects my trail and I come to no harm so long as I keep my course."

"Interesting, interesting."

"Now," said Guyal, "permit me to inquire of you, since there is much I would learn; what is this ghost, what event does he commemorate and what are the portents?"

"You ask beyond my certain knowledge," replied the Saponid cautiously. "Of this ghost it is well not to speak lest our attention reinforce its malignity."

"As you will," replied Guyal. "Perhaps —" He caught his tongue. Before inquiring for the Museum of Man it would be wise to learn in what regard the Saponids held it, lest learning his interest they should seek to deny him knowledge.

"Yes?" inquired the Saponids. "What is your lack?"

Guyal indicated the seared area behind the fence of stone and timber. "What is the cause of this devastation?"

The Saponid looked across the area with a blank expression.

"It is one of the ancient places; so much is known, no more. You will desire to rest and refresh yourself at Issane. Come; we will guide you."

He turned down the trail; Guyal, finding neither words nor reasons to reject the idea, urged his horse forward.

The Saponids walked in silence; Guyal, though he seethed with a thousand questions, likewise held his tongue. They skirted a placid lake. The surface mirrored the sky, shoals of reeds, boats in the shape of sickles, with bow and stern curving high from the water.

So they entered Issane: a town of no great pretense. The houses were hewn timber, golden brown, russet, weathered black. The construction was intricate and ornate, the walls rising three stories to steep gables. Pillars and piers were carved with complex designs: meshing ribbons, tendrils, leaves, lizards. The screens which guarded the windows were likewise carved, with foliage patterns, animal faces, radiant stars; rich textures in the mellow wood. Much effort, much expressiveness, had been expended on the carving.

They proceeded up a steep lane under the gloom cast by the trees, and the Saponids came forth to stare. They moved quietly and spoke in low voices, and their garments were of an elegance Guyal had not expected to see on the northern steppe.

One of the men turned to Guyal. "Will you oblige us by waiting until the First Elder is informed, so that he may prepare a suitable reception?"

The request was framed in candid words and with guileless eyes. Guyal thought to perceive ambiguity in the phrasing, but since the hooves of his horse were planted in the center of the road, and since he did not propose leaving the road, Guyal assented with an open face. The Saponids disappeared and Guyal sat musing on the pleasant town perched so high above the plain.

A group of girls came to look at Guyal with curious eyes. Guyal returned the inspection, and sensed a lack about their persons, a discrepancy which he could not instantly identify. They wore graceful garments of woven wool, striped and dyed various colors; they were supple and slender, and seemed not lacking in coquetry. And yet...

The Saponid returned. "Now, Sir Guyal, may we proceed?"

Guyal, endeavoring to remove any flavor of suspicion from his words, said, "You will understand that by the very nature of my father's blessing I dare not leave the delineated trail; for then, instantly, I would become liable to any curse placed on me along the way."

The Saponid made an understanding gesture. "Naturally; you follow a sound principle."

Guyal bowed in gratification, and they continued up the road.

A hundred paces and the road leveled, crossing a common planted with small, fluttering, heart-shaped leaves, colored in all shades of purple, red and black.

The Saponid turned to Guyal. "As a stranger I must caution you never to set foot on the common. It is one of our sacred places, and tradition requires that a severe penalty be exacted for transgressions and sacrilege."

"I note your warning," said Guyal. "I will respectfully obey your law."

They passed a dense thicket; with hideous clamor a bestial shape sprang from concealment, a creature with tremendous fanged jaws. Guyal's horse shied, bolted, sprang out upon the sacred common and trampled the fluttering leaves.

A number of Saponid men rushed forth, grasped the horse, seized Guyal and dragged him from the saddle.

"Wait!" cried Guyal. "What means this? Release me!"

The Saponid who had been his guide advanced, shaking his head in reproach. "Indeed, and only had I just impressed upon you the gravity of such an offense!"

"But the monster frightened my horse!" said Guyal. "I am nowise responsible for this trespass; release me, let us proceed to the reception."

The Saponid said, "I fear that the penalties prescribed by tradition must first come into effect. Your protests, though of superficial plausibility, will not sustain examination. For instance, the creature you term a monster is in reality a harmless domesticated beast. Secondly, I observe the animal you bestride; he will not make a turn or twist without the twitch of the reins. Thirdly, even if your postulates were conceded, you thereby admit to guilt by virtue of negligence and omission. You should have secured a mount less apt to unpredictable action, or upon learning of the sanctitude of the common, you should have considered such a contingency as even now occurred, and therefore dismounted, leading your beast. Therefore, Sir Guyal, though loath, I am forced to believe you guilty of impertinence, impiety, disregard and impudicity. Therefore, as Castellan and Sergeant-Reader of the Litany, so responsible for the detention of law-breakers, I must order you secured, contained, pent, incarcerated and confined until such time as the penalties will be exacted."

"The entire episode is mockery!" raged Guyal. "Are you savages, then, thus to mistreat a lone wayfarer?"

"By no means," replied the Castellan. "We are a civilized people, with customs bequeathed us by the past. Since the past was more glorious than the present, what presumption we would show by questioning these laws!"

Guyal fell quiet. "And what are the usual penalties for my act?"

The Castellan made a reassuring motion. "The rote prescribes three acts of penance, which in your case, I am sure will be nominal. But — the forms must be observed, and it is necessary that you be constrained in the Felon's Caseboard." He motioned to the men who held Guyal's arm. "Away with him, cross neither track nor trail, for then your grasp will be nerveless and he will be delivered from justice."

Guyal was pent in a well aired but poorly lighted cellar of stone. The floor he found dry, the ceiling free of crawling insects. He had not been searched, nor had his Scintillant Dagger been removed from his sash. With suspicions crowding his brain he lay on the rush bed and, after a period, slept.

Now ensued the passing of a day. He was given food and drink; and at last the Castellan came to visit him.

"You are indeed fortunate," said the Saponid, "in that, as a witness, I was able to suggest your delinquencies to be more the result of negligence than malice. The last penalties exacted for the crime were stringent; the felon was ordered to perform the following three acts:

First, to cut off his toes and sew the severed members into the skin at his neck; second, to revile his forbears for three hours, commencing with a Common Bill of Anathema, including feigned madness and hereditary disease, and at last defiling the hearth of his clan; and third, walking a mile under the lake with leaded shoes in search of the Lost Book of Caraz." And the Castellan regarded Guyal with complacency.

"What deeds must I perform?" inquired Guyal drily.

The Castellan joined the tips of his fingers together. "As I say, the penances are nominal, by decree of the Elder. First, you must swear never again to repeat your crime."

"That I gladly do," said Guyal, and so bound himself.

"Second," said the Castellan with a slight smile, "you must adjudicate at a Grand Pageant of Pulchritude among the maids of the village and select her whom you consider the most beautiful."

"Scarcely an arduous task," commented Guyal. "Why does it fall to my lot?"

The Castellan looked vaguely to the ceiling. "There are a number of concomitants to victory in this contest... Every person in the town would find relations among the participants — a daughter, a sister, a niece — and so would hardly be considered unprejudiced. The charge of favoritism could never be leveled against you; therefore you make an ideal selection for this important post."

Guyal seemed to hear the ring of sincerity in the Saponid's voice; still he wondered why the selection of the town's loveliest was a matter of such import.

"And third?" he inquired.

"That will be revealed after the contest, which occurs this afternoon."

The Saponid departed the cell.

Guyal, who was not without vanity, spent several hours restoring himself and his costume from the ravages of travel. He bathed, trimmed his hair, shaved his face, and, when the Castellan came to unlock the door, he felt that he made no discreditable picture.

He was led out upon the road and directed up the hill toward the summit of the terraced town of Saponce. Turning to the Castellan he said, "How is it that you permit me to walk the trail once more? You must know that now I am safe from molestation..."

The Castellan shrugged. "True. But you would gain little by insisting upon your temporary immunity. Ahead the trail crosses a bridge which we could demolish; behind we need but breach the dam to Green Torrent; then, should you walk the trail you would be swept to the side and so rendered vulnerable. No, Sir Guyal of Sfere, once the secret of your immunity is abroad then you are liable to a variety of stratagems. For instance, a large wall might be placed athwart the way, before and behind you. No doubt the spell would preserve you from thirst and hunger, but what then? So would you sit till the sun went out."

Guyal said no word. Across the lake he noticed a trio of the crescent boats approaching the docks, prows and sterns rocking and dipping into the shaded water with a graceful motion. The void in his mind made itself known. "Why are boats constructed in such fashion?"

The Castellan looked blankly at him. "It is the only practicable method. Do not the oe-pods grow thusly to the south?"

"Never have I seen oe-pods."

"They are the fruit of a great vine, and grow in scimitar-shape. When sufficiently large we cut and clean them, slit the inner edge, grapple end to end with strong line and constrict till the pod opens as is desirable. When cured, dried, varnished, carved, burnished and lacquered, fitted with deck, thwarts and gussets — then have we our boats."

They entered the plaza, a flat area at the summit surrounded on three sides by tall houses. To Guyal's surprise there seemed to be no preliminary ceremonies or formalities to the contest, and small spirit of festivity was manifest among the townspeople. Indeed they seemed beset by subdued despondency and eyed him without enthusiasm.

A hundred girls stood in a disconsolate group. It seemed to Guyal that they had gone to few pains to embellish themselves. To the contrary, they wore shapeless rags, their hair seemed deliberately misarranged, their faces were dirty and scowling.

Guyal turned to his guide. "The girls seem not to covet the garland of pulchritude."

The Castellan nodded wryly. "As you see, they are by no means jealous for distinction; modesty has always been a Saponid trait."

Guyal hesitated. "What is the form of procedure? I do not desire in my ignorance to violate another of your arcane regulations."

The Castellan said with a blank face, "There are no formalities. We conduct these pageants with expedition and the least possible ceremony. You need but pass among these maidens and point out her whom you deem the most attractive."

Guyal advanced to his task, feeling more than half foolish. Then he reflected: this is a penalty for contravening an absurd tradition; I will conduct myself with efficiency and so the quicker rid myself of the obligation.

He stood before the hundred girls who eyed him with hostility and anxiety, and Guyal saw that his task would not be simple, since, on the whole, they were of a comeliness which even the dirt, grimacing and rags could not disguise.

"Range yourselves, if you please, into a line," said Guyal. "In this way, none will be at disadvantage."

Sullenly the girls formed a line.

Guyal surveyed the group. He saw at once that a number could be eliminated: the squat, the obese, the lean, the pocked and coarse-featured — perhaps a quarter of the group. He said suavely, "Never have I seen such unanimous loveliness; each of you might legitimately claim the cordon. My task is arduous; I must weigh fine imponderables; in the end my choice will undoubtedly be based on subjectivity and those of real charm will no doubt be the first discharged from the competition." He stepped forward. "Those whom I indicate may retire."

He walked down the line, pointing, and the ugliest, with expressions of unmistakable relief, hastened to the sidelines.

A second time Guyal made his inspection, and now, somewhat more familiar with those he judged, he was able to discharge those who, while suffering no whit from ugliness, were merely plain.

Roughly a third of the original group remained. These stared at Guyal with varying degrees of apprehension and truculence as he passed before them, studying each in turn... All at once his mind was determined, and his choice definite.

Guyal made one last survey down the line. No, he had been accurate in his choice. There were girls here as comely as the senses could desire, girls with opal-glowing eyes and hyacinth features, girls as lissome as reeds, with hair silky and fine despite the dust which they seemed to have rubbed upon themselves.

The girl whom Guyal had selected was slighter than the others and possessed of a beauty not at once obvious. She had a small triangular face, great wistful eyes and thick black hair cut short at the ears. Her skin was of a transparent paleness, like the finest ivory; her form slender, graceful, and of a compelling magnetism. She seemed to have sensed his decision and her eyes widened.

Guyal took her hand, led her forward, and turned to the Elder — an old man sitting stolidly in a heavy chair.

"This is she whom I find the loveliest among your maidens."

There was silence through the square. Then there came a hoarse sound, a cry of sadness from the Castellan and Sergeant-Reader. He came forward, sagging of face, limp of body. "Guyal of Sfere, you have wrought a great revenge for my tricking you. This is my beloved daughter, Shierl, whom you have designated."

Guyal stammered, "I meant but complete impersonality. Your daughter Shierl I find the loveliest creature of my experience; I cannot understand where I have offended."

"No, Guyal," said the Castellan, "you have chosen fairly, for such indeed is my own thought."

"Well, then," said Guyal, "reveal to me now my third task that I may finish and then continue my pilgrimage."

The Castellan said, "Three leagues to the north lies the ruin which tradition tells us to be the olden Museum of Man."

"Ah," said Guyal, "go on, I attend."

"You must, as your third charge, conduct my daughter Shierl to the Museum of Man. At the portal you will strike on a copper gong and announce to whoever responds: 'We are those summoned from Issane.'"

Guyal frowned. "How is this? 'We'?"

"Such is your charge," said the Castellan in a voice like thunder.

Guyal looked to left, right, forward, and behind. But he stood in the center of the plaza surrounded by the hardy men of Issane.

"When must this charge be executed?" he inquired in a controlled voice.

The Castellan said in a voice bitter as gall: "Even now Shierl goes to clothe herself in yellow. In one hour shall she appear; in one hour shall you set forth for the Museum of Man."

"And then?"

"And then — for good or for evil, it is not known. You fare as thirteen thousand have fared before you."

Down from the plaza, down the leafy lanes of Issane came Guyal, indignant and clamped of mouth, though the pit of his stomach felt heavy with trepidation. The ritual carried distasteful overtones. Guyal's step faltered.

The Castellan seized his elbow with a hard hand. "Forward."

The faces along the lane swam with morbid curiosity, inner excitement.

The eminence, with the tall trees and carved dark houses was at his back; he walked out into the claret sunlight of the tundra. Eighty women in white gowns with ceremonial buckets of woven straw over their heads surrounded a tall tent of yellow silk. Here the Castellan halted Guyal and beckoned to the Ritual Matron. She flung back the hangings at the door of the tent; Shierl came slowly forth, eyes dark with fright. She wore a stiff gown of yellow brocade, and the wand of her body seemed pent and constrained within. She stared at Guyal, at her father, as if she had never seen them before. The Ritual Matron put a hand on her waist, propelled her forward. Shierl stepped once, twice, irresolutely halted. The Castellan brought Guyal forward and placed him at the girl's side; now two children, a boy and a girl, came hastening up with cups which they proffered to Guyal and Shierl. Dully she accepted the cup. Guyal glanced suspiciously at the murky brew. He asked the Castellan: "What is the nature of this potion?"

"Drink," said the Castellan. "So will your way seem the shorter; you will march to the Museum with a steadier step."

"I will not drink," said Guyal. "My senses must be my own when I meet the Curator. I have come far for the privilege; I would not stultify the occasion stumbling and staggering."

Shierl stared dully at the cup she held. Said Guyal: "I advise you likewise to avoid the drug; so will we come to the Museum of Man with our dignity."

She returned the cup. The Castellan's brow clouded, but he made no protest.

An old man in a black costume brought forward a satin pillow on which rested a whip with a handle of carved steel. The Castellan now lifted this whip, and advancing, laid three light strokes across the shoulders of both Shierl and Guyal.

"Now," said the Castellan, "go from Issane outlawed forever. Seek succor at the Museum of Man. Never look back, leave all thoughts of past and future here. Go, I command; go, go, go!"

Shierl sunk her teeth into her lower lip; tears coursed her cheek though she made no sound. With hanging head she started across the tundra. Guyal, with a swift stride, joined her.

For a space the murmurs, the nervous sounds followed their ears; then they were alone. The north lay across the horizon; the tundra filled the foreground and background, an expanse dreary and dun. The Museum of Man rose before them; along the faint trail they walked.

Guyal said in a tentative tone, "There is much I would understand."

"Speak," said Shierl.

"Why are we forced to this mission?"

"It is thus because it has always been thus. Is this not reason enough?"

"Sufficient possibly for you," said Guyal, "but not for me. In fact, my thirst for knowledge drew me here to find the Museum of Man."

She looked at him in wonder. "Are all to the south as scholarly as you?"

"In no degree," said Guyal. "The habitants perform the acts which fed them yesterday, last week, a year ago. 'Why strive for a pedant's accumulation?' I have been asked. 'Why seek and search? Earth grows cold; man gasps his last; why forgo merriment, music, and revelry for the abstract?' "

"Indeed," said Shierl. "Such is the consensus at Issane. But ask what you will; I will try to answer."

He studied the charming triangle of her face, the heavy black hair, the lustrous eyes, dark as sapphires. "In happier circumstances, there would be other yearnings for you to ease."

"Ask," said Shierl of Issane. "The Museum of Man is close; there is occasion for naught but words."

"Why are we thus sent to the Museum?"

"The immediate cause is the ghost you saw on the hill. When the ghost appears, then we of Issane know that the most beautiful maiden and the most handsome youth must be despatched to the Museum. The basis of the custom I do not know. So it is; so it has been; so it will be till the sun gutters out like a coal in the rain."

"But what is our mission? Who greets us, what is our fate?"

"Such details are unknown."

Guyal mused, "The likelihood of pleasure seems small…You are beyond doubt the loveliest creature of the Saponids, the loveliest creature of Earth — but I, a casual stranger, am hardly the most well-favored youth of the town."

She smiled. "You are not uncomely."

Guyal said somberly, "More cogent is the fact that I am a stranger and so bring little loss to Issane."

"That aspect has no doubt been considered."

Guyal searched the horizon. "Let us then avoid the Museum of Man, let us circumvent this unknown fate and take to the mountains."

She shook her head. "Do you suppose that we would gain by the ruse? The eyes of a hundred warriors will follow until we pass through the portals of the Museum. Should we attempt to avoid our duty we should be bound to stakes, stripped of our skins by the inch, and at last placed in bags with a thousand scorpions. Such is the traditional penalty; twelve times in history has it been invoked."

Guyal threw back his shoulders. He spoke in a nervous voice, "Ah, well — the Museum of Man has been my goal for many years. On this motive I set forth from Sfere, so now I would seek the Curator and satisfy my obsession for brain-filling."

"You are blessed with great fortune," said Shierl, "for you are being granted your heart's desire."

Guyal could find nothing to say, so for a space they walked in silence.

Presently she touched his arm. "Guyal, I am greatly frightened."

Guyal gazed at the ground beneath his feet, and a blossom of hope sprang alive in his brain. "See the marking through the lichen?"

"Yes; what then?"

"Is it a trail?"

Dubiously she responded, "It is a way worn by the passage of many feet. So then — it is a trail."

"Here then is safety," declared Guyal. "But I must guard you; you must never leave my side, you must swim in the charm which protects me; perhaps then we will survive."

Shierl said sadly, "Let us not delude our reason, Guyal of Sfere."

But as they walked, the trail grew plainer, and Guyal became correspondingly sanguine. And ever larger bulked the crumble that marked the Museum of Man.

If a storehouse of knowledge had existed here, little sign remained. There was a great flat floor, flagged in white stone, now chalky, broken and grown over with weeds. The surrounding monoliths, pocked and worn, were toppled off at various heights. The rains had washed the marble, the dust from the mountains had been laid on and swept off, laid on and swept off, and those who had built the Museum were less than a mote of this dust, so far and forgotten were they.

"Think," said Guyal, "think of the vastness of knowledge which once was gathered here and which is now one with the soil — unless, of course, the Curator has salvaged and preserved."

Shierl looked about apprehensively. "I think rather of the portal, and that which awaits us...Guyal," she whispered, "I fear, I fear greatly... Suppose they tear us apart? Suppose there is torture and death? I fear a tremendous impingement."

Guyal's own throat was hot and full. He looked about with challenge. "While I still breathe and hold power in my arms to fight, there will be none to harm us."

Shierl groaned softly. "Guyal, Guyal, Guyal of Sfere — why did you choose me?"

"Because," said Guyal, "you were the loveliest and I thought nothing but good in store for you."

Shierl said, "I must be courageous; after all, if it were not I it would be some other maid equally fearful... And there is the portal."

Guyal inhaled deeply, inclined his head, and strode forward. "Let us be to it, and know."

The portal opened into a wall supporting the first floor; a door of flat black metal. Guyal followed the trail to the door and rapped staunchly with his fist on the small copper gong to the side.

The door groaned wide on its hinges, and cool air, smelling of the under-earth, billowed forth.

"Hello within!" cried Guyal.

A soft voice, full of catches and quavers, as if just after weeping, said, "Come you, come you forward. You are desired and awaited."

Guyal leaned his head forward, straining to see. "Give us light, that we may not wander from the trail and bottom ourselves."

The breathless quaver of a voice said, "Light is not needed; anywhere you step, that will be your trail, by an arrangement so agreed with the Way-Maker."

"No," said Guyal, "we would see the visage of our host. We come at his invitation; the minimum of his courtesy is light; light there must be before we set foot inside the dungeon. Know we come as seekers after knowledge; we are visitors to be honored."

"Ah, knowledge, knowledge," came the sad breathlessness. "That shall be yours, in fullness; oh, you shall swim in a tide of knowledge —"

Guyal interrupted the sad, sighing voice. "Are you the Curator? Hundreds of leagues have I come to know the Curator and put him my inquiries. Are you he?"

"By no means. I revile the name of the Curator as a non-essential."

"Who then may you be?"

"I am no one, nothing. I am an abstraction, an emotion, the shake in the air when a scream has departed."

"You speak the voice of man."

"Why not? Such things as I speak lie in the dearest center of the human brain."

Guyal said in a subdued voice, "You do not make your invitation as enticing as might be hoped."

"No matter, no matter; enter you must, into the dark and on the instant."

"If light there be, we enter."

"No light, no insolent scorch, is ever found in the Museum."

"In this case," said Guyal, drawing forth his Scintillant Dagger, "I innovate a welcome reform. For see, now there is light!"

From the under-pommel issued a searching glare; the ghost tall before them screeched and fell into twinkling ribbons like pulverized tinsel. There were a few vagrant motes in the air; he was gone.

Shierl, who had stood stark and stiff as one mesmerized, gasped a soft warm gasp and fell against Guyal. "How can you be so defiant?"

Guyal said in a voice half-laugh, half-quaver, "In truth I do not know...Perhaps I find it incredible that I should come from Sfere, through forest and across crag, into the northern waste, merely to play the role of victim. I disbelieve; I am bold."

He moved the dagger to right and left, and they saw themselves to be at the portal of a keep, cut from concreted rock. At the back opened a black depth. Crossing the floor swiftly, Guyal kneeled and listened.

He heard no sound. Shierl, at his back, stared with eyes as black and deep as the pit itself.

Leaning with his glowing dagger Guyal saw a crazy rack of stairs voyaging down into the dark, and his light showed them and their shadows in so confusing a guise that he blinked and drew back.

Shierl said, "What do you fear?"

Guyal rose. "We are momentarily untended here in the Museum of Man. If we stay here we shall be once more arranged in harmony with the hostile pattern. If we go forward boldly we may come to a position of advantage. I propose that we descend these stairs and seek the Curator."

"But does he exist?"

"The ghost spoke fervently against him."

"Let us go then," said Shierl. "I am resigned."

"We go."

They started down the stairs.

Back, forth, back, forth, down flights at varying angles, stages of varying heights, treads at varying widths, so that each step was a matter for concentration. Back, forth, down, down, down, and the black barred shadows moved and jerked in bizarre modes on the wall.

The flight ended; they stood in a room similar to the entry above, facing another black door, polished at one spot by use. On the walls to either side brass plaques carried messages in unfamiliar characters.

Guyal opened the door against a pressure of cold air, which, blowing through the aperture, made a slight rush, ceasing when Guyal opened the door farther.

"Listen."

It was a far sound, an intermittent clacking, and it raised the hairs at Guyal's neck. He felt Shierl's hand gripping his with clammy pressure.

Dimming the dagger's glow to a glimmer, Guyal passed through the door, with Shierl coming after. From afar came the evil sound, and by the echoes they knew they stood in a great hall.

Guyal directed the light to the floor: it was of a black resilient material. Next the wall: polished stone. He permitted the light to glow in the direction opposite to the sound, and a few paces distant they saw a bulky black case, studded with copper bosses.

With the purpose of the black case not apparent, they followed the wall, and as they walked similar cases appeared, looming heavy and dull, at regular intervals. The clacking receded as they walked; then they came to a right angle, and turning the corner, they seemed to approach the sound. Black case after black case passed; slowly, tense as foxes, they walked, eyes groping for sight through the darkness.

The wall made another angle, and here there was a door. Guyal hesitated. To follow the new direction of the wall would mean approaching the source of the sound. Would it be better to discover the worst quickly or to reconnoiter as they went?

He propounded the dilemma to Shierl, who shrugged. "It is all one; sooner or later the ghosts will flit down to pluck at us; then we are lost."

"Not while I possess light to stare them away to wisps and shreds," said Guyal. "Now I would find the Curator. Possibly he is behind this door. We will so discover."

He laid his shoulder to the door; it eased ajar with a crack of golden light. Guyal peered through. He sighed, a muffled sound of wonder.

Now he opened the door further; Shierl clutched at his arm.

"This is the Museum," said Guyal in rapt tone. "Here there is no danger." He flung wide the door.

The light came from an unknown source, from the air itself, as if leaking from the discrete atoms; every breath was luminous, the room floated full of invigorating glow. Beautiful works of human fashioning ranked the walls: panels of rich woods; scenes of olden times; formulas of color, designed to convey emotion rather than reality. Here were representations of three hundred marvelous flowers no longer extant on waning Earth; as many star-burst patterns; a multitude of other creations.

The door thudded softly behind them; the two from Earth's final time moved forward through the hall.

"Somewhere near must be the Curator," whispered Guyal. "There has been careful tending and great effort here."

"Look."

Opposite was a door which Guyal was unable to open, for it bore no latch, key, handle knob, or bar. He rapped with his knuckles and waited; no sound returned.

Shierl tugged at his arm. "These are private regions. It is best not to venture too rudely."

Guyal turned away and they continued down the gallery, past the real expression of man's brightest dreamings, until the concentration of so much fire and spirit put them into awe. "Great minds lie on the dust," said Guyal. "Gorgeous souls have vanished. Nevermore will there be the like."

The room turned a corner, widened. And now the clacking sound they had noticed in the dark outer hall returned, louder, more suggestive of unpleasantness. It seemed to enter the gallery through an arched doorway opposite.

Guyal moved quietly to this door, with Shierl at his heels, and so they peered into the next chamber.

A great face looked from the wall, a face taller than Guyal, as tall as Guyal might reach with hands on high. The chin rested on the floor, the scalp slanted back into the panel.

Guyal stared, taken aback. In this pageant of beautiful objects, the grotesque visage was the disparity and dissonance a lunatic might have created. Ugly and vile was the face. The skin shone a gun-metal sheen, the eyes gazed from slanting folds. The nose was a lump, the mouth a pulp.

Guyal turned to Shierl. "Does this not seem an odd work to be honored here in the Museum of Man?"

With hands jerking, she grabbed his arm, staggered back into the gallery.

"Guyal," she cried, "Guyal, come away!"

He faced her in surprise. "What are you saying?"

"That horrible thing in there —"

"The diseased effort of an elder artist."

"It lives."

"How is this?"

"It lives!" she babbled. "It looked at me, then looked at you."

Guyal shrugged off her hand; in disbelief he looked through the doorway.

The face had changed. The torpor had evaporated; the glaze had departed the eye. The mouth squirmed; a hiss of escaping gas sounded. The mouth opened; a gray tongue protruded, and from this tongue darted a tendril. It terminated in a grasping hand, which groped for Guyal's neck. He jumped aside; the hand missed its clutch, the tendril coiled.

Guyal sprang back into the gallery. The hand seized Shierl, grasped her ankle. The eyes glistened; and now the flabby tongue sprouted a new member...Shierl stumbled, fell limp, her eyes staring, foam at her lips. Guyal shouting in a voice he could not hear, ran forward with his dagger. He cut at the gray wrist, but his knife sprang away as if the steel itself were horrified. He seized the tendril; with a mighty effort he broke it against his knee.

The face winced, the tendril jerked back. Guyal dragged Shierl into the gallery, back out of reach.

Through the doorway now, Guyal glared in hate and fear. The mouth had closed; it sneered disappointment. From the dank nostril oozed a wisp of white which swirled, writhed, formed a tall thing in a white robe — a thing with a drawn face and eyes like holes in a skull. Whimpering and mewing in distaste for the light, it wavered forward into the gallery, moving with curious little pauses and hesitancies.

Guyal stood still. Fear had exceeded its power; fear no longer persuaded. A brain could react only to the maximum of its intensity; how could this thing harm him now? He would smash it with his hands, beat it into sighing fog.

"Hold, hold, hold!" came a new voice. "Hold, hold, hold. My charms and tokens, an ill day for Thorsingol...Be off with you, ghost, back to the orifice, back, I say! Go, else I loose the actinics; trespass is not allowed, by supreme command from the Lycurgat; aye, the Lycurgat of Thorsingol." This was the voice of the old man who had hobbled into the gallery.

Back to the snoring face wandered the ghost, and let itself be sucked up into the nostril.

The face rumbled and belched a white fiery lick, flapping at the old man who moved not an inch. From a rod high on the door frame came a whirling disk of golden sparks, which cut and dismembered the white sheet, destroyed it back to the mouth of the face, whence now issued a black bar. This bar edged into the whirling disk and absorbed the sparks. There was an instant of dead silence.

Then the old man crowed, "Ah, you evil episode; you seek to interrupt my tenure. My clever baton holds you in abeyance; you are as naught. Disengage! Retreat into Jeldred!"

The mouth opened to display a gray viscous cavern; the eyes glittered in titanic emotion. The mouth yelled, a wave of sound to buffet the head and drive shock like a nail into the mind.

The baton sprayed a mist; the sound was captured and consumed; it was never heard.

The old man said, "You are captious today! You would disturb poor old Kerlin in his duties? So ho. Baton!" He turned and peered at the rod. "You have tasted that sound? Spew out a penalty."

The fog balled, struck at the nose, buried itself in the pulp. An explosion; the face seethed; the nose was a clutter of shredded gray plasms. They waved like starfish arms and grew together once more, and now the nose was pointed like a cone.

Kerlin the Curator laughed, a shrill yammer on a single tone. He stopped short and the laugh vanished as if it had never begun. He turned to Guyal and Shierl, who stood pressed together in the door frame.

"How now? You are after the gong; the study hours are ended. Why do you linger?" He shook a stern finger. "The Museum is not the site for roguery; this I admonish. So now be off, home to Thorsingol; be more prompt the next time; you disturb the order..." He paused and threw a fretful glance over his shoulder. "The day has gone ill; the Nocturnal Key-keeper is inexcusably late... I have waited an hour on the sluggard; the Lycurgat shall be so informed. I would be home to couch and hearth; here is ill use for old Kerlin. And, further, the encroachment of you two laggards; away now, and be off; out into the twilight!" And he advanced, making directive motions with his hands.

Guyal said, "My lord Curator, I must speak with you."

The old man halted, peered. "Eh? What now? At the end of a long day's effort? No, no, you are out of order; regulation must be observed. Attend my audiarium at the fourth circuit tomorrow morning; then we shall hear you. So go now, go."

Guyal stood back, nonplussed. Shierl fell on her knees. "Sir Curator, we beg you for help; we have no place to go."

Kerlin the Curator looked at her blankly. "No place to go! What folly you utter! Go to your domicile, or to the Pubescentarium, or to the Temple, or to the Outward Inn. The Museum is no casual tavern."

"My lord," cried Guyal desperately, "will you hear me? We speak from emergency."

"Say on then."

"Some malignancy has bewitched your brain. Will you credit this?"

"Ah, indeed?" ruminated the Curator.

"There is no Thorsingol. There is naught but dark waste. Your city is an aeon gone."

The Curator smiled benevolently. "A sad case. So it is with these younger minds." He shook his head. "My duty is clear. Tired bones, you must wait your rest. Fatigue — begone; duty to humanity makes demands; here is madness to be countered and cleared. And in any event the Nocturnal Key-keeper is not here to relieve me of my tedium." He beckoned. "Come."

Hesitantly Guyal and Shierl followed him. He opened one of his doors, passed through muttering and expostulating. Guyal and Shierl came after.

The room was cubical, floored with dull black stuff. A hooded chair occupied the center of the room and beside it was a chest-high lectern whose face displayed a number of toggles and knurled wheels.

"This is the Curator's own Chair of Clarity," explained Kerlin. "As such it will, upon proper adjustment, impose the Pattern of Hynomeneural Clarity." He manipulated the manuals. "Now, if you will compose yourself I will repair your hallucination. It is beyond my call of duty, but I would not be spoken of as mean or unwilling."

Guyal inquired anxiously, "Lord Curator, this Chair of Clarity, how will it affect me?"

Kerlin the Curator said grandly, "The fibers of your brain are snarled and frayed, and so make contact with unintentional areas. By the marvelous craft of our modern cerebrologists this hood will compose your synapses with the correct readings from the library — those of normality, you must understand — and so repair the skein, and make you once more a whole man."

"Once I sit in the chair," Guyal inquired, "What will you do?"

"Merely close this contact, engage this arm, throw in this toggle — then you daze. In thirty seconds, this bulb glows, signaling the success and completion of the treatment. Then I reverse the manipulation and you arise a creature of renewed sanity."

Guyal looked at Shierl. "Did you hear and comprehend?"

"Yes, Guyal."

"Remember." Then to the Curator: "Marvelous. But how must I sit?"

"Merely relax in the seat. Then I pull the hood slightly forward, to shield the eyes from distraction."

Guyal leaned forward, peered gingerly into the hood. "I fear I do not understand."

The Curator hopped forward impatiently. "It is an act of the utmost facility. Like this." He sat in the chair.

"And how will the hood be applied?"

"In this wise." Kerlin seized a handle, pulled the shield over his face.

"Quick," said Guyal to Shierl. She sprang to the lectern; Kerlin the Curator made a motion to release the hood; Guyal seized the spindly frame, held it. Shierl flung the switches; the Curator relaxed, sighed.

Shierl gazed at Guyal, dark eyes wide and liquid as the great water-flamerian of South Almery. "Is he…dead?"

"I hope not."

They gazed uncertainly at the relaxed form. Seconds passed.

A clanging noise sounded from afar — a crush, a wrench, an exultant bellow.

Guyal rushed to the door. Prancing, wavering, sidling into the gallery came a dozen ghosts; through the open door behind, Guyal could see the great head. It was shoving out, pushing into the room. Great ears appeared, part of a neck, wreathed with purple wattles. The wall cracked, sagged, crumbled. A great hand thrust through, a forearm…

Shierl screamed. Guyal, pale and quivering, slammed the door in the face of the nearest ghost. It seeped around the jamb, wisp by wisp.

Guyal sprang to the lectern. The bulb showed dullness. Guyal's hands twitched along the controls. "Only Kerlin's awareness controls the magic of the baton," he panted. "So much is clear." He stared into the bulb with agonized urgency.

"Glow, bulb, glow…"

The bulb glowed. With a sharp cry Guyal returned the switches to neutrality, jumped down, flung up the hood.

Kerlin the Curator sat looking at him.

Behind, the ghost formed itself — a tall white thing in white robes, and the dark eye-holes stared like outlets into nonimagination.

Kerlin the Curator sat looking.

The ghost moved under the robes. A hand like a bird's foot appeared, holding a clod of dingy matter. The ghost cast the matter to the floor; it exploded into a puff of black dust. The motes of the cloud grew, became a myriad of wriggling insects. With one accord they darted across the floor, growing as they spread, and became scuttling creatures with monkey-heads.

Kerlin the Curator moved. "Baton," he said. He held up his hand. It held the baton. The baton spat an orange gout — red dust. It puffed before the rushing horde and each mote became a red scorpion. So ensued a ferocious battle, and little shrieks and chittering sounds rose from the floor.

The monkey-headed things were killed, routed. The ghost sighed, moved his claw-hand once more. But the baton spat forth a ray of purest light and the ghost sloughed into nothingness.

"Kerlin!" cried Guyal. "The demon is breaking into the gallery."

Kerlin flung open the door, stepped forth.

"Baton," said Kerlin, "perform thy utmost."

The demon said, "No, Kerlin, hold the magic; I thought you dazed. Now I retreat."

With a vast quaking and heaving he pulled back until once more only his face showed through the hole.

"Baton," said Kerlin, "rest on guard."

The baton disappeared from his hand.

Kerlin turned and faced Guyal and Shierl.

"There is need for many words, for now I die. I die, and the Museum shall lie alone. So let us speak quickly, quickly, quickly…"

Kerlin moved with feeble steps to a portal which snapped aside as he approached. Guyal and Shierl stood hesitantly to the rear.

"Come, come," said Kerlin in sharp impatience. "My strength flags, I die. You have been my death."

Guyal moved slowly forward, with Shierl half a pace behind.

Kerlin surveyed them with a thin grin. "Halt your misgivings and hasten; I wane; my sight flickers…"

He waved a despairing hand, then, turning, led them into the inner chamber where he slumped into a great chair. With many uneasy glances at the door Guyal and Shierl settled upon a padded couch.

Kerlin jeered in a feeble voice, "You fear the white phantasms? Poh, they are held from the gallery by the baton. Only when I am smitten out of mind — or dead — will the baton cease its function. You must know," he added with somewhat more vigor, "that the energies and dynamics do not channel from my brain but from the central potentium of the Museum, which is perpetual; I merely direct and order the rod."

"But this demon — who or what is he? Why does he come to look through the walls?"

"He is Blikdak, of the demon-world Jeldred. He wrenched the hole intent on taking the knowledge of the Museum into his mind, but I forestalled him; so he sits waiting in the hole till I die. Then he will glut himself with erudition to the great disadvantage of men."

"Why cannot this demon be exhorted hence and the hole abolished?"

Kerlin the Curator shook his head. "The furious powers I control are not valid in the air of the demon-world, where substance and form are of different entity. So far as you see him, he has brought his environment with him; so far he is safe. When he ventures farther the power of Earth dissolves the Jeldred mode; then may I strike him with fervor from the potentium… But enough of Blikdak; tell me, what is the news of Thorsingol?"

Guyal said in a halting voice, "Thorsingol is passed beyond memory. There is naught above but arid tundra and the old town of the Saponids. This girl Shierl is of the Saponids; we came to the Museum at the behest of Blikdak's ghosts."

"Ah," breathed Kerlin, "have I been so aimless? These youthful shapes by which Blikdak relieved his tedium: they flit down my memory like may-flies...I put them aside as creatures of his own conception."

Shierl grimaced. "What use to him are human creatures?"

Kerlin said dully, "Blikdak is past your conceiving. These human creatures are his play, on whom he practices various junctures, nauseas, antics and at last struggles to the death. Then he sends forth a ghost demanding further youth and beauty."

Guyal said in puzzlement, "Such acts would seem derangements of humanity. They are anthropoid by the very nature of the functioning organs. Since Blikdak is a demon —"

"Consider him!" spoke Kerlin. "His lineaments, his apparatus. He is nothing else but anthropoid, and such is his origin, together with all the demons, frits, and winged glowing-eyed creatures that infest latter-day Earth. Blikdak, like the others, derives from the mind of man. The condensation, the cloacal humors, the scatophiliac whims that have drained through humanity formed a vast tumor; so Blikdak assumed his being. But of Blikdak, enough. I die, I die!" He sank into the chair with heaving chest. "My eyes vary and waver. My breath is shallow as a bird's, my bones are the pith of an old vine. I have lived beyond knowledge; in my madness I knew no passage of time. Now I remember the years and centuries, the millennia, the epochs — they are like quick glimpses through a shutter. Curing my madness, you have killed me."

"But when you die," cried Shierl, "what then?"

Guyal asked, "In the Museum of Man are there no exorcisms to dissolve this demon?

"Blikdak must be eradicated," said Kerlin. "Then will I die in ease; then must you assume the care of the Museum." He licked his white lips. "An ancient principle specifies that, in order to destroy a substance the nature of the substance must be determined. In short, before Blikdak may be dissolved, we must discover his nature." And his eyes moved glassily to Guyal.

"Your pronouncement is sound beyond argument," admitted Guyal, "but how may this be accomplished? Blikdak will never submit to investigation."

"No; there must be subterfuge, some instrumentality…"

"The ghosts are part of Blikdak's stuff?"

"Indeed."

"Can the ghosts be stayed and prevented?"

"Indeed; in a box of light, the which I can effect by a thought. Yes, a ghost we must have." Kerlin raised his head. "Baton! One ghost; admit a ghost!"

A moment passed; Kerlin held up his hand. There was a faint scratch at the door and a soft whine. "Open," said a voice, full of sobs and catches and quavers. "Open and let forth the youthful creatures."

Kerlin laboriously rose to his feet. "It is done."

From behind the door came a sad voice, "I am pent, I am snared in scorching brilliance!"

"Now we experiment," said Guyal. "What dissolves the ghost dissolves Blikdak."

"True indeed," assented Kerlin.

"Why not light?" inquired Shierl. "Light parts the fabric of the ghosts as wind tatters the fog."

"But merely for their fragility; Blikdak is harsh and solid." Kerlin mused. After a moment he gestured to the door. "We go to the image-expander; there we will explode the ghost to macroid dimension; so shall we find his basis. Guyal of Sfere, you must support my frailness; my limbs are weak as wax."

On Guyal's arm he tottered forward, and with Shierl close at their heels they gained the gallery. Here the ghost wept in its cage of light, and searched constantly for a dark aperture to seep his essence through.

Paying him no heed Kerlin hobbled and limped across the gallery. In their wake followed the box of light and perforce the ghost.

"Open the great door," cried Kerlin in a voice beset with cracking and hoarseness. "The great door into the Cognative Repository!"

Shierl ran ahead and thrust her force against the door; it slid aside, and they looked into the great dark hall, and the golden light from the gallery dwindled into the shadows and was lost.

"Call for light," Kerlin said.

"Light!" cried Guyal.

Illumination came to the great hall, and it proved so tall that pilasters along the wall dwindled to threads, and so long and wide that perspective was distorted. Spaced in equal rows were the black cases with the copper bosses that Guyal and Shierl had noted on their entry. Above each hung five similar cases, precisely fixed, floating without support.

"What are these?" asked Guyal.

"Would my poor brain encompassed a hundredth part of what these banks know," panted Kerlin. "They are repositories crammed with all that has been experienced, achieved, or recorded by man. Here is the lost lore, early and late, the fabulous imaginings, the history of ten million cities, the beginnings of time and the presumed finalities; the reason for human existence and the reason for the reason. Daily I have labored and toiled in these banks; my achievement has been a synopsis of the most superficial sort: a panorama across a wide and multifarious country."

Said Shierl, "Would not the craft to destroy Blikdak be contained here?"

"Indeed, indeed; our task would be merely to find the information. Under which casing would we search? Consider these categories: Demon-lands; Killings and Mortefactions; Expositions and Dissolutions of Evil; History of Granvilunde (where such an entity was repelled); Attractive and Detractive Hyperordnets; Therapy for Hallucinants and Ghost-takers; Constructive Journal, item for regeneration of burst walls, sub-division for invasion by demons; Procedural Suggestions in Time of Risk ... Aye, these and a thousand more. Somewhere is knowledge. But where to look? There is no Index Major; none except the poor synopsis of my compilation. He who seeks specific knowledge must often go on an extended search ..." His voice trailed off. Then: "Forward! Forward through the banks to the Mechanismus."

So through the banks they went, like roaches in a maze, and behind drifted the cage of light with the wailing ghost. At last they entered a chamber smelling of metal; again Kerlin instructed Guyal and Guyal called for light.

At a tall booth Kerlin halted the cage of light. A pane dropped before the ghost. "Observe now," Kerlin said, and manipulated the activants.

They saw the ghost, depicted and projected: the flowing robe, the haggard visage. The face grew large, flattened; a segment under the vacant eye became a scabrous white place. It separated into pustules, and a single pustule swelled to fill the pane. The crater of the pustule was an intricate stippled surface, a mesh as of fabric, knit in a lacy pattern.

"Behold!" said Shierl. "He is a thing woven as if by thread."

Guyal turned eagerly to Kerlin; Kerlin raised a finger. "Indeed, indeed, a goodly thought, especially since here beside us is a rotor of extreme swiftness, used in reeling the cognitive filaments of the cases… Now then observe: I reach to this panel, I select a mesh, I withdraw a thread, and note! The meshes ravel and loosen and part. And now to the bobbin on the rotor, and I wrap the thread, and now with a twist we have the cincture made…"

Shierl said dubiously, "Does not the ghost observe and note your doing?"

"The pane shields our actions; he is too exercised to attend. And now I dissolve the cage and he is free."

The ghost wandered forth, cringing from the light.

"Go!" cried Kerlin. "Back to your genetrix, back, return and go!"

The ghost departed. Kerlin said to Guyal, "Follow; find when Blikdak snuffs him up."

At a cautious distance Guyal watched the ghost seep up into the black nostril, and returned to where Kerlin waited by the rotor. "The ghost has once more become part of Blikdak."

"Now then," said Kerlin, "we cause the rotor to twist, the bobbin to whirl, and we shall observe."

The rotor whirled to a blur; the bobbin (as long as Guyal's arm) became spun with ghost-thread, at first glowing pastel polychrome, then nacre, then fine milk-ivory.

The rotor spun, a million times a minute, and the thread drawn unseen and unknown from Blikdak thickened on the bobbin.

The rotor spun; the bobbin was full — a cylinder shining with glossy silken sheen. Kerlin slowed the rotor: Guyal snapped a new bobbin into place, and the unraveling of Blikdak continued.

Three bobbins — four — five — and Guyal, observing Blikdak from afar, found the giant face quiescent, the mouth working and sucking, creating the clacking sound which had first caused them apprehension.

Eight bobbins. Blikdak opened his eyes, stared in puzzlement around the chamber.

Twelve bobbins; a discolored spot appeared on the sagging cheek, and Blikdak quivered in uneasiness.

Twenty bobbins: the spot spread across Blikdak's visage, across the slanted fore-dome, and his mouth hung lax; he hissed and fretted.

Thirty bobbins: Blikdak's head seemed stale and putrid; the gun-metal sheen had become an angry maroon, the eyes bulged, the mouth hung open, the tongue lolled limp.

Fifty bobbins: Blikdak collapsed. His dome lowered against his mouth; his eyes shone like feverish coals.

Sixty bobbins, seventy bobbins; Blikdak was no more. The breach in the wall gave on barren rock, unbroken and rigid.

And in the Mechanismus seventy shining bobbins lay stacked.

Kerlin fell back against the wall. "My time has come. I have guarded the Museum; together we have won it from Blikdak... Attend me now. Into your hands I pass the curacy; now the Museum is your charge to guard and preserve."

"For what end?" asked Shierl. "Earth expires, almost as you... Wherefore knowledge?"

"More now than ever," gasped Kerlin. "Attend: the stars are bright, the stars are fair; the banks know blessed magic to fleet you to youthful climes. Now... I go. I die."

"Wait!" cried Guyal. "Wait, I beseech!"

"Why wait?" whispered Kerlin. "You call me back?"

"How do I extract from the banks?"

"The key to the index is in my chambers, the index of my life..." And Kerlin died.

Guyal and Shierl climbed to the upper ways and stood outside the portal on the ancient floor. It was night; the marble shone faintly underfoot, the broken columns loomed on the sky.

Across the plain the yellow lights of Issane shone warm through the trees; above in the sky shone the stars.

Guyal said to Shierl, "There is your home; do you wish to return?"

She shook her head. "We have looked through the eyes of knowledge. We have seen old Thorsingol, and the Sherrit Empire before it, and Golwan Andra before that and the Forty Kades even before. We have seen the warlike green-men, and the knowledgeable Pharials and the Clambs who departed Earth for the stars, as did the Merioneth before them and the Gray Sorcerers still earlier. We have seen oceans rise and fall, the mountains crust up, peak and melt in the beat of rain; we have looked on the sun when it glowed hot and full and yellow… No, Guyal, there is no place for me at Issane…"

Guyal, leaning back on the weathered pillar, looked up to the stars. "Knowledge is ours, Shierl — all of knowing to our call. And what shall we do?"

Together they looked up to the white stars.

"What shall we do…"

THE TELEPHONE WAS RINGING IN THE DARK

Chapter I

THE TELEPHONE WAS RINGING in the dark. An insistent jangle. A man climbed out of bed, limped across the room, groped for the receiver: "Hello?"

Remote sounds of gaiety came whispering out into the dark: music, laughter, voices.

"Hello," said Marsh again. Somewhere near the telephone an easy reckless baritone spoke: "For Pete's sake, no! No, no and no! Let her sit."

"Hello," called out Marsh. "Hello!"

There was a confused mumble, then the baritone again, in rueful complaint: "Hell to pay as it is." The voice sounded loud in Marsh's ear. "Boko? Let me talk to Boko."

"You've got the wrong number," snapped Marsh. He hung up, returned to bed, hip aching resentfully.

The telephone rang again. Marsh lay waiting for it to stop. After six rings he heaved himself out of bed, crossed the room. "Hello."

The confident baritone said, "Let me talk to Boko."

"Nobody here by that name," said Marsh. "You've got the wrong number."

He went back to his bed, but almost before he reached it, the phone rang again. He swung around, marched back to the telephone. "Hello!"

The baritone voice had been busy with another conversation, but almost immediately turned itself into the telephone. "Right. Let me talk to Boko."

Marsh rasped, "Are you deaf? Or stupid? Three times now you've called this number. I'm trying to sleep."

There was a short pause. The baritone voice, no longer gay, said, "Don't call me stupid."

"You stupid bastard, of course you're stupid! What number are you trying to get?"

There was no answer. In the background sounded voices and music. Then the line went dead.

With a dour grimace Marsh went back to bed. Now sleep evaded him. The mattress was hard, the pillow hot, his hip ached as it always did in the wake of some unpleasant incident. Not precisely a psychosomatic hurt; the original wound had been real enough. Marsh lay staring into the dark. Presently his eyelids drooped, and he fell asleep.

The telephone rang: a harsh shattering peal. Marsh, startled, jumped from bed, hobbled across the room. He picked up the receiver: "Hello?"

The gay baritone voice, slurred in only the faintest degree, but bright with malice, spoke. "Hey, stupid. Are you awake?"

Marsh paused before answering. "Sure," he said. "I'm awake. Who's calling?"

"This is the voice of your conscience. You go back to sleep. Have a good rest."

Marsh listened. There was still music in the background, but quieter; the voices were either less loud or less numerous. The line went dead. Marsh listened until the dial-sound buzzed into his ear. Then he hung up, returned across the room, looked at the luminous dial of his clock. One-fifteen, of a Saturday night. Sunday morning, June 16th, to be precise. He turned back toward his bed, but paused by the window. Ranked rooftops descended to Lake Merritt, a blankness reflecting a thousand quivering lights. Beyond loomed Oakland's skyline... Marsh heaved a deep sigh, soothed in spite of himself. In general he could take a joke — so long as the underlying motives were genial. He returned to bed, but found that he had forgotten his hip, which now throbbed and ached unmercifully. With a muttered curse he hobbled to the bathroom, opened the medicine cabinet, dosed himself with aspirin. The mirror showed back a rather harsh and brooding face. The cheeks were flat, the nose thin, the mouth wry. The hair was short, of an indeterminate color, already showing gray above the ears. (Ten years before, at the age of twenty-one, Marsh had been half-engaged to an art student, who insisted on his likeness to Rembrandt's Polish Rider. She had cited a mystic, guileless inner destiny common to both faces: an opinion which Marsh had considered over-romantic.) Ignoring the mirror and its rather depressing message, Marsh bathed his face in warm water, went slowly back to bed.

Sleep was far away. His eyes bored the dark. Time passed: half an hour. When the telephone rang, he was over-tense and sat up more sharply than he had intended. He forced himself to walk slowly to the telephone, and answered in a mild voice. "Hello."

"Hey, stupid," sang out the now familiar baritone. "We got into an argument about whether you were asleep or not. If you were awake I stand to collect a buck…Hey!" Someone apparently wrenched the phone away. A girl's voice spoke, "Please say you were asleep, please, and I'll split with you!"

"Sure," said Marsh. "Where do I come to collect?"

But the baritone voice returned. "The bet's off. Say your prayers just once more and hit the sack. A nice good-natured guy like you deserves your rest." The line went dead. Marsh sat looking at the dial of his phone, fingers twitching. After a minute he went back to bed.

Some time later the phone rang again. Marsh did not answer. After an interminable period the ringing stopped. From the next apartment Marsh heard the sound of movement. Apparently the occupants, Mr. and Mrs. Stillwater, who were also his tenants, had been disturbed.

Marsh slipped into a troubled doze. Perhaps an hour later the telephone rang once more. This time, mindful of the Stillwaters, Marsh answered, still keeping his voice even and mild. "Hello."

"Time for you to go to bed, stupid. What are you doing up so late?"

"Nothing much," said Marsh. He listened. The background of music and conversation had dwindled to a murmur. The party was becoming quiet, perhaps breaking up.

"You can go to sleep now," said the voice. "I just wanted to teach you a little lesson, not to call people stupid."

Marsh carefully controlled his voice. His emotion was something not to be squandered in undisciplined invective. He felt something almost like solicitude for the man who spoke with such complacence. This man was doing him a favor: for the first time in a year he was feeling emotion. "What did you say your name was?"

"I'm the voice of your conscience. The next time you start getting salty with somebody, think of me."

"That's a good idea," said Marsh in a far-off voice. But once more he was alone on the line. He wandered back across the room to his bed. Quarter to four.

He had no further calls, though now he would almost have welcomed them. He lay back in bed with his hip hurting badly, but charged with his new mission. A goal, so to speak.

He almost felt sorry for the man with the baritone voice.

⁓

At nine-thirty Marsh arose, showered, shaved, massaged his hip. The Viet Cong bullet had passed completely through his pelvis: shattering, splintering the bone. At least he was alive, as eight other men were not — though Marsh had never found this fact a cause for exultation. Quite the reverse, in fact. He cooked breakfast and ate, watching the telephone, half-fearful that it would ring, with an apologetic baritone to plead excess of alcohol — in which case Marsh's emotion, now hard and heavy, would perforce be frustrated.

The phone remained silent. Marsh methodically washed dishes, poured himself a fresh cup of coffee, seated himself beside the telephone. He considered his telephone number: Clinton 4-2658. A number without pattern or shape, easily to be confused with another.

He opened the directory, consulted the list of exchanges. There were, in addition to Clinton 4, Clinton 9 and Clinton 1. Marsh drew up a list of numbers:

CL 1-2658	CL 4-6528	CL 4-5628	CL 4-8526
CL 9-2658	CL 4-6582	CL 4-5682	CL 4-8562
CL 4-2568	CL 4-6258	CL 4-5862	CL 4-8652
CL 4-2586	CL 4-6285	CL 4-5826	CL 4-8625
CL 4-2685	CL 4-6852	CL 4-5286	CL 4-8265
CL 4-2865	CL 4-6825	CL 4-5268	CL 4-8256
CL 4-2856			

Marsh inspected the list. The first two numbers represented a mistake of exchange, the others were those in which the numbers were confused or inverted. The arrangement, thought Marsh, was more or less in order of probability. He thought a moment, added a few more numbers:

CL 4-1658 CL 4-2668

CL 4-3658 CL 4-2648

CL 4-2758 CL 4-2657

CL 4-2558 CL 4-2659

These were the numbers where a careless, unsteady or distracted finger might dial a digit one removed from the correct number — rather less probable than those of the first list, since a person would hardly make the same mistake three times in a row.

Marsh counted the numbers; there were 33. Among them presumably would be found that number which Baritone had initially tried to reach.

A new idea gave Marsh pause: the entire logic of his procedure was threatened. He opened his address book to the Cs, looked down the page:

Joseph J. Cody,

280 Henry Street, Oakland.

Clinton 4-9690

Cody the apartment house manager occupied Apartment 1. (Marsh had no slightest inclination to burden himself with the details of management.) Marsh dialed, and two apartments distant a bell rang, the sound coming as an unheard vibration through the walls. The vibration stopped; a voice Marsh recognized as that of Mrs. Cody responded.

"Roy Marsh, Mrs. Cody."

Her "Oh, yes?" was vague and incurious.

"I've been wondering who occupied Apartment 3 before I moved in."

"Oh my, let me think." There was a pause. "That would be Mr. and Mrs. Finch. They moved back to Ohio. He works with General Foods and was transferred to Cleveland. Or was it Cincinnati? Somewhere back there, anyway."

"What was Mr. Finch's first name?"

"Joseph, just like Mr. Cody's. She was Evelyn. Very good tenants, quiet and respectable."

"Would you happen to know if he had any friends — young friends — who called him 'Boko'?"

"Well, I wouldn't really know. I'd hardly think so. They weren't very social. I don't believe they entertained once in the two years they lived here."

"Thank you, Mrs. Cody."

Mrs. Cody now was interested. "Is anything wrong?"

"No. Just a telephone call for someone I thought might be Mr. Finch."

"Well, it probably wasn't him."

"I don't imagine so. A wrong number, probably."

"More than likely."

Marsh returned to the list of numbers. Baritone had not called CL 4-2658 hoping to arouse Joseph Finch.

He hitched himself closer to the table, dialed the first number: CL 1-2658. A woman answered. "Hello?"

"Is Boko there?" asked Marsh.

"Who?"

"Boko."

"Nobody here of that name."

Marsh drew a line through CL 1-2658, dialed CL 9-2658. The bell rang. "Hello?" responded a hoarse grumbling male voice.

"Boko?" asked Marsh. The voice sounded as if it might belong to a Boko.

"Who?" rumbled the voice.

"Boko."

"You got the wrong number, buddy."

Marsh dialed CL 4-2568. The line was busy. He tried CL 4-2586. No response.

CL 4-2685. "No, sir. No Boko here. You surely got the wrong number."

CL 4-2865. "Boko? Did you say Boko? How you spell it?" Marsh was not sure, and said as much. "Well, nobody around here with that name."

CL 4-2856. "Wrong number." Curt and definite.

He tried CL 4-2568 again. Still busy.

He worked down the six numbers starting CL 4-6. There were four wrong numbers, one which failed to respond, one connection with a taped message informing him that the number he sought was not in service.

Marsh made himself another pot of coffee, and once more tried CL 4-2568. The dark rich voice of a colored woman responded: "Binkins residence." Marsh asked for Boko.

"Who?"

"Boko."

"Boko? You mean Mr. Binkins? He's not here just now. Gone to his office."

Marsh heaved a deep sigh, hitched himself up to the telephone. "What's his number?"

Another voice came on the line: a quiet controlled voice with cultured intonations. "This is Mrs. Binkins."

Marsh said, "I'd like to speak to Mr. Binkins, but I understand he's not in."

"No, he's out for the day. You can probably reach him at Valley 2-3611. That's VA 2-3611."

Marsh made a note of the number.

"Thank you very much." He hung up, and smiling, sat back. Achievement. He opened the telephone directory to the Bs.

Binkins, B.K.
59 Mowbray Court,
Piedmont CL 4-2568

So there it was. B.K. Binkins. Boko.

Chapter II

Bernard Kelvin Binkins had married a woman eight years older than himself, though when the two were seen together the difference was by no means obvious. Eleanor Binkins, at 44, was a slim woman of medium height. Her skin was flawless, her figure good; her hair had been bleached snow-white by someone obviously competent and arranged in lustrous puffs and swirls: a style which, while dignified, conceded no advantage whatever to time. Her face was rather thin, the eyes narrow and keen, the mouth fastidious, the nose long but well-formed.

Eleanor Binkins had beautiful taste in clothes, and no one, under any circumstances, had ever known Eleanor to be other than elegant, modish, gracious and proper. Her first marriage, to Dr. Wilmuth Gerke, had been something of a trial, and ultimately proved unworkable. Dr. Gerke, a burly black-haired man of vigorous masculinity, had intrigued her with his Viennese accent, his piercing gaze, the glamour of his position as the Bay Area's leading brain surgeon. Eleanor somewhere had acquired the conviction that a surgeon, so intimately acquainted with the human body, would thereby be less inclined to enthusiasm in the bedroom. She also refused to interest herself in chess, mountain-climbing, sailing, calisthenics, abstruse discussion, Indian relics. Dr. Gerke, in his turn, could not adapt himself to the rigorous social schedule which Eleanor maintained. Reluctantly she conceived three children, Nancy, Amy and Maile, and when Dr. Gerke insisted on at least three more, Eleanor moved to her own bedroom. A divorce was arranged, and after a decent interval Eleanor married Bernard Kelvin Binkins. Her friends, the elite of Piedmont and Berkeley, were mildly surprised, and a trifle dubious as to B.K. Binkins' social qualifications. He had achieved notoriety as an audacious and imaginative entrepreneur, having promoted the magnificent Pan-Pacific Hotel on the shores of Lake Merritt. He was also the dynamic force behind Project Forward, which had converted twenty acres of West Oakland slums to a low-cost housing complex. Project Forward had won BK Binkins the cover of *Time*: his face had appeared against an Artzybasheff background of red and yellow bulldozers attacking an army of diseased gray houses. Project Forward, however, had earned him more fame than money; indeed, it had absorbed most of the profits from the Pan-Pacific Hotel venture. Eleanor's nephew Craig Maitland had introduced them at a downtown luncheon. BK had been impressed by Eleanor's appearance, her wealth and her social position. Eleanor considered him carefully.

In many ways BK Binkins made an attractive candidate for a second husband. He was personable, in fact downright engaging: tall, rather loosely put together, with a cinnamon-brown crew-cut going bald at the back. His nose was a big aquiline jut, his eyes were deep-set and quizzical. He wore heavy tortoise-shell glasses, but as often as not carried them in his hand and flourished them for emphasis as he spoke.

The second and possibly decisive factor in BK's favor was his profession. Eleanor herself was a crafty and aggressive business-woman, though she deprecated her activity and spoke of it as "dabbling". Through the offices of her nephew, she had acquired a taste for real estate speculation: why not team her money with BK Binkins' enterprise, contacts and inside know-how?

There were, of course, one or two matters militating against BK. He was a dedicated girl-watcher, and possibly, so Eleanor suspected, a philanderer. Then he had been born in Texas, and though transplanted to California at an early age he had brought with him a set of rather flamboyant habits. His clothes were just a trifle too sporty; his neckties a shade too elemental; his car, a red Pontiac convertible, more than somewhat too bumptious.

Eleanor's final verdict was favorable. When BK Binkins divined that the attractive and wealthy Mrs. Eleanor Gerke would not be disinclined to marriage, he decided to take a chance. What could he lose? Eleanor's children were not unattractive, though the boy Maile seemed something of a "weirdo", as BK phrased it. Nancy, the elder girl, was dark, slender, with the thin face of her mother; like her mother she was at once gracious and formal: a combination of coolness and vivacity like a crème de menthe frappé. Amy, the younger, was quieter, introverted, and in a detached wistful sort of way, almost beautiful.

BK Binkins married Eleanor Hodgson Gerke, and moved into the Piedmont mansion built by Eleanor's grandfather, one of California's first oil millionaires.

By and large the marriage was a success — at least not the fiasco that certain of Eleanor's friends had predicted. Neither had been forced into a radically different pattern of life; each carefully avoided circumstances which might occasion unpleasantness. There was naturally adjustment, and re-assessment. BK found Eleanor to be more independent, subtle, skeptical and secretive than he had expected. To his carefully concealed disappointment, she allowed him no scope in the management of her money — to Eleanor as unthinkable as allowing him to regulate her breath.

Eleanor in her turn had expected new drama and dazzle to her life, which failed to manifest themselves. BK's swagger and magnetic appearance turned out to be superficial; the high point of his life had been the *Time* cover. Events thereafter were anticlimactical. Somewhere Eleanor had encountered the phrase "Brummagem Knight", and it wandered through her mind often. Still she had no real complaints. BK meekly adapted himself to the incessant activity and gadding about of the Piedmont social set. Eleanor would have tolerated no flagrant philandering, but if she suspected BK of occasional gallantry beyond the call of duty, she pretended not to notice. Perhaps she was not unwilling that he expend his energies elsewhere; her own time was more than sufficiently occupied. She was chairman of the Highland Cotillion and the Allegro Ball, on the board of directors of the Ayrton Club, a patroness of the Piedmont Chamber Music Society and the San Francisco Symphony. And then there was the management of her money. Eleanor was not satisfied to let money rest idly and comfortably, she felt impelled to manipulate and nurture it. The oil investments were of course sacrosanct; Eleanor would as soon have blown up the Vatican as meddled with her oil shares. She occasionally participated in one of BK's ventures, but only after consulting her nephew Craig Maitland, whose money derived from the same source as her own. BK controlled his irritation, since the ventures in which Eleanor participated uniformly turned out well. Both Eleanor and Craig had money in his latest project: High Oaks Country Club Estates, a tract of expensive homes in the Orinda Hills, designed for the tastes of upper-bracket executives. Eleanor had been adamant until Craig came in, and BK fumed at the paradoxical situation where a wife trusted the intuition of a dilettante more than the seasoned judgment of her husband. Eleanor, divining his emotions perfectly, laughed in his face, a pleasant clear silvery tinkle without either malice or humor.

Eleanor's children, Nancy, Amy and Maile reacted to BK variously. Nancy preferred "Nancy Binkins" to "Nancy Gerke", and made the change. Amy followed suit, but Maile clung to his patronymic. Nancy and Amy liked BK, rather than otherwise. He could be relied upon to champion their causes against Eleanor. Whenever circumstances permitted he bought them presents. At which Maile sneered, as, less obtrusively, did Eleanor.

Eleanor was 44, BK 36, Nancy 22, and Amy 17: a situation conducive to emotional intricacies. Eleanor stood alert, and BK maintained a nice balance of amiability and detachment. Nancy was enough like Eleanor that there need be no worries on her score, but Amy was vague and dreamy, given to romantic excesses, and beautiful to boot.

Eleanor might have worried more about her girls, but for Maile. Maile was a real problem. His attitudes puzzled and irritated her, often to the point of sheer dismay. As when she found a Band-Aid tin full of marijuana cigarettes in his drawer. Marijuana was a much-maligned substance, so Maile assured her — more salubrious than alcohol (no hangover) and far less dangerous than tobacco, assertions for which he offered to provide documentation. Eleanor's outrage was heightened by Maile's lack of guilt or remorse. Marijuana was illegal, declared Eleanor, a symbol of juvenile delinquency and other forms of depravity. She wanted it stopped. Maile acquiesced too easily, and Eleanor began to supervise his activities with new vigilance. Maile's indifference became sulky resentment. BK was little help in the matter. He pointed out that Maile would only sneer at his admonitions, and in effect washed his hands of responsibility.

The marijuana episode was several months in the past, and the family came down for breakfast on the morning of Sunday June 16th in every outward semblance of amicability.

Breakfast was always served in the morning room: a tall airy chamber paneled in pale green poplar, with a white ceiling and a green Chinese rug on the floor. Sunlight slanted in through a set of French windows, the cleaning of whose innumerable panes was a weekly collaboration between Clara the maid and Sam the gardener. Eleanor had furnished the room with great care. There was an antique French Provincial table painted a dusty ivory, with ornaments and scallops of faded gold, green and blue. Italian marbles and potted ferns filled the window niche; the lighting fixtures were quaint old French sconces.

Eleanor, an early riser, was first to appear. She looked over the table, then stepped out into the kitchen for a word with Marlene the cook, wife to Sam the gardener.

Nancy was next down, then Amy, looking unexpectedly dreary and wan. Then BK appeared, bluff and hearty in a black dressing robe, exuding odors of toothpaste, talcum, soap and cologne. Finally Maile slouched into the room, wearing tan chinos and a maroon shirt — an outfit clashing desperately with the decor of the room. Maile was a dark moody slender youth, with hair worn much too long for the taste of either BK or Eleanor. Frequently they urged upon him a conventional crew-cut, to which Maile's response was typically a twitching cynical grin. His eyes were hazel, set wide apart, and through some unfortunate mannerism seemed always to be glancing sidewise, which made Maile seem at least twenty percent more devious and arrogant than he actually was. Seating himself, he muttered "Good morning." BK, unfolding the Sunday *Tribune*, said "Good morning, Maile." The girls ignored him, Nancy busying herself with the *San Francisco Chronicle*, Amy staring blankly down at the silverware. Eleanor said, "Good morning, dear."

Breakfast proceeded: an assortment of fruit juices, grapefruit in shaved ice, a great platter of eggs, another of bacon, ham and pork sausages, toast, muffins, marmalade, jam, coffee and cocoa in silver urns.

BK read the paper as he ate, occasionally commenting on some aspect of the news which he deemed significant. BK tended to be something of an isolationist and was revolted by the United Nations, where he felt the United States was "sucking hind tit to a bunch of dagos and chinamen". Eleanor, apolitical but with Republican instincts, had no particular quarrel with BK's views; Nancy, a senior at Stanford, frequently took BK to task, and they would argue at length. Amy had little to say — so little indeed that Eleanor often wondered if Amy might not be retarded. Still, her grades at Miss Prince's School were fair to good and she read far too many books. Maile's reaction to the political discussions was a curl of the lip. He attended Piedmont High, where he refused to interest himself in football, drama, publications, in any school functions whatever. But he took the trouble to maintain good grades, as he wanted to enter Cal.

Amy was only toying with her breakfast. Eleanor peered at her sharply. "Aren't you feeling well?"

"I guess not," said Amy. "Not very well, anyway."

"She's got a hangover," said Maile casually.

"Hangover!" exclaimed Eleanor.

Amy turned Maile a curious questioning side-glance: puzzlement rather than accusation or resentment.

"What time did you get home?" Eleanor demanded. She had attended a school reunion in San Francisco and had not returned home herself until the small hours.

"I don't know," said Amy. "It wasn't too late."

"Who were you out with? Randy?"

"No."

Nancy said rather hurriedly, "She was with me. We went to a party. At Craig's. She might have had a highball, but she certainly didn't drink enough for a hangover." She darted a furious glance at Maile, who shrugged and, with his twitching saturnine smile, turned away.

BK rustled the paper. "Jehosaphat!" he groaned. "Listen to this! 'New rains forecast for today and tomorrow. A final faint echo of last week's unseasonable downpour appears likely, as the weather bureau announced a weak storm front easing in from the Gulf of Alaska.'" His voice lost its edge of excitement. "I guess it's not as bad as I thought. Another rain like last week and I've had it. Until that new retaining wall goes in. Nothing has gone right on that confounded job."

Eleanor pursed her mouth — a mannerism which indicated that the subject under consideration was money. She said delicately, "A pity."

BK spoke with artificial cheer, "But we'll pull through, colors flying! Don't worry about that! One or two good breaks, and we'll make all the shopping centers in the world look sick...I'd like to get a few of these sub-contractors off my neck though. That I would."

Eleanor's lips pursed even more tightly, until her mouth resembled a length of old white shoelace. The "shopping center" was a new project of Craig's — the biggest thing Craig had ever tackled: a fifty-two acre complex of department stores, supermarkets, restaurants, an "International Arcade", an ice skating rink, an auditorium, and a permanent "Automobile Fair", at which all makes and models of cars would be displayed and sold under a single roof. This was the dramatic kind of project which appealed to Eleanor. A trifle speculative and visionary, perhaps, but Craig had an absolutely infallible intuition in these matters. High Oaks now — Craig had let Bernard have fifty thousand dollars, on a temporary basis, but had drawn back from any formal association. High Oaks looked good on paper: location, roads, design — all clever and smart and contemporary. But Craig had sensed trouble, how Eleanor could never know. Clairvoyance? Instinct? And Craig had been right. First had come a carpenters' strike, then unseasonable rains — and High Oaks Estates nearly vanished into the mud. Bernard seemed to be hinting that he could use more money, a hope in which he was destined to disappointment. Eleanor doubtless would get back her modest investment — only twenty-two thousand — but with no particular increment. Bernard would be lucky to break even. Why risk money for nothing? The shopping center now: here was real opportunity, with the possibility of profits in six or seven figures. If all went well, naturally. Which reminded her, Bernard should never have mentioned the matter in front of the children. A word leaking out now could mean a world of trouble and expense, with unscrupulous landowners jacking their prices sky-high. This was the current phase of the project: she and Craig were cautiously closing deals and securing options for the low-price land Craig had selected. Not even Bernard knew the exact location. She appraised him from the corner of her eye. Adequate enough, in his own way. Cocksure, glib, personable. Highly personable. Something of a bounder, really, thought Eleanor, with only the faintest rancor. It made no great difference. Anyone who hoped to make money in real estate promotion — herself included — necessarily must condescend. At times. The secret of good breeding was knowing when to condescend, and when not to. Craig knew. Craig had the knack, faultlessly perfect. Bernard was not quite so adroit, not quite the natural aristocrat. How much nicer to be married to someone like Craig. Eleanor turned her attention to Nancy. At one time there had been something of a romance afoot. They were cousins, of course, and cousins married less commonly than in the old days. The interest of both had waned. Nancy now seemed to feel she was too good for Craig. Eleanor sniffed. Nancy was no raving beauty — too slender, nose too long, eyes too close. Still she had a certain piquant attraction. Amy was the beauty of the family. If only she weren't so moony. What on earth had gone on last night? Amy was seventeen — not too young for an occasional cocktail — but Maile might well have called the turn. Amy seemed not only wan and sick, but rather — well, troubled. That particular time of month? Eleanor tried to remember. No, she thought not... Eleanor turned to Nancy, asked casually, "Whose party was it last night, dear?"

Nancy looked uncomfortable. "I told you. Craig's."

Maile laughed — a jeering harsh sound. "Craig still thinks he's a college boy. Big man on campus. Only there's no campus."

Eleanor started to speak, to reprove Maile, but BK's explosive bark of laughter halted her. "By God, there's the best description of Craig I've ever heard!"

Maile grinned, well pleased with himself. He rose from the table. "I need money."

BK blinked and, leaning back in his chair, portentously assumed his role as *paterfamilias*. "What on earth for?"

"I want to build a boat."

"A boat, yet. What kind of boat?"

"A trimaran. Twenty-six feet long."

"Well, well, well, well, well."

"Ridiculous," said Eleanor, then reconsidered. A boat, after all, would at least be healthier than some of Maile's other diversions, which she carefully refrained from defining. She said in a thoughtful voice, "How much money does all this require?"

"Oh — two thousand or so. Not all at once, of course. They're really not expensive boats to build."

"And where will you build this boat?" demanded BK sternly.

"Back in the coach-house." This was an ancient structure behind the tennis court, which Maile had adapted to his own uses.

BK looked toward Eleanor, as if in careful consideration of the request: a pose, as everyone at the table, except possibly Amy — and BK himself — understood. The money, if it came, would come from Eleanor. The decision would likewise come from Eleanor, in one or two cool words.

"We'll see," said Eleanor. "Bring the plans in and show them to your father, and then we'll come to a decision."

Maile turned BK a dark dispassionate glance. "Now?"

BK rubbed his hands together briskly, rose to his feet. "Nope. Haven't time now. Got to get out to High Oaks."

Maile departed.

"The ads started running yesterday, and we might be having some customers," BK explained.

Eleanor looked puzzled. "Customers? You haven't got the place cleaned up after the rain. I should think you'd want to assure people that their house wasn't about to slide down the hill. Or be swamped in mud."

"Well," said BK, "we've fixed up the worst of it. Had a loader and two trucks on the mud all week. And we're putting in that retaining wall. Sixty thousand dollars worth, and believe me, it hurts. So the place doesn't look too bad. The truth of the matter is that I need money."

Eleanor said calmly, "I can't spare anything. Not a cent. I'm strapped. This house costs a fortune to run. Do you know what the bills came to last month? Not counting clothes or taxes? Over eighteen hundred dollars. And that's using every paltry little economy I can think of."

"Liquor included, I hope?" BK asked facetiously.

"A hundred and twelve dollars."

"Money well spent." BK slapped his hands against his black dressing jacket, blew out his cheeks. "Well, my dear, if I bring High Oaks off — not if, when — we'll be in clover. It's bound to go. Absolutely certain. But right now it's all outgo and no income. I won't get any more bank money for a month, and in the meantime there's the payroll, and the sub-contractors are starting to speak up...I could certainly use a temporary loan — not even an investment, in the sense of a permanent outlay — but just enough to ease us by this month."

Eleanor shook her handsome silver head, with the calm irrevocable decision which occasionally irritated BK — though he never allowed the emotion to become evident.

"In fact," said Eleanor, "I wish I had my money out of High Oaks right now."

BK's feelings stirred and smouldered. "For that shopping center business?"

"Yes."

"Have you signed anything yet?"

"Craig's taken up one option, for ninety thousand dollars. Today we take up another for sixty-three thousand."

" 'We'? Craig and you?" BK's tone was delicately sardonic.

"Naturally."

"And that's the entire fifty acres?"

"No. There's one more parcel, of ten acres."

"Hmmf." BK turned half-away, started to speak, but deterred by the presence of Nancy and Amy, said merely, "I think you might have consulted me first."

Eleanor merely stared blankly at him, as if the idea was beyond her comprehension. BK reached down to the table, petulantly drank the last of his coffee, turned and stalked from the room.

Nancy said brightly, "I don't think BK likes Craig."

Eleanor said, "It doesn't make the slightest difference whether he does or not. He doesn't have the responsibility of looking after my money."

"He probably doesn't want it."

Eleanor laughed shortly. "Of course he doesn't. All he wants is the use of it from time to time, to pull his chestnuts out of the fire."

"This is the first I've heard of a shopping center," said Nancy.

"I can't tell you anything about it," said Eleanor. "Not until we have control of all the land, which is a very sensitive business."

"I can imagine."

"It's a beautiful location. I've seen Craig's plans. There'll be all sorts of wonderful features: fine shops, a theater, a supervised playground for children, good restaurants, a cocktail lounge or two. And we've got this wonderful idea of a permanent Automobile Show."

"Heavens, Mother, you and Craig aren't building all this? It would cost millions!"

Eleanor smiled, pursing her lips. "We just—I shouldn't say 'we', since it's really all Craig's project. I'm only putting up part of the initial investment. Craig will put in roads, utilities, supply the master plan, and then solicit tenants, and the banks will lend the necessary money. Craig is certain to become a millionaire, if everything works out well. Naturally I'll stand to make a great deal of money."

Amy looked up from the funny papers, which she had been reading with frowning absorption. "Where is this going to be?"

"That's still top-secret," said Eleanor.

"Highly classified information," said Nancy saucily.

"Oh." Amy rose to her feet, wandered from the room. Eleanor looked after her thoughtfully. Then she turned to Nancy. "What happened last night?"

Nancy shook her head peevishly. "I've no idea. Craig asked us to a party at his house, and we went, and after a while I went off with Dick Jensen. I didn't see Amy. I thought she'd gone home —"

"Now Nancy. That's not true. You simply forgot all about her."

"Well, what if I did? She's old enough to look after herself."

"She's old enough certainly. But you know how vague she is."

"Well, she'd better get her feet on the ground."

"I suppose she was drinking."

"Yes, she probably was. Craig was serving French 75's."

Eleanor sighed. "I'd better talk to her."

She went upstairs, down the green-carpeted hall to Amy's room. This was a pleasant rather untidy chamber decorated in pink and blue, overlooking the tennis court. Shelves along one wall held dozens of dolls and stuffed animals, with bookcases below containing all the books Amy had ever loved and could not bear to part with: the Oz books, the adventures of Nancy Drew, various volumes of fairy tales. Amy was lying on the bed, face down. Eleanor said briskly, "How do you feel?"

Amy stirred. "Oh — I'll be all right."

"What happened?" Eleanor's tone was practical.

"I guess I drank too much," said Amy in a muffled voice. "I wasn't very careful."

"How did you get home?"

Amy paused before answering. "I don't know. Somebody brought me."

Eleanor sniffed. "I hope you didn't make a disgrace of yourself." She turned away. "Take some aspirin and try to sleep. You'll feel better after a while."

Eleanor went to her own room, stepped out on the balcony which overlooked a vast sweep of lawn and the swimming pool beyond. She stood a few moments blinking in the strong sunlight and chewing as if at a piece of thread. Amy, though darkly pretty and with a good figure, had never evinced any great interest in boys. Nancy had been frankly boy-crazy during adolescence, but Eleanor paradoxically had worried never an instant. Nancy was too much like herself: cool and careful. Nancy always knew which direction was up. Eleanor shrugged, returned within. She changed into a gray tweed skirt, a pink cardigan, slipped into a pair of comfortable low-heeled alligator pumps. Returning downstairs, she heard the telephone ring. Clara the colored maid answered.

"Binkins residence...Who?...Boko? You mean Mr. Binkins? He's not here just now. Gone to his office."

Eleanor came forward. "I'll take it, Clara." She spoke into the phone. "This is Mrs. Binkins."

A quiet masculine voice said, "I'd like to speak to Mr. Binkins, but I understand he's not in."

"No, he's out for the day. You can probably reach him at Valley 2-3611. That's VA 2-3611."

"Thank you very much." The telephone went dead. Eleanor hung up, wondering idly as to the identity of the caller. Very few of Bernard's acquaintances called him 'Boko'. Only one, actually, that she knew of. Bernard was generally known as BK...She dismissed the matter from her mind, and returned to the morning room for another cup of coffee and a look at the newspapers before she seriously planned out her day.

Chapter III

BK emerged from the house, wearing a brown houndstooth jacket, beige slacks, a white silk shirt, a tie of nubbly moss-green dacron. He paused on the terrace, half of a mind to return inside for a showdown. The image of Eleanor's face, mildly questioning, cool, indifferent, came to daunt him. He glowered at the 18th-Century fountain — detached by Eleanor's grandfather from a mouldering palace near Würzburg — turned, looked along the façade of the house and back across a half-acre of lawn to the tennis court. He was forced to admit — grudgingly — that the perquisites compensated for the headaches. Still: he was BK Binkins! whose face had graced the cover of *Time*, and who was entitled to more respect than he received. Muttering wrathfully, he turned on his heel, swung down the driveway, past Eleanor's black Continental and Nancy's pale green Corvair convertible, to his own red Pontiac. He pulled out into Mowbray Court, and, still smouldering, drove by twists and turns through the Piedmont hills into Highland Avenue, thence to the freeway and eastward toward Orinda. It just plain wasn't right, he told himself: plain not normal. A woman had no business involving herself with a nephew when her husband needed help. It was, essentially, a form of disloyalty. Not for the world would he have admitted it, but High Oaks was in a bad way. If the sub-contractors decided to turn nasty — look out!

He coasted down the long grade into Orinda, turned left, drove through undulating hills to High Oaks Country Club Estates. Parking in front of the model home which served as his office, he alighted, surveyed the subdivision with hope, doubt and gloom in equal parts. Four other model homes were ready to be shown; a dozen others in various stages of completion occupied sites bulldozed from the hillside. At the moment the scene hardly suggested suburban ease and comfort. Loosened by the rain, a terrace of uncompacted fill had collapsed into Windsor Way. BK shook his head sadly. He could indicate the sixty thousand dollar retaining wall as often as he liked, but the prospective buyer inevitably must be more impressed by the obscene flow of mud.

BK could bear no further contemplation of the scene. It was the most squalid moment of his experience. He was BK Binkins, the hard-driving two-fisted entrepreneur, whose face and fame had been manifested to the nation, but here he stood, strapped for a few thousand dollars to appease his creditors. BK shook his head once more, reverent before the incalculable mysteries of Fate. He turned, went into the model home.

Iola Bunning, the receptionist, summoned for overtime duty, sat at her desk drinking coffee. She perfectly exemplified one of BK's basic principles: with dogs and tomatoes both available for employment, only a dummkopf hires the dogs.

Iola Bunning was twenty-three years old, with a supple and elastic figure. She had a pert round face, a saucy pompadour of shining blonde hair, a manner at once disarmingly shy and provocatively bold. BK walked behind her, kissed her cheek. Iola Bunning smiled vaguely off into space, sipped her coffee. BK sighed heavily, the recollection of his troubles returning to oppress him. He gave Miss Bunning's head a regretful pat, slouched to his desk, seated himself. "Nobody's been out yet?"

"Not a soul."

"It's still early," said BK. He drummed his fingers on the desk. Miss Bunning stretched prettily, tilting up her bosom. She yawned. "Oh, I'm just so tired this morning."

BK regarded her severely. "Too many parties! Not enough sleep! I'll have to take you in hand."

"Gracious," murmured Miss Bunning. "I'm terribly alarmed."

"With good reason. I'm a hard man."

Miss Bunning sipped her coffee. "Someone had better show up pretty soon, or I'll fall sound asleep."

"Someone had better show up pretty soon," said BK, "or I'll fall flat on my face."

"Mrs. Binkins wouldn't come through?" Iola Bunning seemed thoroughly familiar with BK's affairs.

"Not a sou. Luckily I didn't expect it. If a few live ones don't show up, we're dundee."

"Oh come now," teased Iola Bunning. "Surely it's not that bad!"

"At least we'll have no worries about income tax."

The telephone rang, Miss Bunning responded. "High Oaks Country Club Estates... Mr. Binkins? Who's calling, please?" She listened, covered the phone with her palm, looked across the room to BK. "Mr. Marsh."

"Marsh? Do I know a Marsh?" BK hesitated, then lifted the receiver. "BK Binkins here."

A polite voice spoke. "You don't know me, Mr. Binkins. But we have what might be called a mutual acquaintance."

"Oh? Who?"

"Last night someone telephoned you, from a party."

BK frowned, rubbed his chin. "Yes?"

The polite voice hesitated. "I wonder if you can tell me how to get in touch with this man."

A sudden hypothesis flickered alive in BK's mind…"I'm not exactly sure who you're talking about."

"Someone *did* call you last night? About midnight?"

BK said thoughtfully, "Last night I was out pretty late. Someone might very well have called me." Ingenuously he asked, "What's the name of this 'mutual acquaintance'?"

"To tell you the truth," said the voice, "this is what I'm trying to find out."

BK leaned back in his chair, smiled at the ceiling. He opened his mouth to speak, then closed it again. Circumstances were so damnably complicated. He temporized. "I can make inquiries. Will you call me back? Or better yet, let me call you, since I might be anywhere during the next few hours."

After a moment's hesitation the voice said, "Very well. This is CL 4-2658."

BK nodded grandly to himself, in admiration of his own astuteness. "I'll call you back, Mr. Marsh, as soon as I get some information." He hung up, rocked back and forth in his chair. His eye fell on the seated figure of Iola Bunning, effectually roiling the flow of his thoughts. He swiveled about, looked out the window, but the sight of the mud-slide had the same effect. BK swiveled in the opposite direction, faced the blank wall…He had arrived at the party in question — for the second time — at about three. He now knew — more or less — the identity of Mr. Marsh, and why he had called. By and large, he wished Mr. Marsh good hunting — but there remained the ticklish subject of his own activities previous to three. Eleanor's tolerance had its limits…A well-dressed middle-aged couple, apparently affluent, entered the room. Miss Bunning smiled invitingly.

"We saw your advertisement," said the man, "we'd like to look at some houses."

BK, groaning to himself, rose to his feet. What an inglorious situation! He, BK Binkins, forced to show houses like a common huckster! Well, there was nothing to do but put the best possible face on the situation.

The man spoke, "Looks like the rain hit out here pretty bad."

"Yep," said BK confidently. "It sure did. Got us before we finished the retaining wall. Of course nothing like that will ever happen again..."

The man cocked his head dubiously. "Looks pretty bad..."

—

Several hours passed, during which BK and Miss Bunning became very busy. About one o'clock the flow of visitors diminished. BK stood out in Windsor Way, wondering whether or not he should feel encouraged. There had been any number of "be-backs", but only three couples had made what BK called "buying noises". None had signed any papers. Too much to hope for, thought BK, considering the hideous tide of mud. Again and again he had chuckled merrily at the trepidation of prospective buyers. Might not such condition recur year after year? Of course not, of course not! There would be landscaping and ground cover. Look at that new sixty-thousand dollar retaining wall! "We'll control all the mud in the county with that wall!" BK presently began to feel tired and cantankerous. His jaw ached from the confident smile. When the mud was gone, the suspicion of the prospects might diminish...Confound Eleanor, thought BK. Double-confound Craig Maitland and his schemes. If the need for money wasn't so urgent, he'd never have tried selling so soon. Premature, that was the word. All those prime prospects coming out, looking, leaving with unfavorable impressions — merely because BK was so damn strapped for a few thousand dollars. A glistening white Thunderbird nosed into Windsor Way, coasted to a stop. Craig Maitland jumped out with the rakehelly swaggering air BK occasionally found exasperating. BK raised his hand in a mannered salute, rather like a witness taking an oath. "Yay, laddie. You look bright and cheerful. What time did things break up?"

"Good Lord, how should I know? Time means nothing. I just got up an hour ago. Eleanor said you were here."

BK rubbed his chin. "Did you mention I made the bash last night?"

"No. Should I have?"

BK considered. "It's no secret. But just as well let sleeping dogs lie."

Craig nodded without interest. He was broad-shouldered and sun-tanned and looked younger than his thirty-two years. He wore black shorts, a gray polo shirt, white sneakers. His face was square, the slightest trace heavy, with prominent chin and straight heavy nose. His eyes were a clear guileless blue, his brow bland and broad, unfurrowed by care. He looked sidewise at the Thunderbird, patted the gleaming white hood. "How do you like her?"

"New?" asked BK.

"Drove her out of the showroom yesterday."

"Splendid. Real bonzer. Killerino."

"A bomb." Craig looked up Windsor Way. His eye fell on the loathesome mud. He laughed. BK winced.

"How many you sell?" asked Craig.

"No signatures, but all kinds of interest. Highly encouraging."

Craig's face darkened in a frown of startling abruptness. "That's a nuisance. I wanted to tap you for some money."

"Gadzooks, laddie, I can't push a gun in their ribs." Facetiously he reached for his wallet. "I can let you have five, if you're short."

Craig made a derisive sound. "Five what? Five grand I'd go for."

"Not five grand, sorry."

Craig muttered fretfully. "I kinda counted on getting my piece out of here, Boko."

"You'll get it, laddie, don't worry about that. It's safe as Fort Knox."

"That may be so. But I want that gold now. Today. This afternoon."

"What's the wild rush? Give me a month or so and I'll be out of the woods. That mother of a rain —"

Craig nodded peevishly. "Yeah, I know. But I got something on the fire which just can't wait."

"This big-time shopping-center deal, I suppose."

Craig turned his jaw truculently toward the south — presumably in the direction of the projected shopping center. "It'll make me or break me," he said. "I'm going into it all the way, which means that I've got to have some change."

BK shook his head regretfully. "I just don't have it, laddie. I'm for you. If I could produce, I'd produce, so help me."

Craig slowly turned to BK. "I'll tell you exactly how the land lies, in balls and strikes. I'm playing this game all out to score, and score big. I've bought one parcel outright. The biggest section. Call it Parcel A. Cost me ninety-five grand. Land comes high down there in Peralta;

there's housing tracts all over the place. I dug deep, believe me — sold my city bonds and the AT&T my grandfather left me. Everything but the oil shares, which I don't dare touch. I've got an option on Parcel B, and it lapses today. Eleanor's coming in for some of it, but not very much. You know how she is."

"She's cautious," BK agreed.

"That's the situation. I let you have money when you needed it; a short term loan due last month. I haven't pressed you —"

"Right, Craig, you've been damn decent. Damn decent."

"—but now I've come to a spot where it's cold turkey. I want my money, I need it, I got to have it."

"These rains, Craig. They've hurt me, you know that. But that's in the past; things are looking great now. In a week or two I'll have the money — confidently. I need one or two sales — that's all. I had half a dozen prospects today, real hard-breathers; I'll sell this place completely out in —"

"Boko, I hope you sell out tomorrow and make a fortune: great, absolutely great. But I need my money today. You promised me, you signed a note. Legally, I could take over this entire project, if I wanted to be nasty, which I don't. But —"

"Now, laddie, let's be reasonable. If I don't have it, I just don't —"

"You can raise it. Hit up Eleanor."

BK laughed. "*You* hit up Eleanor; you'd get it sooner. Where I'm concerned Eleanor's tight as a two-dollar shirt."

Craig shook his head. "Let's be realistic, Boko. I'm in this game to score. I can't borrow from Eleanor. All I can do is cut her in for a bigger wedge. Which I don't want to do. Eleanor's got all the money she needs. She likes it, sure — who doesn't? But she doesn't need it. I do. It's silly. I have the money. Why should I cut Eleanor in for more than she's in for now?"

"Laddie, if only I could —"

Craig jabbed BK in the chest with coarse emphasis, spoke full into BK's face. "I'll tell you what you can do. These red-hot prospects. Tell two of them you'll sell them a forty thousand dollar job for twenty-five — for promotion purposes — only they got to move and move fast."

BK cried out in anguish, "And I lose thirty thousand dollars?"

"Boko, I don't care what you lose. Either I'm screwed or you're screwed. Since it's my money we're talking about I'd just as soon it was you."

"Well, that's a nice way to talk."

"I'm just being realistic. And you don't need to lose thirty thousand. Charge whatever the market will bear. So you do take a little loss. It's got to be, let's face it. What I want is your check, right now, for fifty thousand, and no bouncer. Right now." Craig glanced at his watch. "Because that option goes up in smoke at five o'clock. I've got to run home, change clothes, meet Eleanor, and get with it."

BK drew a deep sigh. "So be it. So be it." He turned, strode blindly into the office. Craig followed doggedly at his heels.

BK seated himself at his desk. Craig eyed Miss Bunning carefully, who after a swift upward glance through her lashes, ignored him.

BK wrote, stood up, the two went back outside. BK handed Craig the check. Craig examined it, tucked it into his pocket, and became hearty once more.

"Thanks, Boko. No hard feelings about this. I just simply had to have this today."

"No hard feelings, laddie. Business is business."

"You make sure this doesn't bounce now."

"It won't bounce. I've never written a bad check yet, or failed to keep faith in any undertaking."

"That's a good way to be. Well, I really appreciate this, Boko. And now I got to slide."

"Hey. Something funny happened this morning. I almost forgot about it."

"What's that?"

"Some guy telephoned me. Utter stranger. Said you'd called him last night and wanted your address."

Craig stared in perplexity. He frowned, blinked, rubbed his chin. Then he hunched his shoulders aggressively. "What did you tell him?"

BK shrugged, held out his hands. "I thought he was some friend of yours. I didn't think of that guy you were ragging —"

"You gave him my name?" Craig spoke in a dull blurred fury.

"Sure, like I say, I thought he must be some friend —"

Craig turned away, strode to his Thunderbird. The engine started, the wheels bit gravel, the low glistening mass darted off like a swordfish.

BK stood looking after the car, face blank. He licked his lips, sucked them in. He looked at his watch. Fifty thousand dollars, which he didn't have. He drew a deep sigh. "So be it," he muttered. "So be it."

He went to the door. "Iola, you lovely young piece of cheese. I've got to leave. You're in charge. I'll call you later this afternoon. Sell lots of houses."

"Oh, BK — all by myself?"

"Yep. All by yourself."

BK circled the house at a lope, backed around the Pontiac, spun off down Windsor Way.

He stopped at a supermarket, bought two cans of spray enamel, red and black, and then thoughtfully, a quart of corn syrup, and continued at high speed into Oakland.

Craig Maitland rented a small luxurious house in the Berkeley hills. BK swung his Pontiac up narrow tree-shaded lanes, parked cautiously half a block from Craig's house, approached on foot.

Craig's garage was an open-sided frame structure, cantilevered out over the hillside, with steps winding down to the house. Beyond, under a smoky blue afternoon sky, with the sun like a polished brass doorknob, an immense vista of nine hazy cities surrounded the quicksilver bay.

The white Thunderbird seemed to watch BK approach like a skittish horse. With good reason. BK removed the lid to the gas tank. With a quick look to right and left, another down the steps to the house, he poured in the corn syrup. Carefully he replaced the lid. With the can of red enamel he sprayed a message on the gleaming white paint: HELLO STUPID. On the other side he sprayed HOW'S THIS, STUPID? With the black paint he sprayed swirls and daubs and driblets all over the hood, trunk and sides. He opened his pocket knife, reached in, ripped and slit the soft leather seats.

Suddenly nervous, he gathered the paint cans, the empty corn syrup bottle, withdrew. He started the Pontiac, drove away.

Twenty minutes later Craig emerged from the house, wearing a loose easy suit of Shetland tweed. He ran up the steps, swung into the garage, stopped short in utter astonishment. Slowly he leaned forward, eyes bulging as he surveyed the abominable mess. He read the letters printed in dripping red. Words bubbled out from between his teeth: "That son of a bitch…Why, that son of a bitch…" Over and over he muttered the phrase, senselessly, meaninglessly. He discovered the ripped upholstery, and became dead-silent. He heaved a sigh which was almost a whine, looked at his watch, gingerly opened the door, got into the driver's seat. He started the engine, backed out into the street, started down hill.

After a block or two the engine began to sputter and miss. Craig jazzed the accelerator, raced the motor. The sputtering only became worse. There was a whirr which became a thin squealing sound; the engine now caught only in occasional bursts. Black smoke poured from the exhaust. Craig turned off the ignition and coasted, his throat swelled out against his collar, eyes bulging and distended.

The car finally rolled to a stop. Craig alighted and without a backward glance walked away from the humiliated white body.

Ten minutes later he came to a service station. He telephoned the Binkins house and was duly connected to Eleanor. She spoke in a quick sharp voice. "Where are you, Craig? Do you know what time it is?"

"Yeah," said Craig. "I know what time it is. I'm in Berkeley. You'll have to come after me."

"We'll never make it to Peralta by five. We've lost the option."

"It can't be helped."

"What's wrong? Are you well? Did you have an accident?"

"No. No accident. I'll tell you when I see you. I'm at the Shell station, corner of Euclid and Hearst. Just north of campus."

"Very well. I'll be down."

Craig telephoned his insurance agent, who was sympathetic and non-committal. "My word, Mr. Maitland, a terrible outrage…Unfortunately — well, the car wasn't stolen, otherwise there'd be a clear case —"

Craig roared, "Do you mean I can't collect insurance?"

"I know, Mr. Maitland," said the soothing practical voice, "it's a shame. A real shame. But you're not insured against malicious mischief, and that's the whole size of it. Your recourse will have to be from whoever did the mischief. I'm sorry. I'll do everything I can to help, but I'm afraid the company won't give us much satisfaction."

Craig raved, stormed; the insurance agent murmured sympathetically, promised to put Craig's case to the adjusters in the most vigorous terms.

Craig hung up abruptly. He called the Ford agency, gave instructions. Then he went back out to pace up and down the sidewalk.

Eleanor presently arrived, in her sleek black Continental. Craig stepped forward, opened the door, jumped in, slumped down on the seat. Eleanor looked at him with a puzzled frown. "What on earth has happened?"

"Somebody got at my car. Ruined it. Paint. Fouled up the engine. No insurance. It'll cost me a thousand dollars. Two thousand dollars."

Eleanor's eyes narrowed. "Who'd do a thing like that?"

"I know who did it."

Eleanor put her immaculately gloved hand on the drive selector... The car slid slowly forward. She glanced at Craig. "What about Mr. Rosso?"

Craig grunted. "Boko gave me a check. But it's too late. We'll never get down to Peralta in time."

"You shouldn't have waited so long," said Eleanor, in a voice like the tinkle of ice cubes in a glass.

"I didn't have the money before."

Eleanor sniffed. "I could have let you have it."

Craig sat upright in the seat, cleared his throat. "I didn't think it was necessary," he said with dignity.

"Well," said Eleanor practically, "we'd better hurry."

Craig frowned. "No point in rushing down there now. If we come panting up after the option's expired, old Rosso will lower the boom on us. He'll think we're anxious and jack up the price."

Eleanor thought for a moment. "You may be right. But he might sell to someone else."

Craig gave a coarse laugh. "Who else would pay him sixty-five thousand for that old pasture?"

"I hope you're right." Eleanor looked at him dubiously. "What do you want to do, then?"

Craig thought a moment. "Take me home," he said. "I've got a few things to put right."

On the way back up the hill they passed Craig's car. "What a mess," said Eleanor.

"Yes," said Craig. "It's a mess."

"If you know who did it —"

"I don't know his name, but I have his telephone number. I can find him."

⁓

Back in his own house Craig mixed himself a strong highball. He sat thinking, tapping his teeth with a pencil, frowning. Presently he took the phone, dialed a number. A discreet male voice responded. "Hello."

"Virgil?"

"Speaking. Sounds like Craig Maitland. You're too late. Everything's run that's gonna run today."

"I don't want a bet. Just some information."

"Okay, shoot."

"You know all kinds of people in your business."

"I sure do. One of my best customers is a college perfesser."

"Bums, toughs, card-sharks."

Virgil spoke in mild protest. "Here. I ain't some low underworld type. I'm an honest law-abiding bookmaker, if the laws were a little different."

"Here's the deal. There's a guy who's been bothering me — giving me all kinds of trouble. Understand what I mean?"

"These guys exist," said Virgil in a mild voice.

"I'd like to rent a couple real tough guys to put the fear of God into him."

Virgil was silent a moment. Then he said, "Well, Mr. Maitland, I'll give you some advice. Don't get fooling around anything like that. It's poison. Suppose I knew a hoodlum, which I don't. Suppose I sent him to you, and he gave this guy a rough-up job. Suppose his hand slipped and he hurt this other fellow — bad. Suppose this other fellow died. The hoodlum would be a murderer. So would you. It's awful dangerous stuff, Mr. Maitland. Stay away from it."

Craig said in a cold voice, "Let me worry about that."

"So far as I'm concerned, Mr. Maitland, you don't need to worry — because I can't help you."

Craig hung up. After further thought he called another number. A female voice said, "Binkins residence."

"Let me talk to Maile," said Craig.

Maile's voice presently came over the line, cautious and quiet. "Hello."

"Maile, this is Craig."

"Yeah."

"You were saying something the other day about these fellows you know — the guys who would do anything for a buck."

"What about them?"

"I might have a job for two or three fellows like that."

"What's the job, and how much?"

Craig only partially restrained the peevishness in his voice. "I'd rather deal with the fellows directly."

"I don't think it's a very good idea," said Maile.

Craig's temper began to slip. "Why not?"

"Two or three reasons."

"Who do I deal with then?"

"Like I say, what's the job and how much?"

There was a pause. Then Craig said stiffly, "Okay. This is what I want…"

Chapter IV

Royal Garnet Marsh sat idly in his kitchenette, looking out the window. BK Binkins had not called him back, but Marsh had not really expected him to do so. His fury of the previous night had waned to simple indignation, seasoned with a touch of self-contempt. To a certain degree he had only himself to blame, for starting a slanging match with a drunk. So the episode apparently had reached its end. Even had BK Binkins supplied the name of his persecutor, Marsh probably would have let the matter slide. Retaliation just wasn't worth the effort. Nothing was worth the effort… Marsh let the matter drift from his mind.

Automobiles passed below, sentient metallic oblongs, neither bird, beast, fish nor insect, the human polyp within functioning as nerve-pulp. Twelve o'clock whistles from far away blew, hooted, gasped, roared. In a nearby construction project power-saws quieted, hammers stopped pounding. Marsh went to his refrigerator, hacked at a ham, made a sandwich, opened a can of beer.

After he ate, he went into the living room, slumped into an over-stuffed chair, contemplated the remainder of the day. He'd better go for a walk. The doctor recommended mild exercise, and in any event there was nothing else he felt like doing…He dozed, fell asleep.

The telephone woke him. Bleary-eyed he took up the receiver. A familiar voice spoke. It now carried an overtone that sent archaic chills up and down Marsh's back. "Hey stupid."

Marsh had no reply.

"Hey stupid," said the voice. "You had fun. But you know something? It's going to cost you."

Marsh found his voice. It grated harshly in his throat. "You're making a lot of trouble — for me and for yourself."

From the telephone came a thick laugh. "I'm going to show you what trouble means."

Marsh hung up. He sat thinking. It might be wise to notify the police. He himself had no stomach for further contention with an obvious madman.

He looked toward the telephone. What on earth could he tell the police? They'd think he was a crank…Well, what about another go at BK Binkins? He reached out, paused once more, considering the likely course of conversation. The impulse dwindled; Marsh sat with hands limp in his lap. After a while he rose to his feet, walked aimlessly back and forth. He paused before a mirror, stared at the pale young-old face. What was going to become of him? He had no friends, male or female. He had knowledge but no incentive to use it; craft and skill, but no place to apply it. He lacked even the push of poverty. He could suddenly understand how a man could kill himself, for no reason whatever. From sheer boredom, self-hate, self-disgust…Marsh rather hurriedly turned away. He slipped into a jacket, left the apartment and went out on the street.

On the sidewalk he paused. From the construction project came the rap-rap-rap of hammers, the squeal of power-saws. Foundations had been poured, a few concrete-block walls had risen: undoubtedly another apartment building. Marsh turned, walked toward the lake. His hip, which according to expert opinion should be nearly mended, twinged with each of his slow steps.

Marsh watched a chess game in the park. At the public library he checked out a book in which he felt very little interest. The county court-house stood nearby. Marsh wandered into one of the courts, observed the empaneling of a jury. When court was adjourned, he walked west to Broadway, considered and rejected the idea of a movie. In a cafeteria he ate an early dinner, to save himself the effort of cooking at home. Returning to the street he boarded a bus, alighted near the lake, walked up the hill. The time was late afternoon, almost sunset; the sky diffused a wan beer-colored light into Henry Street. There, ahead, was his property, inherited from a father he had not seen in twelve years. It was a building similar to every other along Henry Street: four stories high, with a dignified but nondescript façade. Approaching, Marsh crossed the street to observe it critically, half-expecting to see symptoms of dilapidation: cracks in the stucco, peeling paint, broken glass. The structure, as usual, revealed no serious flaws, and Marsh was forced to the conclusion he owned a substantial and valuable property.

He entered the red-tiled foyer, walked down the hall to Apartment 3. A dark slender youth descending the stairs stopped to watch him. Marsh's attention was caught; he paused with his hand on the doorknob. The youth's face was illuminated by a wall fixture. He peered through the light, trying to see Marsh who stood in the gloom. It was a curious face: poetic, faun-like, but concentrated and intense. Marsh asked in a quiet voice, "Are you looking for someone?"

The youth shook his head, crossed the foyer, went out the front door. Marsh watched the figure bounce jauntily down the steps, then entered his apartment, crossed to the window, looked down into the street. The youth — he was about seventeen, thought Marsh — walked slowly away, head bowed as if in cogitation. He was wearing black slacks, a gray and black flannel sport-shirt, black shoes. As Marsh watched he drew the palms of his hands slowly up his slender hips, squared his shoulders.

He crossed the street. Marsh caught the quick shine of his face as he glanced over his shoulder. He stopped beside a black Ford sedan five or six years old, climbed into the back seat. A minute passed, then the sedan nosed out into the street, accelerated with startling rapidity, swung into the Lakeshore Boulevard traffic, disappeared.

Marsh turned back into the room. He lowered himself into the red overstuffed chair, sat quietly while dusk thickened the window. At this time of day he felt most isolated and alone. Someday, thought Marsh, he would be discovered shriveled, yellow, dead, the apartment choked with old newspapers and balls of salvaged string…

Presently he rose to his feet, went back to the window. Evening had come in all earnestness. Up the street came a car: a black Ford sedan. The dark youth apparently lived in the neighborhood, thought Marsh. A hundred yards up the street the car swerved to the side, parked. No one emerged. Strange, thought Marsh…His attention wandered. He turned away, went into the kitchen, switched on the light, started his percolator, stood watching the hot bubbles rising, dashing against the glass dome, deepening in color…His doorbell rang. Marsh turned. No one had pressed the call button beside his name at the front entrance. One of the tenants? Why should they bother him? Mr. and Mrs. Cody managed the apartment. If they wanted words with him, they would telephone. A salesman? Marsh slowly crossed the living room, reached for the door-knob. Into his mind came a picture of the black sedan, of the intent, impersonal interest of the dark youth… Something stirred in Marsh's viscera. With his hand on the door-knob he hesitated, then slowly withdrew his hand. Again the bell sounded. Marsh put his ear to the panel of the door, and thought to hear a murmur of voices. Marsh waited. Whoever was at the door went away. Marsh went to the red overstuffed chair, sat down, knees quivering…Obviously he should have thrown open the door to confront — whom? The dark youth with the impersonal stare? What of that? But there were at least two, and what business would two, or more, persons have with him this time of evening?…Marsh heaved a sad sigh. A year ago he would have flung the door open, ready for anything.

On sudden thought he rose to his feet, went to the window. The black sedan was parked as before. But even as he watched the lights blazed on; the car plunged off into the darkness.

Marsh went back to his chair. He picked up a magazine, but finding nothing to interest him tossed it aside, and sat sprawled in the chair half-asleep...

Knock-knock-knock at the door. Marsh awoke, sat up in his chair. *Knock-knock-knock* — a soft dainty inviting set of raps, as if from feminine knuckles. Marsh slowly rose to his feet, went to stand by the door. The knocks came again: seductive, intimate. The impulse to reach forward, snatch the door back was almost overpowering. But Marsh stood without moving, corners of his mouth drawn back in a faint grimace.

There were no further knocks. Marsh returned to his chair, sat until one o'clock. Then he went to bed.

Next morning the sun rose into a sky of hurrying fog-shapes, which presently dissipated. By nine o'clock the sky was clear and the sunlight warm. Marsh paid his Tuesday visit to the hospital, submitted to examination and treatment, made his customary responses to the usual questions. The doctor instructed him to maintain the same schedule, gave assurances that sooner or later the hip would mend.

Leaving the hospital, Marsh walked to the bus stop, lowered himself gingerly to the bench. As usual, the visit to the hospital had exacerbated the ache in his leg. A pair of high school girls approached, clear of skin, bright of eye. Hardly glancing at Marsh they plumped down beside him and began to chatter about their private affairs, oblivious to his presence. Marsh frowned, turned them a sharp glance. Their disinterest was both callous and genuine.

Marsh slumped down on the bench. He was a young man. He was not ill-favored. His clothes — he glanced at them: dark gray slacks, a long-sleeved wool shirt of a nondescript blue and green check. Not very dashing. His attitude, the aura of his personality? Marsh nodded grimly. "I feel like a sick old man, I feel and act like a sick old apartment-house manager."

He sprang to his feet. The girls were startled, paused briefly in their conversation to stare at him. Marsh walked swiftly up the street, so vigorously that his hip protested. Damn the hip. Something has to be done. A cab drove past. Marsh signaled; why not? He had fourteen-thousand dollars of accumulated disability pay and income from apartment rentals in the bank. He'd have more after he sold the apartment house. Then what? Who knows? Maybe the stock market. Maybe he'd drive into the far south of Mexico. The cab driver looked at him inquiringly; Marsh said, "Downtown. Anywhere. 14th and Broadway."

At Barclay Brothers, a high-class haberdashery, Marsh ordered three suits, two pair of slacks, two odd jackets, a dozen shirts, a pullover, six neckties, three pair of shoes, socks, underwear. The bill came to eight hundred and twenty dollars. Marsh wrote a check.

Alterations were necessary and Marsh could not throw away his old clothes as he wished.

He walked north along Broadway, to the automobile showrooms. The prices were daunting, despite the fact that the end of the season was at hand. Marsh made no commitments. He'd be a fool to buy a car out of sheer bravado. Or because of two girls at a bus stop.

The hip bothered him not at all.

"The hell with the hip," said Marsh. He dined at a nearby restaurant, emerged into the early evening. Now what? He felt restless. It was far too early to go home. His skin tingled with zest. He wanted a woman. But not just any woman: no flabby-faced drab, no gum-chewing stenographer. His imagination had not run so feverishly since adolescence. He wanted someone beautiful, adventurous, gay — someone to help him explore the sudden new world... For the life of him Marsh could think of no way to locate this paragon. He could hardly approach such a woman on the street... Details, details. Later in the evening he'd wander out to a bar and have a few drinks... Marsh boarded a bus, alighted at Lakeshore Avenue, walked around the lake and up Henry Street. The time was a half-hour after sundown, the sky was a murky blue-gray, streaked with a few high orange wisps. Ahead rose his property, a tall pallid outline faintly tinged with lavender: four floors, sixteen apartments, thirty-nine rent-paying inhabitants. He paused by the new construction, to assess the day's progress. To the front the carpenters had thrown up a skeleton partition; to the side the concrete-block walls rose apace. A girl of perhaps sixteen ran pell-mell out upon the sidewalk. She looked right and left, approached Marsh.

Her face was twitching with emotion, she spoke in a frantic rush, "Mister, please help me; some boys are hurting my sister."

Marsh stopped, looked her up and down. She was a pretty girl in an odd sort of way. Her hair was straight and clung to her head like a cloche. Her cheeks were hollow, her lips wide, her eyes large and wide-set: in the twilight no more than great dark smudges.

Marsh was dubious. Last night there had been a feminine rap-rap-rap at his door.

The girl was watching him from her eery eye-smudges; perhaps Marsh read into her gaze ideas and scorns and challenges she never intended. Marsh said, "Sure, why not?" He looked up the street. There — a half a block away — a dark sedan. He could not be sure.

"Please!" sighed the girl. "Please hurry." She beckoned. "Hurry." She flitted off into the construction area.

From a pile of half-inch reinforcing steel Marsh selected a two-foot length. The girl stopped, looked back. Marsh held the length of steel to his leg. "This way. *Quick!*" came the soft voice. She ran ahead softly, easily, disappeared behind a stack of concrete blocks.

Marsh veered quickly to the left, circled the stack from the opposite direction. He saw the girl. Her head was turned, she looked back the way she had come. Three dark forms stood pressed against the wall of blocks. Marsh approached quietly. The girl saw him, squealed with alarm. The three forms sprang forth. There was a hulking narrow-headed negro, a tall young white man with a face like a bear, and the slender youth Marsh had seen the previous evening. The girl stood to the side, her face luminous with excitement.

The slender youth spoke. "Hey, stupid." The words were flat and carefully enunciated: rehearsed. His two companions came forward. Both carried bicycle chains. Marsh jumped over beside the concrete blocks. The negro raised his arm, the chain hissed. Marsh struck up, caught the chain on the steel bar, snatched it from the black fist, and in the same motion struck down across the cropped head. The negro uttered a poignant sound. Marsh dodged to avoid the rush of the tall young white man, who struck the wall with his chain, then caught Marsh in a crushing hug. The negro staggered close, crying, "He done hurt me; he done hurt me bad." Marsh jabbed up with the point of the rod, caught the white man in the mouth. Teeth grated on steel, the white man choked, gasped; Marsh toppled him in front of the negro, jabbed down as hard as he could into the white face. The steel tore bone and cartilage; the grip relaxed. Marsh struck at the negro who flung up his arm and took the blow on the wrist. Marsh struck again, the rod bending around the side of the black head. The slender youth could not be seen. The girl was standing back, laughing in weird excitement. The white man was on his knees, arms groping; Marsh struck down as hard as he could; an arm fell limp. The negro was crawling confusedly on hands and knees. Marsh struck down, the negro lurched, fell flat.

Marsh was beside himself with fury, the near-orgastic release of tension. He smashed at the white man's shin, then with judicious even-handedness, turned back to the negro, crushed an out-flung elbow. Then back to the white man, whose face was a piteous bloody mess. Marsh raised the rod; the white man brought up his forearm; Marsh struck and the white man fainted.

Marsh paused, a trifle appalled. Where was the slender dark youth? Nowhere in sight. The girl's gaze was riveted upon a spot above him. He dodged, turned. Above him stood the slender form, prying at the pile of blocks with a board. They already were toppling. Marsh stumbled, pressed to the wall, put his hands over his head... An enormous thunderous blow, a series of blows, weight and suffocation. Three-quarters stunned, he heard voices. They came as if out of a chasm. The girl spoke: "I can't see him. Is he dead?"

The boy said, "I don't know. Let's get out of here."

"Dick? And Lundy?"

"We've got to get them to the car before the cops arrive."

The girl's voice quivered. "I can't touch them."

"You've got to." The boy's voice receded into the chasm. "You've got to..."

Chapter V

In the hospital Police-Sergeant Glen Wilson questions Marsh, who recounts everything he knows. Wilson is non-committal. Skeptical? Uninterested? So Marsh suspects.

On his second visit Wilson states that BK Binkins has denied all knowledge of the affair, that no one answering the description of the two thugs have been admitted to any local hospital. If they were injured to the extent Marsh has described — and Wilson is politely dubious — they may have been treated by some private doctor.

Weeks pass. Marsh's hip has been re-fractured. Marsh, nevertheless, is anxious to leave hospital. Doctor is sardonic. "You've been nursing that hip a year. Now with a new fracture you're suddenly anxious to be out helling around."

"I can make it, if I take it easy," says Marsh earnestly.

"Still be two or three weeks yet. And even then — well, we'll see."

Marsh is eventually released. He takes cab to his apartment, limps into living room. Packages on sofa, on floor by door. He opens them — new clothes.

Marsh sits in quiet room thinking. Across hall Mr. and Mrs. William Stillwater have recently moved. Marsh transfers his belongings into Stillwater's apartment, leaves their card in name-plate, removes his own, advertises "Apartment for Rent". Then he gives all his old clothes to Salvation Army.

He buys a new black Buick Special, paying cash. Then he dresses in brown slacks, a jacket boldly patterned in black, white and gray squares, brown brogues, a tan shirt, narrow brown and black striped tie. He looks at himself in the mirror, hardly recognizing himself. He is thinner, his cheeks hollow, his jaw pronounced, his mouth a straight pale line. His hair is longer, he combs it straight back, giving his face a different expression.

He drives out to High Oaks Estates. The tract is sold out: no sign of BK Binkins. In a phone directory Marsh locates the address of the Binkins house in Piedmont: 59 Mowbray Court.

Marsh drives to Piedmont, finds Mowbray Court, parks. He walks into driveway, surveys house. He goes back, sits in car. After a while he gets out again, walks along street, turns corner, finds spot where power and telephone lines lead in toward house, through a copse of cedars, fir, redwoods.

He returns to his car, drives to an electronics supply house in downtown Oakland. He makes a number of purchases and returns to Binkins' house...The time is three o'clock, the streets are quiet. Marsh swings over stone fence, climbs tree, splits telephone wire, scrapes insulation from one of the wires, splices in a shunt, which leads through a detector coil. He ties this to a branch, leads wires to the ground. He connects a small amplifier, one component of a citizen's band transceiver. He climbs tree once more, and using pronged alligator clips, taps the power line. He runs power to his apparatus, switches it on, wraps the whole thing with sheet of vinyl plastic, tucks it out of sight under a laurel bush. Returning to his car, he switches on the other transceiver, waits. About an hour passes. He hears clicking, buzzing sounds, then a voice: "Hello?"

"Alma, this is Eleanor."

"Eleanor dear, how are you?"

"Perking along, as usual. I called to say what a wonderful time we had at your little soirée."

"Yes, I thought everything went well." The conversation rambles on. Marsh listens fascinated. His tap works perfectly. The beauty of the situation, it can't be traced to him. It's a crime, he knows: a felony? Or only a misdemeanor? He doesn't really care.

Marsh drives home. Sound grows fainter, almost dies by time he reaches apartment. He arranges an antenna, and reception improves.

All evening he sits listening to telephone conversations in and out of the Binkins' house. BK telephones home that he'll be late for dinner. Eleanor asks if he and Craig got together. BK says complacently, "If I wanted to commit financial suicide, I'd do what Craig wants me to."

Eleanor sharply reminds him that she's got almost fifty thousand tied up in the project. BK, still bland, remarks that he counseled her against it. "High Oaks was a better bet. It looked bad during that rain, but it paid off. In spite of Craig and his shopping center!"

Eleanor airy, "Any project requires patience. That terrible business with Craig's car cost us a great deal of money."

BK laughs. "That's what options are for. If you let them lapse, then try to buy, you can't expect a bargain. You're just asking for a bath."

A call. Nancy to a girl friend. Chatter, gossip.

A call from Mrs. Grover Brisbane to Eleanor. They chat about Alma's party of the previous evening: "Nancy looked absolutely scrumptious. Such a lovely gown. Is that fabric real? Or should I ask?"

"Yes, it's real. We found it in Rome; in fact it's a Mancini. Somewhere he's laid his hands on a set of priceless old tapestries. I suppose in a way it's a shame to cut them up for clothes, but they do make the most ravishing gowns."

"Oh I agree! Why have beautiful things if they can't be used and enjoyed?"

"Yes. We're having a party for Barbara in a week or two —"

"Barbara? Which Barbara would that be?"

"Barbara Tyburn, my little niece, just graduated from Radcliffe, with all the ambition and drive in the world. She's visiting again this year. Really such a dear. They made everything so pleasant for Bernard when he was back East this winter. So I thought a lawn party would be nice."

"Oh yes! On your wonderful lawn!"

A young man invites Nancy to a party. "What about Amy? I've a friend —"

"Amy's too young for affairs of this sort," says Nancy decisively.

"Come now. Don't be hoity toity. You took Amy to Craig's party. She got squiffed."

"I know. I've regretted it, and so has Amy. She hasn't even drunk wine since, or hardly gone anywhere."

"A pity. She's a cute kid. Why protect and shelter her?"

"Protect her? What a joke. She does whatever she feels like."

Next day Marsh buys a transistorized tape recorder, various relays, sets up a system so that the tape recorder starts whenever someone speaks on the telephone.

Wednesday

A call by Amy to a friend Christina, suggesting a movie.

Christina can't make it. "I've got a tennis date. Why don't you come too? We can always scare up somebody else."

Amy demurs. "I'm just getting over a cold, or the flu. Something or other. I don't feel much like tennis... I'll ask Cynthia."

"Cynthia's in Mexico."

"Lucky girl. When did she go?"

"Last week. With her father and mother. They're staying at some enormous hacienda that her grandfather owns; he's something to do with the railroads. Anyway this house is five hundred years old and covers about an acre, with a court in the center. Cynthia says it's absolutely glorious. Naturally it's all fixed up — fountains and tile bathrooms, rugs, an aviary..."

"Sounds wonderful. I'd love to travel — all by myself, or with just one friend."

"I would too. In Europe girls travel all over and no one thinks anything of it. They stay at Youth Hostels and old inns — sometimes it's pretty ratty, of course."

"I wouldn't mind."

"So long as it's not in Italy. The men simply won't leave you alone. Weren't you in Rome?"

"Last year we flew over, for six weeks. We visited Rome and Venice and Taormina. Nobody paid me very much attention, I'm sorry to say."

"Who's that girl Maile's going with? I saw them on Highland Avenue yesterday. She's so *weird!*"

"Felice? Yes, she's strange. They're out in the carriage house now."

"Oh?"

"They're building a boat. She's helping him. That's what he says they're doing. I hope — I hope..." Her voice dwindled.

"You hope what?"

"Oh nothing... I've got to hang up. Mother's just come home."

Eleanor makes a call. A woman answers. "McGill Investigations."

"May I speak to Mr. McGill?"

"Who's calling, please?"

"My name means nothing to Mr. McGill. I'd like to consult him in regard to a possible investigation."

"Very well, ma'am."

"McGill speaking."

"Mr. McGill, I'd like you to perform an investigation for me."

"That's what I'm here for. Who's calling, please?"

"My name won't mean a thing to you. I can't talk to you over the phone and I don't want to come to your office."

"Shall I call on you?"

"I'd prefer to meet you — say, the lobby of the Claremont. Can you make it today?"

"I'm free during the next two hours."

"In an hour then; the lobby of the Claremont."

"That should do."

"I'll be wearing a light gray suit, white shoes, and accessories."

"It would be a help to know your name."

"Mrs. Eleanor Binkins."

"Very well, Mrs. Binkins. I'll find you. In one hour."

A call to Maile, in a hoarse drawling voice.

"Hey Maile."

"Yeah. How's it going?"

"Not so good."

"Sorry."

"I got to get some more gold. I need it."

"Don't come to me. I told you who to see."

"I can't get near the guy."

"How so?"

"Oh — just the general brush-off."

"Too bad. But I can't do you a bit of good."

"I think we should make out a little better, Dick and me both. We both think so."

"Talk to the guy."

"He says he doesn't know what I'm talking about."

"Natch. That's destiny. With a capital R. For 'Reaming'."

"Maybe so. I still don't like it."

"Charge it up to experience."

"Ha ha! That kind of experience you can keep."

"I got to get back to work."

" 'Work'? You work?"

"I'm working."

"At what?"

"See you, Lundy."

From BK to Nancy.

"Hello my dear. Is your mother there?"

"No. I just came in myself. I don't know where mother is. Nobody's home. Unless Maile is out in the carriage house. With his — ugh — girl friend. Honestly, BK, I wish you'd talk to that boy. He has the worst taste — in everything! Clothes, manners, friends — and that girl!"

"She's an odd one, no denying that."

"She's from a far planet! She's strange!"

"Well, we can't all be alike."

"I know that. I don't want Maile to *conform*, exactly; I just want him to be normal. To get a hair cut and play football and drink beer, and — well, act like the other kids. He's a misfit."

"Yes, perhaps he is — but we're all misfits of one sort or another. None of the family is anything but a real rugged individualist."

"I know that, and I believe in it. Heavens, you should *know* I believe in individualism! But that doesn't mean going really far out!"

"I'll have a word with Maile. One of these days. The boat seems to be occupying his time. It's certainly costing enough money...Where did your mother go? Is she with Craig?"

"I haven't the slightest. I don't think so. Isn't Craig in Portland? Running down the elusive Cazzaro? Or is it Reno?"

Laugh. "Reno. I hope for your mother's sake — and Craig's sake — they find him. There's a lot of money tied up."

"Just where *is* this shopping center? Do you know?"

"No, and I don't want to know. South county somewhere, so I gather. There's lots of new developments down that way — new industries, subdivisions. If they can corral Cazzaro it may turn out to be a good bet. Craig apparently has an intuition regarding these things."

"He only has to be wrong this once."

"I don't want anything to do with the project for just that reason. I won't gamble, except on a sure thing. Craig's a gambler, and, I fear, so is your mother."

"She's been worried about something. Maybe it's the shopping center."

"I can't think what else it could be!"

"Well, I'm worried too. I've got to entertain Barbara and take her around, and she's so pretty I'll feel an utter frump."

"Now, now, honey. You're something to look at yourself."

"Not really, BK. I know it, and I don't worry about it. Well — she'll only be here a month or so. You know, BK? I never feel comfortable with her. She's so single-minded."

"Barbara?" BK sounds surprised. "I've always found her — well, pleasant."

"You're a man, BK."

"I admit to that. Well, I'll be home in an hour or two. I've got a few calls to make. Are you going out?"

"To a committee meeting, for the Clambake. Time's getting short."

Two other calls, both for Eleanor, from social acquaintances, regarding social affairs.

A call from BK to a man BK addressed only as Doc, making arrangements for Sunday golf.

A call to Amy from a boy wanting to escort her to a swimming party in Orinda. After considerable hesitation, Amy accepts.

A call for Maile from a young man who gives his name as Yoke. Amy answers and says that Maile isn't home, and has no idea what time he'll be back. Yoke says, "Who's this talking? Is this Maile's cute sister?", and Amy hangs up.

Thursday

Maile telephones Abe Schuster, inquiring price of fiberglass and resin.

A man calls Eleanor. (Marsh leans forward suddenly. The voice is familiar — but he can't be sure. He's heard so many telephone voices, and it's now been two months.)

Man:	Well, I'm back. (Heavy, disgruntled.)
Eleanor:	And?
Man:	Wild goose chase. No one ever heard of him. I practically went house to house.
Eleanor:	That's discouraging. Have you called Peralta?
Man:	He's still not there and they still don't know when to expect him. No word at all.
Eleanor:	(thoughtfully) I suppose there's not much we can do, except continue the search.
Man:	If I knew where to look. For all I know he's made a trip back to Portugal.
Eleanor:	Portugal? "Cazzaro"? That sounds more Italian, somehow.
Man:	Portugal, Italy — what's the difference?
Eleanor:	I wish I could think of something constructive. Should we hire a detective, do you think?
Man:	Detective, no! They'll blackmail you as soon as look at you.
Eleanor:	(surprised, thoughtful) "Blackmail"? I thought they were licensed, or bonded, or something of that sort.
Man:	Still no security. Some of these guys are pretty shady — real fly-by-nights. It's a dirty game.
Eleanor:	(slowly, thoughtfully) Well, well, well.
Man:	Anyway I don't see what a detective could do that I haven't done.
Eleanor:	I guess we've just got to wait.
Man:	"Wait"? With a hundred and fifty thousand dollars tied up? On one measly little plot of land. What if Cazzaro

dies! Or disappears? What do we do with forty acres of cow pasture, that we've paid through the nose for?

Eleanor: It won't come to that, Craig. So why get excited?

Marsh smiles. His name is "Craig".

Craig: I'm not excited. I'm just — well, disturbed.

Eleanor: What do you think we should do now?

Craig: I don't know. I'm going to forget the whole thing for a day or two. If I can. What's Boko up to?

Eleanor: (voice becomes dry) The usual. He's charging around inspecting properties. He wants to build another tract.

Craig: High Oaks turned out pretty well for him.

Eleanor: I suppose it's really rather common, this kind of money. (Eleanor gives a self-conscious girlish little laugh.) Sometimes I say to myself, "Eleanor, what are you thinking of, grubbing for money like this? Vulgar!"

Craig: It's still money.

Eleanor: Yes. It's still money. Vulgar dreadful delightful money.

Craig: And how I need it. My car still isn't running right. I'd turn it in if I could afford to. Maybe I will anyway. (Voice becomes peevish.) I think I'll do just that, today. There's no reason why I have to drive around in a wreck.

Eleanor: Imagine anyone doing a thing like that, to somebody's car!

Craig: He won't do it again. Unless he's got rocks in his head.

The conversation dwindles off. Marsh, fascinated, returns, plays back conversations. All kinds of knowledge — in tantalizing fragments. Eleanor and Craig seek a man named Cazzaro who stands in the way of some project involving a hundred and fifty thousand dollars. He thinks back to another conversation. "Shopping center", "Peralta". Highly interesting...

Another call comes: for Eleanor.
"This is Mr. McGill, Mrs. Binkins."

"Oh yes." (guarded voice)

"I've had a report from the operative I put on your case. She seems to have had no particular trouble getting the information."

"I'm glad to hear that!"

"I won't mention names over the phone. In our talk you mentioned three possibilities, which, if you recall, you labeled A, B and C."

"Yes. I remember perfectly."

"Possibility C has proved out. Shortly after midnight he left with the girl, who was almost totally incapacitated."

A pause. "Definitely?"

"That's the information the operative received, and according to her, the information was quite explicit."

"Well, well."

"If you like, I'll send you a written report with full details."

"Yes, please. And send me your bill."

"Very well, Mrs. Binkins. Thanks for your patronage; any other time I can be of help, let me know."

Chapter VI

Eleanor turns away from the phone. She's wearing a gown of pale green silk, a jacket of peacock blue with white brocade, a string of pearls. Her hair is swept up into a rather severe and unusual coiffure, which emphasizes the bones of her face and seems to bring them closer to the surface.

She returns from the hall to the living room, a long high chamber, with massive beams, plaster walls hung with paintings. There are a pair of heavy black iron Spanish chandeliers, four Persian rugs, furniture either antique Early California or Spanish, including a chest from Granada, a pair of iron candelabra from Barcelona, a pair of leather and olive-wood chairs from Cordoba bought by Eleanor herself.

In front of the fire sit BK, Nancy and dinner guests: Ralph and Loel Sampson. Loel is the former Loel Hardesty, classmate and sorority sister of Eleanor's at Stanford. Ralph Sampson is member of an old California family, whose great-great-grandfather owned San Francisco's first ship-chandlery, the business expanding into coastal lumber trade, then into lumber and timberlands.

A cart, built of teak and silver to Eleanor's own specifications, carries various bottles, a battery of glasses, a silver coffee urn, warmed by a candle.

Amy comes quietly in, looks into living room, turns to leave. Eleanor calls her sharply, "Have you had dinner?"

"I had a sandwich downtown."

"Where you been, chicken?" asks BK.

"A show with Christina." — lackluster, polite.

Amy goes on up to her room.

"Girl needs a tonic," says BK.

Eleanor compresses her lips, her voice becomes brittle.

Telephone rings. Nancy answers, sits at the little desk in the hall. It's her friend Jane Rush, inviting her to a weekend house-party at Lake Tahoe. Nancy dubious. "I'd love to come. Who'll be there?"

"Oh. Mother and Father, of course. Joyce, Deedee, Bernice, you and I. Richard, Phil, Shaun, Keeler Wilcox, and Chip Boggis. Only I don't think Chip can come. I'll have to think of another man...Ross Hannekin, perhaps."

Nancy demurs. "He's so utterly tiresome. All he can talk about is the stock market. Actually he's just a clerk or a board-marker or something equally ridiculous."

"What about Craig?"

"Craig Maitland? Oh dear. Not Craig. I'd vote for Ross first. Or even Bill Lukens."

"Not Bill Lukens. He's some kind of left-winger. At least that's what Richard says, and Richard is fastidious about things like that. Not that I care personally, but it would be tiresome to spend the weekend arguing about socialized medicine, and you know Richard. Anyway, about Craig. I know what you mean. He *is* rather carnal."

"Carnal, ha! He's plain lecher. We wouldn't be safe in our beds. Especially if he had a few drinks too many."

"I agree entirely. Let's omit Craig. I don't mind living dangerously, but not under my father's nose. Would you believe it, he's becoming an absolute tyrant! You'd think by now he'd relax; after all, I'll be twenty-one in September and I haven't disgraced him yet. Are you laughing? At *me*?"

"Heaven forbid. I'm thinking of my cousin Barbara. She's arriving Saturday, to spend the summer with us. Craig's never met her, he's only seen her picture. But already he's pawing the ground and snorting madly."

"Poor girl."

"Her family is very old Rhode Island. They have a stunning place at Newport. BK stayed there last winter."

"Why is she coming out here?"

"Just a visit. She was out last year too."

"Yes. I remember."

"Well, I'll warn her about Craig and after that she'll have to fend for herself. I'm sure she's had practice…Oh my."

"What's the matter?"

"She's arriving Saturday at two. I should be at the airport to meet her. I really mustn't go to Tahoe."

"Oh Nancy! Please don't say no."

Nancy considers. "I don't suppose it'll make that much difference. I'll tell mother we've been planning the weekend for months."

"It's true! I have. Really!"

"I don't think she'll insist. What time do we leave?"

"Noon Friday. You can drive up with us if you like."

"It sounds much fun."

The conversation ends. Nancy returns to living room. She mentions the house-party at Tahoe. Eleanor coldly asks if she's forgotten Barbara's arrival.

Nancy says, "Heavens, Mother, I'll be back the next day."

"I was counting on you to meet her."

"Ask Craig to go," says Nancy maliciously. "He'll be delighted."

Next day Eleanor telephones Craig, mentions that Barbara is arriving at San Francisco airport at 2:10 PM Saturday, TWA Flight 58. Nancy can't meet her, nor can she herself.

Craig gallantly volunteers.

"Do you think you'll recognize her?" asks Eleanor.

"Certainly. There won't be two girls like Barbara aboard the flight. If there are, I'll surround them both."

"She's dark, quite pretty and pert, blue eyes, not a large girl. I don't know where she gets her coloring. Her parents are both blond."

"I'll meet her. I'll give her a real Maitland-type reception, the works. Caviar, champagne, love and kisses. She'll never forget it."

Later in day comes a call for Eleanor. "Mrs. Binkins, you probably won't remember me. I'm —" here the slightest of hesitations "— William Stillwater, a friend of Barbara's. I've been planning to meet her at airport, but I seem to have misplaced the flight and time of arrival."

Eleanor cool, but polite, gives William Stillwater details. "Someone else, of course, is meeting her. But I'm sure she'll be glad to see you. Have we met? Are you one of the Hillsborough Stillwaters?"

"They're second cousins, something of the sort. We met at last year's Allegro Ball. You were a patroness. I came with the Huysmans." ("William Stillwater" has only this morning searched back files of the *Oakland Tribune's* Society Section.)

"Oh yes. Yes, yes, indeed. I seem to remember. You're the young man who composes for all the strange new instruments."

"No, but I know the man you mean. David something or other. Have you seen the Huysmans lately?"

"Not since — oh heavens, I can't remember when. Last year's season, certainly. But aren't they in Europe now?"

"Yes, I believe so."

"Out of plain unashamed curiosity, where did you know Barbara? Back east? Or when she was out last summer?"

"Originally out here, but I saw her at a party or two back east. Are you meeting her at the airport tomorrow?"

"No, I'm simply too busy. A friend of the family is going out. I'm sure Barbara won't be offended."

"I wouldn't think so. Well, maybe we'll meet again before too long."

"Yes, that would be nice. Do drop by the house, now that Barbara's with us. You have our address?"

"It's right here in the telephone book: '59 Mowbray Court'."

After the conversation Eleanor telephones Craig, who grumbles and glowers when he learns of "William Stillwater". "I'll go anyway. This guy can say hello to Barbara if he likes, and then take off."

Eleanor makes no comment. It's none of her concern; she couldn't care less who meets Barbara, whom she doesn't particularly like.

Two hours later she's called once more to the telephone. A rather uncertain female voice says, "Western Union. Telegram for Mrs. Eleanor Binkins."

"Speaking."

"Shall I read it?"

"Please."

" 'Taking later flight, TWA 111, arriving S.F. airport 4:53 PM. Hope no inconvenience. Love.' Signed 'Barbara'."

Eleanor notes information, relays it to Craig, who laughs in rather crude satisfaction. "This other joker will have a long wait."

"I could try to get hold of him, perhaps through the Huysmans. But they're in Europe."

"I wouldn't worry," says Craig. "If Barbara wants him to meet her, she'll let him know."

Chapter VII

At 2 o'clock Marsh is waiting by the gate. He has taken great care with his clothes: gray flannel slacks, a herringbone tweed jacket, a dark green and gray striped tie. He feels an excitement he has not felt for years.

The plane comes in, Marsh watches passengers alight. Her? Her? No… Indisputably *her!* She looks around expectantly. Marsh approaches. She is even more attractive than he had expected: a girl of twenty-three or twenty-four, immaculately groomed, hair long, straight, rich brown, combed sleekly back in a deceptively artless pompadour. Her complexion clear, faintly sun-tanned, with a minimum of make-up. Her features are even; nose small, almost pert, mouth wide and composed, jaw rather delicate. She is slender, almost boyish; she carries herself with a quaint boyish directness. Her clothes are beautiful: a soft gray coat, black collar buttoned to the neck, with black regimental piping down the front.

Marsh approaches. "You're Barbara Tyburn?"

She gives him a polite smile. "Yes."

"I'm—" he hesitates "— ah, William Stillwater. A friend of Mrs. Binkins. She had some business she couldn't get out of, and Nancy is gone for the weekend. So she sent me to pick you up."

Barbara nods curtly, obviously a trifle annoyed by the offhand reception. "I see. Well, it's very kind of you."

"Not at all."

Marsh picks up her luggage, takes her to his car. She is formally friendly, with the unconscious ease a lifelong background of wealth provides. She's been sheltered and deferred to and while not precisely spoiled, she obviously intends to have her own way.

They drive out Bayshore Freeway. Marsh asks if she's had lunch. "Yes," she says, "on the plane."

They ride in silence. Marsh decides that he rather dislikes this young woman. She's too self-contained, self-assured; he can't warm up to her, he can't make any start at friendliness. The whole ploy is a fiasco.

Barbara actually has hardly noticed him, except to think that Marsh is a quiet, obviously well-behaved young man, undistinguished except perhaps for a certain austerity, a concentration, an intensity. Actually, she's irritated by the casual manner in which Eleanor has sent a stranger to meet her. It's patronizing, condescending, and it bodes not too well for her visit. Oh well, she thinks, this young man — what is his name? — Stillwater isn't to blame. She looks at him, notices that he is frowning. She notices the gray at his temples — but he's obviously young. His clothes are quiet — just clothes — which is good enough. In fact, her whole opinion of Marsh shifts faintly. She relaxes back in the seat, smiles at him. "You're a friend of Nancy's?"

"I'm more an acquaintance of Mrs. Binkins."

Barbara frowns again. The implication seems to be that Aunt Eleanor sent to the airport the first man available. "Strange," she says stiffly, "that she sent you over. If I had known, I could just as easily have taken a cab."

"It's no trouble whatever. In fact, I volunteered."

"Why?" asks Barbara, once more amused.

"Oh — just because." Marsh smiles too. He speaks, stumbling a trifle; he can't bring himself to lie directly to this self-possessed young woman. Her eyes are careless, clear, but also merciless. "You don't remember meeting me before?"

"No." Carelessly forthright. "Have we met?"

"You're a student at Radcliffe?"

"No longer. I'm a graduate. Don't tell me you're a Harvard man. You don't look like one."

"No. I'm not connected with Harvard."

"I'm utterly sick of the word Harvard, of everything connected with Harvard."

Marsh says, "I assured your aunt that I'd met you before — now I'm wondering whether I did or not."

"I'm sorry, but I don't remember. Do you ski?"

"No."

She grins impishly. "Have you ever been a congressman, or a diplomat, or an economist? I've met hundreds."

"No."

"Well, it doesn't matter. When I was here last year I went to dozens of parties. Perhaps we met then."

Barbara isn't really interested. But Marsh is satisfied. He's established himself, provided a past connection for himself, both with Barbara and the Binkinses.

Marsh appraises her. "Are you married?"

"Heavens no," says Barbara primly.

"And you're not engaged. At least I don't see a ring."

Barbara smiles. "I guess I just don't have what it takes. Why do you ask?"

"Curiosity."

Barbara looks away. She's frowning. Apparently she's not bored, just thinking. She gives him a slow calculating look. Perhaps she can use this Mr. Stillwater to promote her own ends. Unfair, of course — but she's already reconciled herself to unfairness. In fact, she's planning absolute ruthlessness. "Do you go to many of Nancy's parties?" Her voice is light, artless.

"No." Marsh is on his guard. "I hardly know her. Or her friends."

"Hm...I wonder...Would you help me?"

"At what?"

But Barbara is silent. She sighs, shakes her head, rejecting whatever plans she has formed. "No, it wouldn't work."

"What wouldn't work?"

"A rather idiotic idea. Please forget it. I just hope that Nancy doesn't have a whole set of galas planned. I'm not in the mood." She says this in a dispassionate voice.

"I see," says Marsh. "You came out to rest."

Barbara looks at him suspiciously. "No. I came out to get a job."

Marsh is surprised. "What kind of job?"

"Something interesting. Not just any job."

"And what interests you?"

"Oh — rather extraordinary things. I love to refinish old furniture." She laughs. "Naturally I wouldn't want to do it professionally. I have an opportunity to conduct a Round-the-World tour, but of course it can be a terrible headache."

"You must be an experienced globe-trotter."

"Not really. No more than anyone else. These would all be younger people, not too demanding, but I'm not really interested. My degree is in Political Science and I'd like to try for a job with the State Department."

"Well — something is sure to turn up," said Marsh.

"Yes, I think so."

Marsh drives on in silence, half-amused, half-irritated. The girl has enormous dignity, she is incredibly adept at maintaining the precise interpersonal relationship on which she has decided.

Marsh turns off the road, to the left. "Where are we going?" asks Barbara at once.

"Across to the Coast Highway. No one is at the Binkins' house, so I thought we'd take the scenic route to Piedmont."

Barbara says nothing, but she evidently is accustomed to being consulted as to her wishes.

They drive along the Pacific shore; ten-foot breakers roar in, rumble up the beach. Overhead streamers of fog thread across blue sky. At the amusement park Marsh stops, buys two bags of popcorn. Barbara thanks him politely as they sit eating and watching the passersby. Marsh ruefully considers the distance between their two lives. Then he feels a surge of anger: at Barbara and himself, both. He's through with defeatism, negativity. Any man by dint of sufficient ingenuity, energy and persistence can accomplish anything he has a mind to. So Marsh assures himself.

They cross the bridge. Barbara chats politely, but always impersonally. They approach the Binkins's house; Marsh parks in the street, and in desperation blurts out a suggestion that they have dinner together in a couple days.

Barbara considers, with a faint smile. "Thank you very much, but I don't have any idea what plans Aunt Eleanor or Nancy might have made. And I'd really better find out before making any commitments."

Plausible, but Marsh feels rebuffed. The whole purpose of today's venture is to secure an entrée to the Binkins's house and their circle of friends. He says doggedly, "I'll call you later in the week."

"Of course," says Barbara. "That would be better."

Marsh turns into driveway, parks. He enters house, meets Eleanor, who graciously pretends to recognize him.

BK greets Barbara with warmth, and holds her hand rather longer than necessary. Eleanor shoots him a cold glance, BK becomes more formal.

Eleanor apologizes to Barbara, for confusion, for Nancy running off over the weekend. "Tonight we've an engagement with Bernard's mother that we simply can't break. Of course you can come along, but I'm sure you'd be bored."

"Don't worry about me," says Barbara. "I'll be quite happy by myself."

"I wonder what's keeping Craig, he'd be happy to help out."

Telephone rings in hall, Amy answers. "It's Craig." Eleanor goes to the phone.

Marsh turns to Barbara. "Have dinner with me tonight."

For the first time — so he thinks — she seems to appraise him as a man, as a person, as an individual.

"No," says Eleanor in the hall. "She came by the original flight, for some reason...I don't know why she sent the telegram, apparently she changed her mind...Mr. Stillwater met her...Oh Craig, don't be stupid." An unfortunate word. Eleanor says in a shocked voice, "Craig! Such language!"

Barbara laughs, and suddenly seems younger, much more delicate and vulnerable. She says to Marsh, "We won't be late, will we?"

"No later than you like."

"Very well."

Eleanor, listening with one ear, tells Craig, "No...I don't think anyone will be home. Barbara is going out with Mr. Stillwater."

~

The evening is relaxed. Barbara, with effortless ease, creates a formal, rather old-fashioned atmosphere, which suits Marsh well enough. He has neither hope nor inclination for an evening of reckless emotionalizing.

They go to a small dim restaurant in Alameda, overlooking the Estuary. Marsh is religiously non-communicative, and Barbara finally is piqued. A man who doesn't try to set himself up in a glamourous role of some kind is almost alien to her experience. She asks, "What do you do for a living, if I may ask?"

"Nothing," says Marsh, "at the moment. A Communist had the lack of consideration to shoot at me when my back was turned."

"Then you were in the army?"

"No. I'm a sort of inventor — research worker, they're called nowadays. I was sent to Viet Nam to check out one of my ideas, a kind of portable radar. The system worked fine the first time out, also the second time. The third time it failed — mainly because I forgot to charge the batteries. Eight men were killed. I was lucky, I got off with a broken pelvis."

"How terrible."

"Yes," says Marsh, capsulizing a year of guilt, pain, demoralization.

Barbara looks out over the water. "Life is so short... I want to do something important and significant with my life. I don't just want to be another housewife. I'm *me*! There's no other *me*!"

Marsh laughs. "I felt the same way once... Now I can't decide what, if anything, is important or significant."

"I don't see why you should feel this way. At least you've created something. That's the main thing! The only people I can respect are the creators, the people with vision. Mr. Binkins for instance: he's famous!"

Marsh, who is unaware of the *Time* cover, is surprised. "Famous?"

"Yes, indeed. He has tremendous energy, and he's confident. The twenty-first century belongs to people like BK."

Marsh says dubiously, "The thing I created — or rather, my inability to use it — cost the lives of eight men. My confidence in myself is a trifle shaken."

Barbara says seriously, "Yes. I can see how it would be..." She shrugs, as if to say, well, it's your problem, I can't solve it for you, and Marsh smiles faintly. Of course she's right, and he's sorry he's told her anything whatever. She doesn't seem too sympathetic. Perhaps she's even something of a fanatic. Why should I care? he thinks. I'm not wooing this girl…Or am I?…No, I'm using her, for a specific purpose, and that's all I want of her. Suddenly he wonders, who is using who?

He makes no effort to prolong the evening, and takes her home after dinner. As they drive she becomes increasingly remote. And Marsh thinks, with self-contempt, well, I've done it. I've bored her to tears, and now she'll never want to go out with me again…

But as they get out of car Barbara says, "I'm awfully sorry I've been so tiresome tonight. I'm usually not quite so dull — but I've really had a terribly long day. And there was a farewell party for me last night."

Marsh feels a flash of sheer warmth. He takes her hand, which he would not have dared to have done, helps her out of the car…But again, he tells himself, this is ridiculous. A girl raised in obviously lavish circumstances, and himself, a man half-crippled physically, spiritually at low tide…He drops her hand, rather clumsily.

She darts him a curious glance, then peers over his shoulder toward the carriage house, where there's a light and the sound of music. "What in the world is going on?"

They wander back, to find Maile, Felice and Lundy working on Maile's boat. Maile is working, fitting a plywood diaphragm into place. Felice, wearing blue jeans and a boy's T-shirt is mixing Weldwood glue, Lundy is leaning against bench drinking a can of beer.

Barbara says hello to Maile, who gives her a curt greeting. He makes no move to introduce Felice or Lundy, who is still plastered and bandaged around the head.

Marsh conceals his recognition, and wonders whether they will recognize him. Maile never actually got a square look at him, nor did Lundy.

Barbara asks Lundy brightly, "What happened to you?"

"Automobile accident," mumbles Lundy in a surly voice.

Felice is looking at Marsh in a puzzled manner. Then she looks away. Apparently Marsh has not been recognized in this new context.

Marsh and Barbara return to house and rather stiffly, bid each other goodnight.

Marsh drives home. He tells himself to put Barbara from his mind, to eliminate her entirely from his plans. At least temporarily. At least until he checks out Peralta, and the shopping center project Craig Maitland has involved himself in... And what to do about Maile, Felice and Lundy? He'd dearly like to see them get what they have coming — but they'll have to wait for a while.

—

Barbara showers, brushes her teeth, gives her hair a few religious strokes. She's very careful, very strict with herself. Perhaps when she's an old lady these traits will make her seem fussy or over fastidious — but now, they merely seem endearing, like a kitten diligently washing itself.

She lies down into bed with a grateful sigh. A tiring day... She thinks of Mr. William Stillwater. She rather likes him, in an offhand way. He seems basically kind, if rather grim and lonely. Strange in a man so young! Barbara can understand how a girl more susceptible than herself might find him attractive... Well, it hardly concerns her. Although he *is* an easy man to be with, one who probably would relax and seem less intense on better knowing... Anyway, she's already in love. Single-mindedly, perversely, achingly in love. Thinking about her lover she falls asleep.

Chapter VIII

Marsh arises early, broods for an hour or two over his coffee, jumps into his car, drives south to Peralta.

Peralta is an artificial construction; a new city incorporating a number of formerly unincorporated towns. It embraces a large area of land, running from the swampy mudflats along the eastern shores of the bay to the tawny hills. There are dozens of housing tracts, almost all low-cost construction, as well as orchards, vineyards, truck gardens, pastures, simple arid land.

In a telephone directory Marsh locates Angelo Cazzaro, at 1416 Ramos Road, asks directions, drives out. He sees at a glance why Craig Maitland envisions the property as a shopping center. First, there is no major shopping area closer than Hayward, or San Jose. Two freeways bring thousands of cars per hour past the site. Cazzaro's six acres are poor, given to scrubby alfalfa, as are the two pieces of land to the north and south — both of which Maitland already owns.

Cazzaro's house is hardly more than a cottage, painted gray with green composition roof. There are withered hollyhocks in the front yard, a tank-house and windmill behind the house, with a clump of bamboo growing around the tank-house. Two pepper trees flank drive-way. The house is empty — locked. No one has been in the house for some time.

Marsh turns away. Across the road, the land changes for the better. Here are ten or twelve acres of vines, green, lush, healthy. The house is larger than Cazzaro's; there are signs of modest prosperity about the place. The name on the mailbox is "Manuel Ramos".

Marsh knocks on door; a fat man with a huge good-natured jowly face, gray hair, a gray stubble of beard comes to the door. This is Manuel Ramos. His shirt can hardly contain a Falstaffian paunch, his trousers seem ready to fall to the ground for lack of purchase. He speaks broken English.

Marsh asks, "Where is Mr. Cazzaro?"

"You want him too? Everybody want ol' Cazzaro. What's he done?"

"Nothing. Do you know where he is?"

"Sure. Where he goes every summer. To the mountains."

"Whereabouts?"

Ramos doesn't know. "He said something about Reno. I think he's joking. Ol' Cazzaro he's pretty tight man." Ramos rubs thumb and fingers together slyly.

"What's he doing in the mountains?"

"He's old-timer. Come out here long ago. Me, I come on later. Land was all cow pasture. Now look. I got nice vineyard, eh? Make good wine. What you want with Cazzaro? He done something wrong?"

"No. I'm a lawyer. Mr. Cazzaro has inherited some money."

"Oh yeah? That's nice. Why don't it happen to me. I need money. Cazzaro don't need nothing. No wife, no family. Every summer he mines gold."

"He's got a mine?"

"Not now. He just look for mine. Prospect, they call it. He's prospector."

"Who runs the place while he's gone?"

Eloquent shrug. "Nothing to run. Vines don't grow over there. Soil too damn alkali. Ol' Cazzaro he try to buy my place, many times. But he won't pay my price. He's pretty tight, ol' Cazzaro."

Marsh considers. "What is your price?"

"Fifteen thousand, twenty thousand. Eight acres in grapes. Good well, good house. Me, I'm getting too old to work. I like to make a trip back to Portugal before I die. Never do it after, that's sure thing."

"I might be able to get you ten thousand."

"Nothing doing. I wouldn't look twice."

Marsh buys property for sixteen thousand, a hundred dollars down, balance to be paid in three months or deal is canceled. In effect, an option. Ramos can maintain residence until purchase price is paid.

Marsh visits several nearby service stations, finally Viera's Super Service, where Cazzaro takes his business. He gets description of Cazzaro's car, an old pink and white station wagon. Viera doesn't know where Cazzaro is prospecting, except that it's somewhere in Mother Lode country.

"I thought it was all pretty well worked over," says Marsh.

"Nah," says Viera, "every ounce of gold they took out there's ten left. But it's hard to get. Cazzaro he tries everything. One year he had what they call a dry-washer. That's a kind of sluice-box without water. Gold supposed to settle by gravity. The man that invents a good one, he can be the richest man in the world. Right now they aren't worth nothing, miss all the fines. This year Cazzaro's got something else up his sleeve."

Marsh either deduces or is told that Cazzaro is planning to skin-dive for gold. "Pretty old man for that, isn't he?"

"Ol' Cazzaro's got a lot of spunk."

Marsh looks in phone directory, locates nearest source of skin-diving equipment, goes asking for Cazzaro. Finally, in Oakland he gets news. Cazzaro has been in with a kid about eighteen. Both bought suits.

"Did he say where he was going?"

"Not to my hearing. He said something about a hundred and thirteen miles. I think he told the kid to get a move on, because they had a hundred and thirteen miles to go before they slept. The kid asked if they were going to camp. Old Cazzaro said no, the hotel was cheap enough."

Marsh goes home, plays the tape recorder. On the tape are conversations:

Between Eleanor and friends, regarding matters of no interest to Marsh: social events, an auction of antique china, general gossip.

Between Craig and Eleanor. Craig complains about his long wait at airport. Eleanor is uninterested. "What about Cazzaro?" she asks.

"He's still prospecting — somewhere. The mountains are eight miles long a hundred miles wide. Patience!"

"Surely someone must know where he is. Suppose his house burned down?"

"I just don't know. But I've got agents in Peralta. They're watching his house and they'll let me know the instant he shows his face."

"Suppose he doesn't show his face?"

"I guess we'll just have to be patient."

"Patient? His land is right in the middle of everything."

"Don't worry, we'll find him."

Between Maile and Felice.

Between Maile and Lundy.

Between Nancy and Jane Rush: gossip. Nancy is having a small folk-singing party. Jane enthusiastic. "I know the most wonderful girl. She's built her own lute, and she sings these tragic old songs in language so authentic you can't understand her!"

Nancy reports that Craig and Barbara and she and Tom Feers are going dinner dancing. Marsh feels a cold pang of — what? Jealousy?

Marsh opens map of California, checks to see which towns in the Mother Lode country are 113 miles from Oakland. There are five, by various routes out of Oakland: Alabaster, Dutch Flat, Mica, Dogtown, and Jonopa.

He goes to telephone, calls Long Distance for the hotel in each of these towns; this eliminates Dogtown and Mica, which have no hotels. He is connected to the hotels in Alabaster, Jonopa and Dutch Flat. He learns that Cazzaro and his grandson occupied a room at the Dutch Flat hotel, but since have set up camp along Rattlesnake Creek.

Chapter IX

Marsh sets out early in the morning, drives to Dutch Flat, gets directions to Rattlesnake Creek. He also learns that Cazzaro comes into town most nights for a few beers and a few hands of poker.

Marsh reconnoiters. He isn't sure how best to approach Cazzaro. From the road he looks down, watches operations: Cazzaro has a gasoline-powered combination air compressor and water pump, a winch which he uses to move boulders.

Marsh goes back to hotel, contrives an approach.

Cazzaro comes in, Marsh introduces himself, says he has bought Ramos' property, but is mainly interested in Cazzaro's, as a place to raise pedigree horses. Cazzaro won't sell. But he agrees to trade. Marsh gets Cazzaro's signature to an agreement, drives back to Peralta, hangs a big sign on property:

— FOR SALE —
Superior Realty Company
P.O. Box 3292, Oakland

Marsh returns to Oakland and listens to his tape recorder.

Nancy talks to Jane Rush: "Barbara wants me to invite this fellow Bill Stillwater."

"Who is he?"

"I don't know. Somebody mother met last year at the Allegro. He's a musician or something. Barbara says he's respectable, but rather remote. Coming from her this must be a compliment, because that's my Barbara — respectable and remote."

"Yes, she is a little stand-offish, isn't she?"

"Why, I can't fathom. Of course there's scads of money in the family. Her grandmother owns half of Rhode Island."

"Including Newport?"

"They do have a home at Newport, absolutely fabulous, if High Victorian. BK stayed there last winter."

"Sounds a bit icky and bothersome. I prefer these contemporary houses, absolutely clean and uncluttered."

"Barbara's not going back. She wants to get a job out here. She's just graduated from Radcliffe and she's bound to be brainy."

Conversation between Craig and Eleanor:

Craig is excited; his agent has reported the "For Sale" sign on Cazzaro's property. "I've already mailed a letter of inquiry."

"Strange a real estate company would use a post office box."

"They might be out of town. Anyway I didn't let on that I was anxious; I asked for their lowest price. You know the drill…Well, let me talk to Barbara."

"She's not in."

"Oh? Where is she, if I may ask?"

"She and Nancy are gadding around somewhere…Excuse me, Craig, I've got to run. I'm taking Amy to the doctor, and we're late."

"What's wrong with her?"

"Oh, adolescent troubles, I suspect, although she's hardly an adolescent any more."

Marsh goes to the post office, picks up his mail. There are two letters, which he reads. To the first, from Craig Maitland, inquiring the price with studied casualness, Marsh composes a reply: "The price to you, stupid, is $120,000."

The second letter is from BK Binkins: "Please regard this inquiry as confidential. I am interested in the property you are selling, and will consider meeting or beating any other offer you may have received."

Marsh considers, then answers: "My asking price is $120,000. I have received no offers as yet, but will keep you informed."

Chapter X

Sunday breakfast at the Binkins's.

BK down first, glances at paper. Eleanor appears, then Nancy and Barbara come down together — white tennis shorts and blouses. Amy comes down — sky blue shorts and a dark blue blouse. She looks red-eyed as if she's been crying. BK glances at her questioningly, then at Eleanor who turns away.

BK says to Amy, "You look peaked, chicken, a little tennis will do you good."

"I don't think I'll play today. I don't feel very well."

"Some kind of summer bug, eh?"

"Yes, I suppose so."

BK looks at Eleanor. "What did the doctor tell you?"

"He gave me the pertinent instructions."

Maile comes in quietly. Eleanor suggests, rather maliciously, that he and his little friend Felice, join the tennis party. Nancy protests. "Not that little creep Felice."

Maile grins his saturnine grin. "She's a swinging chick."

Eleanor says coolly, "You know how I dislike that beatnik jargon, Maile."

"What for? It's just words."

"Yes, but your choice of language places you unmistakably in one or another social class."

"It's not 'beatnik jargon' anyway."

BK says, "The misfits are always with us, no matter what they're called. People with a distorted sense of values."

"They live though," retorts Maile. "They're alive. Not a bunch of phonies and cooky-pushers."

"Are you suggesting that your mother and I, and Nancy and Barbara, are 'phonies' as you put it?"

Maile refuses to make a strategic retreat. "You're all sitting in the middle-class trap, looking out, like young birds in a nest."

"Well, I like that!" snorts BK.

Eleanor smiles a spiteful smile. Barbara stares at Maile with dispassionate curiosity. "It's a matter of viewpoint," she says.

Nancy says sharply, "Maile, when you talk like this, I think you're simply awful. You sound like a — a Bolshevik."

Amy says softly, "Maile thinks anything that isn't weird is square."

"I just don't give a damn," says Maile sibilantly.

"That attitude won't get you anywhere," says Eleanor. "I hope this is just a phase you're going through — because sooner or later you'll have to fit yourself into society. All of us have to compromise."

"Don't I know?" says Maile bitterly.

BK peers through his tortoise-shell Sunday-morning spectacles. His bluff manner only barely conceals a basic rancor. "You just don't appreciate how lucky you are. In India or China you'd be out in the fields on your hands and knees, or carrying dirt in a basket."

"We're all pretty lucky around here," retorts Maile.

BK bites his lip, refuses to answer the insolence.

"Maile!" says Eleanor sharply. "Please mind your manners!"

"My manners are all right."

Craig comes in, gives everyone a breezy salute, sits down. "What's everyone looking so glum about? The stock-market take a dive?"

Nancy says, "We're having a meeting of the Mowbray Court Sunday Morning Debating Society."

"Well, well, cut me in. I love a good argument. What's it about?"

"Middle-class mores," says Barbara.

"The mores and forays of the middle-class!" Craig declaims. "I wrote a theme with that title once, for some English class. Got a B on it too, which makes me an authority."

Maile sneers sidelong at him. "How can a fish know anything about water?"

Everyone blinks at this mordant cut. Craig laughs uneasily. "Come now, old man, relax. The Democrats can't win every election."

Another young man arrives, group goes out to tennis court. BK and Eleanor go out to watch. Craig looks up, waves his hand toward house, to where Amy's pale face shows, rather blurred, behind window of her room.

Craig is jovial, now that he's got a lead on how to acquire Cazzaro's property. BK is quietly watchful. He has no definite plans, but he'll make the most of the circumstances, if somehow he can operate anonymously.

Eleanor is marmoreal. BK asks, "Ah, incidentally, what's wrong with Amy?"

"She's pregnant."

"Pregnant! Good Lord! How? Who?"

"She seems confused. She's two months along. It seems to have happened the night of Craig's party."

BK red in the face. He calls Craig over, breaks the news. Craig gets red in face too. He says, "Nothing like that happened at my party. She got gassed, yes."

"How did she get home?" asks Eleanor silkily.

"I telephoned Boko. He picked her up, took her home. She was plastered when she left, but she wasn't pregnant." He looks at BK. "I don't know what happened to her after she left my house."

BK furious. "Look here, are you implying that I'm responsible?"

"Stranger things have happened."

"Look here, you swine —"

"Don't call me a swine or I'll push your bloody face in."

BK laughs jeeringly. "I took the girl home. Whatever happened to her happened before I saw her. Either by you or one of your buddies."

"Don't go making accusations you can't back up!"

"The same goes for you!"

A terrible scream from the house. Clara the maid comes running out. Amy has hanged herself in her bedroom, with a pair of silk stockings.

Eleanor stands quite still, then turns slowly toward BK, slaps him across the face as hard as she can.

⁓

Ambulances, doctors, police.

In the evening Eleanor, in a metallic voice, says to BK, "Bernard, I think you'd better leave."

BK nods heavily. "Sure I'll leave. You two will be glad to have me out of here."

"What do you mean?" asks Eleanor glacially.

"It makes no difference. In so far as Amy is concerned, I had nothing to do with her, and if necessary I can prove it."

"How?"

"I was in the company of someone else."

"Indeed. Committing adultery, naturally."

Grins. "It's less of a rap than the same thing with Amy."

"You're an utterly nauseating man."

BK turns on his heel, departs.

Barbara appears. Apparently she's overheard conversation, and is uncomfortable. She tells Eleanor she thinks it would be easier if she left too.

Eleanor says, "Just as you like."

Barbara telephones Marsh. He takes her to Claremont Hotel in Berkeley hills. She is melancholy, depressed, unsure. She leans against Marsh's shoulder, starts to cry.

Marsh has a sense of events piling up, one on the other. A pressure... He returns to his apartment, turns on his tape recorder, listens with feeling of queasiness and distaste. Now that he has achieved his primary aim, i.e.: identification of Craig Maitland, listening to the phone calls, while fascinating in a morbid sort of way, now seems merely eavesdropping. He resolves to dismantle apparatus on the morrow.

He listens to various conversations bearing on Amy's suicide, condolences, etc.

Craig talks briefly to Eleanor. They speculate regarding parent. Craig says, "I know that suspicion is bound to fall on any red-blooded man in the neighborhood — and I absolutely deny complicity. That night I didn't leave the house. Boko came for Amy, and she was sound as a drum when she left."

Eleanor talks to one of her friends, who commiserates with no great conviction. Eleanor is business-like. "Naturally, it's a disgraceful business. Still, we've been lucky. The police have cooperated beautifully, and we've kept it out of the papers."

"That's a relief!"

"Nancy is utterly broken, of course. Barbara is planning to take an apartment somewhere."

"What about Maile?"

"Oh — he's just brooding."

Eleanor calls a lawyer, makes an appointment.

Felice calls Maile. She talks in a subdued voice. "It gives me the shivers. Why did she have to be so — so embarrassed?"

Maile laughs sourly. "They think ol' Boko pulled the trigger."

"And did he?"

"Damfino. All I know for sure it wasn't me."

Felice makes a cynical sound between her teeth. "Were you there when your step-father brought her in?"

"Yep. Sitting in the living-room. It was dark and he didn't see us."

" 'Us'?"

"Me and Lundy, drinking gin."

"Did you — see anything?"

"No."

Chapter XI

In the morning Craig calls Eleanor. He's stuttering with fury, over the letter from Marsh. "The son of a bitch — somehow he got word of the deal!"

Eleanor says in fatigue, "Craig, please don't bother me with this anymore."

"But you're my partner!"

"I've got thirty thousand in this scheme. Regard it as a loan to you. I simply don't want to bother with this affair."

"But we —"

"Not we, Craig. You. I'm not putting any more money into it."

"I can't swing it! Not unless I sell everything I own — even the oil shares."

"Please Craig, don't bother me with the affair." She considers and says in a slightly altered voice: "However I will buy your oil shares, if you decide to sell."

Craig mutters, "I'll kill the son of a bitch — except I can't. Not until I get that property."

"Surely he's joking."

"He's not joking."

"Just who *is* this man?"

"I'm going to find out." Craig gives a lame and incomplete version of his relationship with Marsh. "So you see, he hates my guts...I still can't imagine how he learned of Project X. Only you and I knew anything about it."

"I certainly didn't tell him," says Eleanor stiffly.

"I know you didn't. I didn't either."

"Then how did he find out?"

"I don't know...Unless —"

"Bernard."

"That's what I've been thinking. Boko. Good old Boko. Where is he staying?"

"At his mother's house."

Craig drives out to Boko's mother's house, an ancient Victorian castle in a decaying neighborhood. He finds Boko. They quarrel. Craig accuses him of conniving with his enemy.

BK denies all. "— not that it's not a good idea!"

Something occurs — a slip of BK's tongue, or possibly Craig sees a can of red paint — which turns on a light. BK also responsible for sabotaging his car. Craig speechless in the sudden revelation of so much malignance. Then he says in a choked voice, "You think you're the only guy that can play rough? I'll show you something, you God damn skunk! I've got you where the hair is short, only you don't know it."

"How so?" asks BK mildly.

"Never mind, how so," raves Craig. "I'll do my best to put you in San Quentin. I'm talking about Amy, in case you don't know."

BK laughs. "Go right ahead, my boy. I wish you luck."

Craig leaves. Boko thinks. He checks telephone number CL 4-2658 — which belongs to man with whom Craig has accused him of being in cahoots. He telephones. No answer. He sits drumming his fingers; now a call comes in which his mother answers. "A lady, for you, Bernard."

BK answers, with his mother standing nearby; his responses are terse. "Yes…Of course…I'll give you a call shortly."

He hangs up, looks in phone book for the Marsh associated with CL 4-2658, observes the address to be 280 Henry Street.

He finds that Apartment 3, formerly occupied by Marsh is vacant, and for rent. Apartment 2, however, is rented to William Stillwater! — Marsh's off the cuff and too hasty choice of pseudonym.

BK gets in touch with Mr. Cody, rents Apartment 3. Then he calls Barbara at the Claremont. Breezy.

"Hello, young lady. How are you?"

"Very well, thank you."

BK tries to jolly her. "Come now. Just because of, well, circumstances, there's no reason for us to be unfriendly."

"'Circumstances' certainly do exist." — drily.

"You mean — Amy?"

"More or less."

"Why not give me the benefit of the doubt?"

"I'll try to hold an open mind."

"How about having lunch with me?"

"No thanks. I'm with Nancy, as a matter of fact."

"Oh. I see. Well, actually I want some information. This Bill Stillwater — where did you meet him?"

"The first I can remember is at the airport."

"You never met him before?"

"I don't remember. Isn't he a friend of Eleanor's?"

"I don't know. I don't think Eleanor remembers either."

A murmur of conversation. "Nancy wants to know where you've moved to?"

Reluctantly BK says, "280 Henry Street, Apartment 3."

Barbara relays the information.

"About Stillwater," says BK, "I'm puzzled. Has he ever mentioned a man named Marsh?"

"No."

"Very odd. Very odd indeed. Stillwater has Apartment 2 right across the hall."

"Quite a coincidence."

"Yes, isn't it?" BK hangs up. He gets in his car, drives to Peralta, finds Cazzaro, learns details of transaction. Cazzaro mentions that Craig has already seen him. Cazzaro is increasingly bitter; he figures he's been tricked, given a raw deal. "I'm goin' to see this fella; I'm goin' to tell him I want what's comin' to me."

"Well," says BK, "maybe I can tell you where to locate him."

"That other guy, Mr. Maitland, he told me. I know where to find him."

BK Binkins drives back to Oakland. He goes to his new apartment, makes a phone call, "Iola, my little sugar lump. I'm loose as a goose. Wicked old stepmother kicked me out...I'll pick you up in an hour...Sure, why not?...Nope. I'm my own man now. Free, white, twenty-one..."

—

In the morning, Cody, the apartment house manager brings new bed linen to Apartment 3. (BK has rented the apartment completely furnished, and certain of the appurtenances are lacking.) He knocks, opens door with his pass-key. BK dead, shot through neck — floor covered with blood.

Chapter XII

Police come. Detective Inspector Evans in charge of investigation.

There are no indications in the apartment as to identity of murderer. Time of death is approximately midnight.

Police interview members of family. Detective Inspector Evans asks about Amy, wondering as to possible connection.

Eleanor is close-mouthed.

Nancy is tearful, verbose. "It's all my fault. I took her to the party. She drank three French 75's. She got really drunk, and someone took advantage of her."

"Who? Maitland? Or one of his friends?"

"I don't really know. But I don't think so. I don't see how they could."

"Who took her home?"

"BK — my stepfather."

"Did he do it?"

"I don't think he would."

Maile is sulky, reticent. Evans gets nowhere. Afterwards Felice turns on Maile. "You know, I hate you! And your whole stinking family! Your own sister is dead, and you don't turn a hair. Why don't you act decently for once in your life?"

"I don't know anything about it."

"You do too."

"I'm not a damn stool-pigeon. What do I care for the police?"

"What about Amy?"

"She's dead."

But Maile seeks Evans out. "I'll tell you all I know. I was in the living room with a friend of mine, Leon Lundy, when my step-father brought Amy home. She was so drunk she couldn't walk. A woman was helping my stepfather. A young woman with blonde hair."

"What happened then?"

"I don't know. Then I — fell asleep. Lundy and I were drinking gin."

"You mean, you passed out."

"Call it that."

"What about Lundy?"

"I think — he went upstairs, and into Amy's room."

Police talk to Lundy. He curses Maile, admits guilt and is taken off to jail.

Evans interviews Craig, who maliciously directs their attention to Marsh.

—

Eleanor discusses case with Craig over phone. "I've got to see you, I'm so distracted I don't know which way to turn."

"A terrible thing, a terrible thing."

"I just can't believe it. Coming so soon after Amy's death. I'm just stunned. And have you seen the papers! It's unbelievable the way they attack you."

"Yes, they're a pack of jackals, no question about it... I'll be over to see you then."

"Have the police talked to you? That man Evans —"

"He's seen me. He seems fair enough."

"Did he ask about Amy?"

"I told him the truth, so far as I knew it."

Pause. Hollow voice. "Yes, I suppose there's no point in trying to hide anything."

Evans returns to Marsh, whom he has already interviewed. "Mr. Marsh, you're more deeply involved in this matter than I had supposed."

Marsh sees that evidently they want a quick solution to the murder, that his role must inevitably be brought out into the open. He reveals the entire story of how he became involved in the affairs of the Binkins family. He does not mention his telephone tap, but explains his information as derived from observation, and from an informant whom he refused to identify.

Evans polite but skeptical. He drives to Peralta, interviews Cazzaro, who is spiteful, and distorts certain of BK's remarks to him, to the effect that Marsh is made to seem an enemy of BK's.

Evans returns to Marsh. "It's clear, Mr. Marsh, that you haven't told us the truth."

"I've told you everything I know. If I've got my own suspicions, they're my own affair."

"Don't leave the city, Mr. Marsh."

Chapter XIII

Marsh has dinner with Barbara. She's wan and tired, but evidently making an effort to be friendly — even affectionate. Marsh takes her back to the hotel. They have a drink in the bar. Barbara seems distant. Presently she says in her calmest voice, "You can take me up to my room."

Marsh is uncertain what she means, but he takes her up to her room and comes in with her. She is acquiescent and matter-of-fact. They go to bed. Marsh is surprised that Barbara is so easy. She is not particularly emotional, in fact rather prim. The relationship is almost formal. Marsh wants to get dressed and go, but Barbara wants him to stay. He relaxes back into bed. Barbara seems to be weeping. Marsh tries to comfort her. She laughs, in a shaky nervous fashion. Why does she weep? Why does she laugh? What fantastic set of circumstances brings him here in the first place? Barbara goes to sleep, he is left with his puzzle. Either Barbara is a nympho — her lackluster performance makes him dubious of this — or she has fallen in love with him. Possible. Or is it possible that she's simply bored?

In the morning the atmosphere is impersonal. Nonplussed, Marsh returns to his apartment.

Eleanor telephones. In a frigid voice she suggests that he drop out to the house. Marsh does so. Eleanor makes offer for Cazzaro's land.

Marsh refuses to bargain. Craig had him beaten up. "Incidentally, Mrs. Binkins, he hired your son Maile to do the job...The price represents not profit, but punitive damages."

Eleanor practically collapses at news of Maile's involvement. She calls Maile, who admits it. Eleanor summons Sam the gardener. "Go out to the carriage house, destroy the boat. Burn it."

Maile turns Marsh a look of sheer hate. He says nothing.

Eleanor tells Marsh: "You shall have your price. A hundred and twenty thousand dollars. Craig will pay half, Maile will pay half. I am in charge of a fund left him by his father. He will pay sixty thousand dollars. You may assign the property to me, not Craig."

Marsh leaves. On way out he disconnects tap, loads it into his car. He telephones Barbara from a phone booth. The time is noon. There is some difficulty locating her; she's been out shopping, but hasn't found what she wanted and must go out again. He volunteers to accompany her. She deliberates, then agrees. Marsh picks her up at the Claremont. As usual she is dressed beautifully; she is grave and withdrawn. She decides that she won't do any shopping. Marsh takes her to his apartment. Barbara is not in the mood for bed, but sits looking at him, nibbling at her knuckles. Again Marsh is puzzled. Is she looking at him — or through him?

There is a knock at the door: Marsh opens, to find the police, with a search warrant.

They check the apartment, find the gun which killed BK. Marsh sees it, takes deep breath. He sits down. Evans puts him under arrest, asks him to come along.

Marsh shakes his head. "Send your men away. I've something to tell you."

Evans obliges. "A confession?"

"No."

Barbara offers to leave, Marsh gloomily tells her she might as well stay.

"I can help you solve this case," Marsh tells Evans.

"It *is* solved. You're it."

"In the process, I've got to admit to a violation of the law."

"Like shooting BK Binkins?" — cynically.

"No. A technical violation."

Evans gives a tacit understanding that any such violation will probably be ignored. If Marsh is guilty of murder, no matter; if he isn't, then his service to police will overshadow the violation.

Marsh starts playing the tapes of conversations. Evans listens. Barbara sits entranced. Evans says nothing, makes a few notes, asks to listen again.

Evans says, "This is highly interesting. But I don't think it proves anything."

"I think it does."

"What?"

Marsh hesitates. "It proves where I was at the time BK was killed."

"It proves where you *said* you were going to be."

"Ask Miss Tyburn. I was with her."

Evans looks at Barbara. "Well, Miss Tyburn?"

Barbara licks her lips. "Yes. He was with me."

Marsh smiles grimly at Evans. "See?"

Evans snorts. "I don't necessarily believe her. People have lied to protect other people before. If you're not guilty, how did the gun get in your apartment?"

"It wasn't there yesterday."

"You keep your door locked?"

"Yes."

"Are there any other keys?"

Marsh thinks. "Stillwater might have had some extras made. But he's in Texas. There's a master key, but it's never out of the reach of Cody."

Evans calls in Cody who verifies this. Evans clears throat, looks uncomfortable. He takes Marsh aside. "So you're in the clear, and someone has it in for you. Who?"

"Whoever hid that gun here."

"Well — we're back to the question of access again. Who had a key to the place?"

Marsh tells him how to find out. Evans thinks, darts Marsh a wide-eyed glance. He talks into telephone. Then he says, "Let's listen to those tapes again."

An hour passes. Policeman brings a thin old man into the room. "Anyone here you recognize?" Old man points out Barbara. "I made a key for her this morning. From a print in a piece of soap."

Marsh watches her as he might an insect under a microscope. She seems to shrink, to become hard and bright as a brown beetle.

"Well, Miss Tyburn?" asks Evans.

"It's a lie." — calmly.

The old man laughs. "A lie, eh. Very well, young lady, I'll tell you what you were wearing this morning. You've changed your clothes since." He describes clothes. Barbara's face falls.

"Very well. So I had the key made."

"Why?"

"Mr. Stillwater is my — my fiancé. I wanted a key to his apartment."

"Why not ask him for one?"

Barbara thinks a moment. She's harassed. "I was afraid. He attacked me. It was self-defense."

"Who? Him?" Evans points toward Marsh.

"No. BK Binkins."

"So you killed him."

"Yes."

Afterwards Barbara felt the strain of the investigation, imagined the noose drawing tight around her, thought to protect herself. "William Stillwater" seemed an excellent fall-guy. To frame him she had to gain admittance to his apartment, for which she needed a key. She made a mold of the key in soap during the night, in the morning had a copy made. Then while Marsh was at the Binkins house she planted the weapon.

She offers no apology to Marsh, no explanation, but sits stiffly, not looking at him. Marsh jumps to his feet, goes to the bathroom, takes a shower.

When he comes out, Barbara is gone. He explains to Evans, "I probably would have never suspected her — if she hadn't tried to plant the evidence on me. Last night she took the keys from my pocket when she thought I was asleep. She took them into the bathroom, brought them back. I had no idea what she was up to until you found that gun. The tapes surprised her; they indicated the relationship between her and BK Binkins.

"Now here's the grotesque part of the situation: I was obviously not with her when BK was killed. But I said I was, and asked her for verification.

"She had a tough choice. She could agree, give me an alibi and fix up one for herself at the same time. After hearing the tapes she decided she needed me."

Marsh conjectures further. "BK was a real lover-type. Probably last year he and Barbara became friendly, more so when he went east last winter. Perhaps he told her he planned to divorce Eleanor. When she comes out here she discovers that he's carrying on with his secretary."

Later, it develops that Barbara had come to the apartment, listened at the door, heard Iola's voice inside. She went slowly away, seething with anger. At the pay phone in the foyer she telephones BK. He tried to put her off, she said she was coming up anyway. BK makes best of it. Iola leaves, also furious with BK.

Barbara goes back to apartment, enters. She toys with BK, then stabs him.

The weak link is Iola. If it weren't for Iola, she'd be safe. Hence the need for framing Marsh.

Dream Castle

When Farrero first met Douane Angker, of Marlais & Angker, Class III Structors, something in his brain twisted, averted itself; and, looking down at the curl on Angker's tough mouth, he knew the feeling went double. Angker, short and solid, had concentrated in him a heavy unctuous vitality, the same way a cigar stump holds the strongest juices.

Farrero did not, on this occasion, meet Leon Marlais, the other half of the firm, nor did he during the entire length of his job. He would not have recognized him face to face on the pedestrip — because Marlais had an odd mania for privacy, secluded himself behind a coded doorpress, an unlisted telescreen. When he used his private copter stage, a polarizing field jarred the view to dazzle and shimmer.

Angker held to no such aloofness. The panel to his office stood always wide. All day the technicians in the adjoining workroom could look in to see him shouldering, driving, battering through his work; watch him barking orders into the telescreen, flourishing a clenched hand for emphasis.

Farrero stayed pretty well away from the office, appearing only for new assignments, avoiding Angker as much as possible. He assumed his work was satisfactory. If not, he felt sure Angker would have fired him, and with gusto. However, the day he knocked at Angker's door to report on the Westgeller job, he knew he was in for trouble.

"Come in!" called Angker, not looking up, and Farrero sauntered forward — tall, lanky, his face long, droll, wooden, his manner very casual. He had hair the color of wet sand, the mildest of blue eyes.

"Good morning," said Farrero. Angker, after a brief glance upward, grunted. Farrero dropped two strips of microfilm on the desk. "Ready for execution. I've shown them to Westgeller, got his O.K."

"Westgeller? I suppose he can pay for the place." He tipped the strips down the slot in his desk.

"Your credit office likes him," said Farrero. From where he stood, Angker's lowered and foreshortened face looked like a rudely molded mask, with a glazed shapeless nose, thick lumpy lips, eyes hidden under the thrust of his brow. "He makes heavy glass," said Farrero. "The stuff tourist submarines are built from. He's also got a finger in Moon Mining."

The screen on the far wall glowed, ran with blurred colors. Angker, slipping on polarizers, saw a three-dimensional picture — a large solid house backed by a gloomy wall of fir trees. It was an old-fashioned house, warm, Earthy-looking, with high gables and many chimneys, as if it were intended to fight year after year of winter snow. Its colors were a dark red, with gray, white, and green trim, and the sun cells of the roof glowed a rich burnished copper. Behind, the great fir trees marched almost up to the house; and the trunks of many others could be seen dwindling off through the dim aisles. At the front a wide lawn, vivid as argon fire, rolled gently down to a coruscation of bright flower beds. It was clearly a Class III house.

"Ah…ah," Angker grunted. "Nice piece of work, Farrero. Where's the site?"

"Fifty miles from…er, Minusinsk, on the Yenisei." Farrero dropped into a chair, crossed his legs. "Fifty-four degrees latitude, thereabouts."

"Take him hours to get there," commented Angker sourly.

Farrero shrugged. "He says he likes it. Likes the winter — snow — solitude. The untouched forests, wild life, wolves, peasants, things like that. He's got a lifetime lease on three hundred acres."

Angker grunted again, leaned back in his chair. "What's the cost estimate?"

Farrero laid his head back, against the support, half-closed his eyes. "Cost us 28,000 munits to build. Plus ten per cent makes 30,800. I gave it to Westgeller as 31,000."

Angker leveled a sudden under-eyebrow glance at Farrero, squared up in his seat. He pressed a button. A cutaway section of the first floor flicked upon the screen. He pressed again. The second floor. Again.

Detailed wall plans. He looked up, and the lines from his nostrils down seemed to gather, purse his mouth, pull it out into a hard lump.

"How do you fix on that figure?" he jerked a pencil toward the screen. "I say that house'll run upwards of 40,000. Ten per cent puts our bid somewhere near 44,000, 45,000."

"I really don't think so," said Farrero politely.

"What is the basis for your estimate?" inquired Angker, as gently.

Farrero clasped his hands around his knee. "Well—look at it from this angle. One of the shortcomings of modern civilization—ancient civilization too, for that matter—is that the average man never gets all he wants of the most desirable products, never makes his life fit his dreams. Very few people can afford space yachts, Venusian fruit, good film libraries, Class III houses. I suppose it could be said that these always unfulfilled ambitions create an incentive to work, to make money, to—"

Angker made a guttural noise. "Less philosophy, Farrero. Leave that for the college professors. I want to know how you're going to build a 40,000 munit house for 28,000 munits."

"Well," said Farrero, "as a matter of fact, I've worked out a construction technique to bring Class III prices closer to Class I and II."

"Ah—you have indeed?" Angker was still polite. "Perhaps you'll explain?"

"What's the reason for the differential between Class III and Class II? It's that Class I and II houses are largely prefabbed, and the Class III's are individually built and fitted. We still use carpenters, glaziers, masons, welders, electricians. So, the problem was to find a structural method that would preserve individuality, but cut construction costs. I found the answer. So far as I know it's completely revolutionary."

There was a short pause. Angker sat staring like a mahogany jinni.

"I've tried it on a small scale," Farrero went on, his voice rather more brittle. "It works. For foundations, instead of concrete sills or piers, we fuse the earth under the house with an atomic torch. Then on this glass, flint, slag—whatever you want to call it—we joint up a frame of hyproberyl tubing, stretch Caltonite fabric over it taut. Then we spray on the wall—quick-dry. Also the partitions. The floors come as standard steel sections. The wiring, plumbing, radiants, ventilation, filters are naturally laid out first. Frame, Caltonite fabric, spray, and there's the house, everything but the finish."

"Windows? Doors?"

"Slice 'em out with a torch, set the sills in with a little more quick-dry."

Angker nodded. "Sounds reasonable. Seems like you'd save a lot of time with the utilities, too." He scratched his chin with the pencil. He leaned abruptly forward. "You shouldn't have given Westgeller the estimate till you checked with the office."

Farrero opened his eyes, raised his eyebrows. "That's my job," — with a glibness of forethought. "That's what you're paying me for. Designing, estimating, selling."

"This is different. You're not acting for the company's best interests. You've cost us — thirty-one from forty-four — 13,000 munits."

Farrero shrugged. "The company's making ten per cent. My instructions were to quote estimated cost plus ten per cent."

When Angker was aroused, his dog-brown eyes glowed with russet lights. Now he put his hands on the edge of the desk, and Farrero, with an inward quiver, gazing deep into Angker's eyes, saw the russet flicker.

"Ten per cent," said Angker thickly, "is a rough basis for operation. However, you're supposed to exercise judgment. This is a money-making concern. We guarantee our customers quality, nothing else. If our price suits 'em, fine. If it doesn't, there's nineteen other outfits with the same kind of license we've got. I could have sold that house for 40,000 and Westgeller would be getting a bargain. You told him 31,000. You're costing us 9,000 munits. I don't like it."

"You forget," said Farrero, getting to his feet, "that what makes this saving is *my* private idea. *I* worked it out."

"On company time."

Farrero flushed. "I built a small scale section with company equipment, for company protection — to check the idea, and see whether it was a lemon or not. The scheme was completely formulated before I even left the Institute. In any event, the patent is in my name."

"Well," said Angker heavily, "you'll have to sign it over to Marlais & Angker."

"*Hah!*" Farrero thrust his hands in his pockets. "You think I'm crazy?"

Angker wrenched off the polarizers. "Farrero, how old are you?"

"Twenty-eight."

"You've put in four years at the Institute, studying Class III technique, right?"

"That's what my license reads."

"So it would be just four years wasted if you couldn't get a job with any Class III outfit?"

Farrero said, "I've got lots of ideas. Maybe I'll start an outfit of my own."

Angker chuckled. "Your license doesn't say that. It gives you authority to plan, to design, to sell. Marlais & Angker hold the license to build. Those licenses are hard to come by nowadays. Without it you can't contract to build an igloo at the North Pole."

"Very true," said Farrero dryly. "So?"

"So — any process developed during your employment with us becomes our property. You get a bonus, of course. There's a hundred legal precedents to back me up."

"If," Farrero interposed tautly, "I developed the process working for you — which I did not."

"Can you prove it?"

Farrero met the russet lights. "I wouldn't be surprised. I've been talking about it for two years. It's a good idea. It'll bring Class III construction within reach of a lot of Class II incomes."

Angker smiled a glittering hypnotic smile. "Let 'em buy Class II houses — from our affiliate XAB Company. Maybe we'll cut prices in Class II."

Farrero took a half step forward. "What kind of talk is that? Does public welfare mean anything to you, at all? You want to take money without giving anything; you're no better than a pickpocket!"

Angker pushed his knuckles on the desk till they became white buttons. "Get your check from Dempster. You're through, Farrero. You're through in the whole construction game. I'll see ... I'll make it my business to see that you never work for any other outfit in the world."

"You think you'll turn my idea over to your engineers," jeered Farrero. "Go ahead, let 'em try it. Think I was fool enough to tell you anything important?"

"What more is there?" asked Angker, leaning back in his chair with a half grin.

"Ever try to spray a right angle onto a building? No? Go ahead, try." And Farrero laughed. He stopped. "Sure. Go ahead, try. I've got the patent. I'll throw so many writs and attachments and subpoenas at you, you'll think it's snowing."

"We'll see," said Angker. "Meantime, go out and herd sheep if you want to eat — because I promise you'll never work construction again."

Farrero looked at his fingernails. "Remember what I said about organizing my own outfit?"

Angker pursed his thick lips into a ridiculous smirk. "Have you forgotten the little detail of the license? You haven't got one. You can't get one. There's none being issued. Without a license you can't build a doghouse to sell, anywhere on Earth, Venus, the Moon."

"Sounds pretty definite, doesn't it?" mocked Farrero.

"Go back to Tek, Farrero. Put in another four years on something else. Hydroponics. Protolectrics. Because in construction you're done."

"Angker," said Farrero, "you just listened to one of my ideas. I've got others. Better ones. Before I'm done I'll have cost you so much money, you'll wish you'd taken me in as a partner. Remember that, Angker."

He left the office.

Angker sat staring at the screen, where without polarizers, the image was a chaotic blur. He touched a button. A soft voice said "Yes?"

"Did you hear this last interview?"

"No," said Marlais.

"I'll run it off for you — quite a lot in it." He pulled open a drawer, twisted a dial, pulled a knob. The magnowire reeled backward to where Farrero had entered the office; then, pulling its impressions past the detector, it echoed for Marlais' ears the entire interview.

"What do you think?" Angker asked the unseen Marlais.

There was a pause, and Angker waited with an anxiety which might have appeared odd to his subordinates.

"Well, Douane," presently came Marlais' soft voice, "you probably could have handled him more smoothly...aggression, stubbornness, overt hostility —" his voice trailed off to a whisper. Then: "We'd have a hard time proving ownership of the patent. However, it may be for the best. The industry is stable and comfortable. We're all making money. No telling where the disruption might take us. Perhaps we'd better call a meeting of the association, lay the cards on the table. I think everyone will contract neither to hire Farrero nor use his process."

Angker made a doubtful noise.

"You see," said Marlais, with a gentle edge to his voice, "there are twenty companies in the association. The chance of Farrero's approaching any given firm is only one in nineteen. We don't count. Consequently, every operator, to protect himself, will be glad to sign a contract. It might be wise to keep a watch on Farrero, to see what he's up to. He sounded like a young man of determination."

The next day about eleven o'clock Angker called his secretary. "Get me Westgeller."

"Yes, sir…there's a call coming in for you right now, Mr. Angker. In fact it's Mr. Westgeller himself."

"Well, put him on."

Laurin Westgeller's face appeared on Angker's screen — fat, friendly, with little twinkling blue eyes. "Mr. Angker," said Westgeller, "I've decided to have you go no further with my job. You can send me a bill for your work to date."

Angker sat glowering at the image. He had been on the point of notifying Westgeller that Marlais & Angker could not build for less than 45,000 munits, had fully expected a cancellation. Westgeller's beating him to the punch left him puzzled, resentful.

"What's the matter? Price too high?" he asked sarcastically.

"No," replied Westgeller, "the price hardly enters into the picture. In fact, I plan to spend 300,000 munits on a house."

Angker's jaw slacked. "300,000 munits? Who…I mean, shall I send you out a consultant?"

"No," said Laurin Westgeller. "I've already signed — with one of your late employees, Mr. Farrero, who's going into business for himself."

Angker stared. "Farrero? Why, Farrero has no license to build! The minute he drives a stake into the ground he's liable for a ten thousand munit fine!"

Westgeller nodded. "So he informed me. Thank you, however, for your advice. Good day." The screen blurred, sank through the pink after-image to blank ground glass.

Angker blurted the news through to Marlais.

"There's nothing we can do until Farrero tries to fulfill the contract," said Marlais. "When and if he makes an illegal move, we file charges."

Angker grunted, shook his head. "He's got something up his sleeve. Farrero's not crazy."

"*Nobody* who gets 300,000 munit contracts is crazy," said the soft voice. "But all we can do is wait, see what his plans are. You've got an investigator on him?"

"Yes — Lescovic. He worked for us in that New Zealand deal."

"Yes, I remember. I'll be interested to learn what Farrero has in mind."

Two hours later, Angker's telescreen buzzer sounded.

"Yes?" snarled Angker.

"A Mr. Lescovic, sir."

"Put him on." The face of the investigator appeared — a passive, fat, dark-eyed face, with wide red lips and a button nose.

"Well?"

"Farrero's slipped us."

The spasmodic jerk of Angker's arms shoved him back in the chair. "Where…how did this happen?"

"About an hour ago. We dusted his clothes with F-radiant powder, and following him was easy with an F-detector. He walked into the Transport Union, and into a public lavatory. I waited across the lobby, watching the screen. He showed like a big ball of fire. He moved around a little, then was still. When he didn't move after ten minutes, I got suspicious, went to look. His clothes were hung on a hook, but Farrero, no. He gave us the clean slip."

Angker slapped the desk. "Find him, then!"

"There're four operatives on the case right now, sir."

"Call me as soon as you get anything."

Six months later the call came through. The buzzer sounded late in the afternoon. Angker hardly looked up from a model of a Caribbean island. "Yes?"

"Mr. Lescovic calling."

Angker looked up, rubbed his jaw. "Lescovic?"

"The detective, Mr. Angker."

"Oh yes." Angker pulled the case from its mental pigeonhole. "Put him through."

The fat bland face appeared on the screen. "Farrero's back in town."

"When did he get back?"

"Well, evidently during the week."

"Find out where he's been?"

"No word on that."

"What's he doing now?"

"He's calling on Franklin Kerry, of Kerry Armatures. Been there two hours."

"Kerry! Why, Kerry's one of our clients! At least he's looking over our bid for building his house."

Lescovic let a spark of interest show in his careful dark eyes. "He's got plenty of money — registered at the Gloriana."

Angker said, "Hold on a minute." He flipped a switch, reported to Marlais.

Marlais was noncommittal. "We've nothing to go on. We'll have to wait, see what happens."

Angker brought back Lescovic's placid face. "Watch him. Report everything he does. Find out what he wants with Kerry."

"Yes, sir." The screen faded.

Angker slammed into Marlais' office. "Well, he's done it again."

Marlais had been sitting in half-darkness, gazing through the window, out across the many-tiered city, out to the dusk-hung horizon. He slowly turned his head.

"I presume you mean Farrero."

Angker stamped back and forth. "Glochmeinder this time. Last month it was Crane. Before that, Haggarty." He came to an abrupt halt, cursed Farrero with fluid vindictiveness, resumed his pacing. "He doesn't go near any of the small ones, but just let us get wind of a big account —"

"What did Glochmeinder say?"

"Just what Kerry and Crane and Haggarty and Desplains and Churchward and Klenko and Westgeller said. He's given his contract to Farrero, and that's all he'll say."

Marlais rose to his feet, rubbed his chin. "There's a leak in the office. Somewhere."

The muscles roped around Angker's mouth. "I've been trying to find it. When I do —" He slowly clenched and unclenched his hand in the air.

Marlais turned back to the window. "No word from the detective?" — from over his shoulder.

"I gave you his last report. Farrero's been ordering all over the world — construction materials and landscaping supplies. He's got fifteen hundred men working for him, according to the Department of Labor Statistics, but we can't find where — and there's not a job going that isn't a legitimate, licensed affair."

"Clever," mused Marlais, toying with the massive blue spinel he used for a paper weight.

"He's cost us a half million munits," gloomed Angker.

Marlais smiled wanly. "Just as he threatened, just so." And he laughed at Angker's quick glare.

For a moment there was silence. Angker paced the floor heavily. Marlais let the smoke from his cigarette trickle up through his finger, lose itself in the half-darkness of the room.

"Well," said Marlais, tamping out the cigarette, "something must be done."

Farrero found himself an office, a two-room suite in the Atlantica Tower, facing west across Amargosa Park, with the Pylon of All Nations thrusting magnificently high in the distance. He also found himself a receptionist, and this was Miss Flora Gustafsson, who claimed Scandinavian ancestry, and had long birch-blonde hair, with eyes blue as Folda Fjord, to prove it. She was hardly bigger than a kitten, but everything about her matched, and she was efficient with the detectives.

The teleview buzzed. Flora reached over, screened the caller. "Oh, good afternoon, Mr. Westgeller. I'll put you through to Mr. Farrero."

"Thank you," said Westgeller. Flora looked sharply at the image, buzzed Farrero.

"Hello, Mr. Westgeller," said Farrero. "What can I do for you?"

"Farrero, an old friend of mine, John Etcheverry, wants to build, and I'm sending him around to see you."

"Oh … ah, fine, Mr. Westgeller. I'll try to accommodate him, though we're pretty busy."

"Good day, Farrero," and Westgeller abruptly left the screen. Farrero sat stroking his chin, smiling faintly. Then he went into the outer room, kissed Flora.

John Etcheverry was about sixty, tall, thin, pale as a heron. He had a large egg-shaped head, sparse white hair that disobeyed his scalp in damp unruly tendrils. His eyes, set in dark concavities, never seemed to blink. His cheeks were wan, minutely etched. He had large ears with long pale lobes, and a long pale nose that twitched when he spoke.

"Have a seat," said Farrero. "I understand you're planning to build."

"That's right. May I smoke?"

"Certainly. Cigar? Try one of mine."

Etcheverry lit up.

"What do you have in mind? I might as well warn you that my prices come high. I deliver, but it costs a lot of money."

Etcheverry made a brief gesture with his fingers. "I want a country place, seclusion, quiet. I'm prepared to pay for it."

Farrero tapped the desk with a pencil once or twice, laid it down, sat back, quietly watched Etcheverry.

Etcheverry puffed on the cigar. "Westgeller tells me you've satisfied him very well. In fact, that's all he'll say."

Farrero nodded. "It's in the contract. I needed time to protect myself. Now I hardly care any more. I'm just waiting for a call from Capitol City, and then, so far as I'm concerned, I'll drop all secrecy." He leaned forward, pointed the pencil at Etcheverry's narrow chest. "You see, I've got enemies. Twenty Class III licensed structors want my blood. Marlais & Angker in particular. I've had to take precautions. Like for instance —" he pressed the stud and Flora's arch face looked out from the screen. "Get me Westgeller at his office."

Etcheverry chewed his cigar reflectively.

A moment passed. The buzzer sounded. Flora's face returned to the screen. "Mr. Westgeller hasn't been in his office today."

Farrero nodded. "It's not important." He turned back to Etcheverry. "Excuse me … a habit left over from the early stages of the game. Endless caution, endless foresight. It all helped then. You'd be surprised the phonies that Marlais & Angker threw at me."

"You have a license?" Etcheverry delicately inspected the tips of his shoes through the cigar smoke.

"No."

"Then you build illegally?"

"No."

Etcheverry pursed his lips. "You'll have to explain."

Farrero stared thoughtfully out the window. "Um … how much time can you spare?"

"You mean —"

"Right now."

"Well … there are no important demands on my time."

"If you can give me the rest of the day, I'll do better than explain — I'll demonstrate."

"Fine." Etcheverry put out his cigar. "I'll admit you've aroused my curiosity."

Farrero called an air cab. "Purdy Field," he told the driver.

At Purdy Field, Farrero took Etcheverry into the hangar. "Jump in," and he followed the stooped figure into the two-place space boat.

Etcheverry adjusted himself gingerly to the cushions. "If you haven't a license to build, I hope at least you have a license to fly space."

Farrero grinned. "I have. Check it if you care to. It's under the aerator."

"I'll take your word for it."

They rode up off the seared field on snoring atomic jets, beat up, up, up. A hundred miles, two hundred and earth blurred below. A thousand, five thousand, ten thousand miles — twenty, thirty thousand miles, and Farrero kept a close watch on his radar screen. "Should be about here now —" A pip showed yellow-green. "There it is." He swerved the boat, jetted off in the new direction. After a minute:

"You can see it below, off to the left."

Etcheverry, craning his gaunt neck, saw a small irregular asteroid, perhaps a mile in diameter. Farrero edged down the boat, lowered with hardly a jolt on a patch of white sand.

Etcheverry grabbed Farrero's arm violently. "Are you crazy?" he squealed. "Don't open that port! That's space out there! Vacuum!"

Farrero shook his head. "There's air. Fifteen pounds pressure, twenty per cent oxygen. Good breathing. I'm not crazy. Look at the barometer."

Etcheverry looked, watched numbly as Farrero flung open the port. The air was good.

Farrero jumped out of the boat. Etcheverry followed. "But … there's gravity here —"

Farrero climbed to the top of a little hillock, waved an arm to Etcheverry. "Come on up."

Etcheverry stalked slowly up the slope.

"This is Westgeller's estate," said Farrero. "His private world. He paid 300,000 munits for it. Look, there's his house."

Westgeller's house sat on a wide flat field covered with emerald-green turf. Nearby a lake glistened in the warm sunlight, and a white crane stood fishing among the rushes. Trees lined the plain, and Etcheverry heard birds singing across the distance.

The house was a long rambling structure, single-story, built of red-wood planking. There were many windows, and below each, a window box overflowing with floral color. Beach umbrellas, green, orange, blue, rose like other, larger flowers from a terrace.

Farrero squinted across the field, smooth and grassy-green as a golf course. "Westgeller is at home. I see his space boat. Like to call on him? Might like to talk things over with your old friend, eh, Mr. Etcheverry?"

Etcheverry gave him a sharp side glance, said slowly: "Perhaps it would be just as well if —"

Farrero laughed. "Save it. It's no good. You probably don't know I read lips. Well, I do. I was stone deaf the first ten years of my life. And when you flashed Westgeller's picture on my screen, his voice saying, 'I'm sending over my dear old friend Etcheverry,' and his lips saying, 'I've decided to have you stop work on my job, Mr. Angker,' I smelled a rat. I suppose you're Marlais. It's a cinch you're not Angker."

The thin man shrugged, gave Farrero a quick side-glance. "I'm Marlais. Nice set-up you've got."

"I like it," said Farrero. "I'm making money."

Marlais looked around the toy world. "You're spending it too." He stamped his long fragile-looking foot on the ground. "You've got me beat. How do you lick gravity? Why doesn't the air all blow away? Seems as if I'm...oh, about normal weight."

"You're a little lighter," said Farrero. "Gravity here is three per cent less than on Earth."

"But," and Marlais looked horizon to close horizon, calculated, "call this a half mile in diameter — that'll be a half of a half cubed, approximately — one sixteenth cubic mile. Earth is...512 trillion over two is 256 trillion cubic miles. And the gravity is the same. Why?"

"For one thing," said Farrero, "you're closer to the center of gravity — by almost four thousand miles."

Marlais reached down, plucked a blade of grass, inspected it curiously.

"All new," said Farrero. "The trees brought here at no slight effort, I'll tell you. Lindvist — he's a Danish ecologist — is working with me. He figures out how many bees I need to fertilize the flowers, how many earthworms, how many trees to oxygenate the air."

Marlais nodded his head, darted Farrero a look from shadowed eyes. "Very good, very good!"

"There won't be a millionaire living on Earth in another twenty years," mused Farrero. "I'll have sold them all private planets. Some will want big places. I can furnish them —"

"Incidentally, where did you get this one?"

"Out in space a ways."

Marlais nodded sagely. "That's probably where Marlais & Angker will go to find theirs."

Farrero turned his head slowly, looked the man up and down. Marlais met his gaze blandly.

"So — you think you'll cut in?"

"I'd be a fool if I didn't."

"You think," Farrero went on meditatively, "that you'll cash in on my idea. You've got all the equipment, all the technicians necessary for a quick skim at the cream. Maybe you'll even get some laws enacted, barring non-licensees from the game."

"If I didn't — I'd be a fool."

Farrero shrugged. "Well … maybe yes. Maybe no. Like to see another of my jobs? This is Westgeller's. I'll show you Desplains'."

Marlais bowed his head. They re-entered the space boat. Farrero clamped the port, pulsed power through the jets. Westgeller's world fell away beneath them.

They reached Desplains' world half an hour later. "Eventually," said Farrero, "space around Earth will be peppered thick with these little estates. There'll be laws regulating their orbits, minimum distances set for their spacing —" He jerked the controls, threw the power-arm hard over. The space boat fled across Desplains' sky.

Marlais squirmed his long bony shoulder blades, cleared his throat with a sound like a saw cutting a nail, glanced sidewise at Farrero. "Why did you do that?"

Farrero expelled a lung full of taut air. "That was a narrow one. Did you see it slip past?"

"No."

"I forgot that Desplains wanted a moon. It's been installed. We just about rammed it."

He set the boat down on a rocky outcrop. Marlais unsealed the port, angled his skinny legs to the ground. "*Phew,*" he grunted, "Desplains must intend to raise orchids — positively dank."

Farrero grinned, loosened his jacket. "He hasn't moved in yet. We're having a little trouble with the atmosphere. He wants clouds, and we're experimenting with the humidity." He looked up. "It's easy to get a muggy high overcast — but Desplains wants big fluffs of cumulus. Well, we'll try. Personally I don't think there's enough total volume of air."

Marlais looked into the sky too, where Earth hung as a huge bright crescent. He licked his pale old lips.

Farrero laughed. "Makes a man feel naked, doesn't it?" He looked across the little world to the queerly close horizon — barely a stone's-throw off, so it seemed — then back to the sweep of sky, with the majestic crescent of Earth dominating a new Moon behind. "Out here," he said, half to himself, "beauty comes a lot at a time."

Marlais gingerly perched himself on a slab of rock. "Exotic place."

"Desplains is an exotic man," said Farrero. "But he's got the money, and I don't care if he wants the rocks upholstered with rabbit fur." He hopped up beside Marlais. "Desplains wanted something unusual. He's getting it." He indicated a clump of trees. "That's his bayou. Flora from Africa and the Matto Grosso. Fauna from here and there, including a very rare Tasmanian ibis. It's rather pretty, and certainly wild enough — connecting ponds, with overhanging trees. The moss hasn't got a good start yet, and there isn't quite the authentic smell, but give it time. Behind there's a … well, call it a swamp — a jungle cut with a lot of waterways. When the flowers all start in blooming it'll be heaven —"

"Individual worlds to suit any conceivable whim," murmured Marlais.

"That's it exactly," said Farrero. "We've got our largest world — about ten miles diameter — sold to a Canadian yachtsman."

"Fred Ableman," said Marlais dryly. "He canceled his contract with us about two months ago."

Farrero nodded. "He wants his world all ocean — blue ocean, plenty of wind to sail his boats. He wants islands here and there, with beaches and coral banks —"

"Coconut palms too, I expect."

"Right — but no sharks. We won't have it completed for another year and a half. It's heavy and unwieldy — difficult to bring out and get established in an orbit. Then there's an awful lot of water needed."

"Where do you get the water? You can't bring it out from Earth?"

Farrero shook his head. "We mine the Hipparchus ice floe, and every time the moon comes in apposition we shoot across a few big chunks. Slow but sure. It costs a lot, but Ableman makes too much money for his own good. Anyway, how could he spend his money better?"

Marlais pursed his lips in agreement. "I expect you get some strange specifications."

Farrero grinned. "There's a man named Klenko, made his money in fashion design. He's the man responsible for those whirling things women were wearing a year or two ago on their heads. Strange man, strange world. The air is full of thirty-foot glass bubbles, floating loose. Glass bubbles everywhere — topaz, blue, red, violet, green — high and low. It's a hazard trying to land a space boat. He's got a fluorescent forest — activizers in the sap. When he turns ultraviolet on it, the leaves glow ghostly pale colors — silver, pale-green, orange. We built him a big pavilion overhanging a lake. Luminous fish in the lake."

"He evidently plans a lot of night life."

Farrero nodded. "He wants nothing but night. His world won't have any axial spin at all, when we get it trued in its orbit. But he'd better watch his step, or he'll get in trouble with the Anti-Vice League if he goes through with some of his entertainment ideas."

Marlais shrugged, took a cigarette from an onyx case, lit it. "If a man owns his world, I suppose he makes the laws."

"That at least is Klenko's theory."

Marlais blew out a puff of smoke. "One thing has me stumped," and his shadowed eyes calculated Farrero. "How do you beat gravity? So far as I know, artificial gravity has never been discovered."

Farrero nodded. "True."

Marlais made an airy gesture. "Well — whatever the system is, I imagine it will work for Marlais & Angker, too."

"So it would," said Farrero. "Only Marlais & Angker have come to the party late. I don't especially want to drive them into bankruptcy. I don't imagine I could. There'll always be Class III construction on Earth. But Farrero is pulling all the nuggets out of the pan, and he's making an awful dent in that precious twenty."

Marlais shook his head, and a spark appeared back in the depths of his eyes. "You have not quite grasped the idea, my friend. We don't plan to take the back seat. We have the connections, the equipment, the staff. We can bring the asteroids out here cheaper than you can, undersell you four ways from Sunday. We'll even take losses if we need to. But you won't stay in business long. Whatever, however you handle gravity, our engineers can duplicate the conditions."

"My dear Mr. Marlais," jeered Farrero, "do you think I'm a fool? Do you think I'd leave a loophole for you and the other bandits? Have you ever heard of the Norton Space Claims Act?"

"Certainly. It defines and authorizes mining development of the asteroids."

"That's right. I've filed on eleven hundred and twenty-two asteroids. Of a peculiar nature — You see that little black pebble by your right foot. That shiny one, like flint. Pick it up."

Marlais reached, grasped, strained. His mouth slacked in amazement. He pulled again, till his skinny old arms quivered, creaked. He glanced up at Farrero.

"It weighs close to a ton, I expect," said Farrero. "It's star stuff. Matter crystallized at tremendous pressure in the heart of a star. It figures out about a ton a cubic inch. A little bit turns on a lot of gravity. Somehow or other, eleven hundred and twenty-two good-sized chunks of the stuff drifted into an orbit around the sun — not too far out from Earth. They're small and dark and not heavy enough to cause any noticeable perturbations. But when you stand on their surface, the center of gravity is close enough to give you fairly close to Earth weight. I've filed on every one of those chunks, Marlais. Some I'll have to lump together, others I'll have to crust over with a few miles of ordinary matter to reduce gravity. It diminishes, you know, as the square of the distance from the center of mass — But I tell you what, Marlais," Farrero opened the port of his space boat, motioned Marlais in. "I know where you can get all this heavy matter you can use."

Marlais wordlessly climbed into the boat. He eyed Farrero lambently. "Where?"

Farrero clamped the port, swung the power-arm, and Desplains' world fell off below.

"Here's what you do," Farrero confided. "You go out to Sirius, only ten light-years. It's got a small companion. You can cut chunks off the companion, as big as you want, as many as you want. Bring them back to Earth, and then you'll be in a position to compete with Farrero-Styled Worlds."

Marlais stared ahead at expanding Earth, knees hunched up under his sharp chin. Farrero could not resist a last gibe.

"Of course there'll be the detail of cooling off your acquisitions. I understand they're pretty hot. Twenty or thirty million degrees Centigrade —"

About the Author

JACK VANCE was born in 1916 to a well-off California family that, as his childhood ended, fell upon hard times. As a young man he worked at a series of unsatisfying jobs before studying mining engineering, physics, journalism and English at the University of California Berkeley. Leaving school as America was going to war, he found a place as an ordinary seaman in the merchant marine. Later he worked as a rigger, surveyor, ceramicist, and carpenter before his steady production of sf, mystery novels, and short stories established him as a full-time writer.

His output over more than sixty years was prodigious and won him three Hugo Awards, a Nebula Award, a World Fantasy Award for lifetime achievement, as well as an Edgar from the Mystery Writers of America. The Science Fiction and Fantasy Writers of America named him a grandmaster and he was inducted into the Science Fiction Hall of Fame.

His works crossed genre boundaries, from dark fantasies (including the highly influential *Dying Earth* cycle of novels) to interstellar space operas, from heroic fantasy (the *Lyonesse* trilogy) to murder mysteries featuring a sheriff (the Joe Bain novels) in a rural California county. A Vance story often centered on a competent male protagonist thrust into a dangerous, evolving situation on a planet where adventure was his daily fare, or featured a young person setting out on a perilous odyssey over difficult terrain populated by entrenched, scheming enemies.

Late in his life, a world-spanning assemblage of Vance aficionados came together to return his works to their original form, restoring material cut by editors whose chief preoccupation was the page count of a pulp magazine. The result was the complete and authoritative *Vance Integral Edition* in 44 hardcover volumes. Spatterlight Press is now publishing the VIE texts as ebooks, and as print-on-demand paperbacks.

Colophon

This book was printed using Adobe Arno Pro as the primary text font, with NeutraFace used on the cover.

This title was created from the digital archive of the Vance Integral Edition, a series of 44 books produced under the aegis of the author by a worldwide group of his readers. The VIE project gratefully acknowledges the editorial guidance of Norma Vance, as well as the cooperation of the Department of Special Collections at Boston University, whose John Holbrook Vance collection has been an important source of textual evidence.

Special thanks to R.C. Lacovara, Patrick Dusoulier, Koen Vyverman, Paul Rhoads, Chuck King, Gregory Hansen, Suan Yong, and Josh Geller for their invaluable assistance preparing final versions of the source files.

Source: Harrison Watson, Jr.; Digitize: Connie Brown, Richard Chandler, Joel Hedlund, Alun Hughes, David Mortimore, Joel Riedesel, John A. Schwab, Koen Vyverman, Suan Hsi Yong; Diff: Richard Chandler, Damien G. Jones, David A. Kennedy, Joel Riedesel, Steve Sherman, Hans van der Veeke, Suan Hsi Yong; Format: Derek W. Benson, Mike Berro, Evert Jan de Groot; Tech Proof: Ron Chernich, Rob Friefeld, Joel Riedesel, Fred Zoetemeyer; Text Integrity: Richard Chandler, Rob Friefeld, Alun Hughes, Paul Rhoads, Jeffrey Ruszczyk, Steve Sherman, Anton Sherwood, Tim Stretton, Suan Hsi Yong; Implement: Donna Adams, Derek W. Benson, Mike Dennison, Patrick Dusoulier, Joel Hedlund, Damien G. Jones, John McDonough, David Reitsema, Steve Sherman, Hans van der Veeke; Security: David A. Kennedy, Paul Rhoads, John A. Schwab, Tim Stretton; Compose: Joel Anderson, Andreas Irle, John A. Schwab; Comp Review: Mark Adams, Christian J. Corley, John A. D. Foley, Marcel van Genderen, Brian Gharst, Karl Kellar, Charles King, Bob Luckin, Paul Rhoads, Robin L. Rouch; Update Verify: Joel Anderson, Rob Friefeld, Charles King, Bob Luckin, Robert Melson, Paul Rhoads, Robin L. Rouch; RTF-Diff: Mark Bradford, Deborah Cohen, Patrick Dusoulier, Charles King, Bill Schaub; Textport: Patrick Dusoulier; Proofread: Neil Anderson, Neville Angove, Kristine Anstrats, Erik Arendse, Mike Barrett, Karl Barrus, Michel Bazin, Scott Benenati, Malcolm Bowers, Mark Bradford, Ursula Brandt, Angus Campbell-Cann, Deborah Cohen, Matthew Colburn, Robert Collins, Christian J. Corley, Michael Duncan, Patrick Dusoulier, Andrew Edlin, Patrick van Efferen, Joost van der Eijk, Harry Erwin, Rob Friefeld, Marcel van Genderen, Rob Gerrand, Yannick Gour, Tony Graham, Erec Grim, Evert Jan de Groot, Marc Herant, Ruth Hunter, Peter Ikin, Lucie Jones, Jurriaan Kalkman, Jason Kauffeld, Karl Kellar, David A. Kennedy, Charles King, Per Kjellberg, Rob Knight, Chris LaHatte, Gabriel Landon, Bob Luckin, Chris McCormick, Robert Melson,

Michael Mitchell, Mike Myers, Eric Newsom, Till Noever, Michael Nolan, Jim Pattison, Matt Picone, Chris Prior, Michael Rathbun, Glenn Raye, Simon Read, David Reitsema, Errico Rescigno, Joel Riedesel, Axel Roschinski, Robin L. Rouch, Jeffrey Ruszczyk, Mike Schilling, Bill Sherman, Steve Sherman, Mark Shoulder, Steven Smith, Rudi Staudinger, Gabriel Stein, Mark J. Straka, Andrew Thompson, Willem Timmer, Hans van der Veeke, Dirk Jan Verlinde, Paul Wedderien, Dave Worden, Suan Hsi Yong, Fred Zoetemeyer

Artwork (maps based on original drawings by Jack and Norma Vance):

Paul Rhoads, Christopher Wood

Book Composition and Typesetting: Joel Anderson

Art Direction and Cover Design: Howard Kistler

Proofing: Christian J. Corley, Steve Sherman

Jacket Blurb: Steve Sherman, John Vance

Management: John Vance, Koen Vyverman

Made in the USA
Middletown, DE
16 June 2020

97805015R00205